By Your Side

Also by Ruth Jones

Never Greener
Us Three
Love Untold

By Your Side

Ruth Jones

bantam

TRANSWORLD PUBLISHERS
Penguin Random House, One Embassy Gardens,
8 Viaduct Gardens, London SW11 7BW
www.penguin.co.uk

Transworld is part of the Penguin Random House group of companies
whose addresses can be found at global.penguinrandomhouse.com

First published in Great Britain in 2025 by Bantam
an imprint of Transworld Publishers

Copyright © Ruth Jones 2025

Ruth Jones has asserted her right under the Copyright,
Designs and Patents Act 1988 to be identified as the author of this work.

This book is a work of fiction and, except in the case of historical fact, any
resemblance to actual persons, living or dead, is purely coincidental.

The Lyrics on p. 226 are from 'Caledonia' written by Dougie MacLean.
The words on pp. 361–2 are inspired by the song 'Big Spender'
written by Cy Coleman and Dorothy Fields.

Every effort has been made to obtain the necessary permissions with
reference to copyright material, both illustrative and quoted. We apologize
for any omissions in this respect and will be pleased to make the
appropriate acknowledgements in any future edition.

A CIP catalogue record for this book
is available from the British Library.

ISBNs
9781787633896 (hb)
9781787633902 (tpb)

Typeset in 11.25/15.25 pt Sabon by Falcon Oast Graphic Art Ltd
Printed and bound in Great Britain by Clays Ltd, Elcograf S.p.A.

The authorized representative in the EEA is Penguin Random House Ireland,
Morrison Chambers, 32 Nassau Street, Dublin D02 YH68.

Penguin Random House values and supports copyright.
Copyright fuels creativity, encourages diverse voices, promotes freedom
of expression and supports a vibrant culture. Thank you for purchasing
an authorized edition of this book and for respecting intellectual property
laws by not reproducing, scanning or distributing any part of it by any
means without permission. You are supporting authors and enabling
Penguin Random House to continue to publish books for everyone.
No part of this book may be used or reproduced in any manner for the
purpose of training artificial intelligence technologies or systems. In accordance
with Article 4(3) of the DSM Directive 2019/790, Penguin Random House
expressly reserves this work from the text and data mining exception.

Penguin Random House is committed to a sustainable
future for our business, our readers and our planet. This book is
made from Forest Stewardship Council® certified paper.

In memory of my beloved father, Richard Norman Jones.
The best dad ever.

To live in hearts we leave behind is not to die.

– Thomas Campbell

2024

Prologue

The landlord could set his watch by it. Just coming up to 2 p.m. and the pub door opened as it had done on this date every year for the past six, letting in the old fella, coat buttoned up against the gusty gale outside and the dwindling Scottish light of a bleak winter's day. With a welcoming smile, the landlord nodded and took down a seldom-used tumbler from the shelf. He pushed its rim against the optic, once, twice, releasing the dark amber liquid of a single malt. 'There you go,' he said, placing it on the bar and waiting as the man took out some coins from his pocket and handed them over.

'How you been keepin'?'

'Aye, not bad.'

'You managin' okay up there on yer own? You need help with anything?'

'I'm tip-top,' he said and raised his glass with a smile before taking it off to the chair by the fire. The bar was empty apart from a local electrician fixing some light fittings and two Danish hikers sat at a table poring over a map.

The landlord tried not to stare. But this enigmatic once-a-year customer never failed to pique his interest. In all the time the man had lived here, he'd barely spoken a handful of words to anyone. He wasn't rude, just quiet and mild-mannered and had a way of politely batting away chat. The landlord watched now as the man stared at the whisky, swirling it round, deep in thought. Then, muttering something under his breath, he surreptitiously raised his glass and drank. When he wiped away a stray tear, the landlord stopped looking. It felt like an intrusion, an invasion of the man's privacy.

Fifteen minutes later the customer drained his glass, got up and took it back to the bar. Buttoning his coat, he headed to the door and the squally weather outside. 'Take care now!' shouted the landlord. The man raised his hand in response, heaved open the door and left the pub, never to return.

1

Linda

I'm late. Which is so unlike me because I'm usually such a good time-keeper. I thrive on routine and schedule, so being late discombobulates me for the rest of the day. Stopping at the lights on Massey Street, I examine my reflection in the rear-view. It's not that I'm vain. I'm just checking there's no jam on my cheek or toast in my teeth – remnants from this morning's breakfast, and not a good look for what lies ahead. My eyebrows could do with a trim. Going slightly feral. Oh and Lordy, that solitary chin bristle has returned. The bane of my face. I've tried zapping it, plucking it, even snipping it with nail clippers, but it always, always returns. I've contemplated weedkiller. That's how desperate I am. Attempting now to yank it out between finger and thumb, my facial inspection is disturbed by an unnecessarily long beep from the car behind. 'All right, all right!' I shout. One of my pet hates – drivers who think that a micro-second shaved off at traffic lights will make the slightest difference to their journey. In less than three months I'll be fifty-five, so my list of pet hates is getting longer. I'm told they increase incrementally with age until full metamorphosis into *grumpy old womanhood* is complete. Well, that may be so for some, but not for me. Because I, Linda Mary Standish, will not be defeated by age. I'm divorced and single with a job that I love, and a *grumpy old woman* I am not. Nor will I ever be. I intend to live out the rest of my life at full throttle and woe betide anyone who gets in my way. Like the driver behind who's now overtaking. His window is open and he glares as he goes. So I blow him a kiss and shout, 'Show us your knickers, you sexy beast!' His face is a picture.

Fifteen minutes later, I pull – actually, *screech* – into the car park of Boransay Crematorium with inappropriate haste, but the service begins in two minutes and needs must. Hatch open, a plain, unadorned coffin inside, the hearse is parked at the main door. And standing straight as the crease in his black flannel trousers, silently awaiting my arrival, the undertaker nods at me as I approach.

'Linda Standish,' he says sombrely.

'Fergus Murray,' I respond.

We were in school together, me and Fergus. I wouldn't say we were friends as such – we just inhabited the same educational landscape from reception class through to Higher Maths. And we still refer to each other by our full names. It's an unwritten rule. Even at the age of fifty-five. I'm not technically late, so I won't apologize. Especially to Fergus flippin' Murray. To me he'll always be a hormone-fuelled teenager drenched in Lynx, with a light scattering of acne and a habit of self-consciously flicking his fringe. For that reason I can't quite take him seriously.

'Shall we?' I say with a sweep of my hand, and head inside.

As crematoria go, Boransay is rather pleasant. It lacks the harsh, utilitarian feel you get in some of them, and it's tastefully done out. Soft light streams through a modern stained-glass window, accompanied by the gentle organ music now emanating from the speakers. Two pedestals either side of the catafalque boast huge cascading lily arrangements. They're fake, of course, the lilies. But they're good-quality fake. So you'd be hard-pressed to know the difference, especially from a few yards away. I join the only other mourner in there: a small, neat woman at least twenty years my junior standing in the front row. 'Hello,' I whisper. 'I'm from Boransay Council. Unclaimed Heirs Unit.'

We shake hands and she looks confused. 'Unclaimed hairs?'

'No, *heirs*.'

Hairs do seem to be a recurring theme this morning. 'So, are you a relative of the deceased? Because we've been trying to track down the family.'

'Gosh, no,' she says. 'I'm from the hospital. They always send someone if they can. Just out of—'

'Ahem.' It's the unmistakeable throat-clearing of Fergus Murray. Along with his colleague, Old Sam – don't know his surname, I've just always called him Old Sam – they wheel the coffin towards its final resting place, respectfully transferring it from the gurney on to the catafalque. Old Sam removes the gurney and Fergus stands stiffly, hands behind his back, silently signalling to me to begin. I smile brazenly at him, which he'll no doubt find annoying.

Smiling at a funeral director *does* feel a bit wrong, I admit.

Disrespectful, somehow.

I don't mean when they're out and about on their day off, wearing civvies and posting a letter or buying some lamb chops. I mean when they're on duty: facilitating easy passage for the dearly departed as they journey from this world to the next.

Fergus is a fifth-generation undertaker who tried to swerve the inevitable family vocation and took up cycling instead. And I'm not talking bike rides in the park, I'm talking proper full-on professional cycling. He was rather good at it too. Commonwealth Games, Tour de France – he was even heading for the Olympics in 2004 till fate jumped in and knocked him off his bike. This resulted in a sharp exit from the international cycling arena and a slight limp. Which, fair play, he carries well. Gives him the air of a wounded soldier. I respect him for that. Yes, I respect him a lot. It's just, ever since school he's been one of those people who's always got to be right. And consequently, someone you just want to prove wrong.

I tap the microphone to check it's on. A pointless action really: I could whisper my words and still be heard. But it's a habit of mine.

'Friends,' I begin, even though there aren't any there. 'We are gathered to bid farewell to Wendy Maria Taylor, who died peacefully on November the twenty-first.' I say *peacefully* for decorum really. Truth is, she dropped dead drinking Diet Fanta in a transport caff just outside Crianlarich.

The service, if you can call it that, is predictably short. Less than six minutes in total. Still, it's quality, not quantity at the end of the day, and nobody can say I've not given her a decent send-off. I focus mainly on the early days – her job at the supermarket, her collection of matchboxes and her passion for baking. I've surmised all this from the cake tins, pay slips and matchboxes found in her home. I mean, I *presume* she was collecting the matchboxes, but maybe she was just a heavy smoker or a pyromaniac? I avoid the phrases one normally hears at the funeral of a woman her age – 'sorely missed' or 'beloved wife and mother'. I've developed a knack for that now. How to say something without saying very much. How to give the impression of a eulogy without really eulogizing at all.

Because it's difficult to bid farewell to someone you've never met; hard to praise the virtues of a person whose name you first heard only last month; challenging to list the lifetime achievements of a total stranger and make it sound like they were your dearest friend.

Yes, it's a difficult task.

But someone's got to do it. And today, that someone is me.

2

Linda

Wendy Taylor, today's deceased, had lived in a static caravan on the west coast. Me and my colleague Jean went there a week after Wendy's death and scoured the place, looking for scraps of information. Building a picture, or a 'character profile' as we like to call it. We'd started with the cupboards, replacing items with care, removing others we thought might yield vital information. The local charity shop had already been contacted and were due to do a full clearance once our work was done. On Wendy's little cork noticeboard was an overdue bill and a postcard from Scarborough: *Feeling okay now. Would love to say wish you were here, but we both know it's better like this. Ray x*

'Secret lover?' Jean had asked.

'Or estranged relative?'

Sometimes my conversations with Jean sound like they've been lifted from an episode of *Midsomer Murders*. In fact, I think the two of us are prone to embellish our dialogue, just to up the drama. There are elements of my job that I absolutely love. And behaving like a CSI officer is one of them.

Further searching of the caravan had been proving fruitless until Jean found a box file at the back of a storage cupboard. A few minutes later, we'd located Wendy's last will and testament. It was all fairly regular stuff except for one line – that her ex-husband was not to be informed of her death and that *all my worldly goods* were to be bestowed upon a certain Ray Dalgleish from Humberside, 'along with my blessing and forgiveness', added Jean. Half an hour later, having satisfied ourselves we had everything we needed, a man appeared in the doorway. A big fella, shaved head, in a vest and dirty jeans. 'Come for my telly,' he growled, barely looking in our direction and heading for Wendy's flat screen.

'I'm afraid all the items in here are under council jurisdiction,' I said, trying to exude confidence and authority. I don't think jurisdiction was the right word, but it sounded impressive.

'Bollocks,' said the man, proceeding to unplug the back of the telly. I opened my mouth to protest but Jean shook her head at me. As if to say, some battles aren't worth fighting. So we just stood by and let him take it. Literally daylight robbery taking place before our very eyes. Once he had the TV firmly in his arms, he turned to us and burst into spontaneous tears. 'She was all right, was Wendo. Lent her this last Chrimbo.' We all stood there for a few moments as the man pulled himself together. Eventually I found the courage to speak.

'Umm . . . don't suppose your name is Ray, is it?'

He stopped crying as quickly as he'd started. 'No!' he retorted, as if I'd insulted him in the worst possible way. 'Ray's not havin' this, no way.' With that he was gone, him and all his fifty-five flat-screen inches.

We've yet to hear back from Ray, and if we don't, then Wendy's estate goes to the Crown. Which would be a real shame. Because surely the Crown's got enough? I've also still got a box full of Wendy's memorabilia in the office, which I'll have to destroy. Harsh, I know, but if nobody wants it there's nothing I can do. From time to time, despite the frustration, I have to accept that some people's lives remain a mystery never to be solved. I suppose that's where real life differs from *Midsomer Murders*.

I do wonder what Wendy's beef was with the ex-husband and why she didn't want him knowing she'd died. Must have been a very acrimonious split. Me and Douglas are still on pretty good terms, not that I see him that often.

Dear old Douglas.

Aka Dougie MacRae.

Always thought he should have been a country and western singer with a name like that, but fate thought differently and had him selling kitchen equipment to the catering industry instead. I wouldn't say it was ever a head-over-heels kind of relationship between me and Dougie – more a sort of comfortable friendship with added sex. Yes, certainly there was always a lot of wham bam, because the two of us both had very healthy appetites in that department. But in terms of intellectual connection? Spiritual compatibility? Hmm, not really. The upside of all that being that we never had any big rows. So, swings and roundabouts. And like I said, he was good to me during the dark time. As well as being a lovely dad to our boy, Struan. Still is, to be fair.

It wasn't a shock when Dougie told me about Denise. I'd sort of suspected it. She was ten years his junior and a new rep at the company. When he started banging on about her I didn't pay much notice. But then it turned into banging of a different type – late-night 'meetings' to discuss 'sales strategies', even midweek conferences. I mean, seriously, a conference about industrial freezers or turbo ovens? Turns out the 'conferences' had been attended by just two of them and took place in a Premier Inn three miles down the road.

When Dougie finally confessed, I think he was more upset than me. In fact, if I'm honest, I was actually relieved. I made all the right noises, of course – *How could you, Doug? Oh, the deceit!* – but my heart wasn't really in it. I helped him pack up his stuff and reassured him that yes, he *was* making the right decision, when he had moments of doubt. 'I can't bear the thought of hurting you,' he said on the morning he arrived with a hire van to move his stuff. Not wanting to frighten the horses, I just said, 'Look, we'll always be friends. It's all for the best. And Struan's twenty-two now, for God's sake. He's got his own life.'

'I know, but when we made those vows I thought it'd be for ever.'

'Doug, when they invented *till death do us part*, people only lived to thirty-five! And we've had a good run, to be fair.' He looked at me then, all doleful and puppy-dog eyes, and for one awful moment I thought he was going to do a U-turn.

'I'm sorry, Lind,' he said. And pulled me to him, holding me there for a good minute and a half. I'm not sure why I went along with it, but when I felt the familiar stirring inside and a slight thrusting from Douglas, my mind went into pragmatic mode. And I thought – *who knows how long it'll be till I get to have sex again?* I also thought – *may as well, for old times' sake*. And so we did it – a fully fledged farewell fornication. It was rather good, actually. Only problem was that when we were done, I just wanted him to leave the house. For one thing, I'd ordered new curtains for the bedroom – a sort of 'fresh start' purchase – and the woman was due to arrive any minute to measure up. Doug got a bit emotional about leaving. He even started crying. Thank God the doorbell rang. Fully expecting the curtains woman, when I answered the door I said brightly and breezily, 'Hello, are you from Drapes and Capes?', only to be met with confusion.

'No. I'm Denise,' she said sheepishly. 'I promised Doug I'd wait in the van but I thought you and I should meet. I don't want there to be a *thing* between us.' I could see what Douglas saw in her – albeit on a very superficial level. Slim – a size twelve maybe? Around early forties, with excessively highlighted hair, fake tan and a lot of gold. Heavily made-up, with extra-large lips. Y'know, the way these days they get them inflated or something. Looks ludicrous if you ask me, but still. Not for me to judge. I stood there, lost for words, until a panicky Douglas appeared behind me, still a little sweaty after what we'd just done, and presumably his guilt making him nervous that a fight might ensue.

'Come on, girls, I don't want any trouble,' he said unnecessarily. *In your dreams*, I thought.

'Oh, Denise!' I said with a smile, admittedly a wicked smile, given the fact I'd just shagged her boyfriend on the stairs. 'So good to meet you.' And I shook her hand. I think she was a bit thrown by this. Understandably. 'Look, I won't keep you. I think it's fantastic that you're making this move to Spain.'

'Really?' asked Denise.

'Absolutely. Fresh start for us all. Now, do stay in touch, won't you!' By this point I was ushering them back to the hire van, keen to get on with my life. As Dougie climbed into the driver's seat he gave me this meaningful look before starting the engine. And I noticed his flies were undone. But that wasn't my problem.

I think Denise had wanted to suss me out – just to reassure herself that, being the younger and conventionally more attractive option, she could guarantee fidelity from her new man. She probably took pity on me – the older woman who'd gone to seed. *If only you knew*, I thought. Just before she got into the van, I touched her arm and whispered, 'By the way, you might want to invest in a few tubes of antifungal cream for his toenails. Just to be on the safe side.' And with that, they were gone. I waved them off down the road feeling an overwhelming sense of generosity at having *gifted* Douglas to Denise.

That was six years ago. Struan's been out to visit them a couple of times and I think they're doing okay. They run a café on the Costa Dorada called Doolally's. Struan said Denise has gained quite a few pounds. I guess that's what happens when you fall in love.

With Wendy Taylor finally dispatched and sent off to the big caravan in the sky, I head back to my car. Fergus Murray does a slow drive-by in the hearse. He nods at me unsmilingly, so I give him a thumbs-up and a big silly grin. I look at my phone – just enough time to swing by Greggs for a macaroni pie and a fern cake before heading back to the office. I've got a meeting at two with Heather, the new head of HR. This will be our third meeting in two weeks. She's very nice, I must say. Really friendly.

3

Linda

The Unclaimed Heirs Unit is just one of several departments I've worked in at Boransay Council. I started off in transport, then waste disposal, followed by traffic fines, public parks and school catering. The latter coincided with my getting pregnant so they replaced me when I went on maternity leave and promised to find me a new role on my return. That's the great thing about working for the council – you can pretty much slot into a whole array of public-serving roles. Almost a year later, I came back part-time so I could look after the baby. I'd work Monday to Friday, ten till two, which allowed me to do nursery drop-offs and pick-ups, get home and have Mummy time till my husband Douglas got in from work. It was a rock-solid routine and I loved it. They were probably – no definitely – the happiest years of my working life. Happiest years of my ENTIRE life, in fact, let's not beat around the bush.

Then June the second happened.
   1994.
   And my soul collapsed in pain.

Afterwards, I didn't think I'd be able to breathe again, let alone get dressed and go back to work. Because it's not something you ever recover *from*, just learn to live *with*. Douglas, God bless him, kept on at me. Wouldn't let me drown, even though he too must have been suffocating in sorrow. Well, I know he was. But he finally got through and persuaded me to return. 'It'll give you a bit of focus, Lindy,' he'd say.

We've been divorced nearly six years, me and Doug. But his patience back then was extraordinary – taking all sorts of backlashes from me, as if it was his fault, poor man.

It was no one's fault.

That's what they kept telling me.

And eventually I just surrendered and gave up trying to blame.

Of course, when I *did* return to work, I was handled with kid gloves. Nobody knew what to say around me. Or if they did, it didn't matter because I couldn't really hear much anyone said back then. I went in to see the nice lady in HR – which wasn't called HR in those days, just *personnel*. She tried to ascertain where I'd like to work, what interested me.

Nothing, I told her.

Nothing interested me.

But undeterred, like an optimistic careers officer sat across a school desk from a reluctant teenager, the HR lady handed me a list of available roles on offer in Boransay Council, suggesting I went for something benign and uplifting, like Libraries or Adult Learning.

And that's when I first discovered it. *The Unclaimed Heirs Unit is looking for a new team member. The ideal candidate will assist in tracking down a deceased person's next of kin, putting their affairs in order, tidying up and closing down their homes.*

The Unclaimed Heirs Unit. Hadn't even heard of it before! The HR lady looked horrified when I asked for more information, saying that given my recent experience, working in any area death-related might be a bad idea. (These days they'd call it *triggering*. Another one for the pet-hate list.) But I was intrigued, and insisted on talking to someone who worked there.

Josie Byars was the outgoing employee whose job was up for grabs. And as soon as she began describing her work, I knew it was meant for me. 'Giving eulogies for the unmourned and unremembered is not actually part of the job description,' she said. 'But I feel honour-bound to do it. The final piece in the jigsaw, if you like. Doesn't everyone deserve a farewell? Even if there's only one person there to say goodbye?'

Doesn't everyone deserve a farewell?

It helped me crawl back to life. Gave me some sort of purpose. And time passed and I got stronger until everyone expected me to change jobs – like it was something I needed to get out of my system.

Thirty years later, and I'm still here. I've lost count of the number of cases we've handled. Some are straightforward, some quite a challenge. Because you never know what you're going to find when you open up that front door and step inside. Jean and I always gear ourselves up for the worst – y'know, rancid meat in the fridge, overflowing ashtrays and cans of lager strewn across the floor. But more often than not, the homes of the deceased are in order and well cared for. Which makes you wonder why they've ended up alone. Of course, it's very presumptuous of me to judge 'being alone' as a negative. Some people actually *choose* a solitary life. And who am I to say that's wrong?

4

Linda

'No way, Missy!' I declare in a rather melodramatic explosion, instantly feeling a fool for saying 'Missy', as if I'm Erin Brockovich or some other feisty female in a film. Still, I'm in shock. Heather – the 'nice' HR lady – just mooted the idea of my taking voluntary redundancy. 'It's not *you*, Linda, it's the system. With digital footprints being what they are, everything's going more and more online and the role will be better suited to someone with advanced IT skills.'

Well that's not me, to be fair. But *redundant*??

'It's a kick in the teeth, you know. Being told you're no use any more.'

'Oh come on now, Linda, you know that's not what we're saying,' she replies. And I do, but I'm secretly enjoying making her squirm with my passive aggression.

'A computer can't deliver someone's eulogy, Heather. A computer can't attend funerals of the unbeloved.'

Heather sighs and I know what's coming. 'It's lovely that you do what you do, Linda. But we both know it's not actually part of the job description, just a nice little addition.'

I feel utterly patronized. 'And how would you like it, Heather, if nobody turned up to *your* funeral.' I realize what I've just said sounds ridiculous and, mercifully, she moves on.

'Look,' she sighs again, 'it really is voluntary. You're not obliged to do it, but if you decide to stay on we'd have to redeploy you to a different department, that's all. Think about it.'

I nod respectfully and ask if there's anything else she needs to discuss, before turning on my heel and leaving the room. As I do so, Heather says gently, 'No shame in early retirement, Linda. Think of all the hobbies you could take up!'

*

I can barely concentrate this afternoon, mulling the whole thing over whilst writing my name in a two-hundred-gram bar of hazelnut chocolate for comfort. I always keep a good supply in my desk for emergencies.

My desk.

Whose desk will it become after I leave, I wonder? I'm just about to drop into a vat of self-pity – a place I rarely visit – when I get a call from reception to say someone called Ray Dalgleish is here to see me. My redundancy worry is soon forgotten and replaced by a flutter of excitement at the prospect of hearing the end of Wendy Taylor's story. I grab the box of memorabilia and head down to reception, where I berate myself for breaking a golden rule in life: never assume sod all. Turns out Ray is not a man but *Raynor*, a very tall woman in her sixties with spiky red hair and a tattoo on her neck that says *delicious*.

'She was never happy with Rafiq. Told me that from day one. We met in a launderette, you see. And there's always a lot of waiting around in a launderette, so you get to know people quite quick.' Raynor doesn't seem able to stand still. She gives the impression of someone in a hurry, constantly running her fingers through her angry hair and checking behind her. 'Within a week we were sleeping together.'

'Good Lord!' I blurt out. Wasn't expecting that.

'She was amazing in bed,' Raynor continues.

'Well, that's lovely,' I say, a tad self-conscious that we are in a very public place and Raynor is rather loud. I hand her the box of memorabilia. 'Anyway, here are Wendy's things. There's not much in there I'm afraid, but . . .'

'When *he* found out he went ballistic. Looking at it now, I can understand why, but he was vile to her. Made her choose. Said if she chose me he'd cut her off without a penny and chuck her on to the streets. Hideous twat.'

By now I've been drawn in. I no longer care that colleagues are walking past and raising eyebrows. 'She chose him, and he *still* chucked her out. I should have forgiven her, stayed with her, but I was so cut up at the time. I ended up being as big a hideous twat as Rafiq!' At this she starts weeping, burying her head in my neck, leaving me with no option other than to comfort her in an embrace.

'You know that in her will she forgave you?'

Raynor snuffles that she does. 'Yeah, doesn't help though, does it. All too late now. Anyway, cheers for this,' she mumbles, taking the box and shuffling off.

The lives people live. We have no idea, do we?

5

Linda

It's surprising how quickly you can change your mind about something. By the time I get home, I've done a complete U-turn on the whole early-retirement thing. The redundancy package is very tempting, for a start, and it does actually make sense to stop work while I've still got my marbles and the use of my legs. My mother always said I could turn a problem into a gift and so yes, I'm going to accept Heather's offer and embrace this next chapter of my life with joy.

I'd always thought I'd dread retirement, that it would somehow seal the deal on the unavoidable arrival of old age. But now that I've accepted it, I'm excited at the prospect. And I'm already making plans. Most of them will involve my four-year-old grandson Zander, of course: full-time grandmotherhood is beckoning with open arms and I intend to run into them at speed. I'm already very hands-on in the childcare department, seeing as Zander lives with me. As does my son Struan. Thankfully, Struan's wife Lauren – or rather *ex*-wife Lauren – does not. She lives an hour away in her home town of Bordgalsh and has done for the past year, since she and Struan split up. I'm happy keeping that distance, because Lauren is the embodiment of a nightmare daughter-in-law and certainly won't feature in my retirement plans.

*

'Bit out of the blue, Mum, isn't it?' Struan asks later on as he makes our nightly hot chocolate.

'I suppose so,' I say, 'but now that I think about it, Heather's had me in for several of her "chats" of late and I guess she was just testing the water to see how I'd react.'

'And you're sure you're not rushing into it? 'Cos once you've left, you've left.'

'Got to take a few risks in life, Struan, and to be honest, now I've decided, I'm feeling quite excited. I'm gonna do ballroom dancing, bake cakes for the farmers' market – even take upholstery classes!'

'Now *that* I have *got* to see!'

'The best bit is that I can look after Zander!'

'You already do,' Struan replies with a smile.

'But I can have him so much more, Struan. Which will give you more time to yourself . . .' I hesitate and launch in. 'And more time to maybe get out there and meet someone.' I daren't look at him when I say it, because it's a very sensitive area. He knows I know he's still in love with Lauren. I just pretend to be ignorant of the fact. As predicted, he changes the subject.

'Don't you think you'll miss it, though?'

I pause for a moment, because, yes, of course I will. A bit. 'The job's changing, Stru. It's not like it'll be the same there any more.' I think he can see the doubt on my face but decides to move on.

'Go on then, what else are you gonna do?'

'Well, d'you remember I always wanted to go paddleboarding on Loch Braemor?'

'Ah yes.'

Neither of us allude to it, but I'm sure Struan, like me, is remembering an awkward conversation on the subject several months ago at a family pub lunch. Lauren was there that day when I shared my wish to paddleboard. Unsurprisingly, she made a few snide remarks about wetsuits.

'Do they make them in your size, Linda?'

Lauren never passes up an opportunity to point out that I'm fat. Not incapacitatingly so – I mean, I'm still pretty agile for a woman of my heft. I can dance the pants off a twenty-two-year-old, and my downward dog is the envy of many a thin girl. But in terms of actual body mass, I'm definitely the wrong side of a size 20. I'm not pretending when I say I really don't mind being big – yes, being thinner would make life easier. I'd take up less room, I'd get more choice in clothes and I wouldn't run the risk of embarrassment by not fitting into the seat on a ride in Alton Towers. But in general it doesn't bother me.

What *does* bother me is that there's a natural bias against you when you're fat. For one thing, I think people expect you to be a bit thick. They also expect you to cower nervously and feel all self-conscious, pulling down the hem of your top to hide your big stomach or never eating in public for fear of being called Fatty. Well, I'm not that person. But when Lauren first met me, I think she expected me to *be* that person. And although I could bat away her fattist put-downs with razor-sharp comebacks, she still couldn't quite resist sticking the knife in. 'You'll need to be careful, Linda,' she'd continued. 'Woman I know, she was big like you, and they couldn't get a wetsuit to fit her. So she ended up doing it in leggings and a vest, got stung to hell by a jellyfish.'

'They don't have jellyfish in lochs, Lauren,' I pointed out. 'Fresh water, y'see.' As well as being callous, Lauren is also quite intellectually challenged.

She's beautiful, I'll give her that, so I can see why Struan was attracted on a very superficial level. Everything else though? I just don't get it. For a start, I've never really understood what she does for a living and why she needs so much help with childcare. I know she's a sometime hand model because that's her excuse for never doing the washing-up. And I think she's been an energy worker, a dog groomer, a nail technician and a cook. Most recently she's started *influencing*. 'I'm an influencer, Linda. And I'm building up a really good following.' I don't really know what that means. Because for me, work has always been a Monday to Friday office-hours affair. Though not for much longer, of course!

When I go to bed I lie there, eyes open and beaming. This

decision to stop work could be one of my best and I'm almost annoyed with myself for not doing it sooner. Heather suggested February as a retirement date and in my head I've started the countdown. Wendy Taylor will hopefully have been my last case and now all I need to do is enjoy Christmas, tidy my desk and get ready for the next chapter of my life.

6

Linda

A week later, and I'm sucking on a sherbet lemon whilst surfing the net for plus-size wetsuits, when an email comes in from my line manager, Gillian Coles. Bizarre when she's sitting only fifteen feet away, but Gillian likes to get everything down in writing. The heading is 'new case', with a reference number and location: Levi Norman, seventy-three-year-old male, Isle of Storrich.

My heart sinks. *Where's the Isle of Storrich??* I ask, already dreading the answer will mean days away.

Gillian's reply, as ever, is curt and to the point.

Off Roaken. Travel by ferry.

Oh for heaven's sake. It's a bit rich, this. Making me redundant, then sending me off on a big fat case three weeks before Christmas. Talk about getting their money's worth. Also, if I start a new case now it will undoubtedly be left unresolved, and I'll leave at the end of February with a messy desk, so to speak. And it's not like it's down the road. Some godforsaken island that I've never even heard of. In the middle of bloody winter.

Do I have to? I email back like a petulant child. *Can't Jean take Liam?*

Liam on leave. Jean unviable – health issues. Call undertakers to assist. Leave tomorrow. Accom at Storrich Arms.

I wonder if in another life Gillian worked as a telegram writer or a Morse coder. She'd have made a good spy. I reply to her in the language she understands – *Roger. On it* – and spend the rest of the afternoon in a mildly bad mood. I'm doubly miffed when I find out that Jean's 'health issue' preventing her from taking the Storrich case is that she gets seasick. Well, I'm sorry, Jean! Buy a packet of flippin' Sea-legs. See an acupuncturist.

I start googling 'The Storrich Arms' and resentfully book myself a room.

I leave work at four and pick up my little Zander en route. By then, of course, my bad mood has lifted because seeing Zander's little smiling face is enough to bust the biggest of black clouds. I bend down to my beloved grandson and scoop him up into a huge bingo-winged cuddle.

'What have you got there, ma wee pet?' I say, looking at his painting and inhaling the gorgeous scent of his hair. 'Is it a tractor?'

'It's a shark,' says his teacher, and quickly I correct myself.

'Yes a shark, silly Nana Lind. That's what I meant!'

We arrive home to the welcoming sight of Struan's lasagne. I have to say, it's quite a treat having food cooked for me, and an even bigger treat getting to share it at the table like a proper family.

'How long will you be gone?' asks Struan. I've just told him about the new case in Storrich.

'It's a two-hour drive to Roaken, then a ferry to the island. Reckon I'll need at least two days there, maybe three, so all being well I'll be home for the weekend.'

'And you're going alone?'

'No, they're organizing an undertaker to accompany me. It's the woman from Murray's – Ailsa something? She'll pick me up tomorrow first thing and drive me there.'

'God, not in a hearse, surely?'

'Ha! Can you imagine! No love, it's one of those Black Maria-type vehicles – a posh transit van, for want of a better description.

Essentially a hearse, but with no big rear windows or flower arrangements spelling out "DAD". We have to bring the—' I mouth the word *body* so as not to upset Zander, 'back to the mainland, and the cremation will take place in Boransay for efficiency.'

'God, Mum, your job. Honestly. Doesn't it ever creep you out?'

'Well, it's not for much longer, is it? And these are exceptional circumstances: if there was a crem on the island then it'd be done and dusted. It'll be my last case. So.'

Once the dishes are cleared I set about making dessert – strawberries, cream and my own home-made meringues. Can't bear shop-bought, they disintegrate into powder and are crammed with chemicals. My meringues are heaven-sent, soft and sweet and slightly caramelish. I use my mother's recipe – always makes me smile and think of her when I make them. I'm just spooning out the double cream when the bell goes. 'I'll get it,' says Struan and heads to the front door, little Zander in tow. My heart sinks moments later when I hear Zander shout, 'Mummy!' and I dread what's about to happen.

Lauren comes into the kitchen shrouded in an air of self-pity. God, she's good. She should've been on the stage. 'Hello, Linda,' she says solemnly. 'Struan tells me you've been sacked!'

'What?'

'No,' Struan blusters, 'I said *made redundant*, it's not—'

'Same thing,' says Lauren, looking bored.

'Actually, it's neither. I'm taking early retirement, if you must know.'

My reply is stiff. Formal. But I can't help it. As usual she's turned up out of the blue – Christ, that woman is allergic to routine. Doesn't she realize how destructive it is for my little Zander, not knowing if he's coming or going? I try to be friendly. 'Can I interest you in a meringue?'

'God, no. I couldn't eat a thing. Not for Zander either please, too much sugar before bed.'

'Well, I was only going to give him a half portion—' I reply, before Struan interrupts.

'Best not to, eh, Mum?' And in just that one sentence, I feel utterly betrayed. Ridiculous, I know. But the speed with which Struan takes her side is astonishing, and I feel hopeless. Not for myself. For him.

'Actually, Linda, could you give us some privacy?' Lauren asks. And I want to *throttle* her! I know the sensible thing would be to relent, to say *yes of course*, but I'll be buggered if I'm going to let this witch of an ex-wife boss me around in my own home. 'You're very welcome to go in the front room if you want to talk,' I say calmly. And I can feel Struan's eyes on me, as he silently wills me not to start a row.

Lauren sighs. It's that passive-aggressive wearied expression that she's mastered so well. 'Linda,' she says quietly, 'I'm really not strong enough right now for confrontation.'

'I'm not confronting you, Lauren,' I reply, just as quietly. 'But you've not been in touch with your husband or your child for nearly a week and now you come waltzing in here telling me where I can and can't sit. Well, you may think you can bully my son into doing what you want, but you won't bully his mother, got it?'

Lauren gasps and runs out of the room. Struan glares at me before following her. 'Thanks, Mum,' he hisses. 'Look after Zander.' He doesn't quite slam the door but leaves in enough of a fit to make his feelings known.

Me and Zander look at each other and I whisper, 'D'you want one of Nannie Linda's meringues now?' He nods complicitly and we both dive in with our spoons.

Half an hour later, Lauren and Struan are still 'talking' in the front room. I take Zander up to bed for 'wee-wees and teeth', read him a story and settle him down for the night. Then I creep out of his room and into mine, to start packing for my trip to Storrich. I've checked the weather forecast online – Storrich being in the Gulf Stream, the elements there are different from inland. Despite it being December, the temperature is unlikely to be lower than ten degrees, with crisp sunshine and no rain. There's a storm forecast for later in the week, but I'll be back on dry land by then. I pack two pairs of smart trousers, a fleece, a blouse and a jumper, along with two T-shirts and three pairs of pants. I always pride myself on my pants. That's another thing you're not expected to possess if you're fat: glamorous knickers. But my underwear collection is beautiful. Even if I do say so myself. And even if it's been a while since I've been able to show it off to anyone. Wearing nice knickers makes me feel sexy and alive. It's true. And I always wear matching bras. I balk at the idea of wearing a clashing set. It's wrong on so many levels. I put together a small travel washbag and pick out a nice nightie to wear. Then I have second thoughts and the old Girl Guide in me comes to life. What if the Storrich Arms is cold and draughty? Better pack some bedsocks in case. I'm just deciding whether or not to take a hot-water bottle when I hear the front door slam. I roll my eyes at absolutely no one and head downstairs to find out the latest.

'Lauren wants me and Zander to move to Bordgalsh. To be nearer to her and her parents.'

'Struan, it's a whole hour away! And a ridiculous idea!!'

'Not really, Mum, be fair. The travel back and forth is exhausting her.'

'Exhausting her?? When?? On the two or three occasions she's managed to make the journey?'

I. Am. Fuming.

'Don't be sarcastic, Mum, she's not been that bad. And I can see her point – we do all need to live closer, for Zander's sake.'

'So tell her to move back to Boransay, then!'

He stops then and I can see he's choosing his words carefully. 'I think . . . I think Lauren wants her own parents to be more involved in Zander's childcare. It's difficult . . . your relationship with her . . . I mean, it's not exactly . . . Look, you're bound to be defensive of me, aren't you?'

'Well, of course I am!'

'And Lauren senses this, and it makes her anxious. She says she needs to feel she's in a safe space.'

'Oh for the LOVE OF GOD!' I say, too loudly, and Struan shushes me, pointing to the ceiling – a reminder that Zander is asleep. I take a deep breath.

'Where will you live?' I ask mournfully.

'For the time being, Lauren's brother has a friend with a spare room and—'

'You're going to *house share*!?' I don't bother to hide my disgust.

'It's a temporary thing, until I can find somewhere more permanent.'

Permanent. The word punches me in the stomach.

'It's what she wants,' Struan adds quietly.

'So what? What about what *you* want, Struan! You can't just up sticks and turn your life upside down on a whim! What about your job? What about Zander? His school and everything?'

Struan sighs. 'It's not on a whim. She's been thinking about it for a while, she said. She thinks it will make things easier. For everyone. Simon and Lucy can help out, and so can Lauren's old friends. It makes complete sense, when you think about it.'

'Hang on a minute!' I'm nearly shouting again now. 'What about *me*? I help out all the time! I'm helping out right now, for God's sake, you're staying in my house.'

'Mum, calm down. You're getting hysterical.'

I take a deep breath. If there's one thing inclined to make me *not* calm, it's being told to calm down. I shut my eyes and gather myself. This battle will not be won with raised voices.

'Okay,' I say, more to myself than to Struan. 'When is this move going to take place? Surely not till the summer? You'll want Zander to finish the school y—'

'After Christmas,' he says. 'New Year seems as good a time as any.' His voice fades, and he can't look at me when he speaks. I hold my hand up. I don't want to hear any more. It's too, too much. Simon and Lucy are stealing my boys. And my heart is going to break.

'I need to finish packing,' I say, a lump growing bigger in my throat. 'Zander went off straight away. I read him *The Cat in the*

Hat.' I want to cry when I say it. I know Bordgalsh is only an hour away, but it may as well be on the other side of the world. Reading Dr Seuss will become Simon and Lucy's job now, a thing of the past for me. And there was I thinking it was a thing of the future – a regular shared joy in my forthcoming retirement. What's the saying? If you want to make God laugh, tell him your plans.

I rush upstairs and shut the door behind me before I pull my secret supply box from under the bed. Inside are dozens of chocolate bars: Caramels, Wispas, Dairy Milks, Galaxies, Mars bars, Twixes – the lot. Still sat on the floor, I hurriedly rip the wrapper off one and wolf it down almost in a single go, then start on the second. After seven bars, breathless, sweating and nauseous, I shut my eyes and tell myself to stop. Enough now. Enough.

As I clean my teeth in a pathetic attempt to rid myself of the binge after-effects, my eyes are streaming with tears.

7

Linda

The following morning I come downstairs with my holdall to be greeted by Struan and Zander at the breakfast counter, my little man all ready for school. I try and smile when I speak but I'm overcome with a tremendous sense of what must be separation anxiety. My head is dull and my mouth is dry from last night's self-sabotage and there's an ache, a longing, lodged right in the middle of my breast-bone. I manage a 'Have you had enough breakfast?'

'Yes. We had porridge, didn't we, Zand? D'you need a wee before we go?' He's asking Zander, not me. Zander shakes his head. 'Okay, well, let's get your coat on, then, shall we?'

There's an awkward silence as Struan guides his little boy's arms inside the sleeves. I watch Zander chatting away to Foxy, his stuffed vulpine friend who's never left his side since he was born, unaware of the change coming at him over the horizon.

'Will you let me know when you get to—'

'Storrich,' I say.

'Yes. Just text me to let me know you've landed.'

'If they've got reception. You know what the islands are like.'

There's another awkward silence between us. 'I want you to wish us well, Mum. I want you to want it to work.'

I dig deep. Right into the tips of my toes. 'Of course I want it to work. I just don't see how she—'

Struan interrupts me. 'That's all you need to say,' he smiles. 'Thanks.'

We hug and Zander runs up and joins us for a group cuddle. I am fighting not to cry.

'Right, off you go, you two. And stay out of trouble. I won't see you out.' They leave, shutting the door gently behind them, and I stand stock-still, pushing down the tears, breathing away the anger at the injustice and frustration at my son's weakness when it comes to that awful, awful woman. It's moments later that the doorbell goes and I feel a reprieve from my pain – they'll have forgotten something and I'll get to have a bonus hug. But when I open the door it's not Struan standing there but Fergus Murray, the undertaker.

'Linda Standish,' he announces, just as displeased to see me as I am to see him.

'What are you doing here, Fergus Murray?'

He turns to the empty hearse behind him. 'Your carriage awaits,' he says. Without even a glimmer of a smile.

8

Linda

'Mint?'

It's the first bit of conversation we've had for at least forty minutes and even then it was 'let me know when you need a comfort break'. I'd never heard the expression before.

'What's a comfort break?' I asked quite innocently, and he blushed. He actually went red.

'You know, when you need . . . when you want to—'

'Oh! When I need a wee!' I said. And he just coughed a small dry cough before reverting to silent mode.

'Go on then,' I say. And he hands me the packet, keeping his eyes firmly on the road.

I've got at least forty-eight hours ahead of me with this fun-bucket. Ye gods.

It's almost midday when we arrive in Roaken. Being Scotland in December and fairly far north, this is the brightest the day is ever going to get, and it's as gloomy as a tomb. Quite a fitting analogy, considering we're travelling in a hearse. Turns out Ailsa, the undertaker who I'd expected to accompany me, has gone down with shingles and the Black Maria was needed elsewhere, so Fergus was allocated the job. Along with his black Mercedes limousine. I wish I could sit in the back. But I can hardly sprawl out in a hearse. Honestly, the looks we're getting. We're going at a fair pace and I think this surprises people, especially when we overtake on the dual carriageway.

The ferry-port town of Roaken is not a big place. It's quaint and very much a tourist paradise, with visitors passing through in droves every year. And even though it's a good hundred miles away from Loch Ness, the Monster still inhabits all the many gift shops the town offers up. Amazing how Nessie has found her way even this far away from her aquatic home. It must be absolutely bonkers-busy in the summer. People coming from all over the place, catching ferries to the Hebrides and Skye – I take it for granted sometimes, being Scottish. This western coastline is like nothing on earth. Today of course, being mid-December, there are few visitors around and many shops are closed until the season begins again at Easter. The main street has been decorated with pretty Christmas lights and a huge fir tree made from lobster creels dominates one end of the seafront promenade. It still feels alive. No out-of-season bleakness pervades this town like other holiday resorts I've been to mid-winter.

'Do you have your passport ready?' Fergus Murray asks as we approach the parking spaces for the ferry queue.

'Duh, no!' I respond incredulously. 'We're going to a Scottish island twenty miles off the mainland. Why on earth would I need a passport?'

He shrugs and then smirks.

'Oh! It's a joke!' I say sarcastically. 'God, you're a hoot!'

Some kids approach but keep their distance, then take out their phones and start taking photos. I've got used to the fact that we are in a hearse and forget what a novelty it must be for others. Not often you see a hearse on a ferry, I should imagine. I expect Fergus to be outraged. But *I'm* more bothered than he is. I wind down the window and shout at them.

'Have some respect for the dead, will you? Go on, bugger off.' When I wind the window back up I see that Fergus hasn't even looked up from his game of Spelling Bee.

'It's not their fault,' he says. 'Teenagers have become desensitized. They see life as they would a video game. Lockdown has a lot to answer for.' I open my mouth to speak but nothing comes out. I'm both shocked and impressed.

'Those were the most words you've uttered to me on this entire journey,' I say. And still he doesn't look up.

'If you've got nothing worth saying, say nothing at all.'

'And he's back in the room!' I mutter.

An hour later, we are sitting at a table in the ferry's café. Not the most salubrious eatery, to be honest. I was tempted by a custard slice, but the man behind the counter had oil beneath his fingernails and kept rubbing his beard. So I took a rain check. There aren't many other passengers. Hardly surprising for this time of year, and although I'd rather sit somewhere else and read my book, I can't bring myself to be that rude to Fergus Murray. It's not his fault we've been lumped together, after all.

'So let's go through the schedule, then,' I say, trying to sound as friendly as possible. I take out my iPad whilst Fergus dons a pair of reading glasses and produces a small notebook from his jacket.

'I have some information of my own and took the trouble of making a few notes,' he says, turning to the page entitled 'Storrich'.

'That's very old-school,' I comment, pointing at the book.

In turn he gestures at my tablet. 'Well, those things are great until they break down.' I ignore the faint sneer.

'Okay, so we'll be entering the home of Levi Norman, deceased December the second, 2024—'

'Address?' enquires Fergus without looking up, pencil poised.

'Beannach Lodge, Storrich.' He jots this down.

'Postcode?'

'Are you for real? What does the postcode matter – there's only a hundred and fifty-odd living on the whole island, they've probably all got the same one—'

'Which is?'

I sigh, 'Oh for God's sake.' I check my notes. 'RN83 6PJ. Can I go on?'

He nods. 'And for the record, the population is two hundred and seventy-six. Carry on.'

'Right. So he died on the second of December aged seventy-three, and the local undertaker, Hamish Hamilton, has taken charge of Mr Norman's . . . of Mr Norman until we are able to transfer—'

'He's a shepherd,' interrupts Fergus.

'Sorry?'

'Hamish Hamilton is the island's undertaker and sheep farmer.'

'Oh, right. How do you—?'

'Research, Linda Standish. I take my work seriously. Don't just turn up on the day and hope for the best.'

I'm a bit stumped by this. 'Can you actually *be* a shepherd as well as an undertaker?'

'Needs must in these communities, from what I gather. Everyone does more than one job.'

Fair point. I turn back to my iPad. 'Okay, so Hamish Hamilton—'

'He's also an ironmonger.'

'Oh, now you're just winding me up.'

'I most certainly am not. He runs a small ironmongery-slash-chandlery out of his front room and in the back he—'

'Stores the bodies?' I know it sounds grim, but this is where we're at. Fergus Murray gives me evils.

'In the rear of the property he conducts any necessary undertaking, as and when required.' He's ever the epitome of decorum when it comes to discussing all things corpse-related.

'I suppose, given the minuscule population on the island, he couldn't be a full-time undertaker, his business would go under,' I muse.

'Six *feet* under!' smirks Fergus. I pause for a moment and look at him.

'Oh my God, did you just make another joke?'

He shrugs and the smirk drops. And I feel a bit ashamed for

embarrassing him. 'Sorry,' I mumble and move on swiftly. 'Okay, so Hamish is our man and certainly that's who you'll have most dealings with. As for me, I'll be spending the day tomorrow looking through Levi's home. If you feel like helping out, that'd be greatly appreciated. The sooner we wrap this up, the sooner we can get back to civilization.'

'That's very arrogant of you, Linda Standish – to assume that the Storrich islanders are not civilized.'

'Oh shut up, you know what I mean. And don't be such a hypocrite – are you honestly saying you'd rather live on an island than in the thriving metropolis of Boransay?'

'My personal opinions don't come into this,' he says. The pompous git.

We talk over a few more details about the job ahead. I explain that the minister, who lives on a neighbouring island, has arranged for a woman from the kirk to help clear the house and box things up for charity or whatever. After this exchange we go back to our respective silences and I venture out on to the small deck for some fresh air.

I do love a ferry. In fact, I love ferries *and* islands, so this visit to Storrich, although under sad circumstances, and despite my reluctance to leave my boys, is actually a nice little trip for me. Thinking about it, maybe that's one for the retirement list – to visit as many islands in the British Isles as I can muster. I glance at my phone and think about video-calling Struan so I can get my fix of Zander. But there's no signal. And anyway he'll be in nursery till half four. My heart lurches. It's nearly Christmas and with all the kerfuffle of the past week, we've not even discussed any arrangements.

I hate feeling needy. My mood is darkening with the grey December sky as the winter sun creeps over the horizon and the daylight begins to fade. Almost dark and it's only three o'clock. I can see my breath in the cold air, the crystal-white foam splashing out as the bow cuts through the cobalt-coloured water. It will not do to let myself get all maudlin. It will not do one jot. I shake the doldrums away and concentrate on the task ahead. Not far now, Storrich stands large and proud in front of us. It's sort of turtle-shaped from this angle, or to be more accurate, *legless* turtle-shaped, with one end of the island its shell and the other end its neck and head. Despite the fading light, I can still make out the dwellings scattered high and low, a few clumped together but mostly on their own. The lights in the windows peep out as smoke swirls up from the chimneys and the peat fires beneath them. It's quite a welcoming sight, really – despite the lack of trees, just weather-battered grass on the headlands and gorse bushes asleep till spring, the sea lapping gently against the rocks that skirt the island's base. The tinny voice on the tannoy announces in a strong Highland accent that we will shortly be docking and would all car passengers return to their vehicles.

I wonder about Levi Norman and what made him move here. From what I've discovered so far, he was Welsh and had made Storrich his home since 2018. Maybe he'd loved islands and ferries too. Funny to think I will find out so much about him, and yet he never knew of my existence. My job is a kind of legalized voyeurism, I guess. A one-way street into a stranger's life before driving out the other side without them even knowing. Will I miss it when I retire? I sigh to myself and head back inside, where Fergus Murray stands waiting.

'Come on,' he says, 'we've been instructed to—'

'Yes, all right, keep your hair on.' And I notice him surreptitiously touch the bald patch at the back of his head.

9

Linda

'It's nae fancy, but it does the job.' Brodie McLeod, the landlord of the Storrich Arms, is showing me my room. He's made no concession to dressing well, sporting a blue fisherman's smock resplendent with oil stain, green tracksuit bottoms (bearing a white side-stripe) and an incongruous pair of flash Reeboks. I can't quite work out his age – think that's the beard and the salt-and-pepper mop of hair. Combined with the laughter lines and knowing smile, he could land anywhere between forty and sixty-five.

'Oh, it's lovely!' I say. And I mean it. There's a hefty iron-framed bed that looks a hundred years old and as if it has seen some action, covered with a beautiful patchwork quilt. I reckon I'll sleep well in there tonight. It's dark outside now, but Brodie assures me I'll get a great view in the morning.

'On a good day you can see Mull and Iona. On a better day you'll catch a wee glimpse of Skye.' He's a friendly chap, is Brodie. I don't know why, but I'd been expecting distrust and the opposite of a warm welcome.

'Is there a kettle?' I ask.

'No, but there's a kitchen. Help yourself. It's never locked. Bathroom's down the way there. And don't be put off by the brown water – that's just the peat. Good for the skin. You'll be wanting something to eat?'

I make my usual defensive joke that bats away any judgement on my size. 'Ach, indeed!' I say brightly. 'Took a lot of hard work and many meals to achieve this figure!'

Brodie doesn't laugh, just nods sagely as if what I've said is factually correct. Which I suppose it is. 'We've got lamb broth on the go, and Minty's made a cranachan.'

With that, he's gone. I can't quite put my finger on it, but he's left me feeling somewhat discombobulated. And I can't work out if it's a good or a bad discombobulation. There's just something otherworldly about this place. I sit on the bed and take out my phone to text Struan. There's only one bar of signal – *Arrived safe, are you okay?* I watch the screen till the message goes green, then head to the bathroom to run myself a peaty bath. People pay good money at a health farm for a peaty bath. I'm a lucky girl.

An hour later, refreshed and very pink-cheeked, I make my way down to the bar. Fergus is already there, tucking into a bowl of the aforementioned lamb broth. He's changed into 'casual wear' – a polo shirt, cream chinos and a sweater thrown over his shoulders which makes him look like a model in a 1970s golfing catalogue. I wonder how he's managed to be so well turned-out and whether he pressed his clothes before coming downstairs. Though the Storrich Arms doesn't strike me as an establishment that might possess an ironing board. Especially judging by Brodie the landlord's unchanged attire.

'You look very dapper,' I say to Fergus with a smile. But he's got a mouthful of broth and only manages to nod. Without being asked, Brodie places a bowl in front of me and a pile of home-made soda bread. He returns with a small cauldron-type vessel and begins ladling out a steamy serving of lamb broth, which I must say looks very appetizing. 'Thanks,' I say.

'Aye. Beer?'

'Do you have any alcohol-free lager?'

Unfairly, as it turns out, I'm expecting Brodie to scoff at the suggestion of beer with no booze in it. But he offers me a choice of three zero-per-cent beverages plus an alcohol-free gin.

'I'm impressed!' I say, and Brodie looks bemused.

'Lot of folk don't drink these days,' he says. 'Me included.'

'Did you have a problem?' asks Fergus, whilst munching some bread.

'Oh for God's sake,' I scoff. 'Why do people always assume you have a problem with booze if you don't drink?'

'Just that most people do,' says Fergus, taking a big glug of red wine. 'Drink, I mean.'

'And some people choose not to flood their system with sweetened engine oil!' I retort.

'Careful you don't twist your ankle,' says Brodie with a smirk.

'Sorry?'

'When you fall off your wee soapbox.'

I feel stupid now. And even more so when Fergus laughs, as if in collusion with our landlord. I should've known better than to show my feelings about booze. It's just, it's a pet hate of mine – another one to add to the grumpy-old-woman list – this black-and-white attitude towards teetotallers. You're either religious or a recovering alcoholic. I am neither. I simply don't drink.

I tried it once when I was fifteen – a whole flagon of cider. Ended up getting my stomach pumped at Inverness Infirmary. You'd think that would be enough to put me off – but I tried again a year or so later and just, well, didn't like it. I hated the taste and I hated the way it made me feel. I liken it to eating haggis. Some people balk at the prospect. And for some people it's their favourite dish. Well, I balk at the thought of drinking alcohol. Always have done. I glance at Fergus, whose glass, I notice, is being topped up with more red wine, his lips and teeth already stained, giving him a somewhat vampirish air. I shouldn't judge, of course. Because the truth is, I choose to poison myself with a different drug: sugar – mainly in the form of chocolate or Victoria sponge. And people say to me, *Must be lovely not having hangovers any more*, and I smile and think, *You say that, but try waking up in the morning when you've consumed an entire family-sized trifle and a two-litre tub of Häagen-Dazs the night before.* I don't think the urge to binge is likely over the next couple of nights, which is a godsend given the limited menu at the Storrich Arms.

'This is very tasty,' I say of the broth, keen to change the subject.

'Aye. Minty's a fair cook.'

'Is Minty your wife?'

Brodie smiles. 'MINTY!' he calls into the kitchen and Minty appears in the archway at the side of the bar. She's a small, wiry woman aged anywhere upwards of eighty-five, wearing a clean, tight apron and a frown. 'This lassie wonders if we're married!' And Minty stares at me hard, before letting out the heartiest and deepest laugh, revealing the absence of a bottom incisor. Then, shaking her head, she disappears back to her work. I notice Brodie doesn't actually deny being married to Minty, but I daren't ask again. I dive into my broth and let Fergus, now slightly merry, do the talking. 'So your lamb is local, I take it?'

'Oh aye. From Hamish. Slaughters them himself.'

Nice, I think.

'Hamish Hamilton?'

'Aye.'

'He's quite a jack of all trades, this Hamish, isn't he?' I say, juggling a piece of hot potato in my mouth. 'We'll be meeting with him tomorrow to . . . y'know, arrange for the handover of Mr Norman.'

Brodie nods knowingly and an amiable silence descends amongst us, in respect for the dead and disturbed only by the crackle of the logs burning on the fire. Which is throwing out a whack of heat and adding to the whole cosy atmosphere of the pub. There's a fake Christmas tree in the corner and some tacky decorations over the bar that look like they get dragged out every year. A couple of locals sit at a table sipping quietly, not really talking. And I feel overwhelmed with calm. I like this place.

'Did you know him?' asks Fergus, his officiousness spoiling the peace. 'Levi Norman – was he one of your customers?'

'Not exactly. Kept himself to himself, which isnae hard to do in Storrich. He came in just once a year, early November. He'd order a large whisky and sit by the fire. Never exchanged more than a few words.'

'You'd think, though,' says Fergus, 'in a place like this, that you'd need as many friends as you can get. With it being so remote, I mean.'

'That's very arrogant of you, Fergus Murray,' I say, relishing the chance to get back at him for earlier, 'to assume that the Storrich islanders are needy and can't look after themselves.' I wink at the landlord conspiratorially, as if to say, *I'm not like him, I get you Hebrideans.*

But I'm floored once more when he says, 'Well, your friend here is right. We all look out for one another as a rule. Your manny the Taff—'

'The what?'

'The Taff. He was Welsh, was he not?'

'Oh. Yes.'

'Well, it wasn't he was unfriendly as such. Just didnae want the company of others. He'd do what was needed – go the post office every Wednesday, cash his money, buy his food and fuel and what-not – and back home he'd go.'

'Did nobody ever visit him?' I ask.

'Nah, not that we ever saw.'

'And what about the locals?' asks Fergus. 'Did he not make any friends?'

'People tried when he first came here, but he made it pretty clear he wanted to be left alone. He shared a few words with Duncan Logs when he took him his firewood, and the postie of course.' When he says this, he gestures to one of the locals sipping a pint by the fire, a short, round woman with a neat black bob and tight trousers. 'Moira was the one found him. Didn' ye, Moy? Old Boyo Norman.'

Moira gets up and joins us at the bar, keen, it would seem, to share her story. 'Aye. Tuesday last, around ten a.m. Posted the mail – just a council tax bill and a charity letter from Oxfam.' I get the feeling Moira has told this story many times to many people and has now refined it with embellishments and detail.

'Happened to glance through his window on my way back to the van and saw him sat in his armchair by the fire. I don't know what possessed me to knock on the window and wave, because I'm aware he's a man who likes his privacy and normally I'd just post and go. Ask anyone on this island – I see, but I don't tell. I'm not one to go interfering in people's lives like some folk do. But that day I saw him sitting by the fire and I thought, *Ach, why not? It's nearly Christmas, for God's sake!*' Moira pauses to drain her pint and hands her glass over to Brodie for a refill. She's enjoying the audience and making the most of it. 'Anyway, Boyo doesn't wave back. Just stares straight at me. Felt a bit of a numpty to tell the truth and wished I hadn't bothered being nice. So I just turned on my heel and walked away, thinking he was a miserable old git. Then, I'd just got back to the van when I stopped in my tracks. Like this.'

One arm stretched out as if to open the van door and her head turned upwards adopting a quizzical expression, Moira re-enacts the stand-still moment for us, and capitalizes on the drama.

'See, I've always had a bit of a sick sense and it dawned on me: there was no smoke coming out of Boyo's chimney and no flames in his fire. And yet the day was cold! So back I went. And sure enough, I knocked on the window again, waited for him to move, and when he *didn't* my suspicions were confirmed.'

Moira pauses again for effect and by now she has me gripped. Even Fergus looks intrigued, waiting with bated breath for what happened next.

'I called Iona—'

'Community nurse,' interjects Brodie for clarity.

'—and I headed inside. And sure enough, there he was.' Moira looks at us with the gravitas of an archbishop. 'Dead as a door-handle!' she says. And we all shake our heads. I'm expecting more to the story, but Moira's done. She heads back to her table clutching her pint, and an awkward silence ensues. Fergus looks at me and I sense he might be laughing at Moira, which is completely out of order, so I look away and refuse to collude.

Brodie clears away our bowls and Minty appears with two ceramic cups filled with cranachan – a good old traditional Scottish dessert that I suspect is on the menu for any passing tourists.

'You know there's whisky in that, don't you?' says Fergus, with the self-satisfied expression of victory I'm discovering he's fond of employing.

'Your point being?' I say.

'Well, I thought you didn't drink alcohol.'

'I don't. I'm *eating* the dessert, Fergus Murray, not *drinking* it. And I think you'll agree there's a lot more cream and raspberries and oats in here than whisky!' I do wonder why I feel the need to defend myself as I stick my spoon in and savour the deliciousness of the home-made cranachan. Minty's made little shortbread biscuits to go with it. They are irresistibly meltish in the mouth.

'Have mine if you like,' he says, clearly feeling guilty for being a twat. 'I don't have a sweet tooth and I'd rather not offend.'

'Oh okay, if you *insist*,' I say with faux surrender, once again defaulting to my jokey mode when it comes to food and overeating. When I reach over for the second helping, Brodie smiles and says kindly, 'Fill yer boots!' And for a few moments I enjoy the unusual sensation of not being judged as a fat person stuffing their face.

At half ten we call it a night and head up to our respective beds. By now Fergus is more than a little 'merry' and I'm glad our rooms aren't directly next door to each other. I suspect he'll soon be snoring like a walrus, and who knows how thin these walls may be. As we leave, Brodie shouts the offer of a back-up electric heater should I need it, but I tell him I've got my hot-water bottle. The room is indeed on the chilly side and I get undressed at lightning speed before diving under the covers and pushing my hot-water bottle down the bed to keep my feet warm. There's a compensational number of blankets weighing down on me and I can barely move, luxuriating in the warmth and comfort of this glorious bed. Minutes later and only my nose is cold. I take a deep breath. There's hardly any sound – the occasional clink of a bottle or glass from the bar or laughter floating on the air and the not-so-distant waves crashing on the Storrich shore. I am being lulled. That must be where the word 'lullaby' comes from, I think as I drift, contentedly and unresistingly, into a Hebridean sleep.

10

Linda

Goodness only knows how Brodie finds such energy, but this morning he is both waiter and breakfast chef, serving up a humongous plate of bacon, eggs, Lorne sausage – the works. And he looks fresh as a daisy too – clean-shaven and wearing jeans and a red T-shirt devoid of yesterday's oil stains. Fergus Murray, on the other hand, looks a little delicate.

'I slept like a log!' I say brightly and a little too loudly when he plonks himself down at the table. We are, it would seem, the only staying guests at the Storrich Arms today.

'Lucky you,' he replies. 'I think that lamb broth didn't agree with me. I was awake half the night.'

'Nonsense. It was perfectly fine. You just drank too much Merlot.'

'Oh, don't start,' he grumbles, and sinks his teeth into one of my tattie scones.

'Hey! Get your own!' We sound like a pair of squabbling siblings, which doesn't go unnoticed by Brodie.

'Now, now, children, be nice,' he says with a smile as he hands Fergus his full Scottish.

'Cheers,' mumbles Fergus.

'Is Hamish Hamilton's place easy to find?' I ask.

'Aye, follow the track opposite the kirk. Five minutes away. It's Boyo Norman's house'll be more of a challenge. I'll do you a map.'

'No need,' says Fergus. 'The hearse has a satnav.'

'It'll be no use to you here, pal,' Brodie laughs, not unkindly. 'This island is more off the map than Briga-bloody-doon!' And he takes a paper napkin and begins to draw.

Half an hour later, we pull up in front of a solid-looking white-washed cottage with small windows and a slate roof and a sign outside that simply reads 'Chandlery and Funerals'. Hamish Hamilton is late sixties, unshaven, with chaotic hair, surprisingly mismatched with a clean blue shirt and green checked tie tucked into his waterproof trousers. He's also wearing yellow wellington boots and looks not unlike a drawing from a game of Consequences. Two black-and-white collies run up and give us a panting and slobbery welcome.

'Hello, you two!' I say, and bend down to give the dogs a big fuss. Fergus is not so canine-friendly. Maybe because he's back in his 'official' undertaker's gear which he doesn't want covering in dog hairs. He holds his hands up above his head, hoping this will deter the friendly mutts. But no such luck – one of them has obviously taken a liking to her new friend and jumps up at him for affection, the second dog following suit.

'MAGGIE! NEL!' growls Hamish Hamilton, sounding not unlike a dog himself. 'LEAVE NOW.' And instantly they return to their master.

'Lovely to meet you,' I say, holding out a hand to Hamish. 'I'm Linda Standish, Unclaimed Heirs Unit, and this is Fergus Murray from the funeral directors.'

'Aye,' says Hamish, shaking my hand. 'Right. Come in. I've got worming to do.'

I presume Hamish is referring to his sheep rather than any dead people, but who knows. He heads inside and we follow. The place does what it says on the tin. We walk through the 'chandlery' section, stocked to the ceiling with a selection of hardware ranging from light bulbs to garden rakes to baking trays, along with a load of items I don't recognize that I presume are something to do with boats.

'Gosh, what a treasure trove, Mr Hamilton!' I declare. 'How's business?'

'Aye,' he replies. And I doubt I'll get much more conversation out of him.

Through to the back of the house and the mood changes. Hamish opens the door into a small square room containing two wooden dining chairs and a decorator's bench, upon which lies a plain pine coffin. I presume this contains Levi Norman, deceased. Piped organ music is straining to come out of an old CD player on the windowsill, placed next to some dusty plastic flowers in an equally dusty vase. This is Hamish Hamilton's humble attempt at solemnity and funereal respect. He hands me the death certificate completed two days ago by the peripatetic GP. I'm charged with taking it to the register office on our return to Boransay. Turning then to Fergus, Hamish says, 'You'll be wanting to see him?'

Fergus nods and moves towards the decorating bench. 'Just to check everything is in order.'

'He's up there,' says Hamish, pointing to a curtained mezzanine shelf, three feet wide, running above the doorway to the opposite end of the room. The curtain partially conceals another pine casket.

'Good grief,' I blurt. 'Didn't see that there.'

'It's rarely we get a doubler,' says Hamish proudly, as if he's just discovered two yolks in his breakfast eggs. 'But old Molly Mackay went on Saturday. Hundred and one, they say.'

'Oh dear.'

Hamish nips out to the corridor and returns with a stepladder. 'You'll need this,' he says to Fergus, who looks at me, startled, then back at Hamish.

'Up you go, then!' I say with a smile. And watch as Fergus reluctantly climbs the steps.

*

'It was like being in the Old Curiosity Shop,' he says shortly afterwards as we travel along a single-track road, illustrated on Brodie's breakfast napkin map.

'Oh, pull yourself together, man. It's not like you've never seen a corpse before.'

'Well, of course I have,' says Fergus, his voice tinged with bad mood. 'But they're normally kept on ground level.'

The meeting with Hamish was not a drawn-out affair, clearly the worming was weighing heavily on his mind and he was keen to get on. He and Fergus arranged pick-up and transfer to the hearse for two days' time, and off we went. I imagine Fergus would have liked to head straight home today, but he's stuck with me now till the whole Levi Norman case is done and dusted.

'Looks like it's that one ahead.' I've just spied what must be Beannach Lodge, home of the late Mr Norman. It's nestled in the dip of a shallow hill and set against a wintry dark blanket of mossy grass. There's a smattering of snow on the peaks beyond, hardly surprising given the chill in the air. But today the sun is shining and the skies are clear of snow clouds. We turn off the main road and on to the track that leads to Beannach Lodge.

Just like most of the buildings on Storrich, it's a sturdy, thick-walled, white-washed cottage, constructed with harsh weather in mind: small windows so as to keep in the warm and keep out the cold, and modestly designed as a two-up two-down, with a central front door. 'In the olden days,' I say, 'they used to keep the cattle in one of the downstairs rooms and their body heat would rise to warm the bedroom above them.'

'Don't be ridiculous,' snaps Fergus, who I'm now beginning to think must have a bit of a hangover.

'Wanna bet?'

'Ten quid.'

'You're on.'

We pull up outside the cottage and I think how differently a place like this would look down south – probably surrounded by a pretty hedge and gated garden pathway. But here the boundaries are blurred and I imagine sheep in the summer months quite happily ambling past with their lambs, leaving manure-ish gifts on the patchy grass whilst nibbling at gorse. Being December, it feels desolate despite the cold sunshine and clear sky, and I'm glad I'm wearing my thermals. Brodie kindly made us a flask of coffee before we left, and some sandwiches for lunch. I think he knew it was going to be a long day.

'Right then, Fergus Murray. The sooner we get this done, the sooner we can get back to the pub and you can get drunk again.' I get out of the hearse sharpish and slam the door hard, drowning out his protests. That man is sooo easy to wind up.

11

Linda

The door to Beannach Lodge isn't locked. Apparently nobody on the island ever locks their front door and as soon as we're over the threshold I smell it – the comforting, honeyed scent of pipe tobacco, making me instantly nostalgic for my late dad. I've often heard people say they've smelt tobacco when there's been nobody smoking in the vicinity. And they've interpreted it as a 'visitation' from the dead. Or when a robin lands on the windowsill – they think it's their long-departed grandmother. I'm all for it, these inexplicable happenings. Even if they make no scientific sense, they're reassuring. And Lord knows, we all need a bit of reassurance these days. I close my eyes, stand still and inhale deeply.

'Are you all right?' asks Fergus.

'Yes. Just getting a sense of the place before we begin.'

'You look like you're about to conduct a séance or divine water,' he says. I ignore him.

'I'll take the upstairs rooms, you make a start in the kitchen. Pull out all the drawers, check there's nothing stuffed at the back, and try not to make a mess. We're not conducting a drugs raid, Fergus Murray. This is someone's life we're unpicking.'

I've said that line so many times over the years. To so many newbies to the unit. But it needs saying, because respect is important in this line of work. Fergus opens his mouth to protest. Clearly he doesn't want to help, yet he knows if he doesn't he'll be stuck here for longer.

The stairway is small and carpeted in pea-green, leading up to the two rooms above us. On the right is the bathroom, on the left Levi Norman's bedroom. I'm glad he wasn't found in bed. Something so much more dignified about breathing his last fully clothed by the fireside, instead of prostrate in his brushed-cotton pyjamas.

I check the bathroom first and am transported back to the 1960s. A clean but tired primrose-yellow sink stands next to a clean but tired matching bath, the cold tap of which drips and most probably has done for years. A rust-coloured line leads down to the plughole. There are two glass tumblers held in chrome rings attached to the black splashback panel above the sink. One tumbler contains a steel razor and shaving brush, the other a tube of Colgate toothpaste. There is just one of everything – no pair of toothbrushes, no his 'n' hers, no his 'n' his, no sign of any partnership whatsoever. And suddenly it strikes me that my own home will soon revert to the same single occupancy – Zander's little Thomas the Tank Engine toothbrush will be gone from my bathroom, as will Struan's Sonicare. No more socks to pick up off the floor, no more running out of milk or leaving the kitchen cupboards open . . .

Within the week, Mrs MacDonald from the kirk will be here at Beannach Lodge with her helpers, removing all personal effects, all redundant items like Levi Norman's half-used bar of soap and his dental floss, and throwing them into the bin. The last vestiges of this man's solitary life tossed into landfill, and all traces of his existence virtually erased.

Unless I can find a significant other in time. Someone whose life was impacted by Levi Norman.

I tap the bathroom walls in search of any secret panels, but everything sounds solid, convincing me that there are no hidden hollows. There's a bathrobe hanging on the back of the door and I check the pockets: a key ring with two keys, one of which is used to bleed radiators. And a receipt for a packet of digestive biscuits from the Storrich Stores, dated a fortnight since. I keep the keys and put back the receipt. There's a faded pink bath mat hanging on a freestanding wooden rack and a frayed stripy hand towel next to it. Levi clearly took care to keep things tidy, and didn't seem to spend money unnecessarily.

When I open the bathroom cabinet I see it's been neatly stocked with military precision – all the usual necessities, among them two toilet rolls, some Head & Shoulders shampoo, a bottle of TCP, a steel comb and an Aramis shaving stick. I get down on my hands and knees, grateful that Levi Norman appears to have been very houseproud and a regular cleaner of his bathroom floor. It's at times like these I'm glad of my flexibility. Yes, I may be a big girl, but I'm also quite a bendy one! Reaching into the back of the cabinet I check thoroughly for any hidden paperwork. I know it sounds daft, but you'd be amazed at the places people choose to hide important documents. I once found a last will and testament taped to the underside of a lawnmower bin. Covered in grass stains and barely readable. But we found it. And it was the saving grace in a prolonged inheritance dispute.

'Come on, old girl!' I say aloud as I pull myself up from the floor.

'First sign of madness, that.'

'Jesus!' I cry, and my heart races. Fergus Murray is standing in the doorway.

'Talking to yourself,' he clarifies. 'First sign of—'

'Did you *train* in silently creeping up on people?' I interrupt him. 'Is it a prerequisite of being an undertaker?'

'Can't help being light on my feet,' he says and an image flashes across my mind of him dancing the lambada. The image just as quickly disappears when he announces, 'I need the lavatory.'

I can't get out of there fast enough and I head to Levi's bedroom, calling behind me, 'Wash your hands, Fergus Murray!' I don't know what it is about him, but he brings out the worst in me.

*

The bedroom is just as neat as the bathroom, and suddenly the sight of it catches me unawares. Normally I can visit the homes of the deceased, get out my fine-toothed comb and carry out my investigations without so much as a by-your-leave. But this one . . . this one feels different. Maybe it's overwhelm from the thought of Struan moving out and the fact that Christmas is approaching and there's a chance I won't see Zander opening his presents. Or maybe it's a delayed reaction to my – perhaps over-hasty – retirement decision, and the realization that this is likely to be my very last case. Whatever it is, *something* about the demise of Levi Norman is making me less detached than usual. It's breaking my heart that he slept in a single bed and not a double; that on the day he died, he made his bed. And not just a random pull-across of the covers, but a proper neat, hospital-cornered, crease-free, lump-free bed-make. Like he was truly leaving his house in order before he shuffled off his mortal coil.

I open the wardrobe first. Inside a beige suit-carrier with the words 'Howells of Cardiff' printed across it I find a double-breasted suit. I'm no fashion historian, but I'd say this has come hurtling out of the eighties. The smell of naphthalene wafts from the carrier. Levi obviously didn't want the moths munching away at this now-vintage suit. The rest of the wardrobe contents are modest – a dog-tooth-patterned jacket, an old Barbour-style coat and half a dozen shirts – all ironed. *Fergus Murray, eat your heart out*, I think to myself. There are a couple of pairs of corduroys, one in brown, the other in beige, and some black slacks. Such a word of its time – *slacks*. It conjures up images of 1970s comfort-wear. There are no jeans or T-shirts, but several ties, all neatly looped around a narrow rail in the wardrobe. Levi Norman, it would seem, was *proper*. A man who did things by the book, judging by the organization of his clothes. Which makes me very hopeful that his personal affairs and paperwork will be in order too. It's just a case of finding it.

There's a suitcase on top of the wardrobe – the kind that would fetch a fair price in an antiques market. I'm hopeful it may contain something valuable – informationally speaking, not financially – and I haul it down on to the bed. It's very light, and I can tell even before I open it that it's empty.

Next, the chest of drawers. This is always a dodgy one, because drawers are likely to contain the more 'intimate' items. I once searched the home of a retired headmistress, known, according to former pupils, for her ferocity of moral code and strict, Presbyterian outlook. In her bedside cabinet I found a large selection of sex toys and erotica. Another gentleman, in his nineties, had an underwear drawer filled with ladies' silk panties. I make no moral judgement, of course I don't. I just feel guilty having to navigate the intimate and personal territories of lives departed. Thing is, we're none of us ever truly, completely ourselves with anyone. Nobody in the world knows our deepest, darkest secrets or who we really are. Some may get close, but only *we* know the real us. And so wading through the personal effects of someone who has no power to stop me feels at best mildly invasive and at worst downright intrusive. But it has to be done.

The chest of drawers in Levi Norman's bedroom contains nothing so exciting as erotic books or satin knickers. Neatly folded socks and underpants plus one or two vests fill two of the drawers. The third contains half a dozen pullovers. But the fourth and final drawer yields the first proper finding of the day: a photograph album and a biscuit tin full of keepsakes.

Bingo!

The album has not survived well and a couple of items fall out, including a photograph of a young man in graduation robes, and a flimsy square of paper. A receipt. I can just make out the writing – not computerized like a modern till receipt but handwritten. The printed heading says 'The Royal Hotel, Inverness'. Underneath is written the date, 12 March 1984, and *Set Lunch for Two @ £3.00 per person, plus two glasses of Pomagne, two coffees*. It seems such a nondescript item to hold on to, and yet Levi must have kept it for a reason.

1982

12

Levi

Thirty-one-year-old Levi Norman had lived in the first-floor Grangetown flat since his mother's death four years previously. He could've carried on living in the small terrace he'd shared with her, but there were too many memories of her illness and suffering. Her death had left him orphaned. At least, he presumed he was orphaned: Levi had never known his father and so had no idea if the man was still alive. He knew his father's name. Malcolm Fletcher. Owner and director of Fletcher's Haulage Company, where Levi's mother had worked as a secretary. She had caught Malcolm's eye at the office Christmas bash one year and a short-lived affair had begun. It was no secret that Levi's mother was her boss's 'bit on the side' – the term the kids in school had been fond of bandying around, along with 'fancy woman', 'tart' and 'prozzy'. When his mother found herself pregnant at twenty, she'd assumed Malcolm would leave his wife and set up home with her. But Malcolm had very different ideas and offered to pay to 'take care of things'. Horrified at the thought of some back-street abortionist going anywhere near her, Levi's mother turned down Malcolm's offer and not long after was given her cards – how could she work when pregnant anyway? Malcolm handed her a wad of cash on condition she never contacted him again. She duly obeyed. She was a simple woman, really.

Occasionally Levi would wonder if the absence of a father-figure in his life had left a gaping emotional hole. Had he suffered as a result of being the progeny of such a callous man? Even if the answer was yes, there was nothing he could do about it now. 'It is what it is,' his mother had been fond of saying. Levi had inherited his mother's stoicism, and was prone to accepting without question what life chose to throw at him.

Every weekday morning he would walk along the embankment, under the railway bridge and over to the bus stop. There he would wait for the number 27, which would take him almost outside his office at Markby and Lewis Accountancy, where he'd worked since leaving Cardiff university at twenty-one. He had no desire to work anywhere else or even to live anywhere other than Cardiff. Not because he particularly loved Cardiff or his job – he just wasn't ambitious and thrived on routine and security.

During his four weeks' annual leave he would take himself off on his own somewhere. Never abroad. Levi wasn't a sun-seeker. What he did love, though, was nature; his ideal holiday would be hiking in Snowdonia or the Brecon Hills, or birdwatching on the Norfolk Broads. He knew at work they laughed behind his back – not, perhaps, in a vicious way, he sensed that they were fond of him, but they definitely thought he was odd. A loner. Because he didn't fit in. He suspected they thought he should be married by now – they'd known about Sheila, of course, the ex-girlfriend. And the women in the office had all showered him with sympathy when he told them they'd broken up. They'd assumed it was Sheila who'd initiated the split – a fact reinforced by the news that she soon married someone else. The truth was very different. Sheila had been besotted with Levi and had wanted to settle and have 'hundreds of babies'. Well, three, to be exact. And Levi had looked at her one day and seen the desperation in her eyes for him to give her what she wanted, and he knew he never would. Because he simply didn't want what she wanted. And so he'd delivered the news she'd never thought she'd hear – that their relationship was over. There had been tears and admonishments and guilt trips and anger. But eventually Sheila had accepted the situation and they'd parted on good terms. It didn't take her long to find someone else and move away, and within six months she was married and pregnant. And because Sheila had finally got what she was really looking for, she became incredibly well-disposed towards Levi and insisted that they remain long-distance friends. Hence the Christmas cards. And the christening presents and birthday gifts for Sheila's four children.

Since he'd become single there'd been no one else for Levi, despite interest from other women. He wasn't bad-looking, or so he'd been told: still had a good head of dark hair, in thick waves that he'd inherited from his mother, and grey eyes (presumably Malcolm Fletcher's contribution), with a chiselled jaw. Sheila had told him this – it wasn't a word Levi would have used about himself, chiselled. He was physically very fit – not that he went to the gym, but he did walk a lot, and was moderate when it came to food and booze. He was also diligent when it came to keeping up his strength, doing a daily set of press-ups and bicep curls with an ancient set of dumbbells.

There'd been a couple of minor flirtations in shops and at weddings. But these never came to anything. A female accountant at work had taken a shine to him for a while and they even went so far as on a trip to the New Theatre. But when it came to the end of the night and walking her home, he'd turned down the offer of 'coming in for coffee' and thanked her for a lovely evening. She was clearly affronted and for the next couple of weeks ignored him at work, which was very tiresome and resulted in his having to have the 'it's-not-you-it's-me' conversation by the kettle one day. He did what he could to make her feel good about herself and explained that he just wasn't in the right frame of mind at the moment for a relationship. Which was true. Levi was not lying when he said he really did prefer his own company. But nobody seemed to believe him. And then at a recent office bash he'd been approached by a male colleague new to the firm, who, buoyed up by too much Rioja, asked Levi if he'd like to come home with him. Levi had been shocked and politely but firmly said no. The colleague shrugged it off, saying, 'Sorry, I thought you were on my team, that's what everyone said, anyway.' Levi could understand them thinking that. He didn't fit the stereotypical heterosexual family man or Jack-the-lad like the rest of the male staff. And he realized he was fighting a losing battle trying to convince them otherwise. So he just gave up the fight, deciding to let them think what they liked. It was much easier that way.

As he walked through the shared hallway to the front door that morning, he heard them arguing again: the couple in the ground-floor flat. It was an almost daily occurrence. Levi could never make out what they were saying – nor did he want to – but guaranteed there'd be raised voices first thing in the morning and last thing at night. They'd been living there about two months, and yet Levi hadn't met them. And judging by the daily rows, he wasn't sure he wanted to.

He shut the heavy oak door quietly behind him and headed out into the day. Cardiff was buzzing that morning with pre-Christmas jollity.

The bus pulled up at his stop and Levi got out, as he did every day of his working life. He walked the short distance to his office building, as he did every day of his working life, and said good morning to the receptionist before signing himself in – just as he did every day of his working life. There was nothing new in the life of Levi Norman today. Nothing new, and nothing different. Not today.

13

Diana

Diana woke herself up by calling out in her sleep. She'd been dreaming the same dream again – being lost at sea and engulfed by huge waves. She'd only sat down for a minute in between hanging out the washing and changing the bed. *Just catch my breath*, she'd thought. The precious load that she carried was getting heavier by the day, it seemed. Understandable as her time grew ever closer. She wasn't sleeping much at night – couldn't get comfy in that bed, for a start. And there was Jack's snoring, which he denied.

'I'm only twenny, for fuck's sake!' he'd laughed. 'Snorin's for old gits.' She'd threatened to borrow a cassette player and record him. 'Aye, go on then!' he'd dared her, knowing that she never would. So the sleep she missed out on at night had to be made up for in the day. And try as she might to fight it, shutting her eyes for a five-minute snooze often resulted in a two-hour kip. Like today.

She'd slept awkwardly on her left arm, which had gone dead. Shaking it to bring it back to life, she shuffled into the kitchen to make a cup of tea. Diana was only twenty-one – the same age as her princess namesake, who'd had a fairy-tale wedding a year earlier. But this Diana felt more like *ninety*-one. Everything ached. Everything dragged her down. The sooner this baby was out, the better.

As she waited for the kettle to boil, she smoothed her expansive belly and in response the baby kicked back. 'Not long now, sweetheart,' she whispered. For months, Diana had felt the growing bond between herself and her unborn child, often singing to her or him and telling them stories. Some days, her unborn child was the only company she kept. Unless the landlord came round for the weekly rent, which wasn't exactly a social call.

There was no doubt about the fact that she was lonely. The few friends she did have were back in Dublin, the place where she'd met Jack, almost a year ago now. He'd been working on a building site and used to come into the pub where she served behind the bar. He was sweet – she warmed to his Welsh accent and his exceptionally twinkly eyes. It didn't take much before she said yes to a date, and within a fortnight she'd become entranced by this chatty, cheeky Welshman. 'Jeez, I thought it was the Irish had the gift of the gab!' she'd said to him on the night he nuzzled her neck and slowly started undressing her back at his B&B. He'd given this long, impassioned speech about how deeply he'd fallen in love with her and how desperate he was to have her. She wasn't sure she felt the same, but the sex was good and she loved the attention. In her young life, Diana had known many men. She'd lost her virginity at sixteen to a man older than her who she'd met in a Skerries pub. She and her friend had absconded for the night – each claiming they were staying at the other's house and getting the bus out of Dublin to the pretty seaside town. He'd been a farmer called Ruaridh and she'd let him go 'all the way' in the back of his car. All her friends had had sex before her and had all been disappointed with their first time. But Diana thought the whole thing was gorgeous. And once she'd tried it, she wanted to do it again. And again. 'Sure, it's just a natural process, isn't it?' she'd laughed with her friend Molly. She'd always tried to be careful – buying black-market condoms from Molly's cousin and making sure she was well prepared. Sex soon became something of a pastime for her – a hobby she enjoyed every Saturday night, in the same way others might enjoy a game of darts or making patchwork quilts.

She had no home life, after all, having grown up in care. They'd all been kind, her foster parents – she had no nightmare stories to tell. But at the end of the day, she was still a lost soul, rootless and invisible. And Jack's obsession with her made her feel found and rooted and very much seen.

Two months after they first met, when Jack's contract was coming to an end, he cried – actually cried – at the thought of them parting, and pleaded with her to move back to Cardiff with him. Diana was tempted – there wasn't much going for her in Dublin other than that it was all she knew, but she felt completely lacking in any meaningful prospects. She had no qualifications whatever, other than the ability to pour a pint. When else would she get the chance to live abroad – yes, it was only Wales, but it was still across the water, still a foreign country as far as Diana was concerned. She remained undecided for days as Jack's departure fast approached. But the week before he was due to leave, she went to see Dr Elliot about a stomach bug she couldn't shake off, and was given the startling news that she was two months pregnant. She had no choice other than to tell Jack, fully expecting him to want nothing more to do with her. But surprisingly, he was overjoyed. Beside himself with excitement.

'We're too young,' she said, in shock like a headlight-stunned rabbit.

'Bollocks to that.' He beamed, grabbing her around the waist. 'Kid'll be healthier. Course, you know what this means, don't you?'

'I'm coming to Cardiff?' she laughed.

Jack told her how much better her life would be there; how the baby would want for nothing. And she believed him. She packed a small case, handed in her notice and held hands with Jack as they walked aboard the Swansea–Cork ferry.

They moved into a friend's spare room. The friend, Benno, was nice enough, but it was hardly ideal accommodation. Jack said it would be for just a few days. The days passed and turned into weeks. And the weeks turned into months. Benno's patience and politeness understandably began to wane.

All the time, Jack kept promising her their own place. And a wedding. He assured her they'd be married before the baby arrived. But day after day, nothing changed. She'd sit and wait for him to return from work – dusty and tired, quiet and short-tempered. A far cry from the cheeky, chatty chap she'd served at the Dublin bar. He blamed it on feeling hemmed in. No longer seeing Benno as a good and generous friend but rather a pain in the arse who wouldn't get off his case.

Although she'd never admit it to Jack, Diana sympathized with Benno. Jack was a hard worker – true. He certainly wasn't lazy when it came to his job – often getting up at the crack of sparrows, coming home after dark. And he certainly brought in the cash. But when it came to helping out around the place, even picking his socks up off the floor, Jack expected someone else to do it. To keep the peace – and because, being jobless and pregnant, she had nothing else to do with her time – Diana pitched in beyond the call of duty when it came to housework. She actually enjoyed cleaning, tidying up, home-making. The only problem was that the home she was making wasn't hers. It was someone else's. Benno told Diana he didn't know how she put up with Jack. This was after the two men had had another row when Benno had called him a 'selfish, egotistical little shit'. Jack had stormed out to work, and Diana decided to seize the moment.

'I think perhaps we're all just living on top of each other a bit now. You've been very kind, so you have, but me and Jack, we really need to get somewhere of our own.'

'Well, I don't disagree with that,' Benno said, then hesitated. 'Diana, y'know Jack's my mate an' that and I'm made up for him, meetin' you, an' the baby. It's gonna do him the world of good, settle him down a bit, y'know? It's just . . .'

'What?'

He smiled then, and touched her arm. 'Nothing,' he said, though clearly it *wasn't* nothing. 'I hope the best for you, I really do.' She didn't pay it much attention, determined now to solve their accommodation problem herself. For some time she'd been squirrelling away cash from the many wads of notes Jack often left lying around the bedroom. Counting it out, she reckoned she had enough for a deposit on a flat, knowing the only way they'd ever get their own home was if she presented it to him as a fait accompli.

'Guy upstairs is a dream,' the agent had said later that afternoon. 'Keeps himself to himself and won't say boo to a badger. And the great thing about the ground floor is, you got somewhere to hang out the nappies once that little one pops out.' He'd laughed at his own joke. Had he never heard of disposables? What a comedian. But Diana didn't care. She'd finally, finally found them their own place.

She'd done her best to make it as homely as possible, but in her heart she knew she'd failed. Despite having everything set up as comfy and welcoming as possible, Jack still picked holes in it from the day they moved in. And was still picking holes this morning before he left for work. 'This place is a hovel!' were his parting words before he slammed the door. It was far from a hovel. But it was a bit tired, a bit shabby around the edges. The kettle clicked and Diana poured the hot water over the teabag in her mug. It was dark outside now. Only four o'clock. Jack wouldn't be home for at least another three hours. She took her tea into the living room, where the flashing lights from the little Christmas tree she'd set up in the corner attempted to bring some cheer. But there was something nagging her in the pit of her stomach. A feeling she could not identify. And it wouldn't go away.

14

Levi

The thudding sound seemed to be coming from somewhere inside the building. It took him a moment to shake himself awake and look with one eye at the digital numbers on his clock radio: 2.34 a.m. He went out on to the landing and the thuds got louder, then suddenly a moan. 'Aww, come on, mun!' Silence. Then more thuds – angrier this time. Levi went to the bay window of his living room and looked out and down at the front door, where a young man stood – swayed, in fact – leaning against the architrave. He was clearly drunk.

Despite his quiet demeanour, Levi was no coward, and he didn't appreciate being woken from his slumbers by some inebriated interloper. He rammed open the sash window and called down. 'Oi! What are you doing?'

The young man took a while to register where the voice was coming from, then looked up and smiled. 'Sorry, mate! I forgot my key.'

Levi looked at him. The guy would have to do better than that. 'And you are . . . ?'

'Oh, yeah, Jack, I am,' he slurred. 'We're neighbours!'

'I've never met you, so how do I know you're telling the truth?'

Confusion, then irritation, passed across Jack's face. ''Cos why would I bother coming to some random house at three in the mornin' and bangin' the door down if I didn't live 'ere?'

He had a point.

'Look,' pleaded Jack, softening a little. 'My girlfriend's at home but she's not answerin'. Probably out for the count.'

'As was I until five minutes ago!'

'Aw, come on, mate, give us a break?'

Levi looked at him for a moment, then shut the window. He pulled on his dressing gown and slippers and made his way downstairs. But rather than head for the front door, he turned left and went to the entrance of the ground-floor flat. He tapped gently as the thudding continued from Jack. The door of Flat One opened a crack and a pair of pretty green eyes peered out.

'Umm, hello,' said Levi. 'I'm from upstairs, and—'

'I know,' said the voice behind the eyes. 'I'm sorry about his Lordship.' Levi detected a light Irish brogue. 'He's drunk.' *Stating the obvious there*, thought Levi.

'Yes.' He paused. 'You do know the chap, then?'

'Unfortunately.'

'Thing is, I'd really like to get back to sleep. So will you let him in? Or shall I?'

'God, no! He'll give up in a minute and go to his mate's. He's only a couple of streets away.'

Levi glanced towards the front door. He could smell cigarette smoke and decided 'Jack' was now taking a fag break. Thudding on doors was tiring work, after all. He sighed. He couldn't really let the guy in against his girlfriend's wishes.

'Right, well, let's hope for the best!' he said, trying to hide his frustration as he headed back up the stairs. This pair were turning into a bit of a nightmare. The old lady who'd lived there before them had been good as gold. Never heard a peep. As he turned on the bottom step, the young woman came out of her doorway. She was wearing a pink towelling robe and was very heavily pregnant and, despite the time of night, she looked remarkably fresh, an abundance of dark auburn curls tumbling around her shoulders. 'I'm Diana, by the way.'

Levi nodded. 'I'd like to say "pleased to meet you", but I've had better-timed introductions.'

Diana shrugged.

'Anyway, I'm—'

'You're Levi Norman,' she interrupted.

'How did you—?'

'I've seen your name on the mail. I'm not a stalker or anything.'

Levi smiled. At which point Jack yelled through the front door. 'Well, piss off then. I'm goin' to Benno's.'

Levi turned back to Diana. 'Seems you were right!' She shrugged again and went back inside. Just before she closed the door, he shouted, 'Goodnight . . .' But she didn't reply.

The next morning, as he left for work, Levi was half-expecting either to hear the sound of arguing or to bump into a remorseful Jack returning home with his tail between his legs after a night at his friend's house. But the place was silent and Jack was nowhere to be seen. In fact, he didn't see or hear the quarrelling couple the next day or the next, until Levi even wondered if they'd done a moonlight flit. On the third day, Levi had been about to sit down to his TV dinner of tuna pasta bake with a green salad and small glass of red, when a knock came on the interior front door. This was either going to be the landlord making an impromptu visit, or that woman Diana, probably wanting the proverbial bowl of sugar. He thought about not answering, but *Crimewatch* was on the telly, and whoever was stood knocking was sure to know he was in. He sighed, got up and answered the door. Standing there, brandishing a four-pack of Stella Artois, was Jack from downstairs. 'You got a minute, mate?'

'Umm, not really, I'm in the middle of my dinner.'

'Won't take long,' said Jack, who clearly had the hide of a rhinoceros, stepping inside the flat the second Levi relented. Once they were in the living room Jack settled into an armchair and cracked open one of the cans. 'Don't mind me.' Jack indicated to Levi to finish his supper, whilst proffering him one of the Stellas.

'Peace offering!' Jack laughed. And Levi raised his glass of wine in a polite refusal. 'What it is, I just wanted to say sorry, like, for the other night. Wakin' you up an' that. Truth be told, I'd had a skinful.'

'Yes,' said Levi, self-consciously tucking into his pasta.

'Thing is, me an' Di, we haven't been together that long, see, and what with the baby on the way an' that, things get a bit *tense* like.'

Levi nodded and carried on eating. Jack was really spoiling his food and he hoped he'd hurry up with whatever he wanted to say and leave. But two cans and an empty plate later, Jack was still there, bending Levi's ear about the pressures of becoming a dad, earning enough cash for the three of them whilst 'keeping that flame alight', at which point Jack winked at Levi as if to say, *know what I mean?* Levi didn't. And by the time Jack was polishing off the fourth can of the peace offering, he was well and truly spilling his heart out. 'See, I fell really hard for her, I did – Diana, I mean – Irish eyes were smiling an' all that. And y'know, when she first caught with the baby—'

How Levi hated that expression. As if babies could be 'caught', like a head cold or chickenpox.

'—I was dead excited, like! I mean, who doesn't wanna become a dad?'

Me, thought Levi.

'Problem is, now I'm startin' to feel a bit hemmed in, like. She's always on my case: *what time will you be home? I need cash for this, that and the other*, and after a while it gets you down, know what I'm sayin'?'

Levi didn't, but he remained quiet.

'It's why I was out so late the other night. Didn't wanna come home, truth be told.'

'Right,' sighed Levi. 'Look, thanks for calling by, but—'

'Can I share something with you?' Jack interrupted.

Levi so desperately wanted this man to leave.

'There's this other bird, like. That's where I was the other night.

I know. I know exactly what you're thinkin' and believe me, I've tried to end it – several times!'

Levi's expression remained unchanged.

'But she's got her claws into me. Literally like, sometimes. You wanna see the scratch marks on my back – *they*'d take a bit of explainin', I can tell you. Gotta keep my top on at all times. It's a nightmare!' At which point Jack laughed in a man-to-man conspiratorial way that made Levi want to be sick. How on earth had he found himself here with this jumped-up kid who thought he was the big I AM to women, flagrantly cheating on his pregnant girlfriend, sat drinking cans of lager and treating him like some sort of confidant. Unbothered now about causing offence, Levi looked at his watch and interrupted Jack in full flow.

'I'm afraid I have to get on. But thanks again.'

Thick-skinned Jack took no offence whatsoever. 'Aye, no worries.' He downed the remainder of his lager, crushed the can and left it on a pile with the other three empties. He stood up and held out his hand to Levi. 'Cheers, mate. Lenny, isn't it?'

'That's right.' Levi couldn't be bothered to correct him, and, shaking his hand, he surreptitiously eased Jack towards the door.

'Tidy,' said Jack. 'And listen,' he lowered his voice to a whisper, 'keep all this under your hat, won't you? Don't wanna upset the little lady more than necessary. 'Specially with the sprog on the way. I just thought I should keep you in the picture. Never know when I might need an alibi, like.'

Levi watched Jack semi-stumbling down the stairs and heard him greet Diana as he went inside their flat. 'Babe? You okay?'

What an abhorrent little shit, thought Levi as he picked up the discarded beer cans from his living-room floor and put them in the bin. He washed his dishes, re-corked his wine and glanced at the rentals page of the *South Wales Echo*. If tonight's 'neighbourly chat' was a sign of things to come, maybe it was time Levi thought about moving.

15

Diana

The communal hallway was cold, despite the blanket Diana had wrapped herself in to make the call. She rarely used the coinbox phone inside the front door. Sometimes it would ring for the fella upstairs, or a drinking pal of Jack's would call, begging him to the pub. But as it was Christmas Eve, she thought she should try and say hello to her friend Molly back home; they'd only spoken a couple of times since she'd left. She clutched a stack of ten-pence pieces in her hand, but the coin slot seemed to just eat them up – such was the cost of calling Ireland. Barely had she said two words to Molly than the pips went and she had to cram in another coin. At the end of the call, when there were no more ten pences left, she screamed a *Merry Christmas* in unison with her friend, in a show of fake jollity and girlish silliness. Diana had given nothing away of her true circumstances, claiming that Cardiff was fantastic, things with Jack were just peachy and she couldn't wait for her baby to come. She hung up and in the silence that followed, Diana felt more alone than ever, fighting the urge to cry. It probably wasn't helped by the jolly tones of Paul McCartney filtering out of the radio in the flat, encouraging her to simply have a wonderful Christmas time. She shut her eyes and leaned her forehead against the black Bakelite handset.

Try as she might to delete the memory from her mind, it wouldn't go. The sharp shock of the slap. As soon as it had happened, he'd pulled her to him, apologizing profusely, on the verge of tears, almost suffocating her in the tight hold. It had happened two mornings ago. He'd left soon after and when he'd come home later that night had been as gentle as a lamb. She wanted to pretend it hadn't happened. But it wasn't the first time, so pretending was impossible. All she knew was that she was trapped in this now. Maybe when the baby came things would be different.

She was jostled out of her reverie by the sound of a key in the door. Couldn't be Jack – he was on his works bash today and had told her to expect him very, very late. The door swung open and the guy from upstairs stood in its frame, laden with shopping bags, his face almost hidden behind a cardboard box containing what looked like part of a turkey.

'Oh, hello,' he said, bustling into the hall. 'Bloomin' freezing out there today.'

Diana managed a smile. She'd exchanged a few words with him since that embarrassing night when Jack had tried to bash down the door. He was a friendly chap, had a kind face, but understandably he kept his distance. God only knew what he thought of them. Jack reckoned he 'batted for the other side' as he so delicately put it, which was so Jack – things were either black or white with him. Couldn't be different in any way, shape or form. *Different* meant weird. And God forbid you could be weird.

'How are you feeling?' Levi asked as he wrestled with one of the shopping bags threatening to fall from his grip. She thought she might cry again. Nobody ever asked her how she was feeling. And for fear of crying she only smiled, but the smile was wobbly, and the tears were unstoppable.

Levi looked at her for a moment and then said, 'Can I interest you in a mince pie?'

*

She could have stayed there for hours. Not because Levi was particularly scintillating company, but because he was so calm and quiet. His home was clean and undramatic, and his presence just so reassuring. On the few occasions when their paths had crossed before, they'd not exchanged more than a couple of sentences – certainly not enough to reveal any depths to this shy, unassuming accountant. In the corner of his living room was a small artificial tree, under which were two wrapped gifts. When Levi was in the kitchen making the tea, she'd had a quick look at the labels: one was from someone called 'Netty' and the other from 'Sheila, Bill and the kids'. It made her sad seeing them, and she didn't know why. Levi himself seemed content, despite his reserve. He brought the tea in on a tray with two mince pies and half a loaf of stollen. They looked home-made rather than shop-bought.

'Yes, I rather like baking,' he said. 'Not very manly, I know!' He laughed at himself and Diana felt instantly defensive of him.

'I think men who can cook should be given medals!' She imagined Jack in a pinny, kneading dough or whisking eggs. What a joke. The most he'd ever managed was a cup of tea. And even those occasions she could count on one hand.

'Oh, I've just realized,' said Levi, in the middle of slicing the stollen. 'Are you okay to have marzipan? Raw eggs?'

'Yeah, I reckon I'm too far down the road now to worry about stuff like that.' The cake was delicious and she gobbled it up as they shared a very genteel and polite conversation. He asked her where she'd be spending Christmas Day.

'We're going to the pub. The landlord's doing lunch for a few regulars.'

'Will Jack's family join you?'

'Er, no . . .' She looked confused at the mention of family. 'That's one thing me and Jack have got in common. Both sort of orphans, I guess.'

She explained that she'd been brought up in care near Dublin, and had no idea who her parents were. 'And Jack's mother lives in Spain. They fell out a few years ago and he hasn't spoken to her since. His dad's never been on the scene.'

There was an awkwardness then. As if the two of them were

suddenly aware that they were just two strangers making polite conversation.

'What about you?' asked Diana, breaking the silence. 'You got a ma and da?'

Levi shook his head. 'I'm a bit like you and Jack in that regard.' He smiled and told her about his mother, who'd brought him up as a single parent and taught him everything he knew about cooking. Diana thought what a sweet woman she must've been. But when it came to his dad, that was another story. He'd not wanted anything to do with Levi or his ma. 'I only met him the once,' Levi said. 'I turned up at his place of work and introduced myself.'

'You never did!' said Diana, enthralled. 'What did you say?'

'I said *Malcolm Fletcher?* And he said, *Who are you?* And I stammered a bit, lost my way and he said, *Well, spit it out, boy!* And I said, *Your son. I'm your son.*'

'Oh my God, then what?'

'Well, it was all a bit sad really. He got all flustered, looking around to check no one was listening. He thought I'd come looking for money, like I wanted to embarrass him or something, and I said, *No, I just wanted to get to know you*. But he shoved a wad of cash at me, told me to take it and to *disappear*. Only he didn't use the word disappear.'

Diana shook her head. 'What a rotten aul' bastard.'

Well, technically it's *me* who's the bastard.' He smiled, and Diana smiled back because Levi didn't seem too bothered. 'I was a bit thrown at first,' he continued. 'But then I thought what a close shave it had been. Imagine being brought up by someone like him. Me and my mother had a lucky escape, I reckon.'

They sat in comfortable silence for a moment and then Levi asked, 'So what's the itinerary? Tomorrow, I mean?'

'It'll just be a big booze-up,' Diana smiled, 'with tinsel on the top. And board games, apparently.'

'You a fan of Monopoly?'

'Never played it. In fact, the only board game I remember playing is Twister.'

'I should think you might find that one a bit tricky given your . . .' he looked a little embarrassed then, 'your condition.'

'For sure,' she said, and reached over for another mince pie. 'God, these really are delicious.'

'D'you know what the secret is? Make your own mincemeat. Dried fruit and peel simmered for hours in suet – I know, sounds horrible, but the flavours, my God! And then you soak it all in brandy. Lasts for up to two years.'

'Your mother teach you that?'

'Of course!'

Diana savoured the rich sweetness of her second mince pie. 'So what about you?' she asked tentatively. 'You got visitors tomorrow?'

'No, I'll be here,' he said, without a shred of self-pity. 'Just me and my turkey crown!'

'Oh,' said Diana. She hadn't been expecting that.

'It's okay,' he replied. 'I genuinely do enjoy my own company. I can eat at whatever time I want – *in* my pyjamas if I so choose, wolf down *all* the pigs-in-blankets, watch whatever I want on the telly. Plus, I don't have to play any dreadful board games.'

Diana laughed politely, but inside she still felt sad for him. Even back in Ireland, with no family to speak of, she had never been alone on Christmas Day. She'd either spend it with Molly or Deirdre and their folks or do a shift in the pub, where the atmosphere was full-on festive. Never on her own, though.

'I can tell you don't believe me,' said Levi a little more seriously. 'But that's okay. I don't blame you, it's hard to get your head round.'

When she left to go back downstairs, she thanked him and wished him a merry Christmas and Levi gave her a couple more mince pies to take home. Before she'd even reached the bottom step, Diana had decided she would keep the pies for herself. They were far too good to waste on Jack.

16

Levi

On Christmas morning Levi put his turkey crown in the oven and walked to Llandaff Cathedral for the ten o'clock service – the only time he ever went to church. He wasn't particularly religious, he just felt there should be a bit of a nod to Jesus, seeing as the day was celebrating the chap's birthday. Back at home he sat down to a delicious feast, stopping for a break and the Queen's Speech before launching into his Christmas pudding. Home-made, of course. It was the Christmas Day routine he'd had for years, even when his mother was alive. And he enjoyed it just as much as he always did. Apart from a tiny niggle that he couldn't shake off. He found himself feeling disappointed not to have seen Diana. The chat they'd had the day before had been a breath of fresh air – listening to her talk of life in Ireland and relishing her appreciation of his pastry-chef efforts.

Jack, he *had* seen. Looking a little the worse for wear, he'd knocked on Levi's door at midday. Wearing his pinny and holding a roll of tinfoil, Levi had answered, expecting Diana, not her partner. 'Alrigh', mate?' croaked Jack, too many Benson and Hedges the night before having ravaged his voice. 'Merry Christmas, like.'

'Yes! Merry Christmas.' Levi had reached out to shake hands with the younger man, who seemed a bit thrown by the gesture.

'Listen, Di mentioned you was on your own today, so we was wonderin' if you wanna join us, like. At the pub. Haven't asked Clucky yet, but he probably won't mind.'

'Clucky?'

'Mate of mine. Landlord of the Crown.'

The gesture was kind, if a little half-hearted. And certainly unexpected.

'Gosh, that's so generous,' said Levi, detecting a worried look pass over Jack's face, no doubt fear that the invitation was about to be accepted. Levi surmised it must have been Diana's idea. He couldn't imagine Jack thinking about anyone but himself for even thirty seconds. 'Thing is, I've had a late invitation from an old friend of my mother's, so I'll be heading off there later on.' Complete lie of course, and he sensed Jack knew this but was nonetheless relieved.

'No worries,' he said. 'Have a good one.'

'You too. Regards to Diana.'

Jack nodded and, before he turned to go, whispered, 'You didn't say nothin', did you, about what we was talkin' about the other night?'

Levi tried to hide his irritation at being once again drawn unwillingly into his neighbour's web of lies. 'No,' he replied curtly.

'Getting a bit *complicado* at the mo, it is.' And with that, Jack pulled a mock-horror face that suggested the guy was enjoying all the drama.

'Must go,' said Levi, and shut the door before Jack could share any more sordid details. *Poor Diana*, he thought. And headed back to the kitchen to prepare his three roast potatoes, really not wanting to get involved.

He'd fallen asleep after his figgy pudding and woken up with the bowl half-falling out of his hand. After the washing-up, he took himself off for some air and a stroll around the block. It was a nice neighbourhood, usually buzzing. But tonight the streets were deserted. He saw a solitary dog-walker and a girl on a bike whizzing past. There were hardly any cars and certainly no buses. He wondered what sort of Christmas Day Diana had had at the pub and whether she'd been persuaded into playing Twister after all. He seemed to be wondering about her a lot today. How he wished he didn't know that her waster of a boyfriend was up to no good. Because he now felt somehow responsible for her. And that he'd himself been disloyal to his new-found friend. Why the hell had that idiot confided in him?

When he let himself back into the house, all was silent in the ground-floor flat and he presumed the young couple were still out. That evening he watched *Last of the Summer Wine* and *The Two Ronnies* before heading to bed at ten o'clock. He had a restless night – kept thinking he'd heard a noise downstairs, then would drift back to sleep. *Probably just indigestion from the chestnut stuffing.*

Boxing Day was a definite day to get-out-there-and-breathe-fresh-air. Every Christmas, Levi alternated between Barry Island and Cosmeston Lake. This year it was Barry's turn. He was just heading out the front door with a flask and his cold turkey sandwiches when a timid voice called from the hall. 'Levi?' It was Diana. She looked awful.

'I was going to knock, but I didn't like to intrude,' she said. He could tell she'd been crying. He looked at her standing in her doorway, arms folded, slippers on, apparently desperate to talk.

'Is it Jack?' he asked, and she nodded.

'I think he's seeing someone else.'

*

The promenade at Barry Island was surprisingly busy, with families keen to shake off the Christmas Day cobwebs and kids trying out their brand-new bikes and trikes. Although it was cold, it was dry, and the weak sun was doing its best to brighten the morning. Making their way on to the sands of Whitmore Bay, they sat down on the sea wall and looked out. Levi poured them a coffee, opened his Tupperware and offered Diana a sandwich. She'd been very quiet in the car and he hadn't wanted to pry. For one thing, he felt it was up to her to choose what she shared, but for another, he knew the subject was going to make him feel totally compromised and so was in no rush to discuss it.

'Yesterday he disappeared for three hours after lunch,' she said, looking straight ahead. Levi realized how much easier it was to discuss awkward subjects when you didn't have to look the other person in the eye. 'Three hours! Said he was feeling rough and needed fresh air. Then when he came back he was all buoyant and over-friendly. Kept pawing at me. I wondered for a moment if he'd taken something. Cocaine, maybe.'

Levi had never taken cocaine. Nor had he ever smoked a cigarette. He'd tried marijuana once at university. Just the one puff, and it made him go green and vomit on the girl sitting next to him. So understandably he'd never tried it again.

'He was all spiky and jittery,' Diana continued. 'Like he was waiting for someone to tap him on the shoulder. Kept looking at his watch. Even his mates noticed – and one of the girlfriends, she said, *What's the matter with you, Mr Ants in your Pants?* Just being silly, y'know? But he got all cross with her and the next thing, he stormed out! He'd only been back for half an hour. It was like he was looking for an excuse to leave.'

'So what did you do?'

'Well, to be honest, although his friends were kind, and the landlord and his girlfriend – I think they were embarrassed, y'know? – and I just thought I should go. 'Cos otherwise there was this big fat elephant in the room. Like, *What's up with Jack?* I told them I needed my bed. They said I could stay there, but I couldn't bear it. So one of the friends walked me home. Kept apologizing, saying he didn't know what was wrong with him. I felt sorry for them.'

Levi was glad she wasn't looking at him when she said 'big fat elephant' in her beautiful Dublin tones, because it made him spontaneously smile. And he had no wish to make her feel undermined.

'The guy saw me to the door. I think he wanted to come in, check I was okay, but I just had to be on my own. And so I shut the door behind me—'

'What time was this?' Levi interrupted.

'Late – going on for half eleven?'

Ah, so he hadn't been imagining things last night. It must've been Diana coming home. 'Anyway, I'd just shut the door behind me and the phone rang. Christ, I nearly jumped out of me skin.'

'Yes, it's exceptionally loud when you're standing right next to it.'

'I answered, thinking it was Jack, and it just sounded like a party going on in the background. Really noisy-like, music and everything. And this woman's voice was going, *Jack? Jack?* She was obviously drunk, and she goes, *Jack, get your sexy arse back over here pronto, d'you hear?* And I says, *Who is this, please?*'

Levi's heart broke when she said it. He couldn't bear her helplessness and her simultaneous good manners. Diana carried on.

'And she said nothing. And I could just hear the party going on behind her and then she goes, *Oh, sorry love, wrong number.*'

Levi was lost for words. He was filled with anger and frustration at being burdened with the knowledge of Jack's infidelity. He wanted to confirm Diana's suspicions, but it really wasn't his place. On the other hand, he needn't attempt to dispel her fears. He'd just have to try and remain neutral somehow, despite how difficult this was going to be.

'Hmm, doesn't sound good, does it?' he said, sipping his coffee.

'No.'

They sat in silence for a while as the Christmas cheer and holiday bonhomie from the promenade walkers drifted over to them.

'We could head to the Knap if you like?' he asked, thinking a change of scene might lighten the mood. 'It's not too far, and it's a lovely beach. Pebbles, not sand.'

'No, I think that might be a step too far,' she said, and Levi instantly felt like he'd taken liberties.

'Oh, I'm sorry! I hope I'm not—'

Diana laughed, 'I mean, I think my heavy load might get in the way of a long walk!'

'Ah, I see,' he laughed back, noting what a difference a smile made to Diana's demeanour.

'I'll tell you what I do fancy, though,' she said. 'A trip to the flicks.'

'Sorry?'

'That fil-um. Fire Chariots or somethin'. They're showin' it again at the Odeon in town.'

When they got home from the cinema, he waited at the bottom of the stairs and watched her into her flat. She opened the door and called out to Jack. But there was no response. Diana smiled sadly at Levi, 'Not back.'

Feeling like a bit of a spare part, Levi said, 'Well, you know where I am if I can help.'

'Thanks.'

How on earth could he help? What was the point of that offer when there was nothing he could do to alleviate the hopelessness of her situation? He flicked on the TV and hopped from channel to channel, muting the sound every so often when he thought he heard the front door open and shut. Reflecting on the innocence of their day, he held the two cinema tickets in his hand and relived how they'd sat politely watching the film – or fil-um as Diana pronounced it – each with their own popcorn, two friends watching *Chariots of Fire*. He was feeling like a teenager, not a man in his early thirties, and the sensation was so alien to him. His normally firm foundations were being thoroughly shaken. Diana, he could tell, was completely unaware of his losing his footing and he knew that he'd behaved impeccably: that she'd have no reason to suspect that he was falling for her. But he was.

The next morning Levi spent an hour weighing up the pros and cons of knocking on Diana's door. As a friend, he felt he should really check in on her and see if she was okay after yesterday's talk. But he was also startlingly aware that his feelings towards her were more than those of a caring friend. And surely the more contact he had with her, the more danger there was of his being hurt. Or, worse still, making an absolute fool of himself. She was a pregnant woman, for God's sake, ten years his junior, involved with a worthless, faithless waster who she no doubt loved. It would be sheer stupidity to involve himself further, even under the guise of friendship.

But then he felt awful for abandoning her, too. Leaving her to her own devices. She had no one else, after all – that was very clear from their talk on Barry beach. In the end he decided to put Diana's welfare before his own self-protection and say a quick hello. That's all it would be – a swift knock on the door, a quick *just making sure you're okay*. Nothing more than that. He checked his reflection in the bathroom mirror before he left and with a determined step headed to the downstairs hallway. He was almost at the bottom when the front door opened and a sheepish, bedraggled Jack let himself in. For a split second Levi wondered if he could get away with running back upstairs, but he was too late.

'Alrigh', mate,' Jack croaked before heading down the hallway to number one, barely looking up as he went.

Levi remained silent.

'Gotta face the music now, I have. Wish me luck.'

Levi didn't. He just stood stock-still on the stairs, desperately not wanting to hear the door to the downstairs flat open and the muffled sounds of Jack's penitent voice as he smarmed his way back into Diana's affections. Levi felt sick at the thought of her welcoming him home, accepting his apology and all that went with it. Feeling a mixture of rage, jealousy and sorrow, Levi let himself out through the main door, into the cold December day.

On Tuesday Levi was glad to go back to work and the routine he was so accustomed to. He put Christmas behind him, and whenever Diana crept into his mind he made an active choice not to think about her. What happened between her and Jack was none of his business anyway, and thankfully their paths had not crossed since the meeting in the hall. The office, as expected, was quiet, with only two other colleagues of the same mind as him. They exchanged the usual niceties about Christmas and went about their day. Irene, one of the senior managers at the firm, asked him what he was doing for New Year's Eve.

'I might wander over to Cooper's Field and watch the fireworks,' he said.

'Oh, we can do much better than that,' said Irene. 'Come and join us instead. Nice group of people. We're doing boeuf bourguignon with mash and we're asking people to bring a dessert. That's right up your boulevard isn't it, Levi?'

He was on the verge of politely declining the invitation when he thought better of it. He really didn't want to be sat on his own in the flat listening to Jack and Diana either arguing or laughing. So he said yes. And promised Irene he'd bring a crumble. Maybe his New Year's resolution ought to be to get out more.

As well as find somewhere else to live.

17

Diana

When Jack came home the morning after Boxing Day, he looked awful. He smelt awful, too. Diana was putting a wash on when he walked in, making her jump. 'Jesus, Jack!' she exclaimed, but he just leaned his back against the wall and sank down to the floor.

'I'm so sorry, Di,' he said, his voice broken with tears. She didn't know what to do with herself. So she did the best thing she could think of and put the kettle on. Once she'd made the tea, she managed to persuade him to sit at their little kitchen table, where he poured his heart out, head in his hands. He'd been a fool, he said. He'd just got scared. Couldn't handle any of it and wanted to run away from it all. 'The whole baby thing, being a dad. I'm not as strong as you, Di. I'm just a bloody coward. But you . . . I mean, look at you! You're incredible. And beautiful,' he cried. 'Christ knows what you're doing with a prat like me.' Inwardly she couldn't disagree, but it didn't feel nice to tell him so. He was trying his best, she supposed.

'Who is she?' Diana asked eventually.

'What?' He stopped crying and stared at her, confused, bewildered.

'I'm not stupid, Jack. She bloody rang here.'

'Who did? What you on about?'

'Your girlfriend. She called the other night asking for you, then made out she got a wrong number.'

He shook his head. And for a split second she thought he would lash out at her. But instead he reached for her hand. 'No. No! You've got it all so wrong. It'll have been one of them lot down the Crown messin' about, that's all. There's no one else. There's only you. Please! Babe – I swear on my life!'

'All right, calm down,' she said, irritated by his melodramatic outburst. And because she wanted to believe him, because it meant an easier life, she decided to let the whole thing go.

'I just feel like I'm letting you down all the time,' he continued, 'that you deserve better. I'm a coward, yes. But I'm not unfaithful.' She let him stroke the inside of her palm and felt herself begin to relent. She even started to feel sorry for him – he was barely a kid himself, after all. Of course he was scared. Of course he had doubts. And perhaps once the baby came along they'd have a shared purpose, which would bring them even closer together.

He wanted sex. 'You know I'm two weeks off giving birth, don'cha?' she said, hoping to put him off. He wiped his eyes and looked at her, his cheeky smile broadening.

'Don't they call it *wetting the baby's head*?'

'God, you're gross!' She pushed him away, disgusted.

'Ah, come on, babe, I'm only teasing.' And he grabbed her hand again and kissed it. 'I'll jump in the shower and meet you in bed,' he said, winking, without waiting to hear her assent.

She chose to accept his apology. What was her alternative? She couldn't leave him and probably he knew that. Where would she go? A women's refuge in Cardiff? Great. Or back to Dublin? Who would take her in over there? Single mothers in Irish society were hardly welcomed souls. No, her only option was to keep calm and carry on, and hope that Jack's change of heart was permanent.

And for the next couple of days things were okay between them. Pleasant, even. He was kind and attentive, bought her flowers, gave her a foot rub, even made her beans on toast. She dared to think it might be okay, but then the day before New Year's Eve he insisted they go for a drive to Porthcawl in his new car – a Ford Sierra which he'd souped up for extra oomph. She didn't really fancy it but could tell by his excitement that saying no would be a mistake, so she agreed. He wouldn't stop going on about the personalized number plate he'd bought – JAC 80Y. 'Get it?' he said. 'Jack Boy!'

Diana was mortified. She thought personalized number plates were an absolute embarrassment. Why draw attention to yourself like that? But it made Jack happy, and a happy Jack was an easier Jack to live with than a grumpy one.

Of course, his buoyant mood couldn't last and on their way back from Porthcawl they'd been stopped by the police on the A48 for doing seventy in a thirty-mile-an-hour zone. At first Jack had laid the charm on thick, using Diana as his excuse.

'Thing is, officer, she's havin' these pains and I need to get her to the doctor.' Diana knew Jack wanted her to go along with the lie, but she didn't know how, or what to say, so just sat there looking dim.

'Your wife doesn't look like she's in pain to me. Are you in pain?' the police officer said to her, and Diana just shrugged. Something was stopping her from tempting fate by pretending she was going into labour. She knew Jack would be annoyed with her later, but she'd just have to take that risk. The officer got the breathalyser out and Diana sat silently, smoothing her pregnant belly, waiting for Jack to fail the test. Of course, it would be a disaster if he lost his licence. How would they get to the hospital when her time came, for one thing? But miraculously he got the all-clear and a telling-off from the officer not to endanger the lives of others by driving erratically.

As expected, once they'd driven away he had a go at her. 'What was that about? Why didn't you back me up?' She didn't say anything, just sighed and looked out of the window.

And that was when he grabbed her wrist.

'Don't fuckin' ignore me, you ignorant Irish bitch!'

'Jack, stop it!' she screamed, more out of shock than pain. He wouldn't let go, his grip increasing along with the speed of the car. 'Say sorry!' he shouted.

'Let go!'

'Say fuckin' sorry!'

'Okay, okay, I'm sorry, okay?'

He pushed her away then with such force her wrist caught the dashboard and she cried out. 'Oh stop your bloody moaning, it barely touched you.'

They hardly spoke for the rest of the journey home, but once they got there Jack became all sweetness and light again. 'Let me run you a bath, babe,' he said, 'and we'll have an early night, yeah?' She couldn't keep up with his mood swings, but she was too exhausted to question them.

The following evening they were eating pizza and settling down for a night of New Year's Eve telly. Jack had already started on the cider, while she sipped her tea. He'd said he wanted them to stay in tonight: *See in 1983 together, like.* She wouldn't have minded going to the pub. 'We could go for a couple, wouldn't hurt?' she said. But Jack, it seemed, had decided for both of them.

'Nah, it'll be packed and we won't get nowhere to sit.' When the coinbox phone rang in the hall, Jack bolted out of his seat and ran to answer it.

'Blimey, what's the rush?' she said.

'It's just so bloody loud,' he said as he left the room. He was gone less than a minute. When he came back she didn't have time to ask him who it was before he got in there first.

'Someone for Len,' he mumbled and sat back down, immediately starting to tap his toes, a habit she'd noticed he had when he was stressed.

'His name's Levi.'

'What?'

'You keep calling him Len. He's called Levi.'

'Like I give a toss. Fancy some ice-cream?'

'God, what's got into you tonight?' she asked, smiling. 'You can't sit still for five minutes. Look, go to the pub! I don't mind, honest—'

'Will you shut up about the bloody pub, woman!' he snapped, and Diana recoiled. They sat in silence, Jack flicking the channels, a frown on his brow, and knocking back cider like it was going out of fashion. Diana wondered how soon she could get away with saying she was off to bed. But it was only seven o'clock, she'd have to stick it out for at least another couple of hours.

When the doorbell rang he was up and off again. She half hoped it was one of his mates, come to drag him out, and she waited for the inevitable simpering request, *Actually Di, do you mind if—*

But that never came. Instead came shouting; then, before she had time to process what was happening, a woman was barging into the living room and standing in front of her. She was older than Diana – maybe early thirties? Heavily made-up and wearing a figure-hugging dress that clung to her curves. All Diana could think was that the woman must be freezing being out on a December night in such a thin outfit. Her heels were terrifyingly high and she towered over Jack by a good few inches.

'For fuck's sake, Jade!' he shouted, following behind.

She spoke – rather, she yelled, in a broad Cardiff accent – 'He haven't told you, have he?'

'JADE!'

She pushed him away and Diana, feet still curled up on the sofa, looked at Jack, almost laughing, like she was in some sort of weird comedy. *What the hell was going on?*

'Right, well, if he won't say, then I will.'

'Shut it, Jade.' Jack's order went unheeded and he bowed his head as Jade launched forth.

'Him an' me,' she said, breathless, 'we're together, right? And the other night – Christmas night, when he said he was at Darren's? – well, he was bangin' my brains out down Butetown. And he told me—'

'Don't listen to her, Di, she's off her head!'

'—he told me,' Jade continued, 'that he was gonna end it with you but he just had to find the right time, and I'm sorry about the baby and that but it can't be helped, okay? I mean, it's not like I'm not gonna let him see it or nothin', and y'know, like, in time we can all be friends, but for now, he's with me an' the sooner you—'

'Fuck this!' shouted Jack, and he grabbed his car keys and stormed out of the flat. Jade turned swiftly on her heel and followed him, 'Oh! Where d'you think you're goin', you bastard? You don't just walk out on me like—'

And she was gone.

And the front door slammed.

And Diana was left holding a half-eaten slice of pizza in one hand as the fragile future she thought she had secured disappeared down the infidelity drain. On TV Terry Wogan was joshing and joking inanely on *Blankety Blank* and the audience was laughing in waves at everything he said. She didn't move. Just sat there, immobilized.

And then came the pain.

18

Levi

He'd bought a new shirt. New year, new shirt. And now that he'd decided to embrace more of a social life, Levi thought he should make the effort to find a girlfriend. Unlikely – but not impossible – that he would meet someone tonight at Irene's party. He'd been so bothered by the effect Diana had had on him, finding someone to replace her in his thoughts was an advisable idea. He'd been really thrown by the magnitude of feeling she'd elicited in him, and he was well and truly out of his depth. This would not do. Normal service must resume.

   He'd made an apple and blackberry crumble. Very simple, but a sure-fire hit with everyone. To go with, he'd made his own custard using real vanilla pods and added a dash of cream. Although it was New Year's Eve he had no intention of drinking, wanting to have the option to come home early should the party be a bit of a washout. So he also packed a bottle of dandelion and burdock, a favourite of his ever since he was a child. Covering the crumble dish with three layers of clingfilm, he poured the custard into a flask, then neatly packed everything into a zip-up picnic bag. God, he was organized. And boring. And so laughable, he thought. No wonder they thought he was odd at work. Downstairs the front door being slammed – twice – jolted him out of this bout of self-attack. Jack and Diana were no doubt at it again. Arguing. Christ, on New Year's Eve as well. Still, it was none of his business any more.

Checking his reflection in the mirror, he decided he'd made too much of an effort, so he removed his tie and undid his top button, then grabbed his keys, put on his coat and headed out.

He couldn't resist a backward look at the door to the ground-floor flat. It was still open – should he tell them? Should he close it? *None of my business*, he told himself again, and was almost out of the main door when he heard the feeble cry.

*

Understandably, being New Year's Eve, the Casualty Department at Cardiff's Royal Infirmary was already half full, and it was only nine o'clock. He'd been waiting for over an hour now. They wouldn't let him see her yet, even though she'd told them he was a friend. A jolly nurse came by wearing tinsel in her hair. 'They've moved her to maternity now, my love. She's doing okay, but obviously it's all been a bit of a shock for the poor lamb.'

It certainly had been.

He'd found her doubled-up on the sofa, with all sorts of bodily fluids being emitted that he didn't feel it was appropriate for him to see.

'I'm so sorry,' she said and then was seized by another contraction. 'Oh GOD!'

Levi stood there, helpless at first, clutching his picnic bag full of crumble and custard. 'Where's Jack?' he asked, panicking.

'I don't know and I don't fucking care!' screeched Diana.

'Right. Okay. Well, look, I think it might be quicker if I take you straight to the hospital. New Year's Eve, the ambulances will be scarce and—'

'PLEASE!' she moaned. 'Just do it.'

'Yes. Right. Good.' He looked around for something warm for her to wear. It was freezing outside. He grabbed her slippers, glad that she was already wearing socks, a big donkey jacket that was slung over the back of a chair – presumably Jack's – and a padded gilet. 'Come on,' he said, encouraging her arms into the garments. 'Gotta keep you warm.' Thankfully, on their way out he had the presence of mind to pick up her door keys.

With one arm supporting her around her waist and the other holding her hand, Levi guided Diana gently towards the main door, shutting the flat door behind him. Once he'd settled her into the front seat of his car and put the heaters on full blast, he carefully pulled away and headed to the hospital. They'd only got to the end of the road when Diana panicked – 'I haven't got my hospital bag! I haven't even packed one. I'm not meant to even be having this baby yet, oh my God, what am I—'

'Hey! It's all right, it's all right, shhh now,' said Levi, and he grabbed her hand and held it tight. It seemed like the most natural thing in the world to do. 'I can go back and get your stuff later. Let's just concentrate on getting you to the hospital, yes?'

'Levi, I'm so scared.'

'Of course you are. But I promise you – categorically – that you are going to be absolutely fine. Now, try and breathe, long, deep breaths, in through your nose – one, two, three, four—'

And so the short journey continued. With Diana heavy-breathing, trying to stay calm, and Levi consoling her. He did not know where this new-found sense of level-headedness had come from. Because inside he was a complete suitcase of jangling nerves.

And even after he'd got her safely inside the hospital, and knew that she was finally in good hands, still he was a mess. He sat there, watching the people come and go, the minor injuries, the more dramatic ones, the crying, the shouting – even the laughing, 'I know! What a prat! Look what I did!' – all set against a bizarre party backdrop of New Year's Eve bonhomie. He went several times to the public phone and tried calling Jack at the flat. But it rang and rang. God only knew where he'd got to. Probably downing pints in some nearby pub whilst his girlfriend gave birth two miles up the road, terrified and alone. *What an ungrateful, undeserving, selfish little tyke*, thought Levi. How he wished he could be with Diana right now, just to reassure her everything was going to be all right.

At a quarter to midnight the jolly nurse from earlier came back into the waiting room. 'D'you want to come with me, lovely? She's asking for you, she is.' He couldn't move fast enough.

In the maternity suite the atmosphere was surprisingly calm. He'd expected cables and shouting and beeping machines, probably influenced by watching too many medical dramas. He'd also expected Diana to be a mass of tears and wailing, but she too was almost serene. And when she saw him, her face positively lit up.

'LEVI NORMAN!' she shouted. 'Top of the absolute mornin' to ya!' He thought he was in a dream.

The midwife turned to him and explained, 'She's on the gas and air, love. So she might be a bit disinhibited.'

'Oh, right, I see,' he said.

They'd got him 'gowned up' as they put it, insisting his hands were thoroughly washed, and he felt completely out of his comfort zone, especially as he seemed to be looking straight at the business end of things. The midwife, having no doubt dealt before with many confused men at countless childbirths, invited him to move up to the top end of the bed.

'Not far to go now, babes!' she chirped. And Diana groaned, a deep, determined cry from within.

'You're doing really well,' said Levi, finally finding his voice. He felt so inadequate when he said it. Diana grabbed his hand and squeezed, so hard.

'I can't, Levi. I can't do it!'

'Yes, you can! You're amazing! Incredible! Just so . . . so . . .' And to his surprise, he realized he was crying.

'One more push, my love!' said the midwife, her voice loud and confident over the emotions filling the room. In the near-distance the countdown to midnight had begun. *TEN, NINE, EIGHT* . . . and Levi wanted to laugh at the ludicrousness of the situation. He looked down at Diana, the exhaustion of pain marking her face, her hair matted to her forehead, and then she took one final big breath like an athlete about to tackle a challenge . . . THREE, TWO, ONE! HAPPY NEW YEAR!

And on perfect cue, Diana's baby came hurtling into the world. At two seconds past midnight on the first day of 1983.

'It's a girl, my dear! Congratulations!' said the midwife, as she did a quick check and placed her carefully on Diana's chest. 'Here we go, have a little cwtch.'

Diana was crying.

Levi was crying.

And the baby was crying.

To the outside world they must have looked like the perfect newly formed family.

'So proud of you,' whispered Levi, and he kissed Diana's head. She didn't seem to mind one bit. And to him it felt like he was in exactly the right place, even though he was standing in another man's shoes. It should have been Jack who was here now, congratulating and comforting his girlfriend, admiring the tiny form now nestled on her chest. Jack's girlfriend, Jack's daughter. But Jack was nowhere to be found. And Levi was the cuckoo in the nest.

'Congratulations, Daddy!' said the midwife. Diana smiled up at him and neither she nor Levi corrected the mistake.

*

An hour later, they'd been moved on to the ward. Levi tried once again to contact Jack at the flat but still no reply. Even though it was now gone one in the morning. After hanging up, he nipped back to the car to retrieve the picnic bag, Diana having revealed she was absolutely starving. Initially she'd asked for jam sandwiches, but the crumble and custard washed down with dandelion and burdock hit the spot far better.

Although Baby X was doing well, the medics wanted to keep her and her mother in for a couple of days, especially in the light of the early arrival.

'Christ knows how big she'd have been if I'd gone full term,' whispered Diana as she and Levi admired the tiny snuffling bundle in her cot. Her seven pounds and six ounces birth weight was most impressive.

At two fifteen, Diana was almost asleep and Levi told her it was time for him to go. Their farewell was strange. They had been through the most extraordinary shared experience together and neither knew where it would take them. Levi hated mentioning Jack. But he had to.

'He's going to be over the moon!' said Levi, desperately trying to sound excited.

'I don't want to see him,' said Diana. Levi guessed there must have been a row earlier in the evening, but didn't ask for any details.

'Oh, come on,' said Levi, 'you've got a baby now! You can put any silly arguments behind you, can't you?'

'He's a liar. He's with someone else. I never want to see him again.'

Levi felt a strange mixed sensation of elation, concern and protectiveness. He also felt guilty for having known of Jack's secret affair all along. But whatever he thought of Diana and Jack's relationship or the way Jack had behaved, the guy was still the baby's father. And he was out there somewhere, totally unaware of the fact that Diana had given birth.

He had to find him.

1983

19

Levi

Levi could hear the phone ringing as he approached the front door. By now it was nearly four in the morning – the only person it could be was Jack. He fumbled with his keys, desperately trying to make it inside before the call rang off. But in his haste the keys fell from his hand and by the time he'd finally opened the door the phone was silent. He ran upstairs to his flat and quickly wrote a note: *Jack – no panic, but Diana went into labour last night and I took her to the hospital. Mother and baby both doing well. Best wishes, Levi.* He decided not to reveal the baby's gender – it seemed only fair to leave the new father at least some element of surprise. Sticking the note to the door of the ground-floor flat, Levi suddenly felt utterly exhausted and made his way slowly up to his bed.

He was woken several hours later, again by the ringing of the phone in the hall. His first thought was Jack, and he almost slid down the stairs in his eagerness not to miss the call. But it wasn't Jack. It was Diana.

'Hello,' she said softly. 'Is he back?'

'No. How are you? Did you sleep?'

'Like a log, can you believe?' There was a little laugh in her voice – the sweet contentedness of a new mother utterly in love with her child.

'And the baby? Is she . . . ?'

'Oh, she's grand. Aren't you, sweetheart?' Diana's voice muffled as she turned to kiss, he imagined, her babe in arms. 'Will you come and see us?'

Levi stumbled. 'What about Jack?'

'Well, he's not even bothered to come home yet, has he? So.'

This was such a strange situation for him. He felt completely at sea. Torn between sympathy for this poor woman, who appeared to be friendless apart from him, saddled with a boyfriend who'd abandoned her in her absolute hour of need. Though admittedly he hadn't known it was her absolute hour of need. He hated the thought of stepping on Jack's toes, of getting in the way, of going beyond the call of neighbourly duty. But Diana needed help. And right now, it seemed, he was the only person to give it. 'Do you need anything bringing in? Clothes? Baby stuff?'

It turned out the parents-to-be had been ill-prepared for the new arrival. Nervous that Jack would come home and find him rifling through the cupboards, Levi used Diana's key and let himself into the ground-floor flat, leaving the door wide open in the spirit of transparency. There was a good supply of nappies and some rompers, some cotton wool and talcum powder, but that seemed to be the sum total of baby-ware, not a cot or pushchair in sight. He grabbed what he could then headed into the bedroom, feeling really uncomfortable. But what choice did he have? He opened the chest of drawers, and with his eyes half-closed to allay his embarrassment, he pulled out a vest and a couple of pairs of pants and socks. It felt so intrusive, his stomach was turning somersaults. Then in the wardrobe he found some joggers and a T-shirt, along with a sweater. Surely that would do for now. Just as he was leaving, he saw a nightie on the bed and grabbed that too. He couldn't get out of the flat fast enough and was hugely grateful that Jack had not come home at that very moment. What on earth would he have thought? That he was some sort of weirdo.

The phone in the hall remained silent as Levi packed up a bag for the hospital. In a Tupperware he placed some left-over treats from Christmas – mince pies, Christmas cake, a quiche he'd made just the day before, along with some tangerines and a couple of corned beef sandwiches. He stopped for a moment and thought what a bizarre New Year's Day this was turning out to be. Then he showered, shaved and dressed, and headed off to the hospital.

She was feeding the baby when he came into the ward and he nearly turned on his heel and went out again.

'Ah, don't be going all shy on me now, Levi Norman – you saw a lot worse than this last night!'

He blushed and reluctantly made his way towards her, though he still had to avert his eyes whilst they spoke. 'She's feeding really well, aren't you, my sweet?' Diana said. 'The midwife is *really* pleased.'

'That's good to hear. I've brought you some things.' He held up the bag. 'It's all I could find.'

'Yeah, we were meant to go shopping for more stuff this week.' Diana's initial joy began to wane and he felt instantly defensive of her.

'Oh, don't worry, we'll work something out!' he said cheerily. She finished feeding and moved the baby over her shoulder to wind her, taking to it so naturally it was as if this was her fourth baby, not her first. 'D'you fancy a wee hold?'

'Oh no, I might drop her,' said Levi, filled with panic. He'd never held a baby ever in his life.

'Don't be such an eejit, course you won't!' And before he had a chance to protest any more, Diana handed him the precious cargo. He stood stock-still, holding on to the tiny bundle with every bit of muscle he could muster. Looking down at this vulnerable, newborn face, Levi was gripped by a sensation he'd not felt before – a deeply rooted urge to protect this tiny being from all the world might throw her way.

'You are . . . exceptional,' he whispered, and kissed the baby's forehead. When he looked up, Diana's eyes were tear-brimmed.

Trying to lighten the mood, she said, 'You won't be saying that when I ask you to change her nappy!'

He laughed. But actually, inside he disagreed. He already knew he would do anything for this tiny human. When visiting time was over he mentioned Jack again. And he watched Diana's face close down.

'Look,' he sighed, 'you and him, it's none of my business, but he *will* come back. Maybe today, maybe tomorrow. And you *will* have to see him. He's the baby's father, no matter what's gone on between the two of you. And you'll sort it out, y'know?'

'He hit me,' she said. Dispassionate, matter-of-fact.

'What?' Levi could barely speak.

'A handful of times. But a handful of times too many. I kept thinking I would forgive him, but I won't. And I don't want him near our baby.' Levi didn't say anything, but he felt a surge of anger welling up inside him.

'Why didn't you tell me?' he said quietly.

'And what would you have done? He'd have knocked seven bells out of you if you'd so much as questioned him.'

Levi stared at the ground and took several deep breaths. 'What do you want to do?' he asked. 'I'll help you in any way I can.'

She nodded her thanks. 'I've got money,' she said. 'Savings. I need to get stuff for the baby, that's the first thing.'

'I can do that,' he said.

'And then . . .'

'Just say. What?'

'It's a lot to ask.'

He wanted to tell her that nothing, absolutely nothing would be too much to ask. 'Go on.'

She closed her eyes. 'I need somewhere to stay.'

It was to be both fortunate and unfortunate that the January sales were in full swing that day: fortunate because of the bargains, unfortunate because of the crowds. But Levi was filled with a new-found determination that would not be thwarted even by the entire shopping population of Cardiff.

He made his way to Mothercare, where he managed to purchase a cot, a buggy and a car seat – all at half price. Then there were the daily essentials – more nappies, muslin cloths, wet wipes, nappy sacks and a whole plethora of newborn accoutrements. Thankfully, he'd decided to come back by taxi, which meant he could enlist the help of the driver to assist in carrying all the purchases upstairs to the flat, taking the fire exit steps round the back of the building, just in case Jack decided to come home at that moment.

'Congratulations, by the way,' said the cabbie when Levi gave him a tip. 'This is when the hard work starts, mate! Believe me, I know. Got three of the little buggers!'

Levi did not correct the driver's assumption, but instead luxuriated in the warm glow he felt at being mistaken, once again, for a new dad. It didn't last long, though. He must not allow himself these ridiculous thoughts. He had a job to do, responsibilities to fulfil. As a friend.

Once he'd unpacked the shopping he put fresh linen on his own bed, grateful that the place was tidy and guest-ready. The box room, which he used as a study, contained a never-slept-on sofa bed. When he'd set it up, he was impressed at how comfortable it looked. This was to be his temporary new bedroom.

The next morning, he rang in sick to work – something he'd never done in his life before – and made his way to the hospital to collect Diana and her new charge. En route, he wondered if he'd see Jack stumbling drunkenly home, full of regret and apology, ready to beg forgiveness one more time. Levi felt confident that this time Diana would stand strong and not take him back. But human nature was a mystery – who knew what she would do when she saw him face to face. He was appalled at the man's lack of integrity at abandoning the mother of his child the way he had. Okay, so he wouldn't know that the baby had arrived early, but still – he knew she was heavily pregnant, and he knew how upset she would be. How could the guy not care one iota? There really were some selfish people in the world.

'I can sleep on the couch,' Diana said when they arrived back at Levi's and she saw all the rearranging he'd done.

Levi, of course, wouldn't hear of it. 'All you need to think about is resting, and feeding this little one,' he said quietly, and Diana nodded. After clearing out the rest of her clothes and personal items from her flat, he settled her and the baby on the sofa with a big mug of tea and a slice of Christmas cake.

Still the phone had not rung.

'D'you think he's all right?' he asked. 'Jack, I mean.'

'Sure, of course. He'll be with that woman. Jeez, if you'd seen the state of her. Well, good luck to him if that's what he's into.'

20

Diana

Later that evening they were sitting in Levi's kitchen eating spaghetti bolognese, the baby asleep in the Moses basket. Diana loved Levi's cooking. And she loved being in his company. He made her feel nourished, and cherished, and protected. Feelings she'd never known before, not really. He was the best friend she'd ever had, and he'd only been in her life a few days.

'When he comes back, I will be with you. You don't have to see him on your own if you don't want to.'

'I hope he never does,' she said. 'I don't ever want to see him again.'

'I know. But she's his baby. You can't deny him that,' said Levi as he grated more cheese on to her bolognese sauce. 'And you do need to consider how you'll feel further down the road if you don't let him see her. You may regret it, that's all I'm saying.'

'Do you think I'm bad?' she asked, twirling the pasta around her fork.

'Bad in what way?'

'Harsh on him. Cold. Cruel? I mean, y'know, he has his good points. And I reckon he had it tough growing up – it's what made him like he is.'

'Don't!' Levi said, an unexpected anger building inside him.

'Who hits a woman – let alone a pregnant woman! Don't excuse him, please don't do that.'

He looked at her then with an expression she'd never seen before. She'd seen lust in the eyes of many men, the look of *wanting* her, and she'd seen some sort of approximation of love from Jack – though she realized in hindsight that that was just lust as well. But this, the way Levi was looking at her, was pure tenderness. Tenderness and admiration.

'How could you even begin to think of yourself as cold or cruel?' he asked, and seemed genuinely baffled. 'You, Diana O'Donnell, are the kindest, most gentle and compassionate soul I've ever known.'

They were both still for a split second. She stopped twirling her spaghetti, he held the grater in one hand and the Parmesan in the other and she smiled and said, 'And *this*, Levi Norman – this is the best bloody spag bol that *I've* ever had the good fortune to get my chops around.'

He laughed, and they carried on eating quietly. It was Levi who broke the silence.

'Did you and Jack not talk about names, by the way?'

'Oh Christ, yes! Didn't shut up about it. He thought we should call her after his two grandmothers. Said seeing as I never knew my own mam, we should go for double bubble with his lot.'

'And what were they called?'

'One was called Una and the other was a Maud.'

Levi bit his lip. She could tell he was trying not to laugh. 'Sorry,' he said, looking at the baby. 'Una Maud. Mauduna. When you say them together it does sound like a make of car – *the new Ford Mauduna, available from your nearest dealer!*' he joked.

And Diana started laughing too, 'Or Unamaud. Sounds like some sort of Italian dessert. No,' she said softly, looking at her baby sleeping soundly in the basket. 'She's not an Una, is she? Or a Maud.'

'It's sad you didn't know your own mother's name,' he said.

'Ah, well.'

They carried on eating, pensive, but comfortable in each other's company. 'What was *your* mother called?' she asked.

'Mine?' He looked startled, as if he'd forgotten he'd even had a mother. 'Her name was Rachel.'

'Rachel,' she repeated. 'Yes. I like that.' And she looked down at her sleeping child. 'Hello, Rachel. D'you like your new name?' And when she looked back at Levi, she saw him surreptitiously wipe a stray tear from his cheek.

'There's plenty of food and snacks for you,' he said the following morning, before heading off to work.

'You're a gem, Levi, you really are.'

'Just remember, you're perfectly safe. He can't get to you. Try and rest.'

'Me and Rachel might do a bit of baking,' she smiled. 'Give you a run for your money, you watch!' Although she was attempting light-heartedness, it didn't really carry.

He stopped at the door and asked, 'You haven't changed your mind, then?'

'About staying here?'

'No, about the name. *Rachel.*'

'I can't imagine her being called anything else,' she said. And she meant it. He smiled back at her, and she thought she detected a beam of pride. There were good people in this world, she thought. Really good eggs. She waited to hear the front door slam, then began dressing the baby ready to go out. There was something she had to do, before it was too late, and she suspected Levi would dissuade her from doing it if she told him. And yes, there was a risk of bumping into Jack. But she knew if she didn't do it today she might lose the courage.

An hour later she was sitting in the Cardiff Register Office on Park Place, rocking Rachel in her arms as she registered the newborn's birth.

'And the father's name?' asked the registrar.

'I don't know, it was a one-night stand,' Diana replied, filled with an overwhelming sense of liberation: she'd managed to free herself from Jack Blythe at last. She watched as the registrar unquestioningly filled out the appropriate box: *Father unknown*.

Diana was still feeling euphoric when she arrived home, buoyed up by the audacity of what she'd just done, the freshly filled-out birth certificate hidden inside her coat. Creeping in through the common entrance, her heart was racing for fear Jack would appear in the hall. As quietly as she could, she made her way upstairs, shutting Levi's door behind her. Safe again in her friend's lovely home. She couldn't stop smiling then, feeding and changing Rachel before putting her down for her nap. Then she set about baking some rock cakes as promised, poured herself a big mug of tea and joined her daughter for forty winks. The distant sound of the phone ringing in the hall brought her round a couple of hours later. She'd fallen into a very deep sleep. It only seemed to ring a couple of times before she heard Levi's voice answering the call. She looked at the clock – four o'clock. He was home early. The call was short, followed by his footsteps, urgent on the stairs. When he came into the living room his face was ashen, and he was breathless.

'That was Jack,' he said, barely able to get his words out. 'He was arrested . . . New Year's Eve! Says he's been trying for the past two days, says—'

'What are you talking about?! Slow down!' Diana wondered if she was asleep and this was some sort of dream.

'He's in jail, Diana! He's *killed* someone.'

21

Diana

There'd been a crash.

On New Year's Eve, when Jack had stormed out of the flat after the row, he'd got straight into the car with that woman in tow and driven off at speed. He'd jumped the lights at Cathedral Road and smashed into an oncoming vehicle, the driver of which, a man in his seventies, had died outright. When they breathalysed Jack, he was three times over the limit. Arrest was inevitable, and due to a previous drink-driving conviction five years earlier, bail was denied.

'What was his name?' whispered Diana. 'The man who died?'
'Arthur Lloyd.'
'Did he have a family?'
'I don't know, it's not—'
'The poor, poor man.'
'Yes.'

They sat in silence for a few moments, Diana filled with rage at the horror of what had happened: the waste of an innocent life, all down to the stupidity, the sheer recklessness, of the man she'd once thought she'd marry.

'He wants to see you.'
'Of course he does.'

'Will you go?'

'He's nothing to do with me. He *killed* someone, Levi!'

'I know, I know. But not intentionally, it's not like he's—'

'Jesus, you're not defending him?'

'No,' he paused. 'Of course not. It's just . . .'

She could see Levi was nervous about asking, but he did, because he was essentially a good soul, she knew that.

'Look,' he hesitated. 'Jack may be nothing to do with you any more, I understand that. But he's still Rachel's father. He's *always* going to be Rachel's father.'

'Why do you have to keep saying that?!'

'Because it's true!'

'I don't want my baby growing up with a killer for a dad. He may not have *meant* to kill that man, but it's because of him – the stupid bastard – that that man is dead. And I don't want my child having anything to do with him!' Then a thought struck her. 'Does he know? About Rachel? Does he even know she's born?'

'No.'

'Honestly?'

'Honestly! Diana, I barely said two words to him! Came straight upstairs to tell you.'

She nodded and it felt as if they stared at each other for an age; it felt as if they were both thinking the same thing.

Diana's idea was to simply run away – to drop everything, get in the car and just drive. But as Levi pointed out, this would just set up more problems for her further down the road. He also pointed out that she couldn't do it alone. 'So I'll come with you,' he said, matter-of-factly. At first she was confused – she thought he meant he'd drive her somewhere, maybe settle her in, then go back to Cardiff.

'And how will you manage after that?' he asked. 'You may as well go back to Ireland and throw yourself on the mercy of the state. No, we can do better than that, Diana. Just give me a few days to work it out.'

The way that Levi took control, with such confidence and calmness, stirred something in her other than plain gratitude. She was beginning to see him in a new light. He almost *looked* different. His kind eyes, she noticed, were a soft grey, and the way his dark hair curled at the nape of his neck gave him something of an Italian look. It must be her post-childbirth hormones, but she was starting to find him attractive. When these thoughts came into her head, when she observed them, she shook them away and focused on the plan in hand. Which was to get as far away from Cardiff as possible, and start a new life.

*

Levi handed in his notice at work without regret. He told Diana his colleagues were shocked and disappointed when they heard, but understood completely when he explained he'd always had a desire to live in the Highlands.

'Surely it's a bit weird, though, isn't it? I mean, why would you want to?' she asked. But he had his answer ready and waiting.

'They know I'm a wildlife freak – where better than the Highlands to indulge my weirdo hobby?' He'd also mentioned he might go to Australia to live with his cousin Netty for a while. 'Just to keep them off my trail.' And, enclosing a cheque to pay off two months' rent, he sent an explanatory letter to the landlord that repeated the lie about Australia.

Diana was surprised and impressed by his ingenuity. 'You sure you're not a government spy, Levi Norman? Barefaced lying seems to come so naturally to you.'

He raised an eyebrow at her. 'I'm afraid I'm not at liberty to say.'

She smiled at him; then a thought struck her. 'What about me, though? Shall I say I've gone back to Ireland?'

Levi shook his head. 'No, best to say nothing. It'll take a while before he realizes you've gone as well. We don't want anyone linking us together.' To all intents and purposes, Levi succeeded in deleting all traces of his and Diana's existence in Cardiff.

*

Before they left, Levi bought a copy of the *South Wales Echo*, which detailed the story of the crash on its front page. There was a picture of the deceased pensioner and another of Jack, who, it said, faced a minimum jail sentence of eight years for causing death by driving under the influence. Once the car was loaded and they were ready to go, Levi asked Diana one more time if she was sure. 'Because if you have any doubts about going, that's fine and I'll understand, I really will.'

She interrupted him. 'I've never been more sure of anything in my life.'

22

Levi

He arranged a late-night removal van to transfer their possessions. Diana didn't have much in the first place, but Levi seemed to have a whole lifetime's worth of things. And seeing it all boxed up and shipped out upset her. 'What am I doing to you, Levi Norman?' she asked. He laughed it off and told her not to be daft, rapidly changing the subject. Because he daren't start that conversation, daren't think about the answer – what, indeed, *was* she doing to him: this confirmed bachelor, this quiet man who loved his own company, who had never dreamt of sharing his life with anyone else, who'd happily long accepted a solitary, simple life, intending never to change it?

Of course, being in the car together for nigh on two days, heading north in the cold, icy conditions of early January, gave them plenty of time to talk. To get to know each other. And not long after they'd crossed the border into Scotland, she asked him why he was making such a monumental sacrifice in helping her.

'There are three reasons,' he said, as if presenting evidence in court. 'To begin with, I think you've had a rough deal. Jack Blythe is a bully. And I cannot tolerate bullies. They make my blood boil.'

'Well, yeah, I get that,' she said.

'Secondly, I'm a thirty-one-year-old accountant who's lived in the same town all his life, and worked for the same company all his career. I've never done *anything* remotely exciting or different or daring. I am so utterly boring, you could set your watch by the routine of my life. I will never get the opportunity to do something like this ever again, so I'm not going to let the chance pass me by.'

He was silent then, his eyes firmly on the road. He regretted telling her there were three reasons and prayed she wouldn't ask. But she did.

'And thirdly?'

'What?'

'You said there were three reasons.'

'Ah, yes,' he cleared his throat. 'Thirdly . . . well, thirdly, I like you. I like you very much. And Rachel, of course.'

He wanted to tell her that he loved her. That he loved both of them. Because he knew this without a shred of doubt in his mind. But he worried that such a big confession would frighten the poor woman. And he would make a fool of himself in the process. Diana just nodded and said a muted *thank you*. As she looked out of the window she added, 'You're not boring, by the way. You're the most interesting person I've ever met.'

He smiled briefly, hiding the soaring joy he felt inside. Diana turned back to looking straight ahead. They didn't speak again for some time.

He'd found a lovely B&B off the A9 near Perth. The lady who ran it was like something out of a fairy tale – hair in a big white bun, wearing a wrap-around pinny and smiling the most generous of smiles. 'Come on in quick now, before that chill nips at the bairn!'

It was indeed freezing. Levi had thought Cardiff was cold, but Scotland – it was arctic! They'd booked two rooms, even though Diana said she was happy to share if it meant saving money. But Levi wouldn't hear of it. He was nothing if not gentlemanly, and even though he'd been present at the most intimate of life moments when Diana had been in the throes of childbirth, and seen things he'd had no right to see, still he felt obliged to treat her with the utmost respect.

He tried paying for everything but Diana insisted he at least took the small sum she'd managed to save as a contribution to their costs. He realized this meant a lot to her, that her pride was at stake, and so he agreed. They told the landlady they were married but that they needed separate rooms because of feeding the baby in the middle of the night. Which would probably have been true even if they *were* married.

'And Levi needs his sleep for driving,' said Diana, who was becoming rather good at play-acting the young wife.

'These men,' joked the landlady, 'any excuse to get out of hard work, eh!'

Diana smiled, but afterwards told him she'd felt treacherous agreeing with her that Levi was lazy. 'You're anything but!' she said, adding that he'd gone beyond the call of friendship and had helped her in ways she could never repay. When she used the 'friendship' word he felt more relieved than ever that he'd kept his real feelings to himself during the car journey.

The next day they headed towards Inverness and their new home. It was perfect. A small but sturdy two-bedroom terrace within walking distance of the city centre. He'd found it after phoning a local estate agent a week earlier. They'd put him in touch with a retired couple looking for long-term tenants for their 'nest-egg' property. Diana was amazed at how efficient Levi had been in finding it. But he said when the chips were down, he was good at getting things done. It was sparsely furnished, which was a good thing, seeing as Levi had had so much of his own stuff transported up there. When they arrived from Perth, it was lunchtime and still light, and the van and the two removal guys were already waiting for them. With their help, their stuff was transferred and the transition into their new home quickly completed. Diana looked around the cosy living room, Rachel in her arms. The air outside was by now cold and dark, and for the first time in a long time,

Diana seemed relaxed. Levi lit the peat fire and that evening they sat surrounded by boxes, eating tomato soup with bread and butter like a pair of student flatmates. 'It's going to be all right, isn't it?' she asked him.

'I believe so, yes,' he said.

Both bedrooms were a good size, but Levi insisted Diana had the slightly bigger one, seeing as she had to fit the cot in there too. They said goodnight on the landing that first night and went their separate ways. Diana loitered for a moment in her doorway. 'Levi?' she called after him.

'Yes?'

'You have been so incredibly kind to us.'

He simply smiled and said goodnight.

*

Two weeks after starting his job at the Inverness branch of Markby & Lewis Accountancy, Levi's boss said he was delighted with him. 'We'd like to keep you on longer if we can,' he said, 'even when your contract's run out. I know you're thinking of Australia but still, if—'

'That suits me perfectly.' He'd forgotten the lie about Australia, feeling now that Inverness was very much his home. True, he missed his colleagues in Cardiff, but he knew it was only because he had got so used to them. His role here was actually more interesting than the one he'd done before, and the team in Inverness had welcomed him with open arms. He and Diana had agreed their backstory and stuck to it, and before long Levi had begun to believe it himself. That they were new parents who had always fancied living in Scotland. They joked that they wanted to complete the Celtic trio comprising Levi's Welsh heritage, Diana's Irish heritage and their joint Scottish home. And everyone believed their little love story.

They'd settled into a routine with ease, and Levi soon became a dab hand at changing nappies and making up bottles of formula. He even took on the night feeds every other day, despite

Diana protesting. The truth was, he enjoyed it. Looking after baby Rachel made his heart soar. He'd never expected to become a father, and although he still wasn't in reality, in practice this was exactly what he'd become. He sometimes thought about Sheila, his old girlfriend, and how he'd denied her the chance of a family with him. What had he been scared of? Holding Rachel in his arms was the best feeling in the world. He was filled with such gratitude to have been given this opportunity when he could quite easily have lived out the rest of his life never knowing the unbridled joy of parenting. Rachel was almost a month old now and just starting to focus a little, and to recognize him. The happiness was coupled with sadness, of course, because he knew it couldn't go on like this indefinitely: Diana was young and at some point, when she felt settled and confident, she would want her independence. She'd most likely meet someone else and Levi's role as Rachel's adoptive father would become redundant. He pushed the thought out of his mind, knowing that this unavoidable change was not likely to happen any time soon.

Diana seemed to be a natural homemaker and the house was always welcoming. He worried that she felt obliged in some way to 'keep house' as repayment for his help. But as much as he tried persuading her otherwise, she continued to look after all their domestic needs, apparently glad to do so.

'I feel like we're living in the 1950s,' he joked one evening, 'like a traditional nuclear family, the husband going out to work while the little lady stays at home cleaning the house and looking after baby.'

They were facing each other across the little living room and he'd expected her to laugh, but she didn't. 'We're not, though, are we?' she said, her tone unexpectedly serious.

'Sorry?'

'You're not my husband and I'm not your little lady and we are not a family.'

He was thrown. He'd only been joking but he'd obviously hit

a raw nerve. 'It was only me being daft,' he said softly. 'I didn't mean—'

She interrupted him, her face flushed with what seemed to be deep irritation. 'Do you not find me attractive, Levi, is that what it is?'

'I . . . I'm not sure what you—'

'Because for the life of me I cannot see what else I need to do to convince you.'

'Convince me of what?' He was lost now, he really was.

'That I love you! Jeez, talk about talking to a brick wall.'

The logs and peat crackled in the fireplace and the radio in the kitchen was playing a song from the Top Ten. 'I just needed to know, that was all. But your silence says everything.'

Levi opened his mouth to speak. And nothing came out. So he decided to answer her with actions, not words. Crossing the room, he held out his hand to her. At first she didn't take it, just looked at it. Then she put her hand in his and he knew it was up to him. Inside, his soul was churning. He was so completely out of his comfort zone, and yet so completely at home. 'I had no idea,' he whispered, finally finding his voice.

'Well, then you're a lot more stupid than I took you for, Levi Norman!'

He took her face in his hands, marvelling at the sheer gorgeousness of her, then softly, so softly, almost fearful that he would break the spell of the moment, he leaned in and kissed her. She responded with a passion he'd forgotten could exist. In fact, he'd never known such fervour. And hers ignited his, and before he knew it they were making their way upstairs.

To *their* room.

1984

23

Levi

On the last day of February, Levi came back from work to be greeted by the aroma of a chicken casserole and the sight of a prettily laid table. It was covered in a checked cloth with a single daffodil in a vase in the centre and two small candles.

'What's this?' he smiled. 'Early St David's Day celebration?'

'Something like that,' Diana replied. 'D'you want to bath Rachel tonight? And once you've put her down, the food should be ready.'

Bemused, he did what he was told. He picked Rachel up from her rocker and held her up high. 'Hello, little one,' he said, kissing her forehead. 'Have you been helping your mummy make tea?'

'Ah, she's been a delight, so she has. She's not stopped smiling today.'

'Come on then, Smiler!' he cooed. Taking her into the bathroom, he filled the small baby tub, chatting to her all the while. Diana often told him how impressed she was at his hands-on parenting.

'Jeez, you'd not get many men happy as you to do the day-to-day with a one-year-old, especially when—'

He finished the sentence for her. 'Especially when she's not mine?'

Diana looked down, flushed. 'Only biologically, like,' she whispered.

He smiled and kissed her. 'It's okay,' he reassured her.

The meal was delicious, despite Diana being distracted throughout. When it came to dessert – a home-made cheesecake – she plonked it down unceremoniously and said, 'Oh God, I can't do this.'

'What?' he said, confused.

'See, I had this plan how I was going to do it, and now the moment's here, I can't. I don't know how to . . .'

'Diana,' he said gently, taking her hand. 'Take a deep breath. What's wrong?'

She closed her eyes and gathered herself. 'Okay. So yes, St David's Day tomorrow, March the first.'

'Right . . . are you trying to say something in Welsh, because, y'know, it won't matter to me if you get it wrong – I can only say a few words myself and—'

'Hush a minute. So today is February the twenty-ninth . . .'

'Yes,' he said, getting more confused by the second.

'It's a leap year!' she almost shrieked. 'Today is leap day. So that means I can . . . y'know, as a woman, I'm allowed to . . .'

She stared at him. Eyes wide, working out what to say next.

'Yes,' he whispered.

'I haven't asked you yet!' she said, full of mock indignation.

'Well, go on then, but you should know I fully intend to say yes.'

She got down on one knee then, and they both dissolved into laughter when she nearly lost her balance. 'Stop it!' she shrieked again. 'It's meant to be serious, you big loon!'

'That's no way to speak to your fiancé!' he laughed.

'Getting ahead of yourself now, you are. Right. Hush. Let me say my speech.' They were quiet then and he looked at her with such love as she turned her blushing face towards him and said, almost inaudibly, 'Levi Norman, I do not know what I would have done or where I would be without you. You are the most wonderful, special, exciting, loving, kind and sexy man I have ever known and I . . . well, will you do me the honour of becoming my wife – HUSBAND! I mean HUSBAND! Oh, I've messed it up, haven't I?!'

He didn't laugh at her. Just helped her to her feet, cupped her face in his hands and kissed her gently, slowly, sealing the deal. 'Yes, yes, a thousand times, yes,' he said. And he felt the relief relax her whole body as he wrapped his arms around her.

A month later they were stood in front of the registrar at Inverness Town Hall. Levi wore a navy suit he'd bought two years earlier in a Cardiff department store, with a white carnation in his lapel. Diana beamed next to him in a sapphire-blue silk two-piece, wearing a string of antique pearls Levi had bought her as a wedding present. Levi held Rachel – their 'bridesmaid', in a sparkly dress and little white furry coat. They'd asked two strangers pulled in off the street to be their witnesses, one of whom obliged them by taking a couple of shots of the happy family with Levi's Olympus Trip camera. All smiles, the three of them headed over to the Royal Hotel for a two-course lunch accompanied by a glass of Pomagne. Levi quietly made a little speech where he toasted his bride and declared this to be the happiest day of his life. Diana agreed and even Rachel joined in with a loud hiccup, which made them both laugh.

*

Their year continued in a blissful bubble of happy family life. Levi progressed at work and Rachel blossomed into a bonny, healthy baby – every milestone marked and applauded by her mother and stepfather. They celebrated the tiniest of developments – every sound she made, every facial expression.

When Levi's birthday came around in June, he noticed Diana had the deep look of concentration on her face that he had come to know and love so well. He knew it meant she was up to something, and sure enough, when she brought him his breakfast on a tray, Rachel happily sitting up on the bed between them, Diana handed him a card.

'So, I wanted to get you something a bit different,' she said.

Levi grinned. Diana was a big fan of 'different' ideas. 'I take it it's not a Sony Walkman,' he laughed as he shook the envelope.

'Go on, open it. But before you do, honestly, if you don't want to do it, then it's fine. I'll completely understand.'

Intrigued now, Levi opened the card. *To my wonderful husband on his birthday*, it read. Nothing surprising there. But then he opened it and read what was inside:

Appointment: Inverness Town Hall, 2.30 p.m. on Friday, 22 June 1984.

He looked at her, confused. 'Are we getting married again?'

'You know that when I registered Rachel's birth,' she said, 'I put *father unknown*?'

'Yes. You were upset, I get that.' Levi had a sinking feeling. Much as he knew this was the right thing to do, he couldn't help feeling jealous that she'd changed her mind about Jack being acknowledged. It was perhaps something he'd always known would happen.

'I've spoken to them. The registry people. And I want to amend the certificate.'

'Okay . . .'

'Because I want *your* name on there.'

He was silent, taking in what she was saying whilst Rachel gurgled happily on the bed.

'But I'm not . . . I mean, I can't . . . it's—'

'*You're* her father, Leev. We all know that, Rachel especially.'

He looked at Rachel, reached over and pulled her on to his lap, kissing the soft curls on her head.

'It's our birthday present to you . . . if you want it. To be her father. Officially, like.'

And swallowing his tears he whispered, 'It's the best present ever.'

That weekend, they went for a celebratory mini holiday to

Nairn, a pretty seaside town only half an hour's drive from Inverness but which, when the sun shone, could for all the world be on the Cornish or Devonshire coast. They toasted Levi's official fatherhood with plastic cups full of orange squash and he took a photo of Rachel sat on the sand in a floppy sun-hat as Diana built her a sandcastle.

He would look at the photo time and time again in the years that followed – a perfect moment of joy captured in a celluloid square.

2024

24

Linda

'D'you want sugar in that?' asks Fergus Murray, who has just poured us both a mug of coffee from Brodie's flask.

'No thanks.' We're sitting at the blue Formica table in the kitchen at Beannach Lodge. It's bloody freezing, so the coffee is very welcome indeed. Fergus has the Walker's shortbread tin open in front of him, tentatively rummaging through its contents. I'm slowly leafing through the pages of Levi Norman's photo album, making notes on my iPad as I go. I'd really prefer it if Fergus left the keepsake tin to me as I don't trust him to do it thoroughly. Plus, selfishly, *I* want to make all the discoveries myself. I don't want him ham-fistedly announcing his findings and distracting me from the photos. He carries on rifling like a bored teenager. He's not even looking at the items properly. 'Think this lot is a waste of time,' he sighs. 'It's all cinema tickets and library cards and party invitations and nonsense. Not a proper document in sight.' God, he's so black and white. He just doesn't get it. I'm desperate to get my hands on the contents of that tin. But I have to be methodical. Photo album first. 'Though I reckon these might be worth a few quid,' he adds, showing me a blue velvet box containing a string of delicate pearls.

'Tell you what, why don't you see if you can get that wood

burner going?' I say, aware that I'm talking to him like he's six. He gets the hint.

'Okay. But can we have our sandwiches then?' he asks. Sounding exactly like he *is* six.

'Of course. Now off you go.'

I turn back to the album. The pages have lost their adhesiveness, so the once-robust peel-away transparencies have become thin, brittle cellophane sheets. Some of the photographs fall out on to the table. There's one of a young woman with a babe in arms, sat in an armchair with darkness outside. And another of just the baby. The photos look like they were taken at the same time, with the words 'seven weeks today' written on the back of one. I look more closely at the photo of the woman, who's wearing a shoulder-padded red jumper, a kilt-like skirt, woolly tights and Tukka boots. It's grainy, but I can still make out permed hair and heavy eyeliner, so I'd say it was early eighties. She looks happy, this woman. Tired, but happy.

The same woman appears in several other photos taken at different locations and at later dates: there's one at the seaside – this time the baby looks more like a toddler, about eighteen months, playing in the sand and sporting a big sun-hat – definitely a little girl, with dark curls like her mum and a smile that would melt hearts. On the back it says *Beach at Nairn, summer 84*. The remaining photos are still stuck to their pages. The two that really jump out at me appear to have been taken outside a formal building of some kind. The big red door looks familiar, and getting out my magnifying glass (a vital component of the investigator's kit) I decipher the words 'Inverness Town Hall'. Of course. I know it well! The photo is a three-shot this time, the same woman, the same baby – I have to assume – standing next to a man in his late twenties, early thirties. And I know this is Levi, because I recognize the suit from his wardrobe. There's a white carnation in his lapel. I let out a long sigh of satisfaction and gently peel away the transparent sheet, hoping for information on the back of the shot. I'm not disappointed.

Wedding Bells! 12th March 1984.

Ah. So this is why the lunch receipt at the Royal Hotel was so important. That meal for two was effectively Levi's wedding reception. The jauntiness of 'wedding bells' makes me sad again. But at least now I have some solid information.

Levi Norman was married.

And Levi Norman was a dad.

There are a few more photos in the album, but only one more of Levi's wife. She's sitting on a tricycle, her head thrown back in a laugh. There are no more of her after that – mainly single shots of what I can only assume to be the dark-haired baby as she grows up – Levi's daughter. There's one of her dressed as a shepherd in a school Nativity; another of her in a Brownie uniform; one of Levi on his own wearing a paper hat, sat in front of a Christmas dinner; and an accompanying one of his daughter at what looks like the same festive feast. The last photo, halfway through the album before the pages go blank, is another shot of Levi's daughter. This time she's dressed up in party gear, fully made-up and blowing out candles on a big cake. She has friends around her and two big balloons denoting that she is eighteen. On the icing of the cake I can see a name. I turn the album upside down and, magnifying glass once more in hand, I look closer and read: *Rachel*. There's another photo next to it, taken, it would seem, at the same event. Rachel the birthday girl standing in between Levi, a little greyer now, and a woman. Definitely not the same woman as in the earlier photos – could it be a second wife? Rachel's stepmother perhaps? She looks older than Levi, not that I'm judging. I look at the back of the photo and there's writing on this one: *Rachel's 18th – me, Rachel and Mrs McA*.

Hmm.

I put the photo album and the tin into a carrier bag I've brought specially, so I can look through them properly in private. Next, I get the sandwiches out of the Tupperware and set them out on the table. I see Brodie has also included some of Minty's shortbread. What a sweetie. Fergus brings in a few logs from the log shed, announcing that he had a mooch around whilst he was in there – yes, he used the word *mooch*! – and can't find anything useful. He gets the log burner going in the kitchen and I'm rather impressed by his efficiency. 'I bet you were a Boy Scout,' I say, sinking my teeth into Brodie's delicious soda bread filled with strong Cheddar and juicy tomatoes.

'Dib dib dib,' he replies, and does the Scout salute.

'I was a Girl Guide,' I say wistfully through a mouthful.

'I know. We were marching at the same Boransay Carnival in 1979. I remember because you were selling strawberries and cream on a stall with your mother. I bought some from you.'

I'm a bit thrown by this. I remember the stall, I just don't remember Fergus Murray. But then my attention was elsewhere that day – a boy who must've been no more than fifteen was showing off in front of another boy and a couple of giggling girls. He was making fun of me for being fat, called me Frank Cannon – a well-known TV detective who was, shall we say, on the rotund side. It'd be like water off a duck's back if that happened today, but back then I was mortified. I remember very clearly just wanting to disappear. I think I felt that they'd somehow sullied the innocence of my strawberry stall. I'd so been enjoying it up until then, serving the customers, dolloping the cream on to their sugared red fruit. I was horrified that my mother would hear them being mean and confront them. Which would have been unbearable. Why is it that when you're a kid being picked on, it's *more* embarrassing to be pitied by an adult who loves you than to just put up with the persecution? I shake the memory away.

'You seemed a good laugh in school,' Fergus continues. 'You always came across as very confident.'

'Despite being called Fat Belly Standish?' I'm laughing, but Fergus doesn't laugh back – he just looks pensive.

'You weren't thin, but you weren't *fat* fat. I've seen photos. You were just a bit, y'know, *bigger*,' he says. And he's right. I just didn't see it at the time.

'And you were kind,' he goes on. 'You always stuck up for

people. You gave Bruce McAndrew a dead arm once for calling me *Fungus* Murray.'

'Well, it was hardly a very imaginative name. I should think he deserved a dead arm for his lack of originality!' I say, worried that he's going to get all self-pitying on me. But, thankfully, he smiles and nods. 'To be honest, I can't really remember a huge amount about you in school. Were we in the same Maths class?'

'Yes. And we were in the same project group for Biology Higher.'

'Ah, right.' I smile, trying to look like I remember. But I don't.

There's this strange awkwardness between us suddenly and for a moment we are teenagers again, navigating the social landscapes of puberty and the protocols of youth. We finish off the sandwiches in silence. It's getting dark outside and we've still got the living room to search.

'Did you see a stepladder when you got the logs?' I ask. 'Only, there's a loft hatch at the top of the stairs – have a quick check in there, will you, and I'll get on with the lounge. We'll still need to come back here tomorrow for another go.' I'm expecting Fergus to complain, but he doesn't. He's far more amenable than he was first thing. I reckon it must be the sandwich and its replenishing properties. He heads off to find a ladder and I make my way into the living room.

What strikes me about it most is the books. I always think books make a home. A home without books is like a lamp without a light bulb. Impressed as I am by Levi's wide reading, I get sad again when I see his current unfinished book, placed on a small table next to his armchair along with some sort of journal. There's a red leather bookmark keeping his place in the novel and the gold writing on it is almost faded, but I can see it says *Edinburgh Castle*. Did Levi go there, I wonder? Or did his daughter go there and bring it back as a gift? The book is a thriller by someone called Emma McGuire and he was on chapter thirty-three. I open it and look at the previous page – the last sentence he most likely read before he died was, *The day was about to get far worse.* God bless you, Levi Norman. It most certainly did that.

An entire alcove next to the fireplace has been furnished with shelves that in turn have been filled with literature. There are a couple of books about fishing, a *Good Housekeeping* recipe book and a few Ordnance Survey maps. But generally it's fiction that's bursting forth. Lots of classics – and not just for show. You can tell they've actually been read – Dickens, Hardy, Austen and the Brontës as well as the Scottish classics like Lewis Grassic Gibbon. And then the modern stuff – William Boyd, Ian McEwan, Lee Child. There are a few library books, too – which of course will have to be returned. Maybe the women from the kirk can sort that. It's a wonderful institution, the mobile library – dozens of cronky old walk-on vans provided by local councils travel along single-track roads in the most isolated of Scottish areas, sounding their horns as they park up, alerting residents that they've arrived. I've always thought it quite a romantic job, travelling around the Islands and Highlands, lending out books and keeping the love of literature alive. Maybe that's something I could volunteer to help with in my retirement. Yes, I might rather like that.

I begin the arduous but necessary task of taking each book from its place on the shelves and shaking it in the hope that a hidden letter or document will drop out. I'm halfway through, resigned to the fact that the books are unlikely to contain any clues, when something falls from a copy of *Mill on the Floss*. Neatly pressed between tissue paper sheets is a flower, a white carnation in two-dimensional form, its green stem faded and its pale petals tinged with age. But I recognize it instantly as the corsage from Levi's wedding photograph. And it makes me want to cry.

25

Linda

It's quiz night at the Storrich Arms. Didn't see that one coming. Surprisingly, the quiz master is Minty, who for some reason is wearing a clown's hat. And more surprisingly, the bar is pretty full.

'Where have they all come from?' I ask when I come downstairs.

'All locals,' Brodie says. I'm beginning to realize that the word 'local' refers to the entire island, which geographically matches the same surface area as Inverness.

'D'you want a hand behind there?' I offer. 'I've pulled many a pint in my time.' This is true. Hamish Hamilton isn't the only one who can hold down more than one job. From 2008, I worked a shift every Thursday at my local pub – the Fox and Vivian – and I only gave it up when the world stopped in March of 2020. The Fox never reopened after Covid and I hung up my barmaid's apron for good. Maybe that's something else I could put on the retirement to-do list. I rather enjoyed bar work.

'Aye, that'd be grand!' says Brodie and he opens up the counter to let me in.

'Right, who's next?' I call out. And I'm in my element.

I'm much more energetic now than I was three hours ago when we came back from Levi's. It was just gone five and the place was deserted. We would have arrived sooner except that on the road from Beannach Lodge we passed the post van, driven by Moira Mackenzie. She wanted to know how our day had gone – had we discovered anything interesting about Boyo Norman and did we need a hand tomorrow when the ladies of the kirk arrived, because 'some of them wifies can be a bit, y'know, *srònasach*'. Which I took to mean (a) rude, (b) interfering or (c) a bit much. Turns out Fergus – wouldn't you know it – had a Gaelic-speaking grandma. 'It means *curious*,' he told me later, cool as a cucumber. We declined the offer of help from Moira, but out of courtesy took her number and said we'd give her a ring if we needed more troops. We went on our way, but then we got flagged down by Hamish Hamilton, whose dogs Maggie and Nel barked constantly in the back of his shepherd's truck during the entirety of our conversation. Which, to be fair, was pretty monosyllabic from his end. He, like Moira, wanted to know what we'd discovered at Beannach Lodge. And could we keep an eye out for a suit in which to dress the deceased as currently he was lying there in his vest and pants. I was horrified at this thought – the indignity! And what on earth had happened to the clothes he was wearing when they found him? I don't know if I imagined it but I thought Hamish looked a bit sheepish at this point. I guess being a shepherd lends itself to looking sheepish a lot of the time, but still. The jury's out. I must subtly try and find out from Moira what clothes Levi was wearing on that last day and then see if they turn up on Hamish. I promised politely that Fergus would call by tomorrow with a suit and off we went. I gave away nothing of my discoveries, of course. Respect is vital, after all, as is confidentiality.

Anyway, by the time we arrived back at the Storrich Arms, the cold had crept into my bones and I yearned for a peaty bath followed by a nice cup of tea, which Brodie kindly brought up on a tray. I was in my bedsocks and nightie by then but he didn't seem perturbed and I was too tired to be modest. I would've probably had an early night there and then but Brodie handed me my hot drink, sat on my bed and said if we wanted the *menú del día* 'which today is home-made chicken pie and peas', then it'd be best to come down sooner rather than later as the quiz was starting at eight and they'd be sure to run out. I sat bolt upright – 'Quiz? Quiz?!' I said incredulously. Which I think offended Brodie, because he replied quietly, 'Yes. Just because we live on an island doesn't mean we're thick, y'know!'

And now I'm pulling pints. And listening to Minty call out questions over a PA. She's incredibly confident and well-spoken. Clear as a bell. She's just asked the contestants what body part is missing in moths. I'm useless at general knowledge. I'm still trying to list the fifty American states. Good job I'm behind the bar and not competing. Fergus Murray has formed a team with Hamish and Moira and they've called themselves the Postal Dispatchers. Which Fergus seems to think is hysterical. But again, that could be the red wine having its effect. He's ploughing into it again tonight.

The bar is busy and the atmosphere is truly lovely. I can see Brodie is really glad of the help. 'How d'you normally manage on quiz nights?' I ask as I set a pint of Guinness going for a sullen-looking man in his forties.

'People just have to wait.'

The sullen customer takes his pint, and hands his money over without so much as a nod of thanks.

'Don't mind Munro Druinich,' says Brodie. 'He's an angry builder and the world's biggest misanthrope. Thinks he's better-read than anyone, that he knows more than the rest of us.'

'He'll be good at the quiz, then – whose team is he on?'

'He isn't. He won't join a team. Just sits and writes out the answers on his own. He always wins.'

'So he really does know more than everyone else, then?'

'I guess so,' Brodie says easily. 'Did you like the pie?'

'The pie was the best pie I've ever eaten in my life.' And it was. Succulent, flavoursome chunks of chicken, fresh thyme and mushrooms in a creamy sauce. And the pastry. Oh, the pastry was divine. 'Another of Minty's creations?'

'No, all my handiwork,' he says, and blushes with pride. 'I've kept an extra one back for you for later.'

'Why, thank you, kind sir,' I say, and instantly berate myself for sounding twattish. 'I'll take it as payment for tonight.' And Brodie nods back, sealing the deal.

There's a surge of customers then, all clamouring to be served at the end of the quiz as the scores are added up. When Minty announces the results, a cry goes up from the Postal Dispatchers who, to everyone's shock, appear to have won. Fergus Murray is looking manic with joy at the achievement. 'Yes! Yes! YES!' he yells, and for one awful moment I think he's going to stand on the table and do a wee jig. He pulls Moira and Hamish in for a group hug and the rest of the customers applaud them. All except one.

Munro Druinich. Who is staring at them with a face like thunder. He drains his pint, slams down his glass (which surprisingly makes a loud bang but doesn't smash) and shouts over the crowd, 'I DEMAND A RECOUNT!' The momentary silence that ensues is over as quickly as it began and everyone returns to their conversations. I get the feeling there's nothing new here and that Munro Druinich is frequently prone to outbursts like these. But he's not giving up. 'I SAID, I DEMAND A RECOUNT!' he shouts again.

'Easy now, Munro,' says Brodie as he shovels ice into three tumblers to make some gin and tonics.

'The Dispatchers won it fair and square,' says Minty over the PA. 'You got one wrong. They didn't. They won.'

(It was the moth question that did for him, by the way. He claimed moths don't have mouths, but it's stomachs they lack. Absorb nutrients through their flesh, so Fergus told me later.)

'*The Dispatchers*,' hisses the sore loser with disgust. 'Bloody incomers.'

'Fuck you, Munro Druinich!' shouts Moira Mackenzie, clearly affronted. 'I'm not an incomer! Nor is Hamish! What's the matter with you, man?'

I'm getting a little worried now – especially hearing Moira swear like that – but Brodie reassures me as he carries on making the drinks. 'He always gets like this. We just ignore him and eventually he calms down.'

I'm about to take Brodie at his word when suddenly Fergus Murray has put down his red wine and is shouting over the crowd.

'*S e amadan a th' annad. IS CHA GABH THU CALL GU MATH IDIR!*' I have no idea what he's just said, but judging by his body language, it's some sort of Gaelic challenge to Munro's manhood.

'*THIG AN SEO IS CAN SIN!*' comes the reply, and Fergus stands his ground ready to fight.

'*ÈIGNICH MI, SIUTHAD!*' he shouts back. And before we know it, Munro Druinich is charging at Fergus Murray, fully intending a fight. I say fight; it's more of a girlie scuffle, really. Most people are laughing, like it's some form of entertainment laid on by the management. But I'm feeling rather protective of poor Fergus so I'm out from behind that bar in seconds and trying to pull the two men apart.

'Hey hey hey now, stop it, the pair of you!' I say, like a dinner lady in a playground.

'It's all right, Linda Standish,' Fergus pants. 'I've got this!' And he goes in again, grabbing Munro Druinich round the waist in a sort of upright rugby tackle. Munro lands a sly uppercut to Fergus's jaw and the have-a-go undertaker reels back, clutching his chin and emitting a rather pathetic 'Owwww!'

I turn back to Munro. 'Now that's ENOUGH!' I yell, but far from withdrawing, he turns on me! And sneers, 'Ach, get back tae where you came fae, ye fuckin' salad dodger.'

This is such an unexpected outburst that I start laughing. '*Salad dodger?*' I say, incredulously. And in response he puffs out his cheeks, holds his stomach and starts rocking from side to side, doing some sort of an impression of what I *think* is meant to be a fat person.

'Are you all right?' I ask, genuinely confused.

'Hey Fatty Boom Boom!' he sings, and starts prodding my stomach. 'Fatty Fatty Boom Boom!' The man is clearly deranged. I'm just backing away from him when I'm gently moved aside from behind by Brodie, who strides forth, grabs Munro Druinich by the collar, turns him around and literally kicks his arse towards the door, calmly saying, 'On yer way now!' The whole thing happens so fast I don't know if I'm coming or going. Brodie dusts himself down and returns to his place behind the bar. Everyone else gets on with their evening, and from somewhere a guitar is produced. Within seconds of Munro's departure the crowd has started singing 'Wonderwall' and it's as if none of the drama ever happened. Even Fergus Murray appears to have forgotten the punch to his jaw and is belting out the words of the song with Hamish, arm around his shoulder like the pair of them are lifelong friends.

It's midnight by the time the last customer leaves. Fergus Murray and me help Minty and Brodie collect glasses and clear up. Thankfully, having switched to lemonade a couple of hours ago, Fergus has sensibly avoided a hangover tomorrow. He's not fit to drive, but he offers to walk Minty to her home a few hundred yards down the road.

'Ach, get away wi' ye, ye softie!' says Minty, though I can see she's touched by the gesture. The last of the dishes done, she puts on her coat and heads for the door. 'Well done the night!' she says to Fergus, who purrs with pride. I get the feeling achievements mean a lot to him. Probably since the demise of his cycling career. Which I've never had the courage to mention.

'I forgot to ask about the prize,' he says.

'There isn't one,' Brodie says with a laugh. 'Just the satisfaction of beating Munro Druinich.'

'That man is one nasty pasty,' says Fergus. 'Vicious.'

'Ach, he's just unhappy,' Brodie replies quietly as he sweeps the floor. 'Married to a mean wife. We've all got our crosses, eh?'

'That we have,' replies Fergus, heading towards the stairs. 'See you in the morning.'

I put the last of the glasses in the dishwasher and wipe down the bar one more time. 'Right, well, that's me to my bed too, I think!'

'Thanks for helping out.'

'D'you know what, it was really good fun!' I laugh.

'Will you be wanting that chicken pie?'

'No, too late to eat now. Even *I've* got my limits.'

Brodie leans the brush up against the wall. 'Why d'you do that?' he asks.

'What?'

'Get in there quick before anyone else puts you down. Not everyone's like Munro Druinich, y'know.'

'Ach, it's just habit I suppose. Self-defence.' And then, embarrassingly, I do this sort of mock karate pose to illustrate. Thankfully, Brodie finds it amusing. I come out from behind the bar and make my way over to the stairs. 'Another long day tomorrow,' I say. 'Hopefully we'll get it all done.' As I pass him, it doesn't surprise me in the slightest when he reaches for my hand, looks at me straight.

'You're very beautiful,' he says, as if stating a simple fact.

'I am not *very* beautiful,' I correct him. 'I'm *averagely* beautiful. Which is fine.'

We both stand there for a moment, in the middle of the pub, the log fire nearly out, the lights on the Christmas tree flashing – each sussing out the other like a game of courtship poker, wondering who will make the next move. And I think to myself, *Oh fuck it*. I lean in, shut my eyes and kiss him.

I'm a bloody good kisser. Always have been. And when we pull apart I can see he's impressed. 'So,' I say quietly. 'Your bed or mine?'

26

Linda

Fergus Murray is waiting for me at breakfast and I'm not sure which version of him is the more annoying – the snippy, self-satisfied one or the bright and breezy one. 'Well, good morning to ye, Linda Standish!' he declares and begins pouring me a coffee. '*Madainn mhath!*'

'This is how it's gonna be now is it, Fergus Murray? Gaelic every other word?'

'Just tuning in to my ancestral roots!' he says. 'Milk?'

'Yes, please.'

After he pours it, he produces a ten pound note from his pocket and places it before me with an irritating flourish. 'I believe this is yours, m'lady!'

'Eh?'

'You were right. About the cattle keeping the cottage warm. Hamish confirmed it last night, so you win the bet.'

Evidently, and thankfully, he has no inkling about what went on in Brodie's bedroom last night between the hours of midnight and 3 a.m. It wouldn't bother me if he did, but I'm not sure I have the energy to bat away his sarcasms or judgements this morning. Because I won't lie, I *am* feeling a tad tired having had so little sleep. Even though it was a nice sleep. A very, *very* nice sleep.

Brodie's bed is gorgeous. A perfect combination of old-style frame and a new, expensive mattress. He told me – after Round One – that he believed we don't, as a nation, value the importance of a good bed. 'We spend all this money on cars and holidays when it's our beds we spend most time in. This mattress is horsehair, multi-sprung and finished with a premium-quality topper.'

'You should be a bed salesman,' I said. 'You have the gift of the gab.' At which point he sort of stared at my lips as if he was going to devour them. And then we launched into Round Two. Oh, it was marvellous. What a delightful and unexpected, joyful end to the night. He totally celebrated me, delighting in what he called my *proper womanly flesh*. In return I complimented his toned arms and chest. I mean, come on, we're neither of us spring chickens, so I think we can both be very proud of ourselves for the performances we accomplished. I'd say I'm almost as sexually agile as I was ten years ago, and I know for a fact that I gave Brodie a bloody good time. It was a mutually beneficial experience. And when I crept back to my bed at half three I felt *delightfully exhausted*. That's the best phrase I can use. It was nothing more than a right good roll in the sack, and I loved it.

'What are you smiling at?' asks Fergus, and I'm bounced back into the breakfast room.

'Nothing, just thinking about last night.' This is very wicked of me, I know.

'Ha, yes, it was very special, wasn't it?'

'Certainly was,' says Brodie, who's just come in with toast and porridge, which he sets down before me. Fergus doesn't see him wink. Nor does he notice me blush.

'I bet you don't experience nights like that too often, do you, Bro?'

I choke on my coffee. 'Sorry, sorry,' I splutter.

'What's so funny?'

Brodie comes to the rescue. 'I think because you called me "Bro" – makes you sound like a teenager in the Bronx. How's the jaw?'

Fergus rubs his chin, which, thankfully, doesn't show any bruising. 'It's fine, hardly scratched the surface, to be honest. Don't suppose I could trouble you for another banger could I, Brode?'

I bite the inside of my mouth. I daren't look up. I feel like I'm in a *Carry On* film.

*

Before we head off again for Levi Norman's house, I decide to call Struan. 'Just want to catch my son before he heads off to work,' I say to Fergus.

'Whilst you're doing that, I'll pop to the garage.' He makes it sound like a local Texaco filling station with a Spar grocery attached. In reality it's a single fuel pump and a ramshackle workshop owned by mechanic Alasdair McGinty (also known as Al McCanic, which I'm told sometimes gets abbreviated to Al McCan't when he's unable to fix a customer's car). 'Best check the oil in the hearse, and the tyre pressure. These single-track roads take their toll, y'know, and tomorrow the load will be substantially increased, of course.'

Gone is the have-a-go quiz hero from the night before. Fergus Murray has resumed his role of sombre undertaker, taking his work so very seriously. I don't mind. At least he'll be out of my hair for a bit.

I press video call and Struan answers straight away.

'Hi Mum!'

'Sweetheart! You're there!'

'Yep. Just about to do a work Zoom, though. How's Storrich?'

'Yes, all good, all good.' I swallow hard when I see in the background some packing crates neatly stacked and labelled. They're going through with it, then.

'Surely you don't need to pack till after Christmas?' I say. 'You don't want to discombobulate Zander if you don't need to.'

'His room's stayed the same, don't worry, I've just been getting a head start on my stuff, that's all.'

'Ready for your *house share*,' I retort, and I can't hide the venom.

'Mum – please. Don't make this more difficult.'

Silence.

'How's it going over there anyway?'

I take the olive branch. 'We've made a bit of progress,' I say, 'so hopefully we'll be heading home tomorrow.'

'That's great! Take it easy on those roads, won't you?'

'Well, I'm not driving and we're in a hearse. So we're very low risk. Is Zander . . . ?' I can feel a lump rising in my throat. Damn it.

'Zander's really happy, don't worry. I'll get him to draw you a picture for when you get back. It'll probably be a whale. You know how much he loves whales.'

'I'll try not to take it personally!' I laugh.

'Talk when you're back, yeah?'

And I press end call and sigh. I'm not going to cry. I'm not going to cry.

Breathe.

Breathe.

'Ham and pickle today,' says Brodie. He's holding up another Tupperware and I suspect he's just heard the end of my conversation. 'Was that your son just now?'

'Aye.'

He nods and I can tell he doesn't want to pry. I put him out of his misery. 'What was it you said about that Munro Druinich last night? *Married to a mean wife?* Well.'

I don't want to elaborate further. It feels inappropriate to share intimate elements of my personal life with a man I barely know. Which is ridiculous when I consider we were being nothing *but* intimate only half a dozen hours ago. There's a difference though: Access All Areas in the bedroom, but when it comes to my private life it's strictly Entry Forbidden. I force myself to smile. 'Thank you for the sandwiches,' I say brightly. And then to be wicked, I add, 'And the sex. Which was magnificent.' I'm just about to steal a snog when we're interrupted by a toot of the horn. Fergus Murray announcing his arrival. 'I didn't know hearses had horns,' I say. 'I mean, they're hardly gonna use them in a traffic jam, are they?'

'Traffic jam? Traffic jam? What is this strange jam of which you speak?' says Brodie, putting on an extreme Highland accent.

'See you later,' I whisper. And he does a sort of sexy, deep growl. Which, bizarrely, I find attractive.

27

Linda

When we arrive at Beannach Lodge there's a three-person welcome party. Mrs MacDonald from the kirk is waiting in a trailer-towing car. She's accompanied by two assistants – Mrs McVie and Mrs Russell. Lord knows why we can't go by our first names, but that's the way they want it.

'Mrs Standish!' says Mrs MacDonald as the three women struggle out of her Fiat Uno with half a dozen ready-to-assemble boxes and a roll of bin bags. The three of them could have been made from the same mould – each in their seventies, I estimate, each wearing sensible flat shoes, black easy-care trousers and almost identical plain jumpers from the Marks and Spencer 'classic' range – one in mauve, one in grey and one in beige. Even their hairstyles are the same, their white mops coiffed into the same short back and sides with a few permed waves on the top. Manageable. Easy to maintain. And not showy. I imagine they all go to the same hairdresser. Maybe Hamish does a sideline in that too? He'll be used to shearing sheep, after all.

'Gosh, you're in school uniforms!' I say with a smile, but they don't seem to get it and just look confused. I head for the front door of the lodge.

'Now, we won't be wanting to get under your feet, Mrs Standish,' says Mrs MacDonald.

'Oh, it's Miss, actually,' I say. 'I'm a *Miss*. Standish is my maiden name.' The three women look at each other, confused.

'You never married?' asks Mrs Russell.

'Yes. But then I divorced. Been six years now. Fantastically liberating. Shall we?'

I sense their disapproval descend like a mist on the hills, but I don't care. I'm still luxuriating in the raunch of last night. A shiver of thrill runs up my spine when I think about Brodie going at it with all the energy of a thirty-five-year-old. And I look at the three ladies of the kirk and I think, *Oh, if only you knew.*

Then again, who am I to assume they're not getting their fair share every night with their stalwart Hebridean hubbies? No one knows what goes on behind closed doors, after all.

'Start in the bathroom, if you would,' I say firmly. 'And then the bedroom. There's nothing there now of interest apart from Mr Norman's suit, which Fergus will take down to Hamish.' Fergus is manhandling the stepladder he found yesterday up the stairs to the landing so that he can access the loft. He salutes the kirk trio en route with a curt, 'Ladies!'

'But just to point out,' I continue, 'if you *do* find something you think may relate to the estate of Mr Norman, no matter how insignificant it may seem, then please let me know. It's vital that nothing is overlooked.' I try to sound as authoritarian as possible when I say this. They strike me as being in thrall to the law.

'Yes, yes, of course,' says Mrs MacDonald with due reverence, and off they trot up the stairs.

Levi's living room looks different today. Maybe it's the weak winter sun trying to sneak inside – nowhere to be seen here yesterday. I've brought the keepsakes box with me in case there's anything to add to it. On the wall above the fireplace is a painting of a bright blue tropical fish. It looks so out of place in the gloom of midwinter Scotland. I take it down and look at the back – *Bluestripe snapper, Mauritius.* Next to the log burner is a big wooden bowl full of pebbles and sea-glass – all smooth as satin, in greys, pinks, greens and whites. I reach my hand inside, close my eyes and feel the satisfying hardness of the cold, round shapes, all differing in size, all unique. I've always been fond of pebbles. I collect them myself, in fact. I wonder if Levi gathered these up from the Storrich beach. I choose one – a beautiful piece of turquoise sea-glass, not quite egg-shaped, more like a miniature kiwi fruit, polished and soothed by the tides. I lift it out, and hold it up to the light before putting it with the other keepsakes.

On the mantelpiece above there's a copper miner's lamp, a German beer stein, a brass horseshoe and a lidded Chinese-style vase along with two framed photographs – one is of the young woman I now believe must be Levi's wife. It's not a great photo and it looks like it was taken not too long after the 'wedding bells' shot. She has a whisky glass in one hand and a cigarette in the other. And she's laughing. The other framed photo must be their baby, grown up.

Rachel.

She's standing in front of an old-style Ford Fiesta holding up an L-plate that she's cut in half, and looking very pleased with herself. So she'd be at least seventeen and a half. I take the photos from the mantelpiece and put them with the other keepsakes too. These personal items are of no use to any jumble sale or charity shop, and to take the photos out to salvage the frames feels akin to selling someone's fillings. There are no other photos or personal paraphernalia in the living room and it all just feels terribly sad. I still haven't been through the keepsake tin; I must do that this afternoon back at the pub. My optimism that I will find someone to whom these items may mean something does not wane. Not yet, anyway.

There's a cabinet under the windowsill and a small writing desk in the other corner. They seem like obvious candidates for finding any paperwork. I'll give the two-seater sofa a quick check first, though. There's nothing under the cushions or inside the covers, and not a bean down the sides. Not even the requisite two-pence coins that always seem to take refuge in the crevices of everyone's couch. I check the armchair too, opening the zips on the two cushions and looking underneath, but there's nothing.

And so to the cabinet. Inside I find two bottles of malt whisky unopened, three files marked 'household', a light bulb and a small toolbox containing nothing but a hammer and four screwdrivers. There's a set of place mats featuring 'Highland' scenes and I wonder if they were ever used. I doubt Levi was one for holding dinner parties at Beannach Lodge. I take a cursory look through the household files, which contain bank statements and utility bills. The statements will be useful, of course. There's a Post Office account and a life insurance policy and in total it looks like Levi Norman was worth a cool four hundred grand! And that's without the value of the house – if indeed he owned it. All in all, it's clear that Levi was very comfortably off. So why live here, then? In such humble surroundings?

One thing I've learned over the years with cases like Levi's is to look for what's *missing* in a home. Because it's often not so much the clues in what I find, but the clues in what I don't. As far as I can see, Levi Norman had none of the usual accoutrements of modern living: no iPad, no laptop, no desktop computer – and it looks like he had no mobile phone either. There's not even a television set – just an old Roberts radio. This place would be a living hell for any teenager, I should imagine. Even Zander watches CBeebies on Struan's mobile, and he's only four. There's a landline telephone near the window of the living room. Next to it is a handwritten list of numbers:

shop/post office 44786
Duncan Logs 44578
plumber (Gordon) 44655

Just three numbers. The bare necessities for him to get by. I look around for a phonebook, an address book, but there is nothing. It's as if he actively wanted nothing to do with the outside world. And then I wonder . . . I pick up the receiver and hear the dial tone. It's an old-fashioned phone – push-button and digital, yes, but that's as far as his modern technology went. There's no answerphone or fancy messaging system attached. I press the numbers 1-4-7-1-3 and shut my eyes as the ringtone begins. I'm praying the last person to have called Levi might be someone connected to him – a relative, an old friend. A gruff voice answers.

'Aye?'

'Oh, hello,' I say, posh telephone voice kicking in. 'To whom am I speaking?'

'Who wants to know?'

'My name is Linda Standish and I'm calling about Levi Norman.'

There's a beat and then the gruff Scottish voice continues, 'Why? He'll not be wantin' any logs, the manny's deed now.'

'Sorry?'

'Logs.'

I see the handwritten list of names next to the phone and realize I am talking to none other than Duncan Logs.

'Oh, is that Duncan?'

'Aye.'

'Right. Sorry to have disturbed you.' And I hang up.

One thing left to try. This time I press the redial button, which should give me Levi's last *dialled* number. And I'm back in *Groundhog* world again.

'Aye?'

'Ah, hello again. That's Duncan, isn't it?'

'Aye.'

I don't bother to explain and just hang up.

'Anything interesting?'

I jump at the voice. It's Mrs MacDonald, creeping up on me for a nose. I launch into officiousness. 'I'm afraid I'm not at liberty to say. How about you?'

She looks miffed but tries to hide it. 'I've got the suit here. I'll leave it in the carrier, shall I?'

'FERGUS?!' I shout out. 'D'you want to take this suit down to Hamish now?'

He yells back, 'Yep! Nothing to report up here. Not so much as a mouse dropping to be found.'

'Take care coming down.'

*

Everything has been so neatly tidied away. It does make me wonder whether Levi had pretty much packed up his whole life in readiness for his number being called. I suppose some people are better than others at accepting what inevitably will happen to us all. I remember my dad saying on his last birthday with a smile, 'Linda, I'm in the departure lounge waiting for my flight.'

Oh, Daddy, I do miss you.

'Shall I start packing those books up, Miss Standish?' It's the quieter of the three, Mrs McVie, standing in the doorway. She looks harmless enough and I feel like I've been a bit mean. They're only trying to help, after all.

I smile at her. 'Yes, that would be lovely. I've checked through them all.'

Mrs McVie gets on with the task. I sense she knows better than to be too chatty. There are a couple of half-filled-in crossword and puzzle books in the top smaller drawer of the desk. And when I reach in behind them I find a mobile phone! It's dead to the world, of course, but there's a charger next to it. I'll take this back to the pub with me – who knows, there may be some numbers and names on there if I can access them. Then I open the second, much bigger, drawer, and I see it. In all its glory. Crying out to be opened and its secrets revealed. A grey steel strongbox – locked, of course. I've not seen any keys anywhere apart from the two I found in Levi's bathrobe, which annoyingly I've left at the Storrich Arms. I manoeuvre it out of the drawer and put it to one side. There's a small gasp from Mrs McVie, who is reading something in one of the books. 'Let me see,' I say, grabbing the book from her hand, probably a little too enthusiastically. It's a biography of Richard Burton, entitled *Rich*, and written inside are the words, *Happy Birthday Dad – thought you'd like to read about this famous fellow Welshman! All my love always to the best father in the world, Rachel xx*, and underneath that, a date: *June 2002.*

'So he had a daughter after all,' whispers Mrs McVie excitedly.

'Yes, he did,' I say reluctantly. I don't know why, but I resent sharing any information about Levi's life. I feel possessive over his privacy, somehow.

'And do you know where she is?'

'Not yet,' I say. 'But I'll find her.'

1985

28

Levi

That spring Levi secured the purchase on their very own home. Not much bigger than their rental, but it had a small garden and, more than that, it had a neighbour – Mrs McAllister, who was a gem. She took to the young family straight away. A widow in her fifties, with her own daughter living hours away in Glasgow, Mrs McAllister offered herself up for babysitting and general handy help. It was mutually beneficial – Mrs McA appreciated being needed. She adored Rachel and soon became something of a grandmother figure to the 'wee bairn'.

Rachel's vocabulary seemed to grow by the day. It was nearly a year now since she'd uttered her first word: 'cat' – unsurprisingly, as she was obsessed with Mrs McAllister's ginger tom. But her second word had been 'Mama'. Levi's heart had burst with love when he saw Diana's face light up at the sound. He wondered whether the fact that Diana had not been mothered herself made it all the more poignant. Because she was needed. And depended upon. By this beautiful, tiny little soul. 'You really are the most wonderful mother to our little girl,' he'd said, and Diana had beamed back. He would never tire of hearing Rachel call him Dada, but on the day she said 'I love you, Daddy,' Levi thought his heart would stop. That night when they lay in bed, it was Diana who brought up the subject. 'D'you think it'll happen, Leev? A baby sister, y'know, or a little brother?'

Levi stroked her hair. 'There's no rush,' he whispered, though secretly he was desperate for another child.

*

Now that Mrs McAllister was on tap for babysitting duties, it meant he and Diana could enjoy being a couple in a way they'd not traditionally had a chance to do before, having been thrust into the unusual set of circumstances that Rachel's birth had caused. 'We're going on a date!' Levi announced when he came back from work on the evening of their first anniversary. 'Mrs McA is looking after Rachel, and you and I are going to see a fil-um,' he said, smiling.

It was pure happy chance that *Chariots of Fire* was playing again at the local cinema, just over two years after they'd first seen it, as part of their 'Play It Again, Sam' season. He'd put the tickets inside the anniversary card, which proudly bore the words 'Happy First Year' in silver on the front. 'One year of marriage is *paper*,' he said, as Diana took out the tickets and grinned.

'Very clever,' she replied, kissing him. 'I'll get changed.'

They both felt the film was more enjoyable second time round, relishing the trip down memory lane, reliving their first visit to the cinema. 'Did you fancy me then, Levi, did you?'

Levi felt himself uncharacteristically blush. 'It wasn't really my place to *fancy* you,' he said shyly.

'Ah, get away with you,' she laughed.

'But I suppose I was a bit . . . *entranced*,' he added.

'*Entranced!* Very poetic.'

'I thought you were lovely, and I couldn't bear that you were with—'

'Hush now!' Diana put her fingers up to his lips.

They never did mention Jack Blythe. Neither had any idea what had become of him, where he'd been sent or for exactly how long. They both had silently promised to forget the man existed.

*

After the film they went for a pint in a nearby pub and sat together by the fire. The romance of the evening was not lost on Diana. 'Such a special and lovely treat tonight is,' she said, her face pink from the flickering flames. And, cocooned in the warmth of Levi's love, Diana shared with him another of her 'ideas'.

'I've been thinking about starting a little ironing business,' she said. 'It's something I could easily do working round Rachel, and now that we've got Mrs McAllister to help out, I could take on the deliveries and collections.'

Levi nodded. 'Sounds good. But how would you get around?'

'Tricycle.'

'A tricycle?' He laughed.

'Yes! I've seen one advertised in the small ads – cheap and cheerful, and it'll keep me fit.'

'The last thing you need is to lose any more pounds,' he said, not realizing how conscious he was of her weight loss until the words were out of his mouth. There was the tiniest of beats.

'You calling me a skinny-malinky?' she smiled.

'Sorry, no. Course not.' He changed the subject quickly. 'I think it sounds like a great idea. Especially for all those bachelors who wouldn't know one end of an iron from the other.'

'Hey, there's plenty of *women* are useless at pressing clothes as well, y'know. I just happen to find it very therapeutic. May as well make us some cash whilst I'm at it.'

'Ha! I've got the perfect name for your new venture: *Pressed 4 Time*.'

'I love it,' she said, cuddling up to him. 'And I love you.'

Moments like these were commonplace now – something he'd come . . . not to take for granted, because every time he heard it, his heart swelled with love . . . but he always assumed the rest of his life would be filled with such moments: that he and Diana would grow old together, be together always.

How he would, in years to come, long to sit by a fire drinking Guinness and discussing laundry or tricycles; how he would come to know a pain so great he would sometimes be incapable of even getting out of bed in the morning.

29

Diana

'Why didn't you wake me?' Diana asked, sleepy-headed and still in her nightie as she came into the kitchen to see Rachel tucking into her Weetabix and Levi sat next to her making sandwiches.

'Because you need your sleep and today is a holiday!' He looked up and grinned at her. They were off on a family day out to Nairn and a visit to the battlefield at Culloden, something which had become an annual tradition. Diana smiled weakly as she filled the kettle and began making herself a tea.

'I just feel bad leaving everything for you to do.'

Levi licked the egg mayonnaise from his fingers, got up and cuddled her from behind, kissing her neck. 'Will you, for once, let me spoil you? You're exhausted from all that tricycling. And next year we'll have a proper holiday, I promise. Spain or Portugal.'

'But you hate hot weather!' She was laughing at last.

'Marriage is all about compromise. Which is why we're having egg mayonnaise sandwiches.'

True, she wasn't a fan of egg mayo, but she was so touched by these lovely thoughtful things he did for her she was more than happy to eat a sandwich she didn't really like. And yes, she was tired from tricycling around collecting and delivering laundry five days a week. The ironing business had taken off far quicker than she'd expected and it felt like the whole house was continually jam-packed with other people's shirts and sheets. But Levi didn't complain. He said it gave him joy to see her little business grow. 'Inverness today – New York and Paris next week,' he joked.

The day trip was far lovelier than she'd expected. The weather helped, of course. Being June in northern Scotland, the days were long and the nights were short. And as she sat on the beach at Nairn, a light breeze dancing around her and with the sun on her face, she felt content. She wanted nothing to spoil this day, this moment – watching Levi barefoot in the distance, his trousers rolled up to his knees, holding Rachel above his head, then swooping her down to dip her toes in the sea as she giggled with pure delight.

She only wanted to think about that.

Not what was ahead.

Not what Tuesday might bring when she went back to see the doctor.

She had not told Levi of the first appointment, nor the second. Because she wanted to be sure before she turned his world upside down.

At the shoreline Levi looked back at her and waved, beaming as he held their laughing daughter tight in his arms. Diana waved back, and pushed away the creeping fear.

30

Levi

He understood now. Why there had been no baby. The cancer was stage four. And Diana, his darling, beautiful Diana, had been given a meagre handful of months to live.

He had gone with her to the doctor's. She had made him go, because, Diana said, she didn't think he'd believe it coming from her. Looking back now, he should have realized her demeanour was strange – that she wasn't smiling – but did he put that down to nervousness? All she'd said was there was something he needed to know, and Dr Lawson would be the best person to explain it. And the fool that he was, the damn bloody fool, thought she was pregnant, but that maybe something was wrong with the baby. Well, he didn't care. Because it would still be their baby, and he allowed himself a silent inward celebration that he might become a dad again. He'd asked her no questions on their way to the appointment, then just waited patiently with Diana to be called into the surgery.

Time stopped. The world stopped. And he saw their mouths move but didn't hear a word, suspended in a silent fog of incredulity.

'Mr Norman, are you all right?' The voice of Dr Lawson finally made its way through. He nodded, held out his arms to a sobbing Diana, hugged her so tight, muttered pointless, false promises that everything was going to be all right. Of course it wasn't.

He couldn't remember how they got home, but he did remember going next door to Mrs McAllister and telling her the news as Rachel gurgled in her playpen, oblivious to the fact that her mother would be dead within months. For Mrs McAllister he was strong – she may have even thought him heartless, because he didn't cry like she did, just spoke in a monotone and talked of practicalities. But that night he drove his car to a deserted road near the Inverness docks and screamed. Screamed at the injustice, at the pain of what was ahead of him, at the crippling terror of living his life without her.

There were only five months: five months of trying to keep their lives together, going to the office enough to keep his job – though he knew they all pitied his plight and wouldn't think of sacking him. Bringing work home when he could, relying on Mrs McAllister, the only person he could begin to call 'family'. There was no one else. And he hated himself for being such a loner all his life, for never inviting anyone in, for thinking that it was enough, just the three of them. Soon to be two. He barely ate and barely slept – staying close to Diana as much as he could, hardly speaking to the palliative-care nurses who came and went respecting his silence, carrying out their tasks with diligence and compassion.

On the last night, although he did not know then of course that it would be the last night, he was sitting by her bedside at the hospice, willing her as always to come through. Silently praying for a miracle, even though praying was not something he ever did. And for a moment he thought his prayers were being answered, because she seemed to come out of this haze of no-man's-land and focus, her eyes sharp, her breathing less intense.

'Don't be scared,' she whispered. 'It'll all be all right.'

He could only nod in response, his voice deserting him, drowning in grief. He held on even harder, desperate not to hurt her fragile hand, but equally desperate not to let it go.

'Levi, I want you to do something,' she said.

'Anything!' he replied, too loudly, believing that if he granted her request, she may be saved. There was nothing he wouldn't do for her, nothing.

'I want you to tell Rachel about Jack.'

He heard himself gasp.

This was the last thing he'd expected to hear, and he was shocked to find himself annoyed – exasperated – by it. 'But we've always said we—'

'I know what we said. Things are different now. I've thought about it for some time. I want you to do it for Rachel.'

She shut her eyes then and he knew she was in pain. He waited, helplessly, for the pain to pass. 'When she's old enough,' she continued, 'you have to tell her, sweetheart. It's only fair on her that she knows. And only fair on him.'

'Since when does Jack Blythe deserve fairness?' he asked, failing to keep the annoyance out of his voice.

'Don't,' she soothed. 'I know you're angry. But in time you'll understand it's the right thing. You *will* do it, won't you?'

She opened her eyes again and he tried to look away, but the surprising strength in her voice caught him out.

'Promise me?' she said.

He met her gaze, his words barely audible as he made the vow he knew he wouldn't keep.

'I promise.'

*

The service was thankfully short. Mrs McAllister held Rachel for him. She'd tried persuading him not to let her attend, said a funeral was no place for bairns, but he needed her there. Her smile brought a chink of light into the darkness of the day. A handful of people came – mainly people from work, and a couple of women Diana had befriended at Rachel's nursery. Levi couldn't say a word. He let the minister do the talking, though he could have been speaking a foreign language for all it meant to Levi.

He heard nothing.

Felt nothing.

Except the searing pain right in the core of his soul.

At the end he almost collapsed, holding on to the pew. Rachel laughed at her silly daddy. And Levi knew that the only reason left to stay alive was this little girl and her enchanting smile.

Rachel.

His daughter.

2024

31

Linda

Finally, some space to myself. I'm back in my room at the Storrich Arms and my findings from Beannach Lodge are spread out before me whilst Levi's mobile phone charges up on my bedside table. I've put the wedding-lunch receipt in the keepsake box along with the piece of Storrich sea-glass, the two framed pictures from the fireplace, the string of pearls and Levi's pressed carnation. I turn next to the locked strongbox. If the bathrobe key doesn't fit, it's not the end of the world, I'll have to resort to a crowbar. I forgot to pack one this time – very unlike me, but I was rather distracted by the whole Struan-moving-to-Bordgalsh thing. I'll just have to borrow one from Brodie if I need to, though I'd prefer not to have to use it at all – always makes me feel such a vandal.

I've left the three musketeers at Beannach Lodge to finish off the tidy-up. Most of Levi's stuff will be set out in a 'table sale' where people can come and leave cash in an honesty box for the items they select. The rest will be sent to the charity shop in Roaken and, all being well, will have been stacked and packed on to the ferry this afternoon. Mrs McVie is taking it. I reckon the table sale will be an excuse for any nosey parkers to have a mooch round Levi Norman's house, God bless him, but it seems to be what they do on Storrich. Mrs MacDonald is nothing if not trustworthy, so I know she'll conduct the whole process with integrity. 'This time tomorrow,' she said proudly, 'the place will be an empty shell, you'll see.' I'm not sure this is something to be celebrated – the ruthless dismantling of someone's life and home. But there's no way round it. There was a reason Levi Norman lived the isolated life he did, shunning society and family and friends – and mine is not to question why. Mine is just to find his next of kin and ensure their inheritance is claimed. I check the mobile phone and see now that there's enough charge to scroll through. Of course, I probably won't get that far because there'll be a passcode on there which will have to be worked out by someone back in Boransay – it's way beyond my—

'Oh!' I say out loud. The phone has opened with no code and sprung into life. I can feel my pulse get faster at the prospect of finding out more about this Welsh recluse. It's an old phone – not one of these modern smartphones but a good old-fashioned Nokia, like one I used to have. I know I don't know Levi, but I feel as if I'm getting to know him and that he was not someone who liked waste. If it still works, then why not use it? I go into his contacts and am instantly dismayed.

Nothing.

Not a sausage.

As if he'd deleted them all.

Outgoing calls?

None.

Incoming calls?

None.

Blimey, Levi, you certainly didn't want to be found, did you?

And then I look at the texts. There is only one. A solitary reprimand, cold and full of finality.

But I do not understand why you would do it. To lie like that to me – your own daughter. You say you were protecting me. Well, I don't believe you. You were only thinking about yourself. What you have done is unforgiveable. Unforgiveable.

The repetition of the word drives home the certainty of her feelings. I look at the date: 18 September 2018 – not long after he escaped to Storrich. I make a note of the number and try calling it from my own phone, but the signal is rubbish in the bedroom. I head out on to the landing and try from there.

'The number you have called has not been recognized . . . the number you have—'

I sigh, whisper a few expletives and go back into my room.

Maybe this early-retirement thing is a godsend, 'cos I'm feeling my time is up with this job. I've never felt it so acutely. Maybe I've just been party to too many endings, too many sad stories of lonely lives. Suddenly, I'm feeling the cold and I pull on a thick Aran jumper lent to me by Brodie, *just in case*. It smells of him and I find this quite comforting.

I empty the contents of the keepsake tin on to my bed. Just as Fergus said, there is a collection of odds and ends that would mean nothing to anyone except Levi. I put the pearls and the carnation to one side, with the framed photos and the sea-glass, before looking through the rest. There's a red-and-white badge that says '18 today!', a champagne cork with a 20p stuck in the middle and the words 'Dad is 40' written in ink around the base. The cinema tickets that Fergus mentioned were for a screening of *Chariots of Fire* at the Ritzy in Inverness in 1985; a special night out for Levi and his wife, perhaps? There's a Brownie Guide keyring and a Sports Day medal for Rachel Norman coming third in the 100 metres in 1995. There's also a postcard from Paris written in showy round letters – *Bonjour Papa – haha that's all the French you're going to get! Having a brilliant time. I can't stop eating crepes with Nutella! See you soon, love Rachel X.*

It's dated 1995; she'd have been twelve then. Why did she only address it to her father? The answer comes moments later when I pull out a plain folded A5 card from the pile of miscellaneous items.

It's an order of service. And finally I see the name of Levi's wife.

> *In loving memory of*
> *Diana Louise Norman*
> *Who died 3 November 1985, aged 24*
> *Braemor Crematorium, 7 November 1985 at 2 p.m.*

Wham.
  This hits me like a train.
  And before I know it, I'm crying. *For God's sake, Linda!*
  Mine is not to question why.
  Mine is not to question why.
  And yet when I look at the simple piece of card announcing the end of Diana Norman's young life, I am overwhelmed with grief. Twenty-four, ye gods. Twenty-four and leaving behind her beautiful three-year-old girl to a motherless life. It's too much. Too much. And the tears lollop down on to the card, blurring the ink a little. I wipe it dry with my sleeve, but I can't stop the familiar thought from gaining momentum in my head – something I used to say a lot back then when I was drowning in my own pain, desperately searching for an answer, a salve for the stinging heartache that I felt when it first happened, the statement I continually made: that it would have been better if it was me. Who had died.

*

Because in reality, whose life is destroyed more? A three-year-old who loses her mother, or the mother who loses her three-year-old child? That three-year-old could not have known, could she? Couldn't have remembered? Rachel no doubt grew accustomed to her mother not being there. She'd have grown up with Levi, who, judging by what's left from his life, was a kind and loving dad. And they'd have told Rachel that Mummy was in Heaven, living on a big fluffy cloud and looking down on her, forever smiling. Whereas if the situation had been reversed, and Diana had lost her child, *she* would never have forgotten, *she* would never have grown used to her little girl not being there. For Diana there would be no big fluffy cloud on which her daughter sat looking down with a smile. No, Diana would have known the cloud did not exist; Diana would have been left with a lifetime of loss, daily painful memories, a permanently broken heart. And I hate myself for thinking the unthinkable, but I cannot help myself. I am ashamed. And it is so, so wrong of me. But the truth is I am envious that Diana Norman never went through what I did. That *her* three-year-old got the chance to live.

I close my eyes.

Take several deep breaths.

And calm myself down.

Enough now.

These thoughts are pointless. These thoughts achieve nothing.

Come on, Linda. You're better than this.

Think of poor Levi. Of him bringing up that little girl on his own whilst bearing the grief of losing his wife. And think of how he died alone.

It is not mine to question why.

Or is it?

Maybe this is the one positive thing I can contribute to the passing life of Levi Norman. And if there's one thing I'm determined to achieve before I retire and sail off into the sunset on my paddleboard, it's to track down Levi's daughter Rachel and tell her how lucky she is to be alive.

Okay, so I won't actually tell her that.

But I do want to try and reconcile them in some way. For the sake of all those who never got to see their child grow up; for the sake of all those people and life events we take for granted. Yes, this is my mission and yes, I choose to accept it.

1992

32

Levi

'Look! There, Rachel! A kingfisher!'

The magnificent bird was preening himself on the opposite bank, the blue and orange of his feathers vibrant in the April sun. Levi held the binoculars steady for her as she gasped at the sight. 'Is that where he lives?' she whispered.

'It'll be near by, for sure.'

It was the Easter school holidays and their week on the Fens had so far offered up an abundance of wildlife sightings – even an otter. And the weather had been really kind. They'd stayed on a cattle and sheep farm for the first three nights, which nine-year-old Rachel had loved. The two women farmers had invited them to watch the milking and help feed the sheep, even to collect the eggs from the hens. Levi loved seeing the delight and concentration pass over Rachel's face as she processed it all.

In the evenings they'd sat and played Junior Scrabble and Jenga and chatted with the other farm guests, a family of four from Birmingham, the youngest of whom was a boy called Brent, a similar age to Rachel, who'd befriended her straight away. One evening, whilst the children were distracted, the Birmingham wife, Mel, had engaged Levi in a 'hushed' conversation. 'Where's Mum?' she whispered.

At first Levi had thought she was talking about *his* mother – but his confused hesitation was interpreted as embarrassment and Mel had carried on. 'It's okay, bub. Divorce is rife these days – our best friends have just split up, haven't they, Tone?'

Tony, the husband, had nodded sombrely. 'Ten years they was together, and then zip! Over.'

Tony returned to his crossword and Mel continued, 'I think it's great, though, when the dad takes an interest. Most divorced men would be off gallivanting in the nearest nightclub, wouldn't they, Tone?'

Tony nodded again. And Levi hadn't the energy to explain he was a widower. He'd feared Mel and Tone would launch into an overwhelm of condolence and life advice that he might find suffocating. He also intensely disliked the word 'widower'. It was such a loaded moniker. Whenever he could avoid discussing his marital status, he did.

More than six years, now, since she'd gone.

All the usual clichés had been thrown his way over and over again – how *Time will heal* and that *Life goes on*. But he was fast learning that Time didn't heal anything – it just gave him longer to feel sad. What *was* true was that Life did indeed go on. And that was solely down to Rachel, who was the centre of his world.

In the early days he'd relied on Mrs McAllister for the day-to-day care of his little girl. Some days he could barely get out of bed, and he silently thanked the God he didn't believe in when his kindly neighbour took charge. She'd ensure Rachel was fed and bathed and dressed and taken to nursery, bringing her in to see her father still in his pyjamas, his back turned against the world. 'Your daddy's still not quite well,' she'd say quietly as Rachel approached him, tentatively putting out a hand, which Levi took. It felt like some sort of a lifeline.

After three or four weeks – he'd lost count – Mrs McAllister had come into his room, having dropped Rachel off at school. Her energy was different – it could only be described as 'bluster'. She'd paid no heed to niceties, vigorously pulled open the curtains that had remained closed since Diana's death and launched straight in.

'Now then, Levi Norman, I've given you the space and let you be, and it's been my joyful duty to look after that wee bairn of yours, but now it's time for you to pull yourself together and get back on the horse. I know your heart is shattered, and I know you can't see the point in any of it. But that little girl needs her daddy. And you need to wash, and shave, and get yourself dressed.' With that she'd stormed out of the room, shutting the door firmly behind her. Months later she'd shared with him that she'd been terrified going in there that day and giving him the ultimatum. When she'd come out, she said, she'd stood by the door shaking, and listening for signs of life.

At first he'd lain still, taking in her words, and then slowly, slowly, he'd turned over and sat up in bed. He'd stared at his feet on the carpet for several minutes, the words of his mother ringing round his head. 'One foot in front of another, Levi. You can do it.' Mrs McAllister said the relief when she heard him moving around on the other side of the door was intense. 'I knew you were going to be all right,' she said.

And now they were here, nearly seven years and several wild-life holidays later, waiting patiently to see whether the kingfisher had a friend. They were spending the second half of the week in a rented caravan on a campsite near by. Rachel loved the adventure of camping and Levi wondered whether next time they might risk an actual tent. The night before, they'd sat outside, wrapped in blankets and looking up at the clear night sky, a cerulean blue dotted with stars, the quarter-moon smiling down at them, like a giant fingernail clipping. He'd made them hot chocolate, like he did every night, and they talked about the wildlife they'd encountered that week. She'd been particularly taken by a family of ducks and ducklings they'd seen every day. Levi had had to explain why the mummy duck was a different colour from the daddy, and how it kept her safe from predators because she could blend in with the environment. And how the daddy duck was brightly coloured to make him seem more powerful, and also to attract mates. Rachel had nodded thoughtfully, taking in the information, and then from nowhere had asked, 'Will I get another mummy one day?'

His mind had raced, his heart pounding in his head. He'd wanted to scream NOOOOO! with every fibre in his body, but common sense had kicked in and he'd put himself in his daughter's shoes. Taking a deep breath, he'd lied, 'Perhaps, sweetheart, perhaps one day.' And she'd been content with that answer and begun talking about otters.

*

They arrived back home on Sunday afternoon, to be greeted by Mrs McAllister. 'I've put on the hot water,' she said, bustling into the kitchen, 'because I'm sure you'll be needing a bath after all that mud and trampling. And there's a roast chicken and some bits in the fridge.' Mrs McAllister liked to fuss. And despite his being world-class when it came to self-sufficiency, and as a result quite allergic to fuss, he rather liked the mother hen qualities of his next-door neighbour. He knew it was particularly good for Rachel to have this grandmotherly figure in her life. She began chattering away, telling Mrs McA about their week and all that they'd seen. Levi smiled to himself as he went through the mail bundled neatly on the kitchen table. The ubiquitous garden bulb catalogue that seemed to arrive every week, an electricity bill, a postcard from his cousin Netty in Australia, who was currently touring the west coast and was raving about Perth. *It's the most isolated city in the world, you know!* For a moment, Levi had the mad desire to join her: to take Rachel and move to the other side of the world in an attempt to leave his pain behind. He even imagined the scene at the airport where he'd explain what was inside the Chinese vase, and whether or not the grim security guard would believe it contained his late wife's ashes as opposed to Class A drugs.

'I'll take this one up for a bath,' said Mrs McAllister, interrupting his Australian reverie, 'and I'll sort out the washing at the same time.'

'Ah, thank you,' he said, and their voices disappeared up the stairs. Levi returned to the mail. The final envelope in the pile bore the name of his workplace. He wondered why they would be writing to him at his home when he'd be back in the office tomorrow. For an awful moment he considered the possibility that they were making him redundant, but quickly dismissed the thought when he opened the envelope and saw it simply contained another envelope with his name and former work address on the front. A forwarded letter. But who from? He turned over the envelope and saw it, the roughly handwritten address – a street in Cardiff, South Wales, and the name.

That name.

The name he never thought he'd see or hear again.

Jack Blythe.

33

Levi

His initial thought had been to bin the letter. Not even open it. Pretend he'd never seen the bloody thing. Then he could put it out of his mind, forget it had ever happened. But he knew this was an impossibility. Reassured by the muffled sounds of chat between Rachel and Mrs McAllister as they went upstairs, Levi took advantage of the privacy and, hands shaking, sat down to open the envelope. The note inside was short and neat; polite, even.

> *Dear Levi Norman,*
>   *I don't know if you remembers me or not but I used to live downstairs when you was in Cardiff – back in late 82. Lived with a woman called Diana O'Donnell . . .*

When Levi saw her name in black and white on the thin sheet of paper, his head began to spin.

> *Anyhow, I got into a bit of trouble – and I been in and out the Big House on and off, but I won't bore you with that now!*

It all came flooding back to him. The memory from over a decade ago – Jack Blythe's voice on that hallway phone, calling from

Cardiff prison, desperate to talk to Diana. *Where is she? Where is she?* Levi panicking, lying, telling Jack he'd seen her go out, listening to the hideous news of what had happened and hurrying off the call, vaguely promising to pass on the message. He forced himself to carry on.

> *Just last couple of years I've been trying to track her down – Diana, I mean. And the baby. And I was wondering if you knew anything? She disappeared, see. The two of them did. And none of my mates knows where to she went. I think a couple of them knocked on the door for you at the time but no answer . . .*

It was then that it dawned on Levi: Jack Blythe had no idea that when Diana had left, she'd left with *him*! He felt nauseous now – the overwhelming guilt of Jack Blythe's ignorance. Levi had always presumed he'd worked it out – that he'd realized they'd absconded together. But thinking about it, there was no reason *why* he would think that. Jack Blythe had gone to prison; Diana had never visited him. And none of Jack's friends had the first idea where she'd gone. Why should Levi have been put into the mix too? The note continued.

> *So I thought you might be able to help. Only I didn't know where YOU was neither. The only info the landlord would tell me was the name of your workplace. And they said last they heard, you'd gone Scotland. Wouldn't say where but said they'd pass this on. Christ knows, you may not even get this, but I'm desperate, I am. I knows it's a long shot, mate, but if there's anything at all you can tell me – like if she mentioned anything to you before she left – I know it's a few years ago but any help you can give me I'd appreciate it, like. I just wants to get to meet my kid.*
> *All the best,*
> *Jack Blythe*

Levi was so stunned by what he'd read that he didn't hear Mrs McAllister coming down the stairs. Thankfully, she was hidden behind a mound of laundry and didn't see him hide the letter. 'The wee one's in the bath just now,' she chuntered, 'and I'll get this lot on before I'm hame for my tea.'

Levi mumbled his thanks and headed into the living room, calling up to Rachel to check she was okay before closing the door behind him and taking out a writing pad from the desk. He had to reply immediately, before he had the chance to change his mind.

Dear Jack Blythe,
  Your letter was forwarded to me. I am afraid I have no idea what happened to Diana O'Donnell after she had the baby. I got a transfer at work soon after and I didn't stay in touch.

He hesitated then, the pen hovering over the page. He thought momentarily about telling Jack Blythe that Diana had had a baby girl – at least that would give the man some small comfort. But then, why did he want to offer Jack Blythe any comfort? He was a drunk after all, an abusive ex-partner to Levi's beloved Diana, and furthermore had killed a man. Why, indeed, offer him anything? More importantly, why did he want to give him even the smallest of clues that could lead to their discovery? He signed off with,

I'm sorry for your trouble and I wish you well.
  Yours sincerely,
  Levi Norman

With that, he put the note into an envelope, addressed it and stamped it, his heart pounding in his chest. 'Mrs McAllister, would you just stay with Rachel for five minutes whilst I pop out and post a letter?'

'I'll take it, nae bother.'

'No, no,' Levi insisted as he opened the front door. 'You've done enough for us already!'

He didn't await her response, just left the house with a determined step, heading for the postbox at the end of their road.

2024

34

Linda

The key I found does not fit the strongbox and I go in search of Brodie and a crowbar. He's in the kitchen whipping egg whites. So incongruous to see this big, burly, bearded Scot sporting a pink apron – spatula in one hand, icing sugar in the other – but he's a heartening sight after the sorrow of the last hour.

'I'm making meringues,' he declares with a smile and no hint of self-consciousness at his appearance. 'Special farewell dessert for you and Fergus Murray.' I love how he's taken on my habit of calling Fergus by both his first and last names. 'Let me get these in the oven and I'm all yours.' He taps a dollop of meringue mixture on to my nose, then promptly licks it off – an action I find utterly erotic.

'Look at you,' I marvel, trying to contain my response. 'A whizz in the kitchen, a demon in bed . . . Did you never fancy marriage?' I watch him carefully fashion little meringue nests on to a greaseproofed baking tray.

'You may have noticed Storrich isn't blessed with a huge population,' he laughs. 'There's slim pickings when it comes to finding a mate.'

'Euwww, you sound like you're one of Hamish's sheep! Online dating is the way to do it. Spread your net to the mainland!'

'Me? Go on lonely hearts?'

'*Lonely hearts!* What century are you in, man? Seriously, you're quite a catch for the right woman.' I'm fishing for compliments here, in all honesty. I suppose I want him to say something like, *Am I quite a catch for you, then, Linda?* Which is ludicrous. We had a night of unadulterated passion and it was very nice thank you very much, but that's hardly a cause for buying a copy of *Brides Today*. I shake the thought out of my head. I'm capable of getting silly sometimes.

'I'm happy as I am,' he replies a tad seriously. 'Tried marriage, didn't fit.'

And he shuts the oven door with vigour before taking off his apron and rapidly changing the subject. 'Right, let's find you a crowbar.'

Strongbox in hands, I follow Brodie into the workshop at the back of the inn. As he searches amongst the shelves, the wind and rain get up quite a force outside. We've been warned the weather might change.

'Don't be standing half in, half out,' he says. 'Get yourself inside.' He pulls the cord on an ancient wall heater which splutters lazily into life, and I shut the door behind me.

'There's a few folk want to give him a send-off tomorrow, old Boyo Norman.'

'How d'you mean?'

'Well, he may not have had any friends here, per se, but he had no enemies either. And so he was, in effect, one of our own. If he was being buried in the kirk like any other self-respecting Storrichian, we'd have a wake the night before with music and whisky, the lot.'

I think how lovely it must be to be part of a community like that. 'It was his choice not to have friends,' I say, feeling more than ever defensive of Levi Norman.

'Aye, I'm not down on the man. Just seems simpler for him to be buried here, like.'

Brodie has a point. 'Well, it's what happens when there's no one to organize a funeral, no family to take it on. State takes over, so it has to be done as economically as possible. Which means cremation back on the mainland. The slot's been booked for Wednesday. In Boransay.' It sounds so crude when I say it, but facts are facts.

'You know, *we'd* have sorted something out. Between us, we'd have got the plot and the headstone.'

'I'm sure you would,' I say, 'but it's out of my hands. Red tape and all that.' I'm touched by the kindness of this gentle giant and start wondering what he looks like in a kilt.

'Found it!' he announces, and pulls out a small, sturdy crowbar. Within seconds he's wrenched open the strongbox.

I put on my reading glasses to get a better look. The contents are no surprise: deeds to Beannach Lodge, which it would appear Levi has owned since 2018, and his final will and testament. Understandably, he has left everything to Rachel apart from £20,000, which he gifts *'to the community of Storrich in gratitude for the years of peace I've enjoyed as an incomer to your beautiful island'*.

Brodie has a tear in his eye when I read that bit out. 'Ach, that's sterling. Fair play to ye, Boyo Norman.' I find this tender side to him so moving that I reach across and stroke his cheek. He looks at me then and says, 'Those specs really do it for me, y'know.'

We launch into a massive snog and in the process bump up against the shelving, knocking several tools to the ground and causing a huge clatter. Which brings me to my senses. Am I – are we – really doing this? Acting like a pair of teenagers, for God's sake. My professionalism gets the better of me and I pull away with mock outrage, making a show of dusting myself down. 'May I remind you, Mr Brodie McLeod, that I am meant to be at work just now.'

He laughs and I straighten my glasses before looking again in the strongbox. There's just one other item in there. A note.

I wish to be cremated and my ashes scattered together with Diana's, which can be found in the Chinese vase by the fireplace. I have no preference as to where, as long as we're together.

'Well at least we know for sure he didn't want burying,' says Brodie. But I've got something more pressing on my mind – the fact that I didn't notice the lidded vase by the fireplace. Or if I did, why didn't I look inside?! It's so unlike me to miss something like that. And by now the three musketeers will have packed up the house and Diana Norman's ashes could be making their way to a mainland charity shop on the three o'clock ferry.

Deep breaths, Linda, deep breaths. It won't be too late. Of course it won't be. I'm being dramatic.

35

Linda

'I am NOT being dramatic!' I shout. 'The whole thing's a bloody disaster!' I'm pacing up and down the bar of the Storrich Arms, trying and failing to get through to Mrs MacDonald – who I've now learned is called Mary – on my mobile phone whilst Brodie and Fergus try to calm me down.

'Look,' says Fergus. 'Let's be realistic here. As things stand, nobody else knows about Boyo Norman's special request—'

Right now, Fergus Murray is annoying the pants off me. 'Since when did *you* start referring to Levi Norman as "Boyo"? You've only been here five minutes and already you consider yourself a Storrich local!'

'Well, at least I'm not sharing my bed with one,' he retorts, and I'm completely blindsided.

Silence.

'What? How did—'

'The walls may be thick in this place, Linda Standish, but they're not *that* thick. And nor am I, for that matter.'

'But why didn't you mention anything? I've been with you all day and you never said a word!'

'None of my business. I've no interest whatsoever in discussing the sordid ins and outs of your love life. I'm a work colleague, for God's sake. And I use *that* term loosely.'

Embarrassed, I glance over at Brodie, who seems to be finding the whole thing very amusing. Which also annoys the pants off me.

'Let's get back to solving the problem, shall we?' he says calmly. 'Now, Linda, was Mary one hundred per cent certain that the vase—'

'Urn,' corrects Fergus, 'those Chinese-style vases are cremation urns, which any fool could have spotted.'

'Well, if it was so bloody obvious, why didn't *you* spot it?!' I cry, even more infuriated that he used air quotes when he said the word *vases*.

'Because you had me back and forth to log sheds and up and down ladders, if you remember. I didn't go near the living room!'

'Okay, children, time out!' shouts Brodie. 'Was Mary MacDonald sure that this urn—' he glares at Fergus, willing him to silence, 'would have gone with the charity-shop stuff on the ferry?'

'She said she was *almost* certain, but that it could have been picked up with the items in the house. Which is why I'm trying to get hold of her! She was going to find out who came by this afternoon for the table sale.'

Fergus scoffs at this. 'Table sale! Ye gods!! So any Tom, Dick or Harry could have wandered in, picked it up and bunged fifty pence in the honesty box?'

This really isn't helping.

Brodie chips in, 'The good thing about Storrich, though, Fergus, is that everybody knows everybody, including any Tom, Dick and Harry. So all we do is phone the charity shop first thing tomorrow to make sure it's not with them, and start spreading the word on the island in the meantime to see if any of the locals have got it. In twenty-four hours, I guarantee the ashes will be found. It's really not a problem.'

'It *is*, considering we're leaving tomorrow,' I reply.

We look out of the window. It's dark now, but it's also very clearly blowing a gale. 'That's debatable, I'm afraid,' says Brodie, and sneaks a glance my way. Despite the awfulness of the lost – no, *misplaced* – ashes, I'm secretly excited that I might get a couple more nights with Brodie McLeod.

*

I'm calmer now, and more hopeful. Knowing the way this community works, I'm convinced it's just a matter of time before that urn is located. I try not to think of its new – temporary – owner, pouring away the contents, mistaking them for orchid feed or cat litter, rinsing out the urn and sticking a bunch of flowers in it. It's not going to happen. It's going to be fine. I must stop catastrophizing.

I've taken my iPad into the corner of the bar and sat myself down with a hot chocolate. I've not made any progress yet with tracking down Rachel Norman. It certainly seems she and Levi were no longer in contact. Although I don't specifically need his daughter's permission for Levi's cremation to go ahead, it feels like the honourable thing to at least let her know it's happening. If I can find her in time. She does need to be informed of her father's death, regardless of their relationship status during his lifetime, and she also needs to know how much she stands to inherit. There's a possibility she may refuse the money, of course, if things were so bad between them. But I'll cross that bridge when I come to it. At least, a solicitor will. I'll be long off the case by then, and probably paddleboarding the length of a loch somewhere in Perthshire.

My thoughts are interrupted by that familiar 'ahem'. I look up and there's a remorseful-looking Fergus Murray standing there. 'I'm sorry,' he says. 'About earlier.'

I pat the bench seat next to me and he sits down. 'I think we neither of us like being unprofessional, do we?'

'No, but I shouldn't have mentioned the . . . y'know.' He looks in the direction of Brodie, who is behind the bar, chatting amiably with two of the locals – the only customers who've braved the weather tonight. 'All I would say is, I hope you know what you're doing.'

He couldn't resist, could he? Pomposity is in his DNA, I think.

I decide not to rise to it and gently say, 'Fergus, it was a one-off. It was a very unexpected single night of delicious passion.' Of course, hopefully I'm lying about it being a one-off, but he doesn't need to know that.

'Never to be repeated?' He presses his lips together in his earnestness and I'm so surprised by this that I laugh.

'Who are you all of a sudden – the headmaster?'

'It's just that you don't know him – and as far as he's concerned, you're just some passing ship.'

'Charming!'

'I bet when the tourist season starts he has a different hiker or birdwatcher or campervanner in his bed every night!' I'm now laughing even more. Fergus Murray is actually *funny*, but what's so gorgeous is that he doesn't *know* he's funny. And he carries on with his moral diatribe as I try drinking my hot chocolate. 'Have you *seen* the film *Shirley Valentine*? That's what the Tom Conti character does – sleeps with Shirley Valentine and she thinks he's in love with her, but when she returns to the island he's making fuck with another tourist – using the same chat-up lines and everything!'

'*Making fuck?*'

'Yes, it's a line from the film.'

I'm actually laughing so hard now I'm choking on my hot chocolate. And miraculously, as I'm doing so, Fergus Murray's stern expression falls away, and he starts laughing too.

'Oh God, you are priceless, you really are.'

Our laughter subsides and we bask for a moment in bonhomie. 'Where are *you* at on the love front, then? Didn't you marry Beverly Harris?'

'Yes.'

'I always envied her long hair. How is she these days? I ha—'

'We divorced. Last year.' He interrupts me so quickly I sense he doesn't want to talk about it.

'Join the club. I think most people our age are, aren't they?' He shrugs. 'How long did you manage?'

'Twenty-eight years.'

'Wow, that's going some. Me and Doug only made it to twenty-seven.'

He looks sad again now. 'Don't tell me, he traded you in for a younger model.'

'No,' I reply, smiling. 'He traded me in for a cheaper, tackier model who's got him running a chavvy café on the Costa Dorada.'

'Bev went off with a customer,' he says mournfully. 'A widower. Their affair started *in* the actual chapel of rest.'

I try hard not to, I really do, but this makes me start laughing again. It's the way he explains it all – with such solemnity. He's like a mournful puppy. 'Oh, Fergus, no!'

'Three days after his wife's death! Three days!! I couldn't go in there for weeks. The thought of the two of them—'

'You could do stand-up y'know, you're very, very funny.'

He obviously doesn't think so. 'Don't you feel a failure, though?'

I look at him, trying to work out if this is a wind-up. 'Are you for real? Me? A failure? I'm amazing. It's Dougie's fault he can't see that. Not mine.'

I watch as Fergus tries to absorb all this. When he sees Brodie coming over with two big bowls of pasta he turns to me and says, 'Shall I leave you two alone, for some privacy, you know?'

I shake my head. 'Don't be a twat, Fergus Murray.' And when Brodie puts the food down in front of us he says, 'Okay, so d'you want the good news, the bad news or the other bad news?'

'Give us it all in that order,' I say, twirling my fork in some spaghetti. I always eat when I'm nervous. Actually, that's not true – I eat when I'm nervous, when I'm relaxed, when I'm happy, when I'm sad, when I'm angry. In fact, there aren't any conditions under which I wouldn't eat.

'Well the good news is, the ashes have not sailed over to the mainland. The bad news is that tomorrow's ferry is cancelled because of the wind, so you'll have to stay another night.'

'And the other bad news?' asks Fergus.

'The other bad news is that the urn which holds the ashes was indeed bought by a local for a pound in the honesty box at Boyo Norman's house.'

'Why is that bad news?' I ask, confused.

'It's bad news because the person who bought it is the wife of Munro Druinich, and she's refusing to give it back.'

36

Linda

How word spreads so quickly in this place utterly amazes me. But within the hour Brodie is serving drinks to a handful of locals, including Moira the Postie and Hamish the undertaker-slash-ironmonger-slash-shepherd, as well as two of the three musketeers and their husbands. Everyone, it seems, wants to help reclaim Diana Norman's ashes. But nobody is quite sure how. We are joined by a few more Storrichians, including Al McCanic, who's braved the weather with Pat and Bren, his young apprentices. They spend most of the time staring at their phones, to the point that I wonder why they bothered to come. Mary MacDonald recounts the tale to any new arrivals, ending with, 'So I stood there on the woman's doorstep – in the howling wind, mark you – *pleading* with her to return the urn. And d'you know what she said? "I bought that vase in good faith. Paid good money for it. It's staying put." And then she shut the door on me.'

'Well, to be fair,' says Moira, who I notice has a habit of always playing devil's advocate, 'you aren't the best choice when it comes to persuading Lena Druinich to do the honourable thing.'

There are mumbles of agreement.

I find out later from Brodie that Lena Druinich and Bella, Mary's daughter, were once the best of friends. These days they are the worst of enemies. They used to run a business together – a small hair salon set up in Bella's garage and which, given the size of the island's population, did surprisingly well, especially when numbers increased in the summer months. But there was some discrepancy when it came to the end-of-year accounts and, according to Bella, it appeared Lena had been fiddling the books. A huge row had ensued – Lena accused Bella, Bella accused Lena, and the salon was in danger of shutting down. Bella's parents, i.e. Mary and her husband, came to the financial rescue, buying Lena out of her share. She claims to this day she was conned, yet she's never taken any action.

'Which makes you wonder,' said Brodie, 'whether there was any truth in her accusations. But hey ho, twenty-two sides to a story an' all that.'

All I could think when he told me was how exhausting it must be to have a running feud with someone in a community the size of Storrich.

The consensus in the bar is that *someone*, preferably a neutral person, should volunteer to speak to Lena Druinich again.

'Well, it can't be me,' says Brodie. 'Given that I kicked her husband out on his arse last night, I doubt she'd be well-disposed.'

'Aye, and she never understands a word I say,' mumbles Al McCanic in a voice so barely decipherable that I can see Lena Druinich might have a point.

'Hamish?' suggests Mary MacDonald.

'Ach, don't ask me to get involved. I'm Switzerland, me.' And he holds his glass out to Brodie for a refill. I notice he's wearing a smart navy jumper with a crew neck and wonder if it had a Levi Norman-shaped previous owner.

'I'd offer,' says Fergus, 'but her husband is likely to punch me again. And by the sounds of the wife, so is she!'

'Oh look then, *I'll* have to do it,' I say with a sigh. 'I'll just play the official card, show her my council lanyard and mumble something about breaking the law.'

'But she's not breaking the law, is she?' says Fergus.

Nobody seems to know. 'I don't want you going there,' says Brodie, 'not after last night and that idiot Munro insulting you like that.' I feel rather moved by Brodie's chivalry and once again have a flash in my mind of him standing on a hill in his kilt of McLeod tartan, roaring at the invaders in broad Gaelic.

'We'll go,' says Pat without looking up from his phone.

'Aye,' agrees Bren.

Nobody seems to have any objections.

'I'll drive you,' says Moira, 'but I'm not coming to the door. I have to remain impartial, as an employee of the Royal Mail.'

'Fair enough,' I say, and the three of them head off for the Druinich house, which is only a five-minute drive away but in tonight's weather may take a bit longer.

Brodie brings us his version of Eton mess. 'I had to use tinned strawberries,' he says, 'not ideal, but the meringues are good and the cream is from Tessa's dairy.' And he's right. I thought I was the expert when it comes to meringue-making, but my Hebridean friend has knocked it right out of the park.

'This is heavenly,' I say, digging my spoon into the dish for another mouthful. 'Like it was made by angels.'

'I have to agree,' says Fergus Murray. 'Not about the angels, they don't exist. But you're an absolute gourmet chef, Brodie my man. Where's Minty, by the way? Night off?'

'Curling,' he says. 'She's got a competition over in Fife. Represents Islands and Highlands, y'know.' *Wonders will never cease*, I think, imagining Minty, a look of fierce concentration on her face as she elegantly hurls or 'curls' the smooth granite stone along the ice, watched by hundreds of competition spectators. Then I am distracted by the return of Pat, Bren and Moira.

'Well?'

'She wants five grand,' says Pat, climbing back on the bar stool and taking out his phone again. Hamish Hamilton chokes on his drink and there's an outcry of *What the hell?* and *Five grand?!* and *The woman is barking!*

Bren pipes up, 'She said she knows there's money been left in the will. And that she's being fair only asking for a quarter of it.'

Once more I'm amazed that word has got out about Levi's final wishes. 'Look, it's true that Mr Norman left money to the community, but it certainly wasn't intended to buy back his wife's ashes!'

'I should think not!' says Mary, who I've got an inkling may have had one too many port and lemonades. 'There's a number of things that money can be spent on – the roof is leaking on the village hall, for starters!' There ensues a discussion about what else Levi's money could be spent on and I fear we're losing track.

'Hang on, hang on!' I say, tapping a glass with my spoon for attention. 'Obviously, we're not giving that woman a penny. So how else are we going to retrieve those ashes?'

37

Linda

Maybe it's the excitement about tomorrow's plan, or maybe it's the novelty of this mini holiday romance. But after the bar is closed, Brodie and I stay up talking till the early hours. In bed, obviously. I wasn't going to miss out on another couple of hours of glorious passion. I'm not stupid.

It's funny, getting to know someone in a short space of time. When you're only in each other's company for a limited, intense period, you're somehow given licence to open up and share information that in other circumstances might take years to reveal. Almost like *what have we got to lose*, kinda thing. I tell him about Doug and our divorce and how we seem to make it work as friends these days, much to the chagrin of Denise.

'When you've lived with someone for that many years and know their worst habits and their best qualities, it's almost impossible to extricate yourself from them,' I say, cuddled up with my head happily nestled on his broad shoulder, his pint-pulling arm holding me in close.

'Aye, life's too short for holding grudges,' he says, looking up to the ceiling.

'You get on okay with your ex?' I venture.

'We're not in touch any more.' He's reticent at first, but then he starts telling me what happened. How they'd met on holiday in Greece thirty-odd years ago. They connected, being two Scots in the same resort, 'Even though, as you know, Scotland's a big fucking place!' he jokes. 'She was from Glasgow, and there's me from this little island in the Hebrides, and we acted like we were from the same village, living two miles apart.'

He pauses for a moment, gathers his thoughts. 'Anyhow, the holiday came to an end, all tears and promises to stay in touch, et cetera. I mean, we were young – both just turned twenty-four. And for a while, we did. Course, no mobile phones back then – and for people who *did* have them, there was no signal. Not on Storrich, anyway.'

'There's something quite tempting,' I muse, 'about not being contactable, don't you think?'

'Maybe nowadays, yes, but back then it was frustrating. No emails either, so it was all letters and phone calls from the coinbox. Eventually things fizzled out. We just went our separate ways, got on with our lives, you know how it is.' I'm looking at his lips when he says this. He has the most remarkable Cupid's bow and I want to tell him, but now doesn't seem like the right moment. 'And that was it. For ten years. I had other girlfriends – mainly short-lived affairs with tourists.'

'Like *Shirley Valentine*,' I say with a smile.

'Who's she?'

'Nothing. Go on.'

'Well, there was no one special or anything, and I didn't mind. I'd inherited the pub from my folks and was making a go of it. What you see now is dead quiet, but come the summer months it's buzzing.'

'I can imagine that. You've got a captive audience, so to speak.'

'Exactly. So one day I'm collecting the glasses from outside and there's this group of hikers at one of the tables and this voice goes, "Hello Stranger, remember me?" And bloody hell, it's Liz! Looking much the same as the last time I saw her, standing in the Corfu sunshine in 1992.'

'What was she doing there?'

'She was on a walking holiday with her mates. Hadn't been sure whether to phone ahead and warn me she was coming – I guess 'cos she didn't know how the land lay for me by then.'

'That's so romantic!' I say. And it is. 'So, did she stay?'

'Pretty much. She let her friends go on ahead and changed her plans so she could spend some time getting to know me again. It was very much a summer-of-love idea.' Stupidly, I feel a bit jealous when he says this. And I'm also wondering, *Didn't the woman have a job to go back to? Was she going to just leech off Brodie?* But it's not Liz I'm jealous of, it's the youthfulness I no longer possess. He goes on to explain how they decided to make a go of it. 'I couldn't leave the island – I'd not long got the pub going, plus I didn't want to. I've never been a city boy.'

'But she was a city girl?'

'Yes. A city girl who, thankfully, wanted to swap that life for an island one. She said she'd fallen in love again, not just with me, but with Storrich. And she wanted to make it her home. Of course, it was a risk – we didn't really know each other that well – but we both thought it was a risk worth taking. By the end of the season, she'd moved her stuff in, and we were married the following December.'

'But no happy ever after?' I say, because obviously there wasn't, otherwise I wouldn't be lying here now.

'No,' he says quietly, and we're silent till he picks up the tale. 'At first it was great – I'd say the first two or three years? Liz helped me run the pub – she loved meeting the punters, serving pints, cooking the bar meals. And she seemed to have got the balance right between city and island living – travelling back once a month to the mainland to "get her fix of civilization", as she called it. And then one day she says she wants to go home again for a few days. Back to Glasgow. I was thrown, because she'd only been there ten days or so before. I couldn't go. It was hard for me to leave the pub, especially in the season, all hands on deck, y'know? Anyway, we had a bit of a row about it – I thought she was being selfish, she accused me of trying to trap her. Which was insane. I'd always been upfront about Storrich and living here. She knew from the start it was a deal-breaker, so it wasn't like I was shifting the goalposts. But she'd made her mind up. She was going. And the next morning she was on the early ferry over to Roaken. I didn't hear from her for five days.'

'God, you must have been worried, were you? Or were you in a sulk?' He doesn't seem to find this very funny.

'I don't sulk, Linda. Not my style.'

That's me told. 'Go on,' I say.

'When she came back she was different. She said sorry and that she knew she'd been selfish but it was done now and that was that and could we draw a line under it and move on? Well, I'm all for letting bygones be gone, so we just picked up where we left off. But she was never quite the same. She was friendly and loving, but there was a sadness. I'd ask her over and over what was wrong. "Nothing! Stop mithering!" she'd say. Not annoyed or anything, just teasing. I did wonder . . .' He pauses and I finish the thought.

'If she'd met someone else?'

'Exactly. And the doubt was always in my head. Unfair of me, really. Anyway, I guess these things happen almost imperceptibly, like a tiny thread unravelling: before you know it, the whole garment's come apart. And me and Liz, well, that's what happened to us – we just started to come apart. I have to say the drink was a big part of it.'

'I thought you were teetotal, like me?' I say.

'Aye, now I am, but back then I was a bit too fond of my whisky. And it fuelled the paranoia, I'm ashamed to say. So when I'd had too much I'd start questioning her about what *really* went on in Glasgow. And Liz was a drinker too, so between us we were a bit of a car crash.'

'I suppose running a pub isn't ideal if you're fond of a tipple.' I sound so glib when I say it, but I'm feeling a bit out of my comfort zone with all this talk of heavy drinking. It's just not a world I'm used to.

'I've been sober since she left. Well, almost. Stopped drinking three days after, though it was a messy final session. Thankfully, my customers are a good bunch – if it wasn't for them looking out for me, I might not be lying here with you now.'

'And that would be a horrible shame,' I say, desperate to lighten the mood. I can't handle deep and meaningful with close friends, let alone someone I met only seventy-two hours ago.

'The truth came out,' he says, and there's a break in his voice. 'It took four years, but it came out. And it was just too much to take.'

'So she *had* met someone else?'

He smiles sadly at this. 'Sort of. And I could probably have handled it if that's all it was. But it was much worse.'

He's silent again and I tell him he doesn't have to tell me if he doesn't want to, though obviously I want him to because otherwise I will imagine all sorts.

'That time when she disappeared for five days to Glasgow—' He pauses, shuts his eyes for a moment, and the pain is so evident on his face. 'She was pregnant. Eight weeks. And she—'

'She didn't want it.'

'No.'

'And you did?'

This feels so intrusive, this conversation. But it's all gone too far now to turn round. And it's not the sort of subject that can be changed superficially. I'm not surprised to see a tear escape down his cheek. The poor man.

'If I'd known there was a baby, then yes, I would have wanted it. Without a shadow of a doubt. But I wasn't given the option. Not even the opportunity to discuss it . . .' He's actually crying now, and I feel way out of my depth. I suspect he's never told anyone about this since it happened. It feels raw and fragile and new – like it took place only last week. He visibly tries to pull himself together. 'Sorry,' he mumbles, 'sorry.'

'God, don't apologize, please!'

Who am I to judge this complete stranger? This woman I've never met? I don't know what was going on for her. I have no idea what state her head was in or what her history was or how she felt about kids, or anything. But I irrationally hate her for doing that to him. Well, I say *irrationally*: it's a lot more complicated than that. I fight hard to stay quiet.

'Thing is, it was always going to be her choice, wasn't it? Nobody can make a woman have a baby. But the way she just went ahead without telling me and then kept it secret for all those years, with me imagining all sorts . . .'

I think about me and Doug. How we'd always assumed we'd have babies. How overjoyed we were when Struan came along, after what had happened and when we'd thought it would never happen again. How our hearts cracked open with joy. The best gift ever. 'When you got together though, you had all that talk about living on Storrich – did you not discuss having kids?'

'Yes. That was what was so confusing. I mean, don't forget we were in our mid-thirties when we got married, but we both said we wanted them and that we'd see what happened. Let nature take its course, type of thing.'

'So she'd changed her mind about it, then, obviously?'

He shakes his head and wipes his eyes, seeming angry with himself somehow for getting so upset. He pulls away from me and sits up on the edge of the bed, calming himself down. 'It wasn't mine,' he says softly. 'The baby wasn't mine.' And without looking at me he gets up and goes to the bathroom. I watch his reflection in the mirror. He runs the tap and leans over the sink before splashing water vigorously on his face – washing away the tears, and with them the memory of that sad time in his life. When he comes back in he is forcing a smile. 'Too much information, as they say.' It's embarrassing for both of us and I'm not quite sure what to do. Thankfully, he saves us both with a swift and welcome change of subject.

'So, are you ready for tomorrow's mission?' he asks, and the twinkle in his eye is back.

38

Linda

I'm regretting it already. Why I thought we could pull this off, I do not know. I can't even blame it on alcohol. But here I am, behind the wheel of an old Ford Escort, guaranteed to be locally unrecognizable and lent to us by Alasdair McGinty aka Al McCanic, who was more than a little excited at the prospect of being part of the whole plan. 'What you have to understand,' he says to me, 'is that not a lot happens on the island. So we take the drama when we can.' He shows me what to do to make the car temporarily 'not work' and sends me on my way.

Back at the Storrich Arms, my crack team comprises Brodie, Fergus Murray and Mary MacDonald, with Moira Mackenzie on the end of a phone. 'It's more than my job's worth,' she said last night when Brodie finally persuaded her, 'but I can't stand by and let injustice be done.' She's agreed to be a decoy to get Munro Druinich out of the house for twenty minutes. The stakes are now extremely high. Like the wind speed on Storrich.

'I'm not sure the wig is necessary,' I say to Mary MacDonald, who I'm becoming unexpectedly fond of.
  'We cannot risk your being recognized,' she replies, continuing

to stretch the strawberry-blonde bob over my pin-curled head. Behind her, Brodie stifles a laugh and mouths, *You look stunning.* When Mary looks away, I mouth back at him, *Go fuck yourself.* Which makes him laugh even more. I don't know if it's the Storrichian air, or the fact I'm tense as a violin string, but I'm swearing an awful lot this morning, and it's not like me at all. I point out to Mary that there's no risk of my being recognized by Lena Druinich, because the two of us have never met.

'Yes, but Munro has met you. If he comes back early, he'll recognize you straight away. At least with a ginger wig and this fur coat you'll have a fighting chance.' I think the fur coat is just silly. But again Mary convinces me that 'If you're going to lie, make sure you lie big.' She's brought her costume box from home. And is in her element. She's like a Scottish Mrs Snell from *The Archers.* 'What you have to understand, you see, Linda, is that not a lot happens on the island, so—'

'—you have to take the drama where you can?'

'Exactly.'

By the time she's finished with me – there was make-up too, I should add – I look like a cross between a fat Rula Lenska and a red-headed Pavarotti. Minus the beard, of course. And more alive. But I think there's some truth in lying big if you're going to lie at all.

I've got a single AirPod taped to my ear and tucked in under the wig – 'Another reason for wearing one!' said Mary triumphantly – so that I can maintain radio contact at all times with Fergus Murray and Brodie. They are hiding in Hamish Hamilton's sheep-shearing shed, which happens to be conveniently placed within clear view of the Druinich house. Fergus will keep me on speaker phone, and Brodie will stay in touch with Moira. They have binoculars. All being well, it should work like a game of Mouse Trap, where the little steel ball sets the motion going for the whole process. It's 10 a.m., so just about light. It's also an acceptable hour of the day for the set-up we have planned.

'Ready?' asks Fergus Murray.

'Ready,' I say, though inside I'm terrified. I feel like I'm in an episode of *Line of Duty*.

'You've got this, Linda Standish,' says Fergus, high-fiving me. Our hands don't quite meet and the moment is underpowered.

'*Gura math a thèid leat*,' says Brodie, unashamedly grabbing me by the waist and kissing me in full view of the rest of the team.

'My, you're a fast worker,' says Mary MacDonald with a girlish giggle.

Ten minutes later and we're all in place. Brodie and Fergus in the shed, me down the way in the about-to-break-down Escort, Moira in her post van en route to chez Druinich, having messaged to say 'ETA 10.05'. We wait. And we wait. It feels like two hours. It is in fact just four minutes till the post van pulls up. I can't see what's going on, so Fergus is giving me a running commentary from the shed, in hushed whispers. 'Moira has parked and is walking up the path . . . she's knocking on the door . . . she's waiting . . . there's no answer.'

There's a long pause then and it suddenly dawns on me: what if the Druinichs have gone out for the day? Well, that will scupper everything. But surely on a day like this, with the wind a-howling, you'd be a fool to leave the house unless you had to?

'The eagle has landed, the eagle has landed!' screech-whispers Fergus into the phone. Followed by Brodie translating in dry, calm tones, 'He means Munro Druinich has answered the door.'

Oh God, I feel sick.

Fergus again: 'She's explaining to him about the parcel – she's using a lot of hand movements, presumably describing the size of the box. He doesn't look very pleased.'

Brodie adds to this, 'What's new? The man's probably never been pleased about anything in his life!'

Ah. I should explain about the parcel and Moira Mackenzie.

Down at the loosely termed sorting office, which is essentially a store room by the tiny harbour where the Roaken ferry arrives and departs, a large box in a state of disrepair is waiting, along with the rest of the island's mail. Due to her understandably not wanting to lose her job, Moira refused to have anything to do with the actual materializing of said box, but she said if such a box were left there, addressed to Munro Druinich, then she would be more than happy to attempt delivery to the addressee. But if the box were in such a state of disrepair that moving it might damage it in some way, then she would be happy to inform the addressee of the arrival of the box and invite him to come and collect it himself. So last night Pat, Bren and Alasdair McGinty put together a makeshift crate and stuffed it with bubble wrap and several second-hand auto parts taken from Alasdair's workshop. Then they wrapped it in brown paper and wrote Munro Druinich's details in bold letters on the front, before proceeding to hose it down till it became soggy and torn. Moira refused to touch it, but allowed Pat and Bren to deposit it in the sorting room. And that's where it now lies, awaiting collection by Munro Druinich. We all hold our breath. If he refuses to leave the house, then the plan fails before it's even begun.

'Oh, okay, look out. He's gone back inside. Moira is . . . turning to us . . . and is covertly giving us a thumbs-up. So far so good, team. Let's not lose our grip. We've got this.'

'Stop saying "we've got this" all the time, Fergus Murray,' I snap. 'We've far from got anything yet!' I can't help being ratty. I know my cue is coming up. More waiting. And yet more waiting. Then suddenly Fergus's voice, hysterical yet hushed, comes bursting into my ear.

'Okay, he's on his way. The eagle is flying the nest.'

'And shut up with the eagle analogies!' I say through gritted teeth.

'Sorry,' mumbles Fergus. 'I'm just excited. He's getting into the post van . . . and Moira's flashed her lights. Okay, Linda Standish, count to thirty and make your way over.'

I do as I'm told and it's the longest thirty seconds I've ever known in my life. Then I start the engine, put it in first gear and am immediately thrown by Fergus nigh on shouting now – 'Thunderbirds are Go! Go! Go!'

I'm too nervous to respond and I head off slowly down the road. I barely get out of third before I'm outside the Druinichs' home. When I climb out, I glance over at the shed and nod, even though I can't see either Brodie or Fergus, and then, with my heart in my throat, I wander up the path.

39

Linda

'You'll have to wait till my husband comes back. He's gone to pick up a parcel.'

'Oh, I see.' Well, now I'm stumped. Lena Druinich is standing on her doorstep in a purple tracksuit, looking for all the world like she wants to shut the door on me. This is never going to work. I've just explained that my car needs jump-starting, that I have the jump leads, I just need to plug them up to another vehicle, i.e. hers.

'Do you know how long he might be?'

'Half an hour?'

I'm desperate now. I know Brodie and Fergus can hear the whole conversation and am praying they come up with a solution. 'Say you're on a schedule.' Brodie's voice is in my ear. 'That you're visiting your aunt over at Strathcarron Residential Home—'

'Thing is, I'm heading to see my aunty at the care home,' I repeat.

'—and she's about to die!' adds Fergus Murray quickly, and I do an inward tut.

'She's . . . she's on her last legs,' I stammer. 'She could go at any moment.'

'What's her name?' asks Lena Druinich, her eyes narrowing suspiciously.

'Moira,' I reply. A tad quickly. 'Stuart.'

'She's a newsreader.'

'Yes, always been a family joke, that!' I can see she's not convinced.

'Start crying,' whispers Fergus manically in my ear.

Oh, for the love of God.

'Please,' I beg, attempting to weep, and almost wailing. *If you're going to lie, lie BIG* – the words of Mary MacDonald are in my head. 'I'm really fond of my aunt. She was like a mother to me growing up and if I don't see her before she dies, then—'

'All right, all right, calm down.' Lena Druinich grabs a car key and heads outside, me following in her footsteps.

A few minutes later she has positioned her Mondeo nose to nose with my car and pulled open the bonnet. I must keep her attention on the engine, her back to the house. She so doesn't want to be here. She so doesn't want to help.

'Thanks ever so much for this,' I say, faffing around with the cables. Behind her I see Fergus and Brodie niftily sprint from Hamish's shed to the side door of the house. I'm terrified Lena will turn around so I shout dramatically, hoping to keep her attention, pretending to burn myself. 'Oh my goodness, that is hot!' I say. She looks at me like I'm deranged. But at least she doesn't look behind her. Inside I'm counting the seconds. *Please hurry up, please hurry up.* I have no idea what they'll do when they're inside the house. What are the chances she's put the urn on display somewhere? She may well have packed it away out of sight.

'What you doing driving a car like this wearing a coat like that?' Lena Druinich sneers. 'Would've thought a Merc was more your style.'

'I've fallen on hard times,' I say quickly and unconvincingly. I'd have made a terrible actress. The cables are connected, and despite my faffing-slash-delaying tactics, I can't really hold off any longer.

'Right, go on then,' she says impatiently. 'I'm not standing here for the benefit of my health.'

Brodie and Fergus are still inside. I have no option but to start the car. I get in behind the steering wheel and turn the key in the ignition. The engine starts first time. I rev it up a bit and smile, then stick my head out of the window, 'I'd better let it run for a couple of minutes, if that's okay.' She rolls her eyes and looks at her watch. *Don't turn around, don't turn around!* Eventually her patience runs out.

'Right, that's your lot,' she says, and unplugs the cables from her Mondeo. She slams the bonnet shut and leans inside the car to retrieve her key.

Still no sign of Fergus and Brodie. In desperation, I get back out of my car and say, 'Let me give you a hug. You've been so kind!'

'No thanks.'

'Oh come on, please.' I reach out to her, arms stretched wide for an embrace that I want as little as she does.

Where are you? Where the hell are you?

'I said, no!' And she turns on her heels to head back to her house. I shut my eyes, I can't bear to look. Any second now she's going to see them coming out of the side door. And what's worse, in the distance I can see the post van approaching.

This is an absolute disaster.

We're all going to jail.

I unclip the cables from my engine and shut the bonnet of the car, awaiting Armageddon. I want to do a runner, but I cannot abandon the team. We're in this together.

Then I hear it. Brodie's voice in my ear. 'Come and get us.'

'Now! Now! Now!' screech-whispers Fergus Murray.

And just as Lena Druinich goes in through the front, the two men come out through the side, carrying . . .

. . . nothing!

What?? I can't believe my eyes. All this effort, and they didn't find the bloody urn. It's all too much. I feel faint. I'm too old for this malarkey. I zoom up towards them at speed and do a nifty one-eighty turn. They both clamber in and immediately duck down, Brodie in the front, Fergus in the back. None of us speak, too breathless with adrenalin. At the corner I turn left and pass the post van a hundred yards away from the house. Moira is driving of course, and sat next to her is Munro Druinich, looking his usual dour self. Moira doesn't wave. She doesn't know me after all, wink wink. But as our cars pass, she side-eyes me and gives the tiniest of nods. And I'm desperate to say to her – no! Don't nod! Because we've failed! We didn't get it. Mission very, very much *un*accomplished.

40

Linda

At least a minute passes before I think it's safe to stop and park. Brodie and Fergus clamber up from the floor of the car. 'I'm gutted,' I say. 'All that effort.'

But far from sharing my disappointment, Fergus Murray is smirking at me like a schoolboy in my rear-view mirror. And now the two of them start laughing. Which really annoys me. 'Shut up, it's not funny.'

'Oh ye of little faith!' says Brodie. I turn around to look at Fergus and his irritating grin. At which point he pulls from the inside of his coat a thick transparent plastic bag containing what looks like a couple of pounds' worth of white gravel.

'Ta-dah!' he declares.

I stare at him for a moment. Stock-still.

'Please don't tell me those are Diana Norman's ashes?' I say quietly.

'The very same.' He looks so proud of himself. 'The urn was standing on their mantelpiece bold as a badger, wasn't it, Brode?'

'Aye,' says Brodie, smiling.

'So I took an executive decision. I thought, right: we can either grab the whole thing and risk being arrested for burglary, or . . .'

'Oh my God.' I shut my eyes.

'Or we can just snatch the ashes and replace them with something of similar weight so that Lena Druinich would never be any the wiser!'

'So what did you replace them with?'

Fergus Murray smiles back like the cat who got the cream. 'Two tins of baked beans,' he announces. 'Genius, eh?'

I'm lost for words.

*

We'd arranged to reconvene at Levi Norman's house, which we thought was safer than the Storrich Arms in terms of staying under the radar. By the time we arrive, I'm slightly calmer. Mary MacDonald is waiting with a change of clothes and a veritable make-up station to 'de-rig' me and erase all evidence of this morning's disguise. We fill her in on what happened, and she agrees with Brodie that Fergus's decision was actually a good one. Far less likely to draw attention and at the end of the day, it's the contents of the urn that matter, not the urn itself.

'I can furnish you with a replacement once we're back in Boransay,' says Fergus Murray, wearing the mantle of the know-it-all undertaker. 'A simple style, something like the Copperfield. I'll give you staff discount.'

'Plus,' says Mary, clearly wanting to be a part of it all, 'it's not like anyone's going to notice when it comes to the scattering, let's be honest.' She's right, of course. It just feels a bit odd sitting here in Levi Norman's kitchen having my hair unpinned and my false eyelashes removed, with his wife's forty-year-old ashes just an arm's length away from me. Far from being respectfully concealed in a nice ceramic urn, their unceremonious exposure in a clear plastic bag seems rather undignified.

Al McCanic arrives with his pick-up truck to remove our getaway car and wants to know all the details.

'So, it looks like we've managed it,' says Fergus.

'As long as Munro Druinich hasn't had any CCTV installed. Did you think of that?'

'The man's too tight to buy CCTV,' Brodie reassures us.

'Aye, but he's also very paranoid,' Alasdair goes on. 'Remember what he was like with Minty's drone? Accused her of flying it over his house and peering in through his windows when his mother-in-law was visiting?'

'That was an absolute joke,' says Mary. 'The man was completely deluded.'

'He's a lunatic, for sure,' agrees Alasdair. 'And deeply mean-minded. Reported it to The Don and everything!'

Brodie explains that 'The Don' refers to Donald Ferguson, the stalwart and well-loved island policeman. The moniker has an air of the mafioso, suggesting swarthy Italianate looks and a menacing demeanour. But when I say this, they all laugh; apparently, it couldn't be further from the truth. Mary takes out her phone and shows me a video of their local bobby taken at this year's Highland Games. The Don, it appears, is a pale-skinned, ginger-headed Hebridean with a soft, lilting accent and a keen sense of gentle justice.

'Poor Minty,' says Brodie. 'Thought she was after getting a criminal record and everything.'

'Aye, never used the drone again. Sold it on eBay. And it was her pride and joy.'

'Still, she's got her curling now.'

'That she has.'

'Look, we'd better get on,' I say, sensing we're in danger of a Storrich-style digression and keen to put this morning's shenanigans behind me.

41

Linda

We leave Beannach Lodge with heavy hearts. Empty now of all Levi's possessions apart from a few bits of furniture, the place is very much infused with an air of finality. Switching off the power supply and the water, we pull the door shut for the last time. The key that had been on the inside of the door is turned on the outside and hidden under a stone, ready for the estate agent or solicitor or whoever will dispatch this home to its next owners. Who knows what will become of the place after today. Whose spirit will fill it next? Whose laughter will echo round its walls? I can't imagine there's been much of that these past few years. And whose life will tell the next chapter of its story? The optimist in me still holds on to the thread of hope that Rachel Norman will be found and she will one day come here. But the thread is flimsy and beginning to fray.

Back at the Storrich Arms, I've volunteered to go behind the bar again, as Minty is still away on her curling trip. Whilst Brodie rustles up a few home-made pizzas in the kitchen, I serve the dozen or so locals who've arrived. There's a definite party atmosphere. Fergus Murray is playing mine host and clearing glasses, and everyone's talking about the kidnap of the ashes.

'Reclamation,' corrects Fergus Murray. He stands firm in his belief that we did the right thing today.

'Yes, *morally* maybe,' I say. 'It's just, *legally* we didn't.'

'Ach, where's your gumption, Linda Standish?' he says loudly for all to hear. 'Are you a man or a mouse?'

'I'm neither, Fergus Murray. I'm a grandmother on the verge of retirement who doesn't quite fancy spending a few months doing community service for breaking and entering.'

'You only colluded,' he assures me. 'It's me and Brode will serve the time.' I don't know why he's being so jolly about it. He's behaving completely out of character. I had him down as a scaredy-cat jobsworth, the type who duly follows rules and does as he's told. I've certainly seen another side to him on this trip. Must be the Storrich sea air.

Brodie comes out with two massive ham-and-cheese pizzas cut up ready for serving, and the locals dive in like gannets. Everyone sticks a couple of quid in a pint glass to cover the costs. It's like community living is in the customers' DNA – not something they have to think about, they just do it. Helping out when required, and usually without even being asked. Maybe it's what comes from living in a remote part of the world, cut off literally by the sea and where the extremity of weather can exacerbate domestic crises in a way it wouldn't elsewhere. Pitching in seems to be a way of life on Storrich.

As people are tucking in to their pizzas, the conversation turns to Levi Norman and plans for his funeral.

'Well, there aren't any actual *plans*,' I say. 'Fergus Murray and I will travel with—'

I hesitate. Been in this job for years and I still find it uncomfortable to say *body*, or *corpse*. Fergus Murray comes to my rescue, an expert in handling the indelicacies of death. 'We will travel with the casket back to Boransay, where it will remain until the cremation. It's been arranged for Wednesday.'

'That'll give that daughter of his more time to get there, won't it, so that's a wee bonus,' says Gordon, the plumber.

I'm a bit thrown that Rachel Norman's existence is common knowledge.

'Well, actually—' I begin to explain.

'It'll take a fair while if she's driving up from Welsh Wales,' agrees Hamish, who's still wearing the smart blue jumper he had on yesterday but has now paired it with some smart beige cords. They're too long for him and he's turned up the hems and I begin to wonder . . . But as I try to imagine Levi Norman in the same outfit, I'm distracted by Moira, who's guessing the length of the journey from Wales to Boransay.

'At least ten hours,' she suggests.

'Unless she wants to stop off for the night on her way,' says Mary, with all the panache of a well-seasoned travel agent. 'Somewhere just south of Glasgow would be nice.'

'Of course, we're just assuming she lives in Wales because of him being Welsh, but—'

'Actually,' I burst their bubble, 'I've not been able to contact Mr Norman's daughter as yet. And even if I did, I'm not sure she would attend.' The word 'unforgiveable', from Rachel's text to Levi, rings round in my head. 'I suspect they were estranged, you see.'

There's a collective intake of breath, as if such a notion is not credible.

'That's why we're here, after all,' I explain. 'If Levi Norman had had any family, then *they* would be the ones making these arrangements and not—'

'Not a pair of complete strangers,' says Alasdair McGinty, not unkindly, just as a matter of fact.

A silence descends as people contemplate the situation. 'Well, in that case let's give the manny a wake,' says Gordon, full of cheer. 'We can at least drink a wee toast, can we not?'

And all as one, the group raise their glasses and cry, '*Slàinte!*'

'To Levi Noris—' continues Gordon.

'Norman,' I mumble, 'his name was Norman.'

'To the Boyo!'

'To Norman. God be with ye, man!'

'Aye!'

Then seemingly from nowhere, Moira – yes, Moira! – produces a fiddle and starts playing the opening bars of 'Caledonia'. It's astonishing. But as if this wasn't surprise enough, Brodie begins accompanying her with a penny whistle that he's grabbed from behind the bar whilst Mary is marking time with the RNLI collection tin – which I have to say makes a surprisingly good percussion instrument. It's extraordinary. And beautiful. And I'm swept along with it all, singing my heart out.

> *Oh let me tell you that I love you,*
> *That I think about you all the time*
> *Caledonia, you're calling me,*
> *now I'm goin home.*

Even Fergus Murray is joining in. The whole evening has been transformed by this kindly group of Storrichians into an impromptu wake for a man they barely knew; a man who they'd tried and failed to include in their community; a man who chose a solitary existence instead of friendship and camaraderie.

We're three songs down, 'Speed Bonnie Boat' is in full swing and we're just belting out the refrain 'over the sea to Skye' when the door opens and a lone figure stands ominously in its frame, looking straight at us. He's in a police uniform, so I guess this has to be The Don. The music stops and silence descends.

'I'm wanting to speak with a Mrs Linda Standish?' he says, his voice laden with authoritarian doom.

'She's actually a *Miss*,' chips in Mary, nervously wittering. 'Divorced, you see.' Everyone looks at her, then at me. I swallow hard.

'How can I help you, officer?'

42

Linda

Turns out Lena Druinich *did* report the break-in. But the only thing she could say was missing were the contents of her newly acquired 'vase'. She was incensed by the baked beans and the fact that someone had 'come into my home and tampered with my personal belongings!' The Don seems to take delight in recounting the story. I am privately a bit surprised by his indiscretion – surely as a police officer you're not meant to disclose the details of someone's complaint? But nobody else seems bothered, so I put it down to the fact that island rules are different from mainland ones, and like everyone else in the pub, I listen with relish to the story. Nursing an apple juice in one hand and a pizza slice in the other, The Don explains that he was called to the home of the Druinichs an hour or so ago. 'The two of them were effing and jeffing,' he says, 'with Munro shouting, "It's the fat bird from Boransay and the numpty who's with her!"' When The Don quotes Munro, I feel everyone's eyes on me, checking to see if I'm offended. I'm not. Though I notice Fergus Murray flinch a little at being called a numpty.

'She wants me to arrest you for breaking and entering.'
Now *this* I *am* offended by. 'But I didn't even cross the threshold!'
'That was me,' confesses Fergus earnestly.

'And me,' chimes in Brodie, equally as earnest.

It's a very *I am Spartacus* moment.

'Indeed,' says The Don. 'However, she also wants me to arrest you, Miss Standish, for falsely deceiving her with your tale of a broken-down car and an aunt in Strathcarron supposedly at death's door.'

'Well, yes, she's got a point there, I suppose.'

'Hang on,' says Fergus Murray. 'How did they know it was us? Surely they're just making an assumption?'

And there's a chorus response, 'CCTV.'

'CCTV,' repeats The Don sagely. Alasdair McGinty nods at us all in an *I-told-you-so* sort of a way.

'Anyway, I listened to everything they had to say and then I pointed out that entering someone's home when the door is unlocked is not actually a crime.'

Mumbles of agreement ripple around the bar. 'And as for "tampering with personal possessions", well, I said *they* should count themselves lucky not to be arrested for interfering with human remains.' I thought this was a bit dark. And grossly incorrect. But Brodie pointed out later that The Don spends a lot of time watching True Crime thrillers on Netflix and as a result his imagination can be a bit wild. Anyway, I wasn't complaining. It served its purpose. The Don stayed for half an hour, had another slice of pizza, shook hands with me and Fergus and commiserated with us about Levi's demise, as if we were close family relatives. Which I'm beginning to feel we are, quite frankly.

'What an extraordinary day,' I say to Brodie as we lie cuddled up in his vast bed for one last night of gloriousness.

'Aye,' he says.

'Actually, all the days here have been extraordinary, if I'm honest,' I add. 'You'll be glad to get back to normal tomorrow!'

'You fishing?'

I laugh. 'No! It's true, isn't it? Haven't we been something of a disruption?'

He smiles and strokes my hair. 'A very welcome one. I'll miss you,' he says, without a hint of self-pity.

'Will you miss Fergus Murray as well?'

'Of course. He's my bro!'

This is all very pleasant. The mood between us is jocular and light-hearted. Which is just as it should be and just as I want it. Brodie and I have an unspoken agreement that what's happened between us these past few days has been a happy interlude in our otherwise very separate and very different lives. And I'm glad the feeling is mutual. 'I wonder if you'll ever come back?' he muses.

'I doubt it – I've got a target on my back, don't forget, and the Druinichs have their bows drawn and waiting.'

'Ach, they're full of hot air. Won't be long before they have a go at someone else. They'd fall out with their own shadows, those two.'

'I'd have thought, given how small the Storrich population is, they can't *keep* getting cross with everyone? Soon there'll be no one left to hate.'

'That's true,' says Brodie. 'Being angry is so tiring.'

I take a deep breath of contentedness. 'I've really enjoyed meeting you, Brodie McLeod.'

'Aye,' he says in return. And there's a pause. A long pause. And maybe in a parallel universe, this would be the moment for one of us to say, 'Can we stay in touch?' But we both remain silent. Until he turns to start kissing my breasts and I let out a yelp of delight. God, I'm going to miss this.

*

Our ferry leaves at ten. Brodie gives us a final hearty breakfast before we head to Hamish Hamilton's to collect Levi Norman. 'I'll come down to the boat in a bit,' says Brodie as he clears away our plates. 'Wave you off on your way.'

'Aw, that's nice,' I say. 'Fergus Murray, can you put my bag in the car while I settle up?'

'Aye aye, Cap'n!' he replies. He's in an exceptionally buoyant mood this morning. I think he's excited to be going home.

At the till Brodie works out our bill and we wait for payment to go through on the card machine. He hands me my receipt. 'Okay, that's everything, madam.'

'Oh, I forgot.'

'What?'

'I need just one more delicious kiss, please.'

And he smiles such a broad and gorgeous smile, cups my face in his hands and kisses me with gusto. I savour the moment, the taste of his mouth and the tickling of his beard on my lips. When we break away I say, 'Well, that will keep me going for a good couple of days.'

'Glad to be of service,' he says.

An hour later, as Fergus and I approach the little terminal, we are greeted by a small group of locals who've come to wave us off. Moira the Postie, Gordon the plumber and his kids, Alasdair McCanic and Mary MacDonald, as well as a few others from the pub the night before. Even The Don is there, and of course Brodie. It's a strange sensation, because obviously we've now got a coffin in the back of the hearse. So it doesn't quite feel appropriate for them to be waving vigorously with bittersweet smiles and calling out *Bon voyage* and *Haste ye back!* Poor old Levi Norman won't be hasting anywhere. Other than the Boransay Crematorium for a very basic funeral. But whether this farewell party is appropriate or not seems irrelevant. We've been made very welcome on this island, and normal rules do not apply.

As the ferry leaves the small harbour we look back to see the crowd disperse, returning to their day-to-day lives. Fergus and I will soon be forgotten. Part of me is hoping to see Brodie wait until we're out of sight, but he's already turned and left. He has a pub to run, after all. And I have a home to get back to and a job to finish. The island gets smaller as the ferry picks up speed and gains distance, and as the detail of its landscapes fades, its silhouette against the clear December sky once more takes on the appearance of a giant turtle. I feel a lump in my throat. What a special place is Storrich. What a privilege to have stayed there.

We order coffees in the seen-better-days on-board café, and I sign in to the wi-fi to check my emails. Several work messages have come in this morning, two spams telling me I've won an air fryer and another urgently requiring payment for a TV licence that's lapsed. The giveaway is always in the spelling. Air fryer written as 'air frAYer'. And TV licence written as 'licInce'. I have been known – foolishly, I agree – to reply on occasion, pointing out that if the sender really does have their heart set on stealing my bank details, the least they could do is learn to spell.

'What are you doing for Christmas?' I ask Fergus.
   'Skiing,' he says. 'French Alps.'
   'Oh.'
   I wasn't expecting that. But I always forget that he's been a professional sportsman in his time, has Fergus. 'Can you do it okay, then? Y'know, with the leg?' Am I being a bit insensitive, mentioning his cycling injury back in the day?
   'Oh yes. I've learned to compensate.'
   And he returns to looking at his phone and another game of Spelling Bee. I'm surprised he doesn't ask me what *my* Christmas plans are. Then I realize I'm glad he doesn't. Because I might cry, thinking of little Zander moving away so soon after Christmas. Maybe I'll just invite myself to theirs for New Year. Not the most tempting of prospects, but I would quite happily unicycle blindfolded across an oily tightrope fifty feet in the air whilst declaring Lauren the kindest, most intelligent and generous person in the world if it meant getting to spend time with my precious Zander.
   'Can I come with you, Fergus Murray?'
   'Afraid not,' he replies rather too quickly. 'We're a party of six and all the rooms are taken.'
   'It was a joke,' I say. But part of me secretly wonders if it was,

and I'm suddenly gripped by a terrible loneliness. Thankfully, he doesn't pick up on this, returning to his game and clearly happy not to talk.

I take myself up on to the deck and give myself a good talking-to about Struan and his move to Bordgalsh. Why am I being such a wimp about it all? Come on, Linda Standish, get a grip! I pick up my mobile and Facetime my son. He answers quickly and I can see he's not at home. 'I took yesterday off,' he says. 'We travelled down to Bordgalsh, started moving some stuff.'

I'm a bit thrown by this. Why didn't he mention it last time we spoke?

'Oh, I see.'

'Lauren says it's best we do it in stages.'

Probably doesn't want to risk breaking a nail by carrying too many boxes. Actually – Lauren? Carry a box? Pull the other one.

'You haven't changed your mind, then?' I say stupidly, because I know what the answer will be.

'I know it's hard to take, Mum, but it really is for the best. And you'll only be an hour away. It's hardly the other side of the world!'

What he doesn't realize is that it may as well be.

'And it's what Lauren wants.'

I'm pinching the skin on the palm of my hand when he says this but outwardly nodding in agreement and saying, 'Yes, of course. I completely understand.'

'Thank you,' he replies. 'We're heading back in an hour or so, okay?' I can see he's exhausted by the whole thing. So it behoves me – I've always wanted to use that word – it behoves me to be accommodating and flexible and as helpful as possible.

'But I've been thinking,' I say, ready to plunge in with my idea. 'Why don't we all have Christmas at my place? And make it really special? Invite Lauren's parents – even her grandmother, if you want? I'd do all the cooking, Lauren wouldn't have to lift a finger.' Inwardly I am *hating* myself for being such a damn fraud.

'That's really kind of you,' he says, and I can see he likes the idea. 'Obviously, I'd need to check Lauren is okay with it.'

I bite my tongue. 'Obviously!' And smile.

'And . . . thing is, Mum, Lauren can be a bit funny if she feels she's been coerced into doing something. But if I let her think *she's* come up with the idea, it's far more likely to go ahead.' I decide to be the bigger person – literally – and let her take the credit. Because quite frankly my capacity for humility and self-flagellation knows no bounds when it comes to my grandson.

'Absolutely,' I say with a rictus smile. 'Y'know me, I'm easy!'
You big liar, Linda Standish.

43

Linda

When we get back to Boransay, Fergus Murray and I part company at the funeral home. I watch as he and his colleagues transfer poor old Levi's casket inside, where it'll remain until the cremation next week. Fergus offers to take me home once everything's been dealt with, but I'd rather not hang around. I opt for a taxi instead and we bid each other a curt, polite farewell. We didn't talk much on the way back from Roaken: apart from the fact that it felt disrespectful with a coffin in the back, I think – dare I say it – that we've both got a form of post-holiday blues. Sounds ridiculous, I know – I mean, how can a three-day trip in a hearse to the Outer Hebrides for a corpse repatriation be described as a holiday? Maybe because it ended up being so much more than a work trip. Yes, for me there was Brodie of course, and lots of fabulous sex. And Storrich itself was so special, so magical, even in the depths of a Scottish winter. But it is Levi Norman who has had the most profound effect on me. It keeps niggling away at me – why would this quiet Welshman choose to live so far away from his home, and why, when by all accounts he was a gentle soul once much loved by his daughter, did he end up alone and cut off from the world? What did he do six years ago that was so 'unforgiveable'?

I try to put him out of my mind as I climb out of the taxi and make my way to the front door. It's lovely coming home to my boys rather than an empty semi-detached house. Struan has made me a big bowl of chilli and put the heating on. He'd make someone a lovely husband, would my son. Ha! What irony.

I tell him all about my Hebridean adventure – minus the sex. I mean, that would be very wrong. Struan definitely thinks I'm past all those sorts of shenanigans. And I'm not about to disabuse him of that belief. I tell him the sad story of Rachel's mother dying when she was only three. 'I'll never track her down before the funeral, and even if I did it's unlikely she'd come, not if they were estranged.'

'God, that's rough,' says Struan. 'So he brought her up on his own, then?'

'Yes. Not an easy call for anyone, but especially for a man.'

'That's a bit sexist, Mother!' he teases.

'True. And you, my boy, are living proof that I'm wrong. I know I'm biased, but I do think you're a far better parent than Lauren—'

'Mum!' he cautions me, aware that I'm about to rant.

'Well, it's true. You're not neurotic, you care about other people – you're aware other people exist! – and you're not a drama queen.'

'Okay, enough now,' he says gently, and swiftly changes the subject. 'So, what chance is there of you finding her, then? The daughter, I mean?'

'Well, once I'm back in the office I've got more means at my disposal. But at the moment there's nothing – no address book to be found, no letters – nothing whatsoever to suggest which country she might be living in, let alone which town. The only thing I've got is a postcard from her, sent over twenty-nine years ago, with Levi's old address on it. But I doubt that'll prove useful.'

'You wanna get Davina on the case, or that Nicky Campbell.'

Struan knows me so well, he knows how much I love *Long Lost Family* – a real busman's holiday, I admit, but I just love having a good blub at the reunions. I think it's because I always fantasize that's how my cases will turn out. They seldom do, but

I live in hope. I also find Davina McCall very watchable. She has amazing eyelashes.

'Fancy having a lifelong rift like that. Families, eh?' says Struan. We share a look that says he knows his ex-wife is one big pain in the arse and that I wish he'd never married her. But we say nothing and carry on with the chilli. 'Shame you can't locate her before the funeral, though. If there's been some big rift, at least that would give her closure . . .'

'Oh, don't!' I say, irritated.

'What?'

'I *hate* the word "closure",' I say. 'Or more to the point, I hate the phrase "get some closure". It's so . . .'

'American?' he says.

'Pretentious. It's one of those expressions we only started using in recent years. Along with *reaching out*—'

'Well, that *is* American!'

'—and *circling back* and *jumping on a call*. I mean, who in God's name *jumps* on a call? I had an email from a solicitor's office the other day in Fife, and this young thing, she wrote, *Let me know if anything's unclear, am always happy to jump on a call.*'

Struan is smiling at me – he knows I'm on a roll.

'And don't get me started on *a hundred per cent*. When did that happen? *A hundred per cent!* Everybody seems to say it nowadays. What's wrong with a simple "yes"? Do you take sugar in your tea? *A hundred per cent.* Do you watch *Strictly* on Saturday nights? *A hundred per cent.* Don't you think video games are at the root of the increase in violence amongst young people? *A hundred per cent.* NO! Just say YES! Yes – a simple yes!'

Struan is now laughing.

'Oh, and *perfect*. Why does every man, woman and dog have to say everything is *perfect*? Would you like bread with that? Yes please. *Perfect.* Would an eight p.m. appointment suit you? Yes please. *Perfect.* Would you like a window or an aisle seat? Aisle please. *Perfect.* SHUT UP!!! IT'S NOT PERFECT. NOTHING'S BLOODY PERFECT.'

Struan manages to stop laughing long enough to ask, 'How's the book coming along, Mum?'

'What book?'

'The *Linda Standish Guide to being a Grumpy Old Woman?*'

I flick a piece of rice at him.

44

Linda

I'm just leaving for work on Monday when a WhatsApp message comes through from Lauren. Well, I say message, it's more of a thesis. I skim through the blah blah blah and pick out the bones of what she's saying, which is essentially – *I've had this incredible idea which I think could be really healing for all of us as a family. What if we had Christmas Day at yours? And invite everyone. Granny Moss included?* Whilst I'm impressed by Struan's canny manipulation and success in achieving his goal, it still sticks in my craw that Lauren will get all the glory for this family Christmas. But I swallow my pride and message back – *What a super idea!* – before heading off to the office. I can't ever remember using the word 'super' before. And I actually wouldn't have the first clue as to the whereabouts of my craw.

The festive atmosphere at the Unclaimed Heirs Unit this morning has decidedly ramped up a gear. We don't officially close for the holidays for another week. But the end-of-term feeling is rife amongst us normally conservative council workers, who don Christmas jumpers, Santa hats and antlers and walk between each other's desks with a little holiday spring in our steps.

Gillian Coles is wearing an actual full elf costume. Which is a surprise. But she's nothing if not unpredictable. 'Secret Santa.

Wednesday. Two p.m.,' she says, looking at me in a meaningful way which makes me assume she picked *my* name out of the hat back in mid-November. There's a fifteen-pound limit to the cost of the gift. We do it every year and I have to say, I think it's a rather lovely tradition. I picked out Liam's name – he's taking over from me in February, so it's rather apt, now I think about it. I was quite excited at first, as I'd sourced a brilliant calendar online featuring photographs of male undertakers in varying states of undress. I know! Who'd have thought such a thing existed, but it absolutely does. January depicts two shirtless funeral directors in black trousers and tail jackets, standing either side of a mahogany casket. They're wearing black top hats and leaning on silver-topped canes and smiling. February shows a naked undertaker concealing his modesty behind a huge wreath of red roses. I think that's meant to combine Valentine's Day with funeral ware. It's the tackiest thing I've ever seen in my life, and it's hilarious. All of the undertakers featured are actual real-life undertakers! At first, I couldn't wait to see Liam's face when he opened it.

However, when I showed it to Struan he thought it might be misguided and could be interpreted as homophobic or sexually harassing. 'Ye gods!' I said. 'On what planet could I be seen as being either of those things?' I was genuinely confused. But my lovely son is far more aware than I am of potential offence-causing. He's had to do 'sensitivity training' at his place of work and often passes on to me what he's learned. So it was back to square one and, with my gift-choosing confidence being severely knocked, I ended up buying Liam a cheese plant. Which I shall give him next Wednesday at 2 p.m. I asked Struan if he thought it would be all right to just *tell* Liam about the calendar in a 'you-should-have-seen-what-I-*was*-going-to-get-you!' kind of a way. But Struan gently suggested I keep it to myself.

Isn't it funny how we parents swap places with our children on the advice-giving front? When does that changeover happen, I wonder? When do we stop 'knowing what's best' and hand over that mantle to the next generation? It's like with crossing the road.

For years we hold our child's hand to keep them safe from traffic. And then, boof! As if overnight, it is *they* who are taking *our* arm and protecting us from speeding cars.

That afternoon I'm at my desk and once more looking through the box of keepsakes, which I'd brought with me from Storrich. Diana's ashes are now with Fergus Murray, who has promised to transfer them into a nice new urn. The hope is that if – no, *when* – I find Rachel, she will reclaim them along with those of Levi and they can be scattered together as per Levi's wishes. I take out the postcard Rachel sent him in 1995 on her school trip, and I copy the address, composing a short note to 'the occupiers' of 26 Strathan Street in Inverness. On the electoral register, there's no one by the name of Rachel Norman living there, but maybe the current inhabitants will have a forwarding address. I've also found on the register a Jane McAllister living on the same street. I'm hoping this is the Mrs McA whose name appeared on the back of Rachel's eighteenth-birthday photograph. She looked like she was in her sixties then, so surely she'd be pushing ninety now? Still, worth a try.

To date, the records have come up with a list as long as my left arm of current Rachel Normans around the age of Levi's Rachel, but none seem to match any in Inverness. She could've moved, of course. And she could've changed her name. I'll get there, I just need a bit more time.

It certainly doesn't feel like a very satisfactory ending – all terribly broken and unhealed. I've accepted I won't find her before the cremation. But I've got to find her before I retire, and that's only weeks away. It feels absolutely sacrilegious to hand the whole thing over to Liam and never find out what happened. No, that will not do. That will not do at all. Maybe it's my ego or my control-freakery taking over, but I am absolutely determined to find Rachel Norman and break the news to her about her dad. If she doesn't want to know, then that of course is her prerogative. But at least I'll feel I've done my bit for Levi. He deserves to have someone on his side, no matter what he and Rachel fell out about.

2001

45

Rachel

The party had been everything she'd wanted it to be. Her dad had gone all out – as he always did – to indulge her every wish. 'I want it to be perfect,' he'd said. 'Your eighteenth is such a special birthday.'

Rachel had laughed when he'd said it. 'You say that about every birthday!' And he'd pulled his daft face that he always made when he was being silly, then hugged her to him.

'What can I say?' he'd asked. 'I *like* spoiling you!'

And this was true. All her friends had said she was the luckiest of all of them. That her dad pretty much gave her everything she wanted. The year before, when she'd turned seventeen, he'd bought her a little red Fiesta in readiness for when she passed her test. On her sixteenth he'd said she could get her ears pierced and bought her a beautiful pair of custom-made platinum earrings which she adored. For her fifteenth he'd taken her and a friend to see U2 in concert in Belfast. Her fourteenth had been a trip to Alton Towers with three friends, and when she'd become a teenager, he'd taken her to Disneyland Paris. In fact, every birthday had been made special in some way.

He never held back about mentioning her mum – especially on these big occasions. He'd tell her how proud Diana would be to see her now all grown up. Every year he said the same, whether she was seven or seventeen. He'd always cry when he said it, and she'd wonder how a human heart could survive the pain of loss like his did. She couldn't remember her mum. She desperately wished she could, because the guilt of not missing her was overwhelming sometimes. Especially when she witnessed Levi's grief, always so raw and deep, as if he'd lost his wife just a few days previously. Rachel would often catch sight of him looking at a small framed photo of the three of them – taken on her parents' wedding day, Levi in a smart suit with a carnation in his lapel, Diana, her mother, beaming with joy and holding baby Rachel in her arms. And he'd stare at her incredulously sometimes, and whisper how like her mother she looked.

Rachel's eighteenth was held at the Stromness Hotel in Inverness, and because her actual birthday was on the first of January, Levi had booked it for Hogmanay, which would imbue it with even more specialness. She'd invited eighty-five guests, and there was a full buffet as well as a live band. Everyone had had the best time – even her dad, normally quite a shy chap, had danced for a couple of songs, his 'dad dancing' being the funniest ever. He'd made a short speech about how she was the biggest joy in his life and how proud he was to have such a beautiful, kind and brilliant daughter. They all drank a toast to her health and happy future and Rachel was on Cloud Ninety-nine all night. 'Thank you sooooooo much!' she'd said to him when it was over. 'You're the best dad ever.' And he'd had tears in his eyes when she said it.

She couldn't understand why two days later Levi's mood had so suddenly changed. No longer the over-emotional, smiley, proud dad but a painfully shy, nervous man who barely said two words to her. She asked him what was wrong and all he would say was that he had stuff on his mind but nothing that she should worry about. Then out of the blue – on three separate occasions – he'd looked her in the eye and told her that he would always protect her: that to keep her safe was his primary goal in life. This strange phase lasted for about ten days, until eventually he seemed to relax again and return to his old self. Rachel wondered if it was some sort of depression – her schoolfriend's mother had behaved in a similar way and been put on tablets that seemed to sort her out. Or was he worried about the fact that she'd be leaving home in September and heading off to university? But that was months away. When she tried talking to him about it he brushed it away and changed the subject, leaving Rachel feeling very out of her depth. It was too big for her eighteen-year-old mind to deal with and her relief when Levi seemed to 'get back to normal' was huge.

46

Levi

It had been almost a decade since he'd received the letter from Jack Blythe. A letter that had turned his world upside down. He'd wished in a way that Jack had replied to the note back then. At least Levi could've put the worry to bed – just something along the lines of, *Oh, okay, so you don't have any info, sorry for bothering you, have a good life* . . . But the silence and lack of response had left the door open to the possibility that one day Jack Blythe would come looking for his daughter again.

The first two years had been the worst: every morning Levi would check the mail, his heart racing as he scoured the envelopes for a Cardiff postmark. It was a ludicrous fear – the only way Jack could possibly get in touch was via Levi's place of work. And no such letter ever arrived there. But still he worried that he would eventually be tracked down to his home. When the phone rang, he'd jump – and pressing play on the answer machine made him overly anxious. He always did it out of earshot of Rachel, in case there was a message from the man he feared the most.

They moved house.

It was a bigger, detached property, further out from the city centre, with spacious rooms and a beautiful garden. Rachel loved it. Her friends would frequently have sleep-overs and Mrs

McAllister continued to be part of their lives, twice-weekly taking the number 10 bus and the half-hour journey to visit them. She'd become family, after all.

For a while he'd wondered about coming clean and seeking legal help – hoping to be reassured by a solicitor that Levi's name was on that birth certificate and, being the parent who'd brought her up, Jack Blythe didn't have a leg to stand on. But in his heart, Levi knew that even this reassurance wouldn't solve the problem: the fact that Jack was Rachel's real father, that was never going to change. More than that, he was forever haunted by the fact that he had broken his promise to Diana on her deathbed and chosen not to tell Rachel about Jack. Rachel was his most precious, precious girl – his reason for living, the biggest and only joy in his life. He could not risk even the slightest possibility of losing her, but more than that, he dreaded the thought of even sharing her. Or of her feeling that, despite herself, blood being thicker than water would bring her closer to Jack than she was to Levi. It simply could not be allowed to happen. He would rather die. With every year that passed, Levi felt safer: that the chances of Rachel's biological father turning up were now reduced to none.

He'd done his absolute best to make her eighteenth a night to remember. Despite not being much of a social butterfly himself, he'd dug deep and welcomed all her friends with a big, beaming smile and made an effort to join in, even dancing into the early hours. It was a fantastic party. Mrs McAllister had wished him a happy new year and they'd all linked arms to sing 'Auld Lang Syne', followed immediately by 'Happy Birthday'. A huge cake with eighteen candles was wheeled in and Levi had stood back and watched his daughter's beaming face as she blew them out and made a wish. Every year he'd silently wish along with her – that Diana was watching them now. And every year he'd remember the first time he'd looked down and seen the tiny little newborn bundle who would grow up to be the most important person in his life. He'd had no idea then, of course. No idea of the love and the grief that lay ahead, or the joy that Rachel would bring in compensation for his loss.

The start of the new year gave him a spring in his step. He felt an overwhelming sense of achievement that he'd brought Rachel up to be a happy, well-balanced, gentle and generous human being. She'd reached adulthood with hardly a bump in the road, no major obstacles. She'd enjoyed school, taken a gap year, had a place all ready for her at the nursing school at Dundee University, and was blessed with friends and good health. Yes, Levi thought. He'd not done a bad job. As he headed back to work three days after the party, he felt buoyant. Approaching the office, he waved to a couple of colleagues arriving at the same time as him. 'Happy New Year!' he called out to them and they returned the greeting, joking about sore heads and post-Christmas weight gain. He was about to mount the steps into the building when a voice called out to him, 'Levi? Levi Norman?'

Still laughing from his colleague's joke he turned on his heel, expecting to see another workmate returning to the nine-to-five of office life. The face was familiar indeed; Levi recognized him straight away. But it wasn't someone from work. Older, yes: greyer around the temples, lined at the eyes and with a paunch that had come with age, along with the loss of that swagger Levi remembered so well.

It was Jack Blythe.

The two men stared at each other for a matter of seconds that felt for all the world like an hour. Jack spoke first. Tentatively he walked towards Levi, holding out his hand as if approaching a nervous dog. He was clutching an envelope.

'I was gonna . . .' He paused. 'I've written this letter, I was gonna leave it at the reception if I couldn't see you . . .' His voice still had the Cardiffian twang Levi remembered so well.

'What do you want?' Levi eventually spoke.

Jack looked at him, the cockiness he'd once possessed now vanished. He seemed to struggle to find the words. 'Thing is . . . I know.'

Levi swallowed hard. Every muscle in his body seemed to strain in readiness to . . . to what? To run? To fight? His head was spinning and he thought for a moment that he might pass out.

'Look, I know why you did it,' Jack continued. 'Why you lied about Diana. You didn't want me near the kid an' that – I do understand. I'd probably have done the same, mate.'

Levi cringed at being called Jack Blythe's *mate*. 'But I found out. With the internet an' all that, it's easier now, like, to track people down. And I found out you and her got married. And that the kid—'

'Rachel.' The name was out of his mouth before he could stop himself, and when he said it, it felt like a cry for help.

'Rachel, yeah.' They stood in silence again, until Jack seemed to come to his senses and thrust the letter he held in his hand out to Levi. 'All I'm asking is that you give her this. I waited till she was eighteen – I wanna do it all properly. Don't wanna tread on no one's toes. You have to believe I don't want any trouble. I'm not wanting a fight or anything like that, I just want her to know about me and maybe, in time, to agree to meet me.'

Levi took the letter from Jack and looked at it held in his shaking hand. 'I'll leave you alone,' Jack said softly. 'I won't hang around, you have my word.'

The two men stared at each other.

'You behaved appallingly,' Levi said, barely able to get his words out for the tears clogging his throat. 'You hit her. You *hit* her.'

'Yes.'

'And you killed someone – you killed a man!'

Jack looked up as if preparing to face his demons, swallowed hard and said, 'And I've lived with the shame of it for decades.'

'As you should.'

'But I'm not that person any more. I don't even know who that person was, like.'

Levi remained silent.

'And let's face it, none of us is perfect, mate. We all do things, don' we, that we regret?'

Levi thought he detected a small threat in what Jack was saying, as if he was comparing the two men's actions and finding fault in both.

'I've never hit a woman in my life,' hissed Levi.

'And I've never stolen another man's child.'

It came from nowhere, the punch. Landing squarely on the right side of his jaw. Jack Blythe reeled from the force but did not retaliate.

'I deserved that,' he said, his tone conciliatory. He nodded and turned to go. 'Just, please, mate – give her the letter, will you?'

Levi watched him till he was out of sight. It was only the arrival of another colleague that brought him back to earth.

'You all right, Mr Norman?' It was Zoe, one of the clerical assistants from along the corridor.

'What? Yes. Sorry,' he stammered.

'Happy New Year!' she replied. 'Did you have a good one?'

'Yes . . .'

He spent the work day in a daze. The change in his mood from the start of the day could not have been more pronounced, and no matter how hard he tried to concentrate on the job in hand, all he could think about was the letter from Jack Blythe burning a hole in his coat pocket.

He didn't read it straight away. He waited till lunchtime and headed down to the riverbank. It was freezing, but he knew he wouldn't be disturbed there, and was unlikely to bump into anyone from work.

Inside the envelope were two more, one bearing Rachel's name and one addressed to him. It contained the same points Jack had made to Levi in person by the steps of his work building, ending much the same way as their conversation had: *Please do this for me, just hand her the letter, that's all I ask.*

The envelope addressed to Rachel sat in his lap. He tortured himself by staring at it, mulling over his choices. He could go home that night and give it to her, explain the whole sorry mess. Or he could just dispose of it, burn it, and trust that Jack Blythe would keep his word and stay away. In the end, he did neither.

In the end, even though he knew it was wrong, he opened the letter to Rachel and read what Jack had written:

Dear Rachel,

This ain't an easy thing to write. Truth be told, I don't really know where to start. God only knows what you must think of me for staying away all these years, but it was a bit awkward, bit sensitive. I'm sorry about your mum. She was a lovely woman, was Diana. I didn't deserve her, no way. And I let her down big time. I only found out recently that she'd died – when you was, what – two? Three? I tried lookin for you years ago but didn't have no luck. Then when I found out where you was, I wanted to come straight away. But I didn't want to tread on no toes. By the looks of things, Levi Norman's done a crackin job bringing you up and he's your dad, to be fair. I'm not tryin to change that. But I'm just wonderin if there might be space in your life for me as well. I know it's a lot to ask. Levi's probably filled you in on what I used to be like so you're probably in no rush to get to know me. But I've turned things around, Rachel. I'm not the same bloke your mother would remember – or Levi for that matter. I did a bad thing and I paid the price for it. Prison taught me a lot. I don't drink no more – started going to AA when I was inside. Saved me from myself, to be honest. I'd like to tell you about my life. I'd like to get to know you. Would you think about meetin me? I can come to you or if you wanted you could come Cardiff with Levi? What d'you think?

Best wishes,
Jack Blythe

For three days Levi walked around in a daze of trouble, barely speaking, jumping at the smallest noise. Rachel asked him several times if he was okay. He tried to brush it off, attempted vague lies about January blues. He could tell she didn't believe him, but he simply couldn't find it within himself to pretend convincingly. Three times he couldn't hold it in any longer, grasping her by the shoulders as if she would be snatched away from him at any moment, looking her straight in the eye and telling her he would always protect her: that her interests were all he cared about.

It wasn't sustainable, of course. His life would be on hold until he found the courage to reply and put himself out of his own misery once and for all.

Dear Jack Blythe,

I cannot deny it was a shock to see you last week. Whilst I appreciate how you must be feeling, I hope you too will understand that your turning up like that has put me in an awful position. As requested, I gave Rachel your letter. I was with her when she opened it and I'm afraid her reaction was not the one you are hoping for. Whilst she has always known about your existence, and whilst I have always answered any questions she's had about you, I cannot force her into changing what she feels. I have tried my best, but she simply does not want anything to do with you. She is legally my daughter and I must look after her interests. I hope you can understand this. I do not wish to make this any more difficult than it has to be, but I must warn you that if you persist in attempting to contact Rachel, I will have no other option than to seek legal advice. I'm sorry that this is not what you are hoping to hear, but I'm afraid it's how things stand. Please do not contact us again.

Yours sincerely,
Levi Norman

He knew it was wrong. But he also knew it was right.

He posted it at the main post office and recorded the delivery so it was guaranteed to get there. And as he walked out on to the high street, his heart felt a little lighter.

Lighter, but never free.

2024

47

Linda

Boransay Crematorium is particularly cold this Wednesday morning. Not just because of the time of year and it being Scotland. It's cold in tone, in atmosphere. Of course, being empty also doesn't exactly jolly things along. The hearse pulls up outside the main doors and I'm there, ready to greet it, wrapped in my black faux-fur hat with matching faux-fur coat, effecting the look of a chubby Anna Karenina. It's keeping out the chill, but more importantly it hides what I'm wearing beneath: a scarlet woolly dress with a laughing reindeer emblazoned on the chest. I won't have time to go home and change, and it's our office Secret Santa straight after this: festive frocks are obligatory. When the reindeer's nose is pressed, his antlers start flashing and he declares 'Merry Christmas One and All' in a deep American accent. I've worn it for the past three Secret Santas and it always engenders a smile from colleagues. Not sure Fergus Murray would find it as entertaining, though, so it's best to keep it hidden under my coat. I watch him climb out of the hearse along with Old Sam and they head to the rear. I'm surprisingly overcome with delight at seeing my old Storrich travel companion and I go straight in for a hug. Which of course irritates him, this being a funeral service after all, and he being ever the Professional Undertaker.

'Time and place, Linda Standish,' he mutters, subtly pushing me away.

'Oh, cut the act,' I whisper so that Old Sam doesn't hear. 'You know you like me, really.' He doesn't let me hug him, but he does twinkle a little and I'm sure I detect a small smile.

We are here, of course, to finally bid farewell to Levi Norman, God bless him. Despite putting the death notices online and in both the Cardiff and the Inverness local press, I've heard nothing from anyone remotely connected to the man. So apart from Old Sam pushing the gurney and driving the hearse, and Joseph, the crematorium operative who's lurking in the background ready to facilitate the *actual* cremation, me and Fergus are the only people in attendance. Just as I'd expected. I stand aside to let them wheel Levi in and I follow at a respectable distance.

I take a seat in the front pew, though it's only for a matter of seconds whilst Fergus settles the gurney, bows and stands aside. Then I take my place at the lectern, looking out at the empty rows ahead of me. It all feels pretty pointless, but as I say time and time again, everyone deserves a proper farewell. I've written quite a nice eulogy, even though I do say so myself. It's only a few lines, but I'm pleased that it's quite specific to Levi and not some generic one-size-fits-all blurb.

'Levi Norman was born in Cardiff in 1951,' I say to the four of us, 'where he lived until his early thirties, when he met and fell in love with Diana, whom he married in 1984. They then moved to Inverness, where they brought up baby Rachel together until Diana's untimely death in 1985. Levi was a very successful accountant and—'

Just at that moment the door at the back opens and of course the incorrigible optimist in me expects the very same Rachel Norman to appear. I look up. Fergus Murray turns around and we stare at the young man framed in the doorway. He's in his early twenties, I'd say, fighting a dark suit that does not want to be worn, hair swept back into a loose ponytail, a tattoo of a Celtic cross on his right cheek.

'See, I'm lookin' for Stuey Blair?' he says in a booming Glaswegian brogue. I'm so shocked by the interruption and the lack of respect or decorum that I'm left speechless. Fergus Murray is silent too. As is Old Sam (though to be fair, I've never actually heard him speak).

'He's dead, like,' continues the Glaswegian, just in case this clarification helps us identify the missing Mr Blair. It's Joseph the crematorium operative who pipes up, equally as indecorously, I feel.

'He's on next, pal. Y'can stay in the waiting room just now.'

'Cheers, pal!' he booms back – all pals together – and waves at us, as if giving his blessing for us to carry on. So I do.

'Since 2018, Levi made his home on the Hebridean island of Storrich, where he would take long walks and watch the wildlife through his binoculars.' I've made this bit up. But in all fairness, seeing as he kept himself to himself, I didn't have a huge amount to go on so have given myself artistic licence. 'He would occasionally visit his local pub, the Storrich Arms—' Okay, so 'occasionally' is more than once a year, I know, but I'm scraping the bottom of the PR barrel here. 'The locals said he was a quiet and thoughtful man—'

That's actually true.

'And he will be sorely missed by the island community.'

Okay, so that's *not* actually true. I mean, you don't miss what you don't have, do you? And the island community didn't have Levi Norman. He wouldn't let them near him. I catch Fergus Murray surreptitiously look at his watch. I say surreptitiously, but he knows I've seen him do it and he knows I'll get the hint.

'And so we bid farewell to this remarkable man,' I conclude a tad speedily, 'who leaves this world a better place.'

I always say that at the end. Even though I *do* have a bit of a problem with it as a phrase. I know it's *meant* to mean that your presence in the world has improved it, so you're leaving it in a better state than before. But it could *also* be interpreted as the world is a better place now that you've gone. I give Joseph the nod and press the discreet button under the lectern. I always try and choose a piece of music that might relate to the deceased. In Levi's case, I was inspired by the cinema tickets found in his keepsake box, which I decided must have been from a date he had with Diana. It's not until the curtains open and the casket slowly moves out of sight that I realize the inappropriacy of my choice: the theme from *Chariots of Fire*. Fergus Murray shuts his eyes momentarily, no doubt despairing of me. Oh well. Nobody's perfect.

Outside, he's a little more friendly, I guess now that his work is finished. But also, he's in a bit of a holiday mood. 'That's me done now till January,' he says, and mimes skiing slalom.

'I'm surprised at your going away at Christmas. Isn't it an undertaker's busiest time of the year? Bit like Santa?'

'You're right there, Linda Standish. Not ma problemo though 'cos I is outta here!' I find it disturbing at the best of times when British people Americanize. But Fergus Murray *really* shouldn't do it. To alleviate the moment's awkwardness I quickly open my coat to reveal my Christmas dress. Fergus does a double-take.

'Press his nose,' I say.

'What?'

'The reindeer. Go on. Press it. Firmly.'

He's torn, I can see that. But curiosity gets the better of him and he does what he's told. 'MERRY CHRISTMAS ONE AND ALL!' booms the reindeer, and to my delight Fergus bursts out laughing.

'Ha! I love it!' he cries. But his joy is shortlived when he's admonished by a mourner heading into the crem for the next service. It's the tattooed bloke from the Blair party.

'You wanna show some respect, pal!' he shouts in Fergus's direction. 'Some of us are bereavin'.' And before Fergus can apologize the man is gone. I turn to Fergus and shake my head.

'Yes, Fergus Murray, where's your damn respect?'

*

At the office Secret Santa that afternoon, I'm gobsmacked by two things: Liam – my giftee – says he can't accept the cheese plant because he suffers from botanophobia. Seriously! It's an actual thing – some people are scared of plants. He clearly feels bad about it, and now I'm gutted I didn't give him the bloody naked undertaker calendar after all. Hey ho. I'll give the plant to Lauren as a Christmas present. That'll earn me some Brownie points. And then the other surprise is that Gillian, my line manager, has given me the most unbelievable gift. I know we're not supposed to know who gives what to whom in a Secret Santa, but because we're all public servants, we have to have a policy of absolute transparency, which is fair enough. Anyway, she's given me a gift that I could not imagine anyone actually inventing: it's tacky, trashy and naff and yet absolutely extraordinary. It's a personalized garden gnome. When I say personalized, it's actually a mini-me! The likeness is incredible – it's even got the little beauty spot beneath my right eye.

'Gillian!' I say. 'This is remarkable!' I love how excited gifting it to me has made her, and I sense a lot of thought went into it. Which, as the old adage goes, is what counts.

'Your photo, department website – strictly no-no but needs must. Local firm, made gnome, hey presto.' I think it's the most amount of words she's ever said to me in one go.

'I shall treasure this for the rest of my days, Gillian. Thank you.'

People never cease to amaze me. And as I head home at the end of the working day with my gnome in one hand and a cheese plant in the other, having broken up for school holidays as it were, I feel filled with Christmas spirit and an overwhelming love for my fellow man. There *is* sadness in the world, yes. That was my last work Secret Santa, for one thing. And then there's poor old Levi Norman – he certainly had his fair share, judging by what I've learned of his life, and it can't have been plain sailing for his daughter. But we have to look for the good bits, don't we. Otherwise, what's the point?

48

Linda

Christmas Eve has arrived and I'm just getting into *Carols from King's* and peeling carrots when the doorbell goes. It'll be Struan with Lauren and my little man, earlier than expected but who cares. Drying my hands on a tea towel and singing along to 'While Shepherds Watched', I head to the door full of Christmas cheer.

'Good grief!'

That's the best I can come up with, given the shock of what I'm looking at on my doorstep. Or rather *who* I'm looking at.

'Merry Christmas, Lindy. Any room at the inn?'

Yes, it's Douglas. My bloody ex-husband! *Sans Denise.*

*

Twenty minutes later we're at the breakfast bar finishing off a pot of tea and he's already getting on my wick. He's ruined my *Carols from King's*, and I've still got to finish the carrots. But he's in a bad way, so I'm cutting him some slack.

Turns out him and Denise have been having problems for a while and have been building up to a trial separation. 'Don't tell me, you've met someone else,' I say with a sigh, and offer him a slice of panettone.

'No, I bloody have not!' he says indignantly, as if *he'd* never dream of being unfaithful. 'And nor has she! We just . . . I dunno, don't seem to have much in common any more.'

'Well, she *is* a completely different generation from you, Doug.' (I can't help myself.)

'Don't be mean now, Linda, it doesn't suit you,' he chastises.

'Sorry.'

'The café is hard work, and she won't make any effort to learn Spanish.'

'That's hardly grounds for divorce.'

'I know, but I think it's the . . .' and then he whispers, though Lord knows why because no one is listening, '. . . it's the You Know What.'

I *don't* Know What so I take a guess at (a) hot weather, (b) consequences of Brexit or (c) the seven-year itch. None of which, it seems, is correct.

'The BLOODY MENOPAUSE!' he almost yells. 'It's making her erratic, bit looney tunes.'

Always been sympathetic to the female condition, has Douglas. We launch into a whole conversation about HRT (I'm a *big* fan) and how it might help, but it all seems a bit beyond Douglas and, thankfully, we are interrupted by the arrival – finally – of Struan.

I whisper to my lovely son at the front door, 'Your father's here!'

'What??' he asks, confused. But I don't explain, just turn to greet Lauren with a huge smile (I've been practising for days in the mirror) before reaching down to engulf my Zander in a massive Nana hug.

'My parents aren't far behind,' says Lauren, who doesn't seem remotely bothered at Douglas's presence. 'They had to fetch Granny Moss. Which room are we in?'

She addresses me like the receptionist of a Holiday Inn. *Do not react, Linda, do not react.* 'All sorted, my dear. There's a Z-bed and a futon in the study for you and Granny Moss, and your parents are on the sofa bed in the front room. As for our *extra visitor*,' I say pointedly, nodding in Douglas's direction, 'he'll have to sleep on a Li-lo in the conservatory.'

'Don't you think, Linda,' says Lauren in that simpering voice she frequently adopts, 'that my parents ought to have *your* room rather than a sofa bed downstairs?'

How on earth am I going to survive three days with this woman? 'Well, I did think about that, Lauren, but it would mean clearing out my drawers and I've got that many sex toys and fantasy costumes in there, it—'

'Stop your nonsense, Mum,' says Struan, evidently on high alert for any wife-and-mother clashes. He glares at me.

'Only joking,' I laugh (falsely). 'Thing is, the sofa bed really is very comfortable, it's an expensive one from John Lewis and I thought your dad might appreciate being close to the downstairs loo.'

'I know the feeling!' chirps Douglas, glass in hand. He appears to have discovered my Christmas brandy, which doesn't bode well. Douglas can get quite amorous when he's had a few. And seeing as his current relationship status is 'temporarily single', he could turn out to be an almighty pain.

'Right, let me get these carrots done and we can all settle down to a game of Trivial Pursuit,' I announce as Douglas has an emotional reunion with his son. I fight the urge to go upstairs and dive under the bed for my giant bar of Galaxy, which I've got saved in my box of supplies. For emergencies such as these, when the realization dawns that I actually have to spend Christmas with my ex-husband, highly irritating ex-daughter-in-law, her parents and grandmother. And there's the doorbell. Full house!

I make broccoli wrapped in ham with cheese sauce for our Christmas Eve supper, a favourite recipe stolen from my Aunty Lynne. Of course, Lauren is a vegetarian, *quelle surprise.* She's got a degree in being different, that woman. I mean, don't get me wrong, I have absolutely nothing against vegetarians. But Lauren eats fish! So how does that compute? I've made her salmon en croûte and I manage not to say anything provocative. Unfortunately – or fortunately, depending on which way you look at it – Douglas has imbibed quite a bit of Dutch courage by now and launches in with, 'How come you eat fish, then, Lauren, if you're a so-called vegetarian?'

She sighs. 'Don't be pedantic, Douglas. It's just easier for people to understand if I say I'm veggie. And I hardly eat fish anyway.'

'Don't fish have feelings too, though?'

'Dad.' Struan's got that warning tone in his voice, which I'm glad is being directed at someone other than me for a change. Lauren's parents are lovely, and very accommodating; Simon, especially, is a dab hand at changing the subject.

'What's the plan for tomorrow then, Lindy?' he says with an all-hands-to-the-pump attitude.

'Well, pressies and breakfast in the morning, a walk to the reservoir to get up our appetites, and then we'll eat around two?'

'Granny Moss won't want to walk to the reservoir,' says Lauren, instantly putting a downer on things.

'How do you know?' pipes up Granny Moss, who up until now has been silent, focusing hard on chewing her ham.

'Look, nobody has to do anything they don't want to do, I just want it to be a lovely, relaxed, family day. It's all about Zander, after all. And the fact that you're taking him away from me!' I attempt to put a laugh into my voice so it sounds like I'm being ironic. But it just comes out bitter and needy and I suddenly feel hijacked by tears. I manage a garbled, 'Ooh, excuse me a minute – I need to check on the . . . pillows.' I run upstairs, desperate for a little oasis of calm in my bedroom. This farewell Christmas was such a bad idea. I reach under the bed, grab the giant Galaxy and wolf down a quarter of it in less than a minute, still lying on the floor with my head stuck under the valance. 'Enough now,' I whisper, knowing full well that I could actually finish the lot if I let myself.

The rest of the evening passes off without incident. I persuade Douglas to switch to gin, which he does willingly. This gives me the opportunity to secretly ply him with Gordon's Zero and, thankfully, he can't tell the difference. Without realizing it he is getting sober, even though he believes he's getting more drunk. I've made up the Li-lo for him with a sleeping bag, lots of blankets and an electric radiator. He excuses himself for a 'wee lie-down' at seven o'clock, but we don't see him again for the rest of the evening.

'Shall I check he's all right?' asks Lucy after an hour, but the snores coming from the conservatory reassure us all.

Simon and Lucy head off for an early night, and Lauren eventually persuades Zander that it's bedtime. I help him put out the carrot for Rudolph, the mince pie and a glass of milk: I know it's meant to be sherry or whisky, but it sticks in my craw, turning Santa into a raging alcoholic. I point out that if Santa had a wee dram at every house he visited, then he'd be too sloshed to drive the sleigh and might get breathalysed by the polis. But it goes over Zander's head, his eyes drooping with sleep now as Lauren whisks him away to bed, followed closely by Granny Moss.

Only me and Struan are left, and there's a comfortable silence between us as we clear away the dishes. I resist the urge to continue my campaign of persuasion against the house move and decide just to make the most of his company. Times like this are such a rarity.

'I know you wish I was with someone else, Mum,' he blurts out, unprompted.

'Well, yes, I won't deny it.'

'But hard as I've tried, I can't stop loving her. And I think . . .'

'What?'

'I think we might have a fresh chance, when Zander and I move. When we're all living in the same town again. I reckon that will make her more relaxed and we can . . . y'know. Have another go.'

I swallow back my sorrow at how pathetic my lovely son is making himself sound. I knew it. He'd go back to her at the drop of a hat.

'Your divorce, though, that's all through now.'

'Doesn't mean we can't start again? Might be quite romantic.'

The hope in his voice is excruciating. 'You could have so much more though, Struan, so much—'

'I don't want so much more, Mum. I want Lauren.'

'*Awww, isn't this lovely!*' slurs Douglas, who has woken from his slumber and waded into the kitchen from the conservatory. He puts an arm each round me and Struan and pulls us in for a family hug. 'I really miss you both, d'you know that?'

'Have some water and go to bed, Douglas,' I say snippily, really cross that he's interrupted us at such a crucial moment.

'Awww, Lindy, don't be like that now!' he says and actually *nuzzles* my neck. There's only one thing for it. Firmness.

'Douglas!' I bark. 'I have given you a bed for the night and welcomed you into my home to celebrate Christmas. Do not be an absolute twat or I will have to ask you to leave.'

'Fair point,' he says, holding up his hands in surrender. I can see Struan smirking out of the corner of my eye. 'But can I get some hot milk?' says my ex-husband, who appears to have reverted to being six.

'I'll do it for you, Dad,' says Struan. 'You go back to your Li-lo and I'll bring it in.'

'Thanks, son,' says Douglas, who does as he's told. But the moment between Struan and me is lost.

49

Linda

Yes, I finished the Galaxy. Of course I did. My son's still in love with his horrible ex-wife, and it's breaking my heart. I'm bound to eat chocolate. So I wake up Christmas morning feeling rotten, down a couple of paracetamol and drink a pint of water before heading for the kitchen. I've never had a hangover from booze, but if it's anything like a sugar hangover, then they are as hideous as people say. It's only half six so I'm hoping I can grab a bit of time on my own before the tribe emerges. I give myself a stern talking-to whilst I sip a mug of good strong tea.

Much as I try to switch off from work, I keep wondering about Rachel Norman. What will she be doing this Christmas morning? Will she be thinking about her dad? It's so strange that I know he's died and yet she has no idea. Does Christmas remind her of him more? And what about Beannach Lodge? I can't bear to think about it empty and dark and cold up there on Storrich. It feels so desolate, so bereft.

A second mug of tea helps me feel a bit more human and I switch on the oven in readiness for the turkey. Almost on cue, there's a screech of delight and a very happy little boy comes trundling down the stairs to see what Santa has brought him, his mother and father in tow, in pyjamas. We exchange Christmas

Day greetings and I hug Struan tightly, silently communicating my love for him. Then I put on my best smile, boil the kettle and make everyone a cup of coffee before kneeling down next to Zander. I watch the wonder on his face as he unwraps the scooter I've bought him. His smile simultaneously breaks and gladdens my heart. I am going to miss this little man so much.

Granny Moss *does* come on the walk, and what a surprise she turns out to be. She's an absolutely fascinating woman. I tell her so and she comes back at me with, 'Aye, people write you off once you're past seventy. Think you've nothing of interest to offer the world. You'll find it yourself, Linda, once you retire – you'll become invisible.'

'Oh well, that's nice to know,' I say with a smile.

'That's if you don't fight back. Why d'you think I'm wearing these clothes?' I haven't liked to say, but she is dressed most outrageously, in a flamingo-pink fluffy jumper and red slacks under her yellow duffle coat. She's brought her binoculars in case she sees anything of interest at the reservoir. 'CORMORANT!' she yells at the top of her voice. You certainly couldn't miss her. And no, she's not particularly fast on her feet, but she's quicker than Douglas, who's either hungover or moping or both.

'Have you rung Denise this morning?' I say to him, as if talking to a broken-hearted teenager rather than a fifty-five-year-old man. He walks behind the rest of us, dragging his feet, so I join him to try and chivvy him along.

'She text me.'

'Texted.'

'Yeah, that's what I said.'

'No you didn't, you said she *text* you. But it's past tense, so it should be *texted*. Like *post*. I *post* – present tense; I *posted* – past tense. You wouldn't say, *She post me a letter yesterday*, you'd say, *She posted me a letter yesterday*.'

Douglas stops walking and stares at me. 'And you wonder why you never found a man after we split!'

I don't take the bait. 'Oh, I've had plenty of men after you, Douglas. Much more manly men, who know how to speak English properly.'

'Yeah, right,' he scoffs.

'Anyway, I hope you *texted* her back and wished her a Merry Christmas?'

'What do you care? You don't even like the woman!'

'Nor do you at the moment!' I retort and Struan, as if his antennae have started buzzing, turns round and interrupts his parents' lovely little chat.

'Come on, you two, no squabbling today, it's Christmas!'

I roll my eyes and stride ahead to catch up with Zander, who's concentrating hard on balancing on his scooter. 'That's it, darling, you've got it!' I say as I watch him wobble and gain speed.

'Nana Lind, look at meeeeeeeee! I'm zoooooomin'!'

Oh, my heart.

*

Lunch is a huge success. Douglas has perked up (mainly due to too much Rioja but also because he's had a long video call with Denise), and even Lauren is half decent. She's nice about the salmon and backhandedly compliments me by telling me that she approves of a lot of my child-rearing techniques, despite our being 'complete opposites'. I'm just basking in the warmth of a Christmas Day gone well and gearing up for a game of charades when the doorbell goes, followed by the muffled sounds of carol singers. Struan goes to answer it as I'm pouring Granny Moss some more tea. Strange, getting carol singers at all, let alone on Christmas Day itself. They're very much a dying breed, like 'penny for the Guy'. I doubt kids these days even know who Guy Fawkes was!

'Mum?' shouts Struan. 'Have you got any change?' I notice the singing has already stopped – not very good value for money.

Struan has invited the carollers into the hallway, only fair given how cold it is outside. They're covered up against the winter weather, their faces partially hidden by scarves.

'Merry Christmas, Linda Standish!' says a familiar voice. Yes, Fergus Murray is standing in my house, wiping his feet on my mat. 'Our flight to France has been delayed until tomorrow so we're at a loose end.'

'Fergus Murray!' I say. Bit thick, I know, but I'm feeling very confused.

'Indeed!' he says. 'Fergus Murray and—'

He stands back like a magician's assistant presenting on stage, '—Brodie McLeod!'

If I was in an American sitcom right now, I'd faint. But I'm in a semi-detached house in Boransay, Scotland, so I just screech, 'Well don't just stand there, take your coats off and come in!'

50

Linda

Well, I am *delighted*. But first of all, why is Brodie going skiing with Fergus? No, they've not been having a secret affair. Turns out, Robbie, one of Fergus's ski party friends (not the sharpest pencil in the pack, according to Fergus), has broken his arm skiing. Yes, I know, right? It was on the practice slopes, of all places, at the ski centre down the road. It only happened on Friday, and they were all at a loss as to who could replace him. They asked around (notice they didn't ask me, but Fergus said it was men only, at which point I told him he was sexist), and nobody was game. Fergus remembered a conversation with Brodie about skiing and that he'd expressed an interest in going again some time; turns out he used to go quite regularly when he was married to Liz.

'But what about the pub?' I say.

'Oh, I've left it in the hands of the Storrich Collective,' he says. 'Minty's in charge and between them they can man the bar. They won't fiddle me – it's not worth their while for the Arms to go under.' When he says 'arms', I think about his. And remember what it felt like to lie encircled by them in his bed. 'Anyway, we were meant to fly today but the flight's been delayed till tomorrow. So here we are!'

Fergus hands me a bottle of Nosecco and a small square box wrapped in Christmas paper. 'Just a little something,' he says. I open it as I make my way to the kitchen. It's a set of glass coasters depicting the Scottish Hebrides. Very thoughtful, and quite unexpected from Fergus Murray, I must admit.

I try really hard to hide the thrill of seeing Brodie again. But it's not easy. I'm desperate to get him on his own. Whilst Simon's working out the teams for charades, I ask Brodie to join me in the kitchen to get top-ups and Christmas cake for everyone. It's a little oasis of canoodlance and I make the absolute most of it, shutting the door to protect our privacy. We have a delicious kiss whilst the tea is brewing and I relish the feel of his beautiful bulk of a body.

'Well, this is a lovely Christmas gift!' I say.

'Certainly is,' he whispers, going in for another smooch.

'Stay tonight!' I whisper, totally uncaring that I may sound needy. 'I can take you to the airport in the morning.'

'Don't think Fergus would approve. There's a minibus picking us up and it's all part of the camaraderie. Y'know, lads together and all that.'

'Well, meet me in the shed then, when no one's looking,' I laugh.

'The shed?'

'Oh, it's a really nice shed,' I say. 'More of a summer house, really. There's heating and everything. And then you can go home.'

'Oh I see, have your wicked way with me then chuck me aside is it, Linda Standish?'

'It's exactly that!' I can't keep the smile off my face. And having sealed the deal for our 'date night', I pick up the tray of goodies and head back into the living room, where charades has already started.

Granny Moss is pulling her right ear and pointing at her nose, to a chorus of screeches from her audience. 'Sounds like . . . pimple!'

'Wimple!' shouts Fergus Murray.

'Dimple!' yells Doug.

And Granny Moss despairs, her frustration transforming her into quite a silent tyrant.

Because of my innate Christmas obsessiveness, it goes against my grain not to give presents to a guest in my house on Christmas

Day. I mean, I've already fallen short of my standards with my rushed purchases for Lauren's family. Although, weirdly, Lucy and Simon really liked their fondue set and even played a game with the Travel Scrabble earlier. As for Granny Moss, she couldn't have been happier with her knife sharpener. Though I was slightly disturbed when I asked her whether she did a lot of cooking, because she replied rather hurriedly, 'I gut fish.' And left it at that.

Thing is, Fergus and Brodie are in danger of going home empty-handed, which I can't bear. Especially as they gave *me* something; at least, Fergus did. So whilst the gang finish the last round of charades, I nip upstairs to grab a couple of emergency gifts for my latest visitors. I find a fridge magnet of Boransay for Brodie – I know, awful – but for Fergus, I'm delighted to say, I've found a home for the naked undertaker calendar! Hurrah! I quickly wrap them and rush downstairs. Their faces when they open them are a picture. Brodie laughs and says it's the worst present he's ever been given but loves it. And Fergus is completely bemused. He turns his head at different angles as if trying to work out how the various model funeral directors managed to achieve such poses. 'Good God, you should see April!' he declares. At which point Granny Moss grabs it off him and says, 'Give us a gander!'

An hour later and Struan puts a very overtired Zander to bed whilst Lauren has a bath. Granny Moss plays her accordion – yes, she brought an accordion with her – and Fergus and Lucy are singing along to Don McLean's 'American Pie'. Douglas, who's a bit the worse for wear, has fallen asleep and is leaning his head on Simon's shoulder, and Simon – also quite tipsy – is half-asleep but still tapping his fingers along in time to the music. So whilst the coast is clear, Brodie and I put on our coats and sneak out the back to the summer house. I get the heater on quick and it soon warms up, though I think that's more because of our enthusiastic passion than the electric radiator. It's absolutely marvellous having a good old bit of festive raunch, especially as it's so unexpected, and it tops off my Christmas perfectly.

*

Afterwards, we cuddle up together on the two-seater futon. 'Sorry about the fridge magnet,' I say.

'Well, it's more than I got you. Though actually, I do have something. It's not a present as such.' He rifles in the pocket of his big parka coat and pulls something out.

He hands me an unopened letter. It's addressed to Mrs Rachel McKenna at a home in Inverness, but it's been 'returned to sender, recipient unknown'. Ah, so McKenna is her name now – presumably she married. On the reverse are the sender's details: *Levi Norman, Beannach Lodge, Isle of Storrich RN83 6PJ.*

'Moira the Postie asked me to give it to you. She knew it was pointless redelivering it because, well, he's not there any more, is he?' I look at the postmark and I go cold, despite the warmth from the electric heater.

'Oh my God.'

'Yeah,' sighs Brodie. 'Looks like he posted it the day he died.'

I hold the envelope in my hands, turning it over, taking in the neat, considered handwriting. What must it have taken for him to write this, if he and Rachel were no longer in touch? And yet it was all for no good: the letter has remained unread.

'Are you going to open it?' Brodie asks quietly. I think for a moment and sigh. It feels like trespassing. Even though it's what I do day in, day out, searching for clues to someone's life.

Minutes later I'm holding Levi's letter over the boiling kettle, watching as the envelope begins to wrinkle and curl, the sealing glue softening until access is granted to its contents. Carefully, I take out the letter inside and we read.

Beannach Lodge, Storrich.
December 1st, 2024.

Dearest Rachel,
 This letter is so very long overdue. I cannot apologize enough for the time it has taken for me to find the courage to get in touch.

I am writing to you from Storrich – this most beautiful part of the world, nestled in the Hebridean Archipelago – an island I have made my home for the best part of six years. It has been the perfect place for me to hide from the world, from the lies I told you, from the pain I would feel if I'd stayed to face the truth. I chose to live in denial, in solitude, rather than accept the consequences of my actions.

Why now, you are probably wondering. What is different now? Well, I guess it is the passing of time, and also the reality of getting old. I shall be seventy-four next birthday. I have nothing left to lose in contacting you and I will of course completely understand if you wish to have nothing to do with me. But I would dearly love to make peace with you, sweetheart, and to see your smiling face again. To be reminded of my darling Diana, whose likeness you most certainly inherited. And so this is my invitation to you. To come and visit me here in Storrich – I think you would love it. And I would so love to share its beauty with you. Christmas is not far off now and I'm sure you have plans. But if you wanted to come here for Hogmanay, there is a lovely little pub called the Storrich Arms where I'm sure you could enjoy a lively New Year's Eve and of course celebrate your forty-second birthday.

The invitation is open. I would just so dearly love to see you again, Rachel, and to say sorry to you in person for all the hurt I have caused you through my lies.

My love always to you,
Dad x

We sit in absolute silence, taking in what we have both read. This poor, poor man. To have suffered like this. To have finally found the courage to contact his daughter in search of reconciliation and to die hours after sending it.

'You realize there is one small consolation,' says Brodie quietly.

'What?'

'Well, he never received the rejected letter. He never knew Rachel had refused to read it.'

I think about this for a moment, and then I nod. 'So he will have died at least knowing that he wrote to her, that he said sorry, that he sort of explained—'

'Yes. Yes he did.'

51

Linda

Two days later I say an early-morning farewell to Lucy, Simon and Granny Moss, followed soon after by Lauren, Struan and my little Zander. Douglas groans goodbye to everyone from his Li-lo. Having celebrated reconnecting on Facetime with Denise last night, he's hungover and still half-asleep.

I cry buckets when they leave, much as I try not to because I don't want Zander to get confused as to why his Nanny Lind is all upset. So I do this sort of weird hysterical snorty-laugh-cry, which probably upsets him even more. And I keep hugging him till the very last moment. Lauren's already ensconced in the front seat, AirPods inserted – which I think is a bit irresponsible, seeing as her four-year-old will need to be listened to and engaged with, but then that role has probably been left to Struan, as usual. Even though he's driving.

'Doesn't Lauren believe in talking whilst travelling?' I ask sarcastically, once the passenger door is closed and Struan shuts the boot.

'She's listening to a podcast,' he says, 'about mindfulness.'

'Oh, right.' I'm not impressed and I whisper, 'Please call me when we can talk properly, sweetheart. I don't want you going through all this on your own.'

'It's fine, Mum. Honestly. The place I'm staying—'

'The *house share*.'

'It's only ten minutes from Lucy and Simon.'

'Good. That's good,' I say, though I don't feel very honest saying it. We hug, an overly long hug, and I think I'm going to start crying again until Struan brings me back to earth with a bump.

'Look out, the bear's left his den,' he says, and we both turn to the front door, from where a very dishevelled Douglas comes stumbling.

'Sorry, sorry!' he shouts, and launches in for a big man-hug with Struan, who's nearly knocked off his feet by the force of it all.

'You already said goodbye in the house!' I say, irritated that this cuckoo in the nest is stealing my hostess thunder.

'I know, but I felt bad not seeing them off properly.' He knocks on Lauren's window then and I can see she's annoyed at being disturbed, even more so when Douglas leans in and gives her a slobbery, hungover kiss on her cheek. I think I see her visibly recoil. 'Bye, babe! Come and see us in Spain!'

I roll my eyes at Struan, who's obviously finding the whole thing amusing.

'Take care, you two!' he shouts as he gets behind the wheel. I stand there waving them off, with Douglas unwelcome by my side. Once the car is out of sight I turn to him, trying to hide my impatience. 'Right, what's happening?'

'Well, I was thinking a nice fry-up?' he says, completely oblivious to my hinting it was time he left.

'No, Douglas, I meant what's happening with you? In other words, when are you off?' He does this hurt-puppy look then, and for a moment I worry I'll never get rid. But thankfully, he informs me he'll be leaving at twelve.

'After a nice fry-up,' he repeats.

To be fair, he does do the cooking. 'You've done enough this Christmas, Lind! Put your feet up and let me spoil you.' I was always a bit suspicious of Douglas when he offered to cook. It used to mean he had an ulterior motive. Though I can't think what it might be. It won't be sexy-times, seeing as he and Denise are now back on track and he's heading home to her on a Glasgow flight at 6 p.m. But it soon becomes apparent: he's just being nosey.

'So,' he says, smiling and putting down a full Scottish breakfast in front of me, 'tell me how you feel about this Brodie fella.'

'Ah, so that's what this is all about.'

'I'm just looking after your interests, Lind, that's all.'

'You should have asked him what his intentions were,' I joke.

'Well, I sort of did.'

'*What??*' I'm horrified to hear this. 'When?'

'I followed him and that Fergus out to the car when they left. I said I'm sure he's nice enough 'n' all that, but if he hurts you, he'll have me to deal with.'

I'm absolutely lost for words. I literally open my mouth and close it several times before I finally manage, 'Douglas, you are such a knob.'

'Oh, well that's nice!' he says, sticking his fork in a cherry tomato too hard and sending juice across the table.

'What *is* this – a Jane Austen novel? I don't need you "looking after my interests" – Brodie isn't even . . . I mean, he's . . .'

And then I falter. Because I really don't know *what* Brodie is. A friend? A passing ship? 'He's just someone I met through work and got on with.'

'Who you subsequently slept with. And we both know, especially at our age, that sex is to be cherished. It's not just something we do for the hell of it.'

'Yes it is!' I say, and I mean it.

'Linda.' He looks at me then, all serious, and for an awful moment I think he's going to take my hand. So I grip my cutlery and quickly fork a chestnut mushroom. 'I know you must be lonely sometimes. You're bound to be. But hey, this is *me* you're talking to, remember?'

'How could I forget?' I bluster through a mouthful of toast. 'You gate-crashed my Christmas, slept on my Li-lo and now you're wolfing down my Lorne sausages. Brodie McLeod, for your information, is a lovely man, a wonderful shag and a fantastic interlude in my working life. I do not need protecting from him, nor do I need you embarrassing me like that. So subject closed,' I announce. 'And if you're not eating that tattie scone, pass it over.'

We're fine by the time he leaves. That seems to be the way of things with me and Douglas. We're more like argumentative siblings than ex-partners. When he says goodbye I wish him luck with Denise. I have a vested interest in their staying together; I couldn't bear the drama of them splitting up – especially as he might turn up on my doorstep for solace and succour. Euwww.

'Oh, and don't worry,' he shouts as he gets in the car. 'I *didn't* embarrass you with Brodie. He told me it was just a harmless fling and that it meant nothing.'

'Exactly!!' I shout back indignantly. Though inwardly I feel unexpectedly upset by this.

52

Linda

I've not heard from Struan and co. since they left the day after Boxing Day, apart from a text saying they'd arrived in Bordgalsh. I feel so dreadfully alone without them, but I'm just going to have to get used to it. And throw myself into dessert- and cake-making – my 'happy' place. Yes, I love *Bake Off*, of course I do. There's a scary place inside where I think I might eat all that I've baked, but I just pray a few neighbours will pop round to say Happy Hogmanay. And if they don't, well there's no point in wasting it all, is there?

I spend the afternoon making a key lime pie, a chocolate chip cookie cake, profiteroles and a big trifle. As I do so, my head is whizzing round – jumping between Struan's sad relationship with his wife and Levi's broken relationship with his daughter. When I'm back in the office next week I can start a new search for Rachel McKenna, as opposed to Norman. It's not really up to me to fix either situation, I know. But it's my default. I like to know everything's *okay*. I'm probably – no, definitely – a control freak. When I had a brief spell in therapy, the counsellor said my overeating was related to a deep-seated need to control. Which I thought was a bit weird, seeing as my overeating is so chaotically *out* of control. But she thought it related to my past. And I suppose she might have been right – certainly, food wasn't a problem for me when I was younger. And yet now? Now it's where I turn when I think I can't resolve things. When I can't see an answer. When I feel completely bereft.

I take out the sponge tins from the oven and turn them on to the wire rack. They'll be going in the trifle later – no shop-bought fingers for me, I make the whole thing from scratch. Inhaling the delicious syrupy aroma of freshly baked cake, I'm tempted to wolf down the whole lot, but that would be really annoying. I'd have to start all over again. Instead, I make myself a hot chocolate and head up to bed. I cleanse my face and apply a bright green face mask from an organic 'pamper' kit I was given for Christmas by Lucy and Simon. It has to stay on for twenty minutes, so I sit on the bed, sip my hot chocolate and start scrolling through photos of Zander (I have about three thousand on my phone). When a Facetime call comes through, I'm thrown. It's Brodie McLeod! And I'm understandably feeling very self-conscious about my appearance – should I just ignore the call? That seems a bit mean. And anyway, what does it matter how I look? He's seen me in pin curls and a ginger wig before now. And bedsocks. *He's a friend, for God's sake!*

'Hello there!' I say, attempting to be jaunty and full of bonhomie. It's not easy, as the face pack has made my cheeks and chin go taut. I start to explain, 'I'm doing a—' but I'm cut off.

'Sorry to interrupt,' he says quickly, 'but I'm afraid we need your help. It's Fergus Murray. He's broken his leg.'

*

'That's it, go slowly now.' It's teatime the next day and I'm holding open my front door as Brodie McLeod helps the casualty – aka Fergus Murray – over the threshold like an unlikely bride. He grimaces in pain and even though most days the man annoys me, today I can't help feeling sorry for him. 'Now, I've made up the sofa bed in the front room so you'll have access to the downstairs loo – will you manage that on crutches? Or shall I try and source a bedpan—'

'I do *not* need a bloody bedpan,' he snaps and I turn my face away so he doesn't see me laugh.

Brodie helps him on to the big chair in the back room where the telly is, before heading out to the car to fetch their bags. I keep the door open for him and say in hushed tones, 'Was it the same leg? That he broke before – y'know, when he was a cyclist?'

'No, it's the other one,' says Brodie. 'I don't know if that's a good or a bad thing.'

Poor Fergus Murray.

'To break one leg may be regarded as a misfortune,' I whisper as Brodie comes back in, 'to break both looks like carelessness.' And he stops for a moment as if seeing me for the first time.

'Didn't have you down as an Oscar Wilde fan.'

'I could say the same for you,' I reply with a cheeky grin.

'Hello,' he says.

'Hello.'

We look at each other for a moment, stood on the doorstep enjoying this unexpected happy reunion despite the unfortunate circumstance that has brought it about. 'Any chance you could shut the front door?' shouts Fergus Murray from the living room. 'It's blowing an absolute gale in here.'

'We'll have our work cut out with this one, matron.' We both laugh and head back inside. Thankfully, Fergus Murray will not be my patient for long. He is here because his sister – the only person who could feasibly look after him – is away till January the first. They did try asking other friends of his to take him in, but they were all either similarly away or had relatives clogging up their spare beds and sofas. So Brodie suggested asking me. Which is a bit bizarre, seeing as I don't really know Fergus Murray. But the added bonus of seeing Brodie again makes me forget that minor detail and I've welcomed the luckless undertaker pretty much with open arms.

When I point out to Brodie that he could have played nursemaid at Fergus's own house until the arrival of Fergus's sister, Brodie actually goes a bit coy and says, 'Yes, but then I wouldn't have got to see you. If I'm ending my skiing trip three days early, I'm after some compensation.' Which in turn makes *me* a bit coy. Honestly, like a pair of soppy teenagers, we are.

I'm excited at the prospect of impressing my Hebridean friend by cooking up a storm, so I splash out on a good-quality côte de boeuf along with stem broccoli, and get going on a potato dauphinoise. For dessert there's obviously plenty of choice, seeing as I had a bake-fest yesterday.

Over supper Fergus and Brodie tell me all about their trip – how it had been going so well, how Fergus had met a woman on the second night who he'd been rather taken with, 'And it was clearly mutual,' adds Brodie. I am struck by a ridiculous feeling of jealousy, wondering if Brodie had also been drawn to any lithe female skiers on the piste. But I just smile and brush the thought aside. Fergus admits he was showing off to said lady – whose name was Anthea – and attempted something far too ambitious, resulting in a nasty femur-fracturing fall.

'I'll be out of action for eight weeks, they reckon, so they'll be sticking me behind the desk instead of mingling with the punters.' Brodie and I share a sneaky smile at this – it sounds so bizarre, describing mourners as 'punters', though I guess in one sense that's what they are.

By nine o'clock Fergus seems to be dropping off, so I make a start on the washing-up whilst Brodie helps him into bed, which is a step too far for me.

'He's out like a light,' says Brodie when he comes back into the kitchen and wraps his arms around me from behind. It's such a lovely, gorgeous feeling to be cuddled like this, and I realize how much I've missed being held. You sort of get used to being self-sufficient, managing without. But meeting Brodie and having these recent little interludes of interaction has brought home to me that there's a vacuum in my life. A vacuum that I've learned to tolerate.

He nuzzles my neck, which is delightful. 'God, you smell good,' he says, and I turn around and kiss his face off.

'You'll be pleased to know you've been upgraded from the shed to the bed,' I say, pausing for breath. 'Unless you want to sleep downstairs on the sofa, next to your patient?'

'I've told him to call my mobile,' says Brodie. 'Or ring that little handbell I found in your hall.'

'Well, we might be in for an interesting night,' I say, taking his hand and leading him upstairs.

53

Linda

New Year's Eve is upon us and Brodie helps Fergus to get dressed after he navigates the downstairs shower room. There's something amusing about a man so conscious of his neat appearance being dressed by another who couldn't care less. Though to his credit, I've not seen Brodie in a single oil-stained sweater so far this holiday. At the breakfast table Fergus does look a little dishevelled, which makes me think how complicated it must be getting dressed with a leg in plaster.

'Maybe you should invest in a sarong. Like David Beckham wore that time. Be easier to get on and you wouldn't have to worry about trousers.'

'I'm not wearing a sarong, Linda Standish.'

'Or a shroud? I bet you'll have a few of those kicking around at the office?' I tease. He ignores me and starts playing Spelling Bee.

As we're bound to the house by our patient, Brodie and I spend the day tackling *the list*: things in the house I keep meaning to do and never get round to. Like cleaning the oven (me), fixing the loose hinge on the bathroom cabinet (Brodie), replacing the batteries in the smoke alarms (me) and tightening the screws on the garden pagoda (Brodie). Fergus Murray, meanwhile, watches Netflix and rings his bell when he needs attention. I give him a bag of socks to pair up. 'Your hands still work okay, don't they?' I say when he tries to object.

Later, Brodie comes in from the garden, where he's been mulching, and I hand him a cup of tea. 'You're very handy to have around the house,' I tease. 'Every girl should have a Brodie McLeod in their cupboard.'

He smiles and engulfs me in a big Brodie embrace, 'You make me sound like some sort of sex toy!'

'Which in many ways you are,' I laugh. And we kiss, just affectionately at first. But it soon turns into a delicious full-on snog and we run upstairs for a quickie, shouting down to Fergus that we need to 'pop up to the attic for five minutes'. Fergus Murray is oblivious, I think (I hope). And a new euphemism between me and Brodie is born: *popping up to the attic.*

Afterwards – we were gone quite a bit longer than five minutes – Brodie checks in on the Storrich Arms, where everyone seems to be managing perfectly well without him. 'I'm surprised at you, going away at what must be your busiest night of the year,' I say, as I get going on our Hogmanay supper: roast lamb and colcannon mash, with Brodie doing dessert.

'Can't keep doing the same thing over and over, can I? Got to take a few risks in life. Anyway, by the time I get back on Monday they'll probably still all be at it.' Brodie has agreed to stay until Fergus's sister can pick him up tomorrow morning. 'D'you think I've done enough shortbread for the cranachan, by the way?' He shows me a mountain of biscuits.

'Just one *tiny wafer-thin* shortbread?'

Brodie smiles in recognition and I feel a deep glow. It's not lust or even affection, but a sense of camaraderie between us that we share this Monty Python code of reference. That we may be in our fifties, but we can still enjoy a joke as if we were teenagers. Oh heck, this is not good, this glow. Not good at all.

*

At five minutes to midnight, we offer to help Fergus up and outside into the garden to watch the fireworks from my neighbours' garden. 'I'll watch the ones on TV, if you don't mind,' he says. 'The Edinburgh display is out of this world.'

'Oh well, we'll stay in here with you,' I say.

'Don't be a fool, Linda Standish. Get outside before you miss it all.' At first I take him at his word, but then I realize he's being kind: giving me and Brodie a little bit of Hogmanay romance on our own. I'm touched by the gesture. I hate to admit it, but I've got a lot of affection for Fergus Murray now, and I never thought I'd see the day.

Brodie and I wrap up and head into the back garden. Alan and Matthew next door always have a fine display, and live music to boot. They *did* invite us over, but given the circumstances we had to decline. And to be honest, I'm actually quite glad. Because I'm stood here in the dark of my garden, lights from the conservatory Christmas tree cheering us on from inside, and I'm huddled up next to this gorgeous man. And I think, *How lucky are you, Linda Standish?*

The countdown from next door reaches us loud and clear: *Five, four, three, two – ONE! HAPPY NEW YEAR!* The band starts playing and me and Brodie link arms in an intimate two-person rendition of 'Auld Lang Syne'. The cheers after the final refrain are echoed around the town it seems, and the fireworks, perfectly timed, top off the whole night. Brodie turns to me, cups my face with his gorgeous weatherbeaten hands, and we kiss. Oh, such a beautiful kiss. How I adore those lips. 'I don't think I've had a Hogmanay snog like that since I was a teenager!' I whisper, with the whoops and celebrations going on around us.

'Ha, yes,' replies Brodie, 'when you're young you get given some sort of licence on New Year's, don't you? To kiss whoever you want. No rules.'

'Ah, to be young again.'

I refuse to get sad about the passing of time and the sorrow that accompanies getting older, because right now I feel sixteen again.

And it strikes me, too, that this might be the first New Year's Eve I've not felt the secret ache in my heart that visits me on occasions such as these: happy family occasions, milestone events, times when missing loved ones come so crashingly to mind. 'It'll never go,' the therapist had told me back then, 'but it *will* get less . . .' Me and Douglas shared a tiny moment together before he got too drunk on Christmas Day. It was a rare connection, when he wasn't annoying me. Just held my hand and nodded. Some feelings just can't be put into words. We just both understood that we were both remembering.

'Would you really want it?' Brodie asks, breaking me out of my reverie. 'To be young again?'

I think for a moment and say, 'D'you know what, no. I don't think I would. The here and now is just peachy for me.' And I mean that. I really do.

*

Fergus Murray's sister is at my doorstep the next day at 10 a.m. on the dot. I suspect punctuality runs in the family, as does a precise dress sense. She apologizes profusely for the inconvenience her brother may have caused and it's very entertaining to see the two siblings in action together – sniping, sarcastic, with an obvious underlying affection for each other.

'Thank you to both of you,' says the casualty before he clambers into his sister's car. Once he's settled, he turns to us and says, 'So what's gonna happen with you two, then?'

'What d'you mean?' I ask, knowing *exactly* what he means and feeling very awkward and wishing he'd shut up.

'Well, I have to say . . .' he starts.

'Do you?' I plead, and I look at Brodie, who remains inscrutably silent.

'Yes, Linda Standish, I do,' continues Fergus. 'When we were skiing our man Brodie here talked about you a lot. A *lot*. And I know that you feel the same, so when are you both going to get your act together?'

'Right, well, thank you for that!' I say. 'Now bugger off.'

We watch them drive away, waving till they're out of sight.

'I was thinking that I might stay a couple more days,' says Brodie.

My heart skips a beat when he says it. But I manage to keep my cool and strike just the right note of friendly nonchalance. 'Oh, that'd be nice,' I reply. 'You know you're very welcome.'

'You could sound a *bit* more enthusiastic,' he laughs.

I want to tell him that I just can't go there. I can't go where I really want to. I have to keep a lid on it. Rein it in. Because there's a door that will always remain locked as far as Love is concerned. I dare not even think about turning the key. Best to stay safe, protected and well-hidden within my carefully constructed walled world.

'Don't be so needy, Brodie McLeod,' I say, as we head back inside arm in arm. In the kitchen my mobile is ringing. It's not a number I recognize.

'Is that Linda Standish?'

I can't bear it when people calling me don't announce their names first, so my answer to 'Is that Linda Standish?' is always, 'Who wants to know?' Which makes me sound a bit like a gangster.

'Oh, sorry.' The female voice on the other end is timid and I instantly regret my bolshiness. 'You sent a letter,' she says. 'I'm Elaine McAllister. I'm sorry to call on New Year's Day, but it seemed urgent?'

'Oh! Oh my goodness!' I wave frantically at Brodie and get him to stand next to me, sharing the phone so he can hear. 'You sound a lot younger than I thought,' I say, realizing that I'm speaking to none other than Rachel McKenna's babysitter.

'I'm sixty-three,' she says, confused. 'You sent a letter to my mother's house.'

'Yes,' I reply. 'Yes I did!'

'Well, Mum died last year, but I live here now.'

'Right . . . ?'

'I take it you'd like to know where Rachel is?'

2018

54

Rachel

'Oh my God, I thought I was going to pass out in there!' Emily had just emerged from the steam room to join the other three hens in the relaxation zone of the Courtfield Hotel Spa.

'You are such a drama queen!' laughed Nikki, handing Emily a glass of champagne. 'You were only in there for forty-five seconds.'

'That was long enough,' Emily gasped, gulping her drink. 'It's not natural, sitting in a room full of steam. And it's dangerous! You could slip and break your back, or catch a disease!'

The others laughed as they sipped their champagne. They were used to Emily's dramatics. She was always the one in the group who had a problem, an extreme situation to overcome, and it had been that way for as long as they could remember. All four friends, Emily, Nikki, Kerry and Rachel, had known each other since school – and all four played their unofficial individual roles: Emily was the dramatic one, Nikki was sensible, Kerry the romantic and Rachel the quiet one. And it was Rachel's hen night the four women were celebrating today.

They were having the best time. An entire day being pampered and spoiled, getting their nails painted, their faces cleansed, their backs massaged and their bodies steamed. All in preparation for dinner at Glasgow's Michelin-starred restaurant, La Divine.

'What's the odds on Emily getting ill from a dodgy prawn?' Rachel said when they booked the table.

'I don't think La Divine would sell dodgy prawns,' Kerry replied. 'She's far more likely to get bitten by one, knowing her.'

'You lot would all miss me if I wasn't here,' said Emily. She enjoyed playing up to her role as the class clown.

'Yes, we bloody would,' said Rachel, pulling her friend in for a big hug.

The Glasgow weekend was just what Rachel had wanted for her hen party. At thirty-five, she felt she was a bit past L-plates and chocolate willies. And the thought of having dozens of women trailing from club to club or pub to pub with a strip-o-gram at the end of the night was completely anathema to her. She just wanted to be with her three best friends on a weekend away, with dinner, pampering, fine wine and laughs. They'd decided on Glasgow because not only was it such a buzzing city offering all that they wanted from the weekend, it was easy to travel to from their home city of Inverness. And as well as this, Rachel's father Levi was paying for the whole thing, so she didn't want to take advantage.

He'd tried persuading her to go further afield. 'What about Paris?' he'd said. 'Or Morocco? I really do want you to have the best, best time. Please say – whatever you want!'

'Dad!' she'd said. 'You've already been too generous with the wedding. I don't want you wasting your money on somewhere ridiculously extravagant. Glasgow will be lovely.'

He'd relented then and stopped trying to persuade her. 'As long as you're happy, sweetpea. That's all I care about.'

This was true. All her life, her beloved father had spoiled her without making her spoilt. She'd never taken anything for granted and she knew she was the apple of his eye. Always had been. At school she'd been pitied. The only one in her class without a mum. It had given her some weird kind of status – the notoriety of bereavement. As she grew up, Rachel understood better what the circumstances surrounding her mother's death had been: the pain of terminal illness, of losing a family member so young.

It felt strange now that at the age of thirty-five Rachel was eleven years older than her mother had been when she'd died. How unfair that she'd been granted a longer lifespan than Diana. And how arbitrary was the selection of who would make it and who wouldn't.

At La Divine that evening, Rachel and her friends laughed until they cried, remembering silly jokes and events from school and their teenage years. Rachel was the only one now living back in Inverness. Nikki had gone to university in London and had stayed there ever since. Kerry had married young and moved to her husband's home town of Ullapool. And Emily had been living in Edinburgh since coming out ten years previously. She said there was far more scope for romance in the capital than in the less-populated Inverness. 'Plus, I don't have to face my mother on a daily basis, crying about me being gay,' she said. They all moaned at different points about their parents and their families. All except Rachel. Who genuinely didn't have anything to complain about when it came to her dad. Her friends agreed.

'You definitely struck gold on the parent front,' said Emily, immediately biting her tongue. 'Oh shit, sorry. I mean—'

'Shut up, Emily, you donut,' snapped Nikki.

But Rachel smiled. 'It's fine! I know what you mean. I *am* lucky. I think my dad's had to do a sort of two-for-the-price-of-one special offer, y'know, making up for my mum not being around.'

'He's so lovely, your dad,' said Kerry.

'Yes. He is.'

'Let's drink a toast,' said Nikki, rescuing the mood. 'To our beloved friend and hen, Rachel Norman.'

'RACHEL NORMAN!' the friends cheered.

'And Levi, who has so generously paid for this spectacular weekend!'

'To Levi!'

'And to Diana,' added Rachel quietly, glancing up above her.

The women clinked their glasses, teary-eyed and full of love for each other.

'To Diana,' they said.

'Right,' Kerry declared, trying to lighten the mood. 'What time's the stripper due?'

55

Levi

They'd persuaded him to go on the stag night. David, his future son-in-law, was desperate for him to join them. 'Oh come on, Levi! It'll be decent. Golf up at Kingsmills, dinner at the Thai Garden, followed by karaoke in Tiger Tiger. Nothing extreme.'

In all fairness, most stag nights Levi had heard about were far more full-on than what David was proposing. At work there'd been young ones who'd gone to Prague for five-day stag parties and even one chap who'd gone to Las Vegas with a dozen friends. It made Levi feel very old. Like he came from a different planet. Apart from anything else, he couldn't understand why they'd spend all that money just on a lads' holiday, when surely newly married life would be financially challenging enough. It certainly was in his day. When he and Diana had got married, they'd lived in their tiny little terrace and saved every week to buy things that would turn it more and more into a home. Most of their money went on baby things for Rachel. There certainly wasn't any spare cash left over for extravagant jaunts to exotic places. Levi smiled when he remembered those early days of new marriage. In fact, he'd never felt anything *other* than newly wed. Diana had lit up every room she walked into. And for Levi that had never changed.

'Just come for the golf, then,' pleaded David. 'You're gonna be my father-in-law. You're *meant* to come on the stag. Even if it's just part of it.'

'Okay, okay!' said Levi, relenting. And David beamed.

Levi liked David. A Maths teacher at the secondary school, he was patient with his pupils and passionate about his subject, but more importantly he was just a kind man who adored Rachel. Yes, Levi liked him a lot. Good job, seeing as he was marrying his precious daughter. What would he have done if Rachel had fallen for some self-congratulating arse or a politically correct bore? Anyway, he didn't need to think about that, because it wasn't happening. Rachel had chosen well, and had, thankfully, fallen in love with a kind, funny, gentle soul, whom Levi knew would look after her.

Levi had insisted they have a big wedding. 'I've been saving up for it since she was a baby!' he'd laughed. 'I want it to make as big a splash as possible.'

'In that case,' joked David, 'shall we go for one of those big pink carriages like Katie Price and Peter Andre had?'

'If that's what you want,' Levi said and Rachel hit David playfully on the arm.

'Don't be daft! Can you imagine?!'

In the end, they'd agreed on Inverness Cathedral for the ceremony, with a reception at Achnagairn Castle. 'A far cry from mine and your mother's wedding,' Levi said. 'Just me and her, with you a babe in arms and two strangers as witnesses off the street. All done and dusted in twenty minutes at Inverness Town Hall.'

'So you're making up for it now, then, Leev,' said David. 'Vicariously having a big bash through us. Good for you.'

It wasn't really vicarious. Levi wanted Rachel to have the best of everything. And he knew Diana would have wanted the same. But it wasn't just a big wedding Levi wanted to bless the couple with. Being savvy with money came naturally to him as a long-in-the-tooth accountant. And having researched the tax issues and his own financial status, Levi had decided that he would sign over his house to the newly-weds as a present.

It took a long time for Rachel to accept his gift. 'Dad, it's your house! Where will you live, for God's sake?'

'It's been your house, too, Rachel. And you'd get it after my days anyway. I'm just handing it over to you a bit earlier and saving you a big chunk that would otherwise go to the tax man.'

His decision wasn't rash. Now aged sixty-seven, Levi had retired two months previously and was planning to travel. Not that he would go abroad. Just visit places in Britain that he'd always fancied. Maybe take six months off to do it, then settle down in a little flat near Rachel and David. Maybe one of the new ones on Broch Lane. Who knew, there might be grandchildren on the way. Not a subject he ever brought up – it was too private, he felt. But deep down he hoped more than anything to become Grampa Levi one day.

Eventually Rachel and David accepted the gift of the house. Levi's plan was to wait until the couple returned from their honeymoon before setting off on his own *trip of a lifetime*.

The simultaneous stag and hen were held three weekends before the wedding. Seemed mad to think that in the olden days there was no such thing as a hen night. And the stag night was always held the night before the big day. Why would anyone in their right mind, Levi wondered, want to get married with a raging hangover?!

He was nervous about going on the stag. But it was, after all, only a round of golf. He knew Archie, the best man, and David's father of course. So he wouldn't be a complete Billy No-Mates. It was just that Levi was very much a solo soul. He kept himself to himself most of the time, always had done. Was he shy? A bit, yes. But ultimately, he just preferred his own company. Still, David would be gutted if he didn't go, now that he'd promised he would, so he got up early on the morning of the stag to polish his barely used golf clubs.

He was awake bright and breezy when the bell went. Still smiling as he opened the door, it took several seconds for him to process who was standing there.

'It's okay,' said the visitor. 'I know she's not here, I've seen on Facebook and—'

'No. No!' They were the only words Levi managed to utter as he tried to close the door on Jack Blythe, a shadow of his former self, desperately but not violently placing his foot in the way of the door.

'Please,' Jack said gently. 'You *know* we have to talk.'

'How did you get this address? This is harassment, it's—' But Levi couldn't finish the sentence because he didn't know exactly *what* this was.

'Does it matter? Look, mate – I promised you I would stay away, and I have. She didn't wanna know me. Fair dos. I accepted it.'

Levi shook his head, unable to look Jack Blythe in the eye.

'But I want to know about *her* life.'

'So that's why you're stalking her on Facebook?' demanded Levi, and immediately regretted the harshness of his words.

'It's not *stalking*,' said Jack, 'it was the only way I could follow her life, without actually making contact. And now I know she's getting married, I just want to see her, just once, on her big day.'

'Are you out of your mind?' Levi was outraged. The audacity – the unbelievable nerve! He just wanted him to leave, to say his piece and go. This was unbearable.

'Please,' Jack said, 'grant me this one thing, will you, mate? And I'll leave you alone.'

'You said that last time. You say you've kept your promise but you haven't really, have you?'

Jack sighed and looked down. 'No. I suppose you're right there, and I'm sorry. But look, I'll be discreet. I won't draw attention to myself. I'll slip in at the back and I won't talk to anyone.' He reassured Levi that if any of the guests asked him who he was, he'd say he was a tourist visiting the cathedral.

Levi's mind was racing, torn up by the knowledge that he should just surrender to this request, make good on his broken promise to Diana and let this man into his daughter's life, albeit anonymously. He could feel the fight in him seeping away and, with barely a nod, he signalled his agreement to Jack Blythe's request. It was enough encouragement for Jack to turn to leave.

As he headed down the path, Jack looked back at Levi. 'I have to ask you this, I promised myself I wouldn't but now I'm here I have to . . .'

Levi braced himself. He had no idea what Jack was going to demand of him next.

'When you told her, back then, about me, I mean—'

Levi felt suddenly nauseous.

'What did she say?'

Taking a deep breath, Levi struggled desperately to find the right words. Words that avoided the truth without being an out-and-out lie.

'What do you *think* she said? Who would want a lying, abusive drunk as a father? A lying, abusive drunk who killed a man. *What* do you *think* she said?'

Jack nodded, sheepish, accepting, ashamed. 'Yeah, I get it,' he muttered. And headed out of the door.

Levi called after him, 'You promise me, don't you, that you'll watch the ceremony and leave straight away?'

'I promise,' said Jack. And as Levi watched him go, he hated his own hypocrisy – that he could expect another human being to keep their promises, when he himself had broken his.

56

Rachel

Rachel and David had decided it was ridiculous to ban contact between each other on the stag and hen weekend, despite their friends' best efforts. They thought it was a load of superstitious nonsense and secretly arranged to sneak off for a call at half five before going out for their respective evening events. 'It was great! I just wish your dad had turned up,' said David.

'What? He didn't come?'

'No! And I really thought I'd persuaded him.'

Rachel was worried. 'Well, did you call him?'

'Of course! He said he had some sort of bug, but to be honest he sounded okay, so I didn't push it,' said David. 'Thing is, I don't think in his heart of hearts he wanted to be there.'

'I'll call you back,' said Rachel.

She hung up and pressed dial on Levi's number. He answered straight away. 'Dad? Are you okay?'

'Hello, sweetpea.' He sounded weak, broken. 'Sorry . . . I . . .'

'Daddy? What is it? David said you were ill.'

There was a worrying pause and then, 'To be honest, I just couldn't face it in the end and I thought with all the excitement he wouldn't really notice if I wasn't there.'

Rachel felt simultaneously angry and sad when he said this. Like her father didn't think he mattered.

'Stop worrying,' said Levi. 'Just go and enjoy yourself!'

Rachel wasn't convinced. But it was pointless trying to argue with him.

The three weeks since the hen party flew by, and now the wedding day was upon them. Her father had been very quiet since she'd returned from Glasgow. And despite her endless enquiries as to how he was, he always gave the same reply. 'I'm fine! Just nervous about my speech.' She could believe that to an extent, as public speaking wasn't exactly in Levi's comfort zone. There was just something niggling away at her. Something wasn't right – was it overwhelm from the forthcoming wedding and the stark reminder that her mother wasn't there to share it all? Well, there was nothing she could do. If he wouldn't tell her what it was, she'd have to just take his word for it that he was nervous about his speech.

Rachel's maids of honour, Nikki, Emily and Kerry, arrived early at Levi's house to get ready for the big day ahead. Rachel had moved back to her childhood home for the run-up to the wedding. There were two make-up artists there to do their hair and faces, and the house was buzzing with nuptial excitement and pre-wedding activity. Levi wandered around in his smart suit looking for ways to help but there was nothing for him to do – everything had been taken care of. The florist arrived with the bouquets and his buttonhole, which she pinned in place for him.

Rachel, still in big curlers and a cotton robe, make-up done to perfection, took in the sight of her lovely father. Fighting tears, she took his hand and said, 'You look brilliant, Dad.'

'I'll do, then, will I?'

And they stood there silently for a moment just holding hands, unable to speak. Eventually Levi cleared his throat. 'There's something I want to give you,' he said.

'Don't you think you've given me enough? Like a big fancy wedding and a house?!'

'This is more . . . personal,' he said. And reaching into his pocket he took out a blue velvet box, which he handed to Rachel. Tentatively, she opened it. Inside was a string of antique pearls, nestling on a bed of blue silk. Rachel gasped at their beauty.

'They were your mum's,' he said. 'I bought them for her to wear on our wedding day. I thought they could be your *something borrowed*. Not sure I'm quite ready to part with them for good.'

'Oh, Dad,' she whispered. Taking them from the box, she tried to put them around her neck.

'Let me help you,' said Levi, and he clipped the pearls in place. 'They look lovely!'

'Oh God, my mascara is going to run,' said Rachel as she checked her reflection in the hallway mirror. 'Thank you!'

Something flashed across Levi's face then. Rachel would've said it was fear, but fear of what?

'Sweetheart . . .' he said.

'Yes?'

'No matter what happens, y'know, in life, please remember that I'll always love you. And always *have* loved you.'

'Er . . . yes,' she said, confused and wary. A flash, then, a memory of something she couldn't quite place. But it was an overwhelming sense of déjà vu, as if she'd had this conversation before. 'Dad . . . you're not ill or anything, are you?'

He smiled. 'No, no. I just . . . ah, I don't know, just being a soppy old father of the bride on his daughter's wedding day. Now, come on. Chop chop. The car's about to arrive and you're still in your dressing gown!'

57

Levi

It should have been one of the happiest days of his life, taking his daughter to her wedding, the father of the bride, yet Levi was filled not with joy but despair. Because of the face in the congregation that he didn't want but would inevitably have to see.

He tried so hard to be upbeat, engaging in light banter with Rachel, who joked that it was *she* who was meant to be nervous – that *he* was meant to be reassuring *her*! 'We're in reverse, Dad,' she teased him. 'I've never known you look so white, you're almost the same colour as my dress!'

When they arrived at the cathedral there was a flurry of excitement as the maids of honour greeted their dear friend and Reverend Jameson checked that they were all ready to begin. A few photographs were taken, Levi trying his damnedest to smile and banish the turmoil going on inside him.

'Right, then,' said Rachel, taking command. 'Let's do this, shall we?' And she took her father's arm and headed inside to the beautiful sound of Jeremiah Clarke's *Trumpet Voluntary*.

Everyone turned as they began their journey up the long aisle. The hundred and fifty guests took up the seats at the front section of the cathedral – a sea of hats and fascinators and bright, happy colours, smiling faces and cameras, tissues and gasps of delight.

And for a few seconds, Levi thought Jack hadn't gone through with it. That he'd decided not to come. Maybe he'd realized it was for the best. But then as they approached the chancel, where Reverend Jameson greeted them, Levi caught sight of Jack Blythe. He was sitting in the side seats, away from the rest of the guests, discreetly, as promised, looking down at the order of service, for all the world as if he wanted to be invisible. And then, as if sensing that Levi was looking at him, he raised his head and met his gaze, nodding almost imperceptibly.

'Looks like the father of the bride wants to hang on to his daughter a bit longer!' announced the Reverend, and the congregation laughed.

'Dad?' whispered Rachel, drawing him out of his reverie.

'Let's try again,' said Reverend Jameson. 'Who gives this woman to this man?'

'Oh, sorry. Me, yes, I do.'

And again the congregation laughed.

During the ceremony, Levi didn't dare risk looking again at Jack Blythe, and yet he didn't stop thinking about him for the entire time. He could not escape the fact that in another existence, it should be Jack and not he, Levi, walking Rachel up the aisle, giving her away. The father of the bride. It was a ludicrous thought, of course, but he couldn't get it out of his head that he was an impostor. Only once the organ announced the conclusion of proceedings and the happy couple turned to walk down the aisle arm in arm did Levi's eyes wander to where Jack Blythe had been sitting. And saw him still head down, seeming weakened with emotion; a pitiful sight. There was no sense of victory in Levi's heart, just overwhelming guilt at what he'd denied the man now shuffling discreetly towards the cathedral's east door.

2025

58

Linda

'We're a bit like Cagney and Lacey, aren't we?' I say to Brodie as I pass him another fruit pastille. On the road to Inverness, picnic packed, satnav programmed, we are off in search of Rachel McKenna, Levi Norman's daughter.

'Sure, yeah,' he laughs. 'We're both female American police officers working the streets of 1980s New York. The similarities are astounding.'

I hit him playfully on the arm. 'I think your sarcasm is perhaps one of your least endearing qualities,' I say. 'Along with your terrible driving.'

'What? My driving is superb.'

'You are deluded, my dear. You brake too late and you don't check your mirrors enough. Still, I guess that's what comes of living on an island all your life.'

'Harsh, Miss Standish. Very harsh.'

It's so comfortable between us, me and Brodie. Funny really, like we've known each other for years rather than a few weeks.

The phone call with Elaine McAllister had left me excited and hopeful, and Brodie, bless him, seemed equally as enthusiastic. Elaine explained that her mother, Jane, had known Rachel all her life. 'She was like a kind of grandmother to her. When Levi and Diana first moved in next door, mid-eighties I think, she used to babysit. Then when the poor woman passed away, my mum helped out even more. She said Levi was a lost soul – I suspect he might not have coped if it hadn't been for Mum.'

'There are good people in the world,' I said.

'Yes, Mum certainly was one of those. She and Rachel stayed in touch right up to Mum's death. Even after they moved. Her and David, I mean. Rachel was always inviting her round for lunch and family occasions and stuff. Sometimes I even used to feel a bit jealous.' Elaine gave a small laugh. 'As though she'd stolen my mother. Though to be fair, with us living so far away, it was reassuring to know that Rachel was keeping an eye on her.'

'But what about Levi?' I asked. 'Why didn't your mother stay in touch with him?'

'Because she had no idea where he'd gone! It was really upsetting for her, to be honest. I mean, she never had any grudge against him. Said the row that went on between him and Rachel was the family's business, not hers. She took people as she found them, and she was always very fond of Levi. Though if I'm honest, I think she found it hard to forgive – him just disappearing like that. With no explanation.'

Elaine went on to explain that Rachel and David moved house about a year after Levi disappeared. I quickly scribbled down the address. 'Mum reckoned Rachel couldn't live there any more. Made her feel too sad, so she needed a fresh start. Funny, really. I'd have left Inverness if I was her, but she only moved a couple of miles away.'

'Did your mother ever tell you what went on? Y'know, *why* Levi and Rachel fell out?'

'Not really. She was quite discreet, my mother. It just never got discussed, as far as I know, and if my mother knew the reason, well, she didn't tell me. Must've been pretty major though, don't you think?'

And so here we are, me and Brodie, travelling just over the speed limit down the A9. The journey from Boransay to Inverness takes ninety minutes and I must say I am having a lovely, lovely time despite the purpose behind our trip. At the end of it, if we succeed, we will find Rachel Norman and hand her the letter from Levi that she never got to read.

But we will also have to break the news to her of his death.

And to top it all, it's the poor woman's birthday.

In truth, I probably wouldn't be making this journey if Brodie wasn't with me. I think I'd be a little wary of the unknown. But with him by my side, it all feels a lot more doable. And it's a bit of an adventure for both of us. To be fair, he's been involved in Levi's story just as much as me – for longer, in fact, as Levi was technically his customer, albeit a once-a-year patron of the Storrich Arms.

*

'I'm sorry, I don't understand.'

Rachel Norman is in her early forties, medium build, with dark hair like the grainy photos of Diana, her mum, and a small gap between her front teeth. We have been standing on the doorstep of 25 Sutherland Avenue for several minutes. I've explained we're here in connection with Levi Norman and a letter he sent her, which had been returned to sender. She takes the envelope and examines it.

'Why didn't they forward this to me? We moved from there five years ago, but the people who bought it knew the forwarding address.'

'Maybe there are new occupants,' I say, trying to sound cheery, though I'm dreading what has to come next.

'Darling? You okay?' A blond man with a neat beard and bright blue eyes comes out into the hallway. This, I'm presuming, is her husband. She ignores him and looks up at me.

'I still don't understand – if you've got my proper address, why didn't you just post the letter on? And why do *you* have the letter in the first place?' She doesn't wait for an answer, just begins reading. And we stand there, watching her absorb Levi's words, watching her hand go to her chest, as if her heart is beginning to break.

'Would it be possible for us to come in?' I ask gently. 'There are a few things I need to tell you.'

We're sitting in the kitchen, having just told Rachel the news. Her husband, David, is with us. Nice guy, very calming. Wish I could say the same for their dog, who is *huge* – a Weimaraner, I think – and who will not leave me alone. It's really not appropriate to be breaking the news of a parent's death to someone with a large dog literally sticking its nose in where it's not wanted. I catch Brodie trying to hide a smirk as he watches me struggle to divert the dog's attention away from my private areas. Thankfully, David comes to the rescue. 'Oscar! Away!' he says firmly, and the dog lopes off to his bed.

'It must be so difficult for you,' I say, after what feels like an appropriate amount of time.

'I can't believe the funeral's already happened,' Rachel says quietly. 'And I wasn't even there! This is awful, just awful.' She turns to her husband for comfort. He pulls her to him and strokes her hair.

I don't really know where to put myself. By rights we should leave, I know this. But I just feel there is so much still left to tell her – about the will, the ashes . . . Plus, I won't beat around the bush, I want to know what happened.

The awkwardness is interrupted by a small child coming in. He's in pyjamas, sleepy-headed, with tousled dark hair like his mum's. 'Can I have some milk?' he asks quietly, and I'm reminded of my little Zander.

David scoops him up in a big hug. 'You go on up and I'll bring it to you, okay, bub?'

The little boy nods and goes, not remotely interested in the two strangers sat in his kitchen.

'After he left, we never heard from him again,' says David, once his son is out of the room.

'And we spent all those years apart and out of touch . . . all those years where we could have been in each other's lives.' Rachel is crying now, full-on sobs. 'He never even got to meet Ellis.'

David reaches out and holds her again, letting her cry into his chest and be comforted. We all sit there, not knowing where to look. *What a way to start the year.* And I wonder, as I look at Oscar in his bed, whether it would have been best to let sleeping dogs lie. But curiosity has got the better of me. 'You don't have to explain if you don't want to,' I lie. 'Though you might find it helps . . . ?'

2018

59

Rachel

The wedding was spectacular. Rachel hardly drank, barely ate, laughed, cried and loved. The October sun shone bright, the night-time fireworks dazzled, and everyone said it was the best wedding they'd ever been to – including their own! Her father's speech had had everyone in tears and the best man's was hilarious.

The one hundred and fifty guests almost completely comprised their friends and David's family. Rachel tried not to dwell on the fact that the only relative of hers was Levi's cousin from Australia. 'Sorry to be so scant on the family front,' Levi had joked when they'd done the guest list. But what she lacked in relatives, she made up for in friends. All her nursing colleagues from the hospital were there, along with her uni friends from Dundee and neighbours from their old house in Strathan Street. Mrs McAllister, now in her eighties, was also there as a sort of pseudo-grandmother. And David's family more than made up for the lack of her own – they were loud and boisterous and emotional, and they smothered her in love, welcoming her into the bosom of the clan.

'Are you sure you don't mind?' David asked her when they lay on the vast bed of the bridal suite at the end of their glorious wedding day. 'Giving up your surname and becoming Mrs McKenna?'

Secretly, she did mind a bit. She felt she was abandoning Levi, somehow. Maybe because of him being an orphan and so lacking in family. She was all he had, after all.

But Levi seemed adamant that she shouldn't keep her maiden name and so she'd agreed.

'You can always become a *Norman* if you like?' she teased David.

'Ach, that would be a step too far!' He laughed and adopted a strong, growly Scottish accent. 'And a gross insult to ma clan, ye ken!'

They left on the Tuesday after the wedding for their honeymoon in Mauritius. Her friends were there to wave them off at Inverness airport, as were Levi, and David's parents. It was a tearful farewell. Happy tears. Rachel hugged her dad tight and there was such desperation in his response. As if he never wanted to let her go. 'Be safe,' he said, 'be happy.'

'By the time I get back I want to see that travel itinerary of yours all mapped out, okay?' She sounded like *she* was the parent, and he the child. But she felt so sad for him and could not help but worry whether he would be okay with her gone. It was another milestone in their lives. She knew this. And she knew Levi did, too. They just didn't want to acknowledge it out loud. David had asked his parents to 'keep an eye' on Levi. 'They'll invite him over for supper and things, and Dad said he'll get him round for a poker game.'

Rachel knew that Levi wouldn't go, but she appreciated her in-laws' kindness. As she went through the security barrier, she turned one final time to wave. Levi was still watching and waving and smiling, but behind the smile was a deep sorrow, she could tell. And despite the warmth within the airport building, Rachel shivered.

60

Levi

Levi decided to be proactive and take Rachel's advice. Even before he returned home from waving off the newly-weds at the airport, he called in to a travel shop in the city centre. He would indeed begin mapping out his expedition plans and set a departure date for the week after Rachel and David returned from honeymoon. Yes. He would be positive. He might even take up the offer of supper from David's parents on Friday evening.

With absolute determination, Levi put the vision of Jack Blythe at the wedding out of his mind. He would surely leave them alone now.

Rachel phoned him twice whilst they were away. 'Just checking in!' she said, after sharing with him all the excitement of the place they were staying.

'Well, I've been very industrious,' he said. 'I've begun the big clear-out, ready for you and David to move in.'

'But the house is big enough for all of us. You don't have to go, you know that, don't you?'

'Sweetheart,' he said softly, 'I know you mean well, and it's lovely. But you have to live your own life and I need to start the next chapter of mine. I've seen a few possible properties near by, but I'm not going to start the search properly until I'm back from my travels. I'm thinking of doing the entire coastline of Britain.'

'Wow, Dad, that's phenomenal!'

'Yes, probably too ambitious. And it would mean I'd miss out an awful lot in the middle – the colleges of Oxford, the car industry of Coventry,' he laughed at himself. 'Not forgetting Shropshire and mid-Wales . . . and in the meantime, I'm doing a really good job of sorting out the house. I've already burned a load of old paperwork that was up in the attic doing nothing, and I've taken six bags of clothes to the charity shop. It all feels very feng shui.'

This was absolutely true. He'd been brutal in his clear-out, setting aside just a minimum of items to put into storage until he found his new home. He kept one storage case for treasured items such as his own wedding photograph and Diana's 'something borrowed' pearls, which Rachel had returned to him as promised. He was taking life well and truly by the horns.

But that night, Levi slept badly. He dreamed of being chased, of being continually on the run, out of breath, hiding behind trees and cars, down alleyways and lanes, always with a hunter at his back. He knew it was guilt. No matter how he dressed this up, Levi's past was coming back to haunt him. The secret he'd kept all these years had sunk its teeth into him and would not let him go. He woke at half five, bleary-eyed and agitated, and made himself a strong coffee, praying that when the daylight came it would banish his determined demons.

61

Rachel

Did she feel different now that she was married? Yes, she actually thought she did! Sort of safe. Well-founded. Part of a double act. They were such good friends, she and David. Friends with lots of other benefits. Many of which had been explored over and over again on their exciting honeymoon. She didn't feel sad to be home, though. Home looked different now, but in a good way. Home was shared. Home was her and David, David and her.

They got a taxi back from the airport, wanting to take their time and settle home, just the two of them. Their one-bedroom flat by the river had spectacular views over the city and she would miss it when they moved. But Levi's kind gift – that of passing on their former family home – was beyond generous and couldn't possibly be refused. A four-bedroom detached house in one of the leafier suburbs – well, she couldn't ask for anything more. The plan was to move in the following weekend, once they'd had a chance to get into the routine of a working week again, settle into some semblance of 'normal' married life. There was something reassuring about moving back to the home in which she'd spent many of her teenage years. She and David would redecorate of course, make it their own. But it would always be a house full of love, a family home.

David carried her over the threshold of their flat, pretending she weighed a ton, her giggling, him huffing and puffing. They put the kettle on, made steaming mugs of tea and cracked open the chocolate digestives. Then they sat down to open their huge pile of cards and presents, which David's parents had brought round the day before their return, ready for them to open.

It was five o'clock by the time they headed over to Levi's. Both tired, Rachel told David he didn't have to come but he insisted. 'I know you need to check on him,' he said, and Rachel kissed his forehead, 'and so do I.'

'You're so lovely,' she said.

'I know,' David laughed. 'I'm absolutely glorious.'

*

Levi had made a delicious ham, leek and turkey pie. 'With home-made pastry!' he declared. Rachel loved how committed her dad was to his cooking. 'Bet you didn't have this in Mauritius,' he said, laughing.

After supper they showed him their honeymoon photos on David's laptop, and Levi was particularly interested in all the underwater shots they'd taken when snorkelling.

'We've got you a present,' said David, producing a square package wrapped in tissue paper. 'It was done by a local artist.' Levi unwrapped it to reveal an oil painting of the most beautiful tropical fish.

'It's a bluestripe snapper,' said Rachel. 'We just thought the colours were astonishing.'

'I love it,' said Levi. 'Will I need to buy a tank to put it in?' They laughed and Levi looked at it long and hard. 'This will look perfect in my new home.'

'You've found somewhere?' said Rachel excitedly.

'Not yet. When I get back. I'll help you move in on Saturday and then I'm going to head off beginning of next week. Now, who's for some ice-cream?' When Levi got up to clear the plates away, the doorbell rang. 'That might be Mrs McAllister. She mentioned she might pop over,' he said, heading out into the hallway. 'Desperate to hear about the honeymoon, no doubt.'

Rachel took David's hand across the table. 'He seems all right, doesn't he?' she whispered.

'Completely on form,' said David.

And then they heard raised voices coming from the front door.

'You gave me your word. You said that was it, that there'd be no more—'

Rachel flinched, exchanging an anxious look with David.

'I know what I said,' the stranger's voice continued. 'But when I left I thought, why can't she tell me to my face? I should at least give her the chance to meet me and say it to me straight!'

The man's accent was faintly similar to her father's. Rachel had always known Levi was from Cardiff somewhere. But she'd never really noticed his accent before. It was just the way he spoke.

'You can't do this. You can't just turn up at my home and—' and then he paused.

'Look,' the other man was saying gently. 'It's not like she doesn't know about me, she's known for years. And to be honest, it's not been fair on you, having to be the go-between all this time. Seeing her at the wedding I thought would be enough, but it's never gonna be enough, is it? Let's be honest.'

'Please go,' pleaded Levi. 'Now is not convenient.'

'I will. But just let me meet her the once. I need to hear it from her. Come on, mate, have a heart—'

In the kitchen, Rachel and David were struck dumb by what they were hearing, trying to process the exchange. Rachel stood up. David tried to stop her. 'Maybe we should stay out of this—' But Rachel's innate sense of protectiveness where her father was concerned kicked in, and, ignoring her husband's advice, she left the room.

'Dad?' said Rachel, coming into the hallway. Her father was facing someone she didn't recognize. Younger than Levi, but with a face that had seen better days. Levi turned around, looking terrified.

'No, Rachel, don't! Go back, please—'

The other man's face crumpled into tears and he whispered, 'Hello, Rachel.'

She would never forget that image: her father, her beloved father, withdrawing into himself, a broken man, surrendering to what she later discovered was his obligation to confess the truth. She stood, stuck to the spot, looking from the stranger to her father.

'What's going on?'

'Rachel,' her dad said eventually, barely audible.

'Please, Levi. Just say it,' the man said quietly.

'I . . . I can't.'

'Who are you?' she asked, so, so confused.

And then Levi turned to her, his voice cracking with tears, a man destroyed, delivering the bombshell that would define her life from that moment on.

'Rachel, this is Jack Blythe. He's . . . he's your real father.'

She felt dizzy, a loud hissing in her ears. From somewhere behind her David said something, but his voice was muffled. She held out her arm, and the next thing she knew, he was holding her and leading her gently to sit on the stairs. The man at the door didn't move, and Levi sank to the floor, his back against the wall. Everything seemed to be moving in slow motion. Thank God for David. Of the four adults stood in that hallway, he was the only one with an ounce of capability to deal with this most extraordinary of situations.

'Look,' said the man at the door softly. 'I know you never wanted to meet me, and I *do* understand that. I'm just asking you to give me a chance, that's all.'

'What d'you mean, Rachel never wanted to meet you?' asked David. 'What are you talking about?'

'That when she found out, she didn't want to know me, which is fair enough, I—'

He stopped in his tracks, realization crossing his face. He turned to Levi.

'Christ! You didn't tell her, did you? She . . . never knew . . .'

All eyes were on Levi. His voice breaking with pain, he managed, 'I'm sorry . . . I'm so sorry.'

62

Rachel

They hardly slept. During the night, Rachel kept voicing her worries, her questions, and David patiently answered her. How could this be happening? And why, after such a blissful couple of weeks, the most wonderful wedding and beautiful honeymoon, was her life being turned upside down in such a gargantuan way?

This sensation was so alien. She thought about *The Truman Show*, the extraordinary experience of Truman Burbank discovering his life was not what he'd thought it was. That everything he'd believed to be true about his existence was a lie. That's how she felt. Except this – this was real. *The Truman Show* was a film. How could she look at Levi in the same way ever again? She'd always felt so connected to him; that they weren't just father and daughter but really good friends. She'd always looked up to him, always turned to him for advice. He was her rock, her constant, her beloved Daddy. But now she was being asked to see all that in a different light; that it didn't count any more, that none of it had been true. Because he was not to her what she'd always thought he was, and neither was she to him. And yet it wasn't just that he wasn't biologically connected to her, it was that he'd carried this huge lie all of her life. She thought about contacting him, but something was stopping her. She felt so confused.

And now they were on their way to the Lochmuir Hotel, where Jack Blythe had told them he was staying. The night before, when David had advised him to leave, Jack had conceded without complaint, but he'd begged Rachel to come and talk to him the next day. She'd been in no state to respond, and David had said they might come, but he was making no promises.

'I think I should meet him on my own, first. You can wait in the car. We don't know anything about this man and—'

'You mean my father. He's my father. Apparently.' Rachel couldn't hide the bitterness in her voice. When they arrived at the hotel, Jack was outside, smoking. He didn't see them at first and Rachel had a moment to take in the sight of him. The night before had been such a blur – his appearance had barely registered with her. He was in his fifties, she guessed, but he had not aged well. His cheeks were ruddy and his eyes a little bloodshot. He was clean-shaven, but his hair was thinning and he smoked nervously, as if the harder he sucked on his rollie, the calmer he would become. His clothes were clean but creased, and his trainers had seen better days. He looked up as they approached and quickly extinguished his cigarette.

'Ah, sorry, I tried resisting but I'm that nervous!' He held out his hand to David, and Rachel could tell David was reluctant to shake it, but, ever the gentleman, he did. Then he turned to Rachel, open-armed. Thankfully, David stepped in.

'Let's take this slowly, shall we, Jack? How about we go inside? Get a cup of tea.'

Jack obliged, and they found a table in the corner of the hotel's coffee shop. A waitress came over and they ordered drinks. David paid. Rachel couldn't think of anything to say. She watched this man, her own flesh and blood, as he talked nonsense to her husband. Nervous, pointless small talk. And all the while she tried to absorb the sight of him.

What freaked her out the most was his laugh. Not just because it felt so inappropriate for the situation, but because it revealed the physical confirmation that he was indeed her father – the small gap between his top front teeth. Identical to her own. She looked so much like him; it was glaringly obvious.

In stark contrast, she now realized she looked nothing like Levi. But why had she never noticed it before? Had she just assumed she took after her mother?

'I'm sorry you had to find out this way,' said Jack, his hands grasped tightly around his coffee cup. 'He said he'd told you about me, see. Years ago.'

'Yes, Levi explained,' said David.

This was an exaggeration. After Jack had left the night before, the three of them had sat in silence for some time, until eventually Levi uttered just a handful of words. 'I should have told you,' he said, his voice flat and devoid of any emotion. 'But I knew I would lose you if I did.'

'That wasn't your decision, though, was it?' Rachel had responded, unable to look him in the eye. Moments later she said she wanted to go home, the subject left undiscussed.

And now here they were, in the company of her biological father, her life dismantled in the space of twelve hours.

Jack began a rambling monologue, telling them how he'd met Diana when he was just twenty and working in Ireland.

'She was an absolute cracker, your ma,' he said, turning to Rachel. 'Them Irish eyes were smilin', too right. Had me from the moment I met her, she did.'

Jack Blythe was not the most eloquent of men, but he was earnest, and had a rough honesty in the way he spoke. 'There are things you need to know about me. Difficult things, like.' Rachel and David sat in silence as Jack told his story. He pulled no punches, told them of his infidelity to Diana, the drink-driving the night Rachel was born, the pensioner who had died and the six years he'd spent in prison. He told them he was lost when he came out and ended up back inside for another two years on a charge of GBH. 'It was a fight that went wrong. I'm not proud of myself.'

Rachel couldn't believe that this man sat next to her drinking coffee, whose life was so alien to hers, actually shared her DNA. 'I want you to know everything there is to know about me,' he said tenderly. 'I was not a good person back then. Levi will tell you things about me, and they'll be true.'

'What things?' asked David.

'How I behaved. I wasn' just unfaithful to your mother, Rachel. I . . .' He hesitated, clearly finding it painful to confess, but clearly needing to, too. 'You need to know that I hit her.'

'Jesus.' David sat back, shocked. Rachel was too stunned to speak.

'Yes. It in't an easy thing to hear, I knows that. An' I can't pretend it didn' happen – can't cover it up. But I can tell you, hand on heart, that that is not who I am now. An' I'd like to think I've made up for it over time.'

'How?' asked Rachel, desperately trying to process what she was being told.

It was the first time Rachel had been able to find her voice, and both David and Jack looked startled when she spoke.

'Well,' Jack began, 'one of the good things about being inside the second time was that I started going to AA meetings. I think that probably saved my life, to be honest. Been sober thirty-one years next month.'

'That's some achievement,' said David.

'It's a cliché, but it really is one day at a time.' Jack paused. 'I don't know how much you know about twelve-step programmes, but a lot of it is about being accountable for past wrongs and making amends for them. So when I got released, I knew I wanted to find you, Rachel. And Diana, of course. And I wanted to say sorry . . .'

'Rachel's mother passed away a long time ago,' said David. 'When Rachel was three.'

'I know.'

'Who told you?' Rachel felt uneasy that this stranger seemed to know so much about her life and yet she'd only become aware of his existence in the last few hours.

'Like I said, I tried finding you when I got out. Would've been in '92. And I managed to track Levi down through his old place of work. They passed on my letter.'

'And he replied?' asked David.

'Yes.'

'Oh my God,' Rachel said, barely audible. 'And said what?'

There was silence as Jack appeared to be choosing his words carefully. 'You have to understand that at that time, I didn't even know your mother and Levi were married. I only got in touch with him because he'd been living in the flat above when me and Diana were together. I thought he might have some info about where she'd gone back then. I had no idea he'd gone *with* her.'

'In 1992 I was nine,' Rachel said.

David squeezed her hand, sensing her shock at what she was hearing.

'What did Levi tell you?' David asked.

Jack cleared his throat, seemingly embarrassed at having to expose Levi's behaviour. 'He denied knowing anything about either of you. Said he moved away with work and never stayed in touch.'

Rachel could not believe what she was hearing. That the man she had known as her father all her life – the kind, honest, wise man whom she'd respected and loved, was not the person she'd thought he was. She felt sick at the thought.

'But that still doesn't answer the question,' said David. 'If Levi denied knowing anything about Rachel or Diana, how did you find out?'

Jack sighed and took a big gulp of coffee, as if seeking support in the bottom of the china cup.

'Okay, so after that first reply I sort of gave up. Thought I'd exhausted all the avenues, kinda thing. I didn't stop thinking about you, don't get me wrong. I just didn't know where else to look. Don't forget, people didn't use the internet like they do these days. It was all quite new back then. But years later, that started to change, didn't it? Facebook an' all that. Friends Reunited . . . ? Births and Deaths register online. Well, I had a mate who was into all that stuff and he helped me out. He could look up all these things.'

David nodded. 'And you looked up Diana.'

'Yes. I knew *her* name, didn't I? And I knew she'd have had the baby in the CRI – y'know, the Infirmary. So I had some details, and I got this mate to check out the records. And that's when I found out about you, Rachel: I found out I had a daughter.' Jack's voice choked with emotion when he said this, and he cleared his throat before going on. 'Your birth certificate was amended in 1984. Levi Norman is down as your father. But it should really be my name on there.' There was a hint of petulance when he said this. 'My mate, he found out they was married. In Inverness. And he found out Diana had died too . . . All this was happenin' around 2001 – you'd have turned eighteen by then and I thought I had to try again to find you. Now that I had all this info.'

Jack took a deep breath and carried on.

'I managed to get Levi's work address and I went to Inverness. I wasn't angry or nothin'. I said I knew about him and Diana – I mean, I understood why he'd lied, course I did. But I still wanted to see you. To meet you. That was all I cared about, the rest was behind us, like. Stupid of me, really, I just assumed that you'd always known about me. Never questioned it for one second. And he didn't say otherwise, so when I gave him the letter to give you . . .'

'The letter I never read—' said Rachel.

Jack continued, barely audible, 'He threatened me with legal action if I made contact ever again.'

'Christ!' said David. 'I can't quite believe all this.'

'I did make contact,' said Jack. 'I came to your wedding.'

'What?' Rachel was incredulous.

'Stayed at the side, like, saw you make an honest woman of her!' He was joking, but the humour didn't land and even Jack didn't seem to have his heart in his smile. 'Yeah. Just one of them milestones. I reckoned I'd missed enough of you growing up – your wedding was a big one—'

'Oh my God, you were there!'

Rachel shuddered. There was something so disturbing about hearing all this.

Jack stood up and put on his jacket. 'It's a lot to take in, I know. And I need a fag. Give me five minutes, yeah.'

'You okay?' asked David, putting his arm around her shoulders.

'How could Levi have lied like that?'

'Raych, you're calling him "Levi", listen to yourself. He's still your dad, y'know, he's the one who's brought you up.'

Rachel shook her head. 'It's too much, too much.'

When Jack came back in, he seemed more grounded, serious even. His gallows humour was no longer on show. 'Look,' he said quietly. 'I'm not stupid, y'know. I can guess what you think of me – you two, you're obviously doin' all right, you talk posh, you look posh – and me, I'm just scrapin' by, tryin' to stay on the straight and narrow, not a lot goin' for me. But I'm not a bad person. Not any more. You have to believe that.'

He didn't wait for an answer. Just reached into his pocket and took out an envelope. 'I've written my number down, and my address if you felt like comin' down Cardiff. I know it's a schlepp, but I'd be made up if you came for a visit. I know we gotta take things slow an' that.'

She nodded. 'I'm sorry. For what you've been through.'

Her words seemed to floor him, and he swallowed nervously.

'Er, cheers. That's . . . that means the world. But, y'know, don't be hard on Levi Norman. He's given you more than I ever could. He done good, like. Bringin' you up.'

They stared at each other. 'Can I . . . can I have a cwtch?'

'A what?'

'A cwtch. A hug.'

'No,' Rachel said suddenly, backing away. 'Sorry, I didn't mean to offend, it's just—'

'Probably a bit soon, Jack,' David intervened. 'Give it time, yeah?'

'Yeah, I get that. Ball's in your court, like.' And he handed Rachel the envelope.

Rachel stood up and David followed, taking her cue. There was something in the envelope. A photograph. A Polaroid.

'It's the only one I have,' Jack said quietly. 'My mate gave it me. I want you to have it. Whatever happens from now, I want you to know that me and your mum . . . there were some good times. Not many, I admit. But some.'

He stared at the two of them, uncertain of the territory, then turned and walked away. Rachel watched him go, then looked down at the photograph. Two young people – Jack Blythe with a shock of dark hair, slimmer, younger, his arm around the young woman she recognized from Levi's photos: her mother, Diana. Heavily pregnant, laughing, both wearing Christmas cracker hats, sitting at a table weighed down with the remains of a turkey dinner, in the company of a couple of friends. It looked like they were in a pub. On the bottom of the Polaroid it said, *Xmas 1982*. An unknown part of her little-known mother's life.

She looked at the pregnancy bump and said, 'I was there. I'm in this photo.' How strange this all felt.

'Can we go home now?' she asked David, and he took her hand.

63

Levi

A week had passed since Jack Blythe turned up on his doorstep. David called the next day to explain about the meeting planned at the Lochmuir Hotel and that maybe it would be a good idea to give Rachel a bit of space. 'So that she can make sense of it all,' he'd said, not unkindly. Levi completely agreed, and was glad to be left alone, mainly because he couldn't handle the immense shame he felt at deceiving them all: his daughter, his wife and Jack Blythe. He'd only met the man a handful of times and owed him nothing. But he'd deprived him of his chance to know his daughter.

    He'd tried to convince himself that what he'd done had been for the best – that he was protecting Rachel from being hurt. That despite Diana's dying wish that he should tell Rachel about Jack, Levi had felt he knew better: that Diana's intentions, although well-meant, were misguided. And probably heavily influenced by the morphine. Yes, this was what he'd told himself over the years. But now in his heart he knew he'd only done it for the most selfish of reasons: because he didn't want to lose his precious, precious child to another man.

    After three days, he'd phoned her. It rang out and the voicemail kicked in, but he chose not to leave a message. The same thing happened the next day, then the next. 'Darling, please call me. I just need to know you're okay.' Levi kept telling himself that it would all be all right; that nothing could erase the thirty-five years they'd spent as father and daughter, and that she just needed more time. That she would understand why he did what he did.

Levi called David, too. He was sympathetic but non-committal. All he'd say was that Rachel would get in touch when she felt ready.

To distract himself he spent his days packing up his things ready for storage before his trip. He was going through the motions. The thought of travelling right now held little joy for him. Still, it gave him something to do whilst he waited to hear from Rachel.

The clear-out he'd begun when the newly-weds were on honeymoon had resulted in a grand-scale diminishing of his possessions. On the sixth day, he found himself surrounded by packing cases and feeling terribly lonely. And it struck him how much his bringing up Rachel single-handedly since she was three had not only been a joyful privilege but had filled the void left in his life after Diana's death. He was jolted out of his sad reverie by the sound of the front door opening, and Rachel's voice calling out to him.

'Hello?'

He rushed out into the hallway and they stood facing each other. 'I'm so glad you came,' he said, swallowing down unwelcome tears at the sight of her.

He wanted to reach out and hold her, his little girl. How many thousands of times in thirty-five years had he comforted her, cuddled her, reassured her? And yet now she stood before him with a defensive body language that silently warned him off going anywhere near her personal space. He wanted her to move through into the kitchen, just like she always did when she called by; to flick on the kettle, to open the cupboard and take out the biscuits. But she just stood there, stock-still.

'I've spoken to him a lot these past couple of days,' she said. 'He gave me this.' She handed him the Polaroid Jack had given her.

Levi felt sick, suddenly filled with the rage that injustice brings.

'D'you know where he was the same night this was taken? With his bit on the side. His *lover*.' Even as the words came out he realized how petty it sounded, like he was in some sort of playground argument. But instead of shutting up, he was like a runaway train; he couldn't stop himself. 'The woman he was with, she was there that night. Did you know that? The night he *killed* someone. That's the sort of person he is! A killer!' He knew he sounded melodramatic and needy and he hated the person he'd become in that moment.

'But he's paid the price for that. Hasn't he?' Her voice was quiet but firm.

Levi nodded. She was right, after all.

'And he came to the wedding,' she said, her voice shaking.

'Yes.'

'Hidden away like some sordid little secret because *you* decided he shouldn't be part of my life.'

A silence ensued and then she spoke again. 'I'm struggling to understand why you would do it? To keep me from knowing – to not let me make up my own mind.'

Levi shrugged, helpless.

'Was it my mother? Did she . . . I don't know, did she say something? Did she tell you to keep it all from me?'

Levi raised his head and met Rachel's gaze. He knew now that he could save himself, at least lessen the pain, if he just told one more lie. It was within his grasp – to redeem their relationship, to put the blame on Diana so that Rachel could at least understand a motive. But he also knew he had told enough lies now. He'd hidden the truth for all these years, and it was time to be honest. He took a deep breath.

'Please understand,' he whispered, 'the thought of losing you was too much, and I couldn't take the risk.'

'You haven't answered me, though.'

He bowed his head again, shame flooding his body. 'Your mother wanted me to tell you. When you were old enough to understand.'

'And did you promise her you would?'

'Yes,' he whispered, unable to look at her.

Rachel stayed calm. 'But you chose not to.'

'I chose not to.'

She nodded, as if making a decision. 'Well, you wouldn't have lost me. Not then. But you have now.'

They both stood in silence until Levi found his voice.

'I'm so ashamed.'

'As you should be!' she shouted, tears in her eyes. 'Playing God like that! Stopping him from seeing me when he'd searched for me all that time, pretending you knew nothing about me! It's appalling. Breaking your promise to my mother. You kept it from me *all* my *life*.'

She turned to go, heading straight for the front door. 'I don't know who you are!'

'I'm your dad,' he whispered and she turned to face him, her hand on the door.

'That's not true, though, is it? None of it is *true*. Our whole relationship is a lie.' And with that she left, slamming the door behind her.

2025

64

Linda

'I was so angry with him,' Rachel says, almost to herself as she recounts what happened. 'I really did feel betrayed – you *do* understand that, don't you?'

'Yes,' says Brodie, unexpectedly joining in the conversation. 'Betrayal is a bugger.'

'But I should have been kinder,' she adds, close to tears. 'He deserved better from me. Because he was the sweetest, loveliest soul and I hurt him so much. I sent him horrible texts, changed my number, was just so awful to him, so he couldn't call me!'

'Hey, come on now,' comforts David. 'You can't keep beating yourself up for this. There was nothing you could've done.'

'Yes there was! If I'd listened to him – if I'd just given him more of a chance – then he wouldn't have gone, would he? I can't bear thinking how rejected he was, how bad I made him feel . . .' Rachel sobs, and David holds her tightly, kissing the top of her head.

'You should know,' he says to me and Brodie, 'that *that* day was the last time Rachel ever saw Levi.'

We sit there in silence for a couple of minutes. I catch Brodie's eye and we exchange a look of incredulity at what we're hearing. I sense that, like me, he's desperate to know how things turned out the way they did. But we can hardly nudge Rachel into explaining. We have to let things unfold in their own time. And eventually they do.

'It was a tricky time for me,' David says. 'My main concern was Rachel in all of this and I didn't want to get in the way of what could be a relationship with her real – or should I say, her *biological* father, if that was what she wanted. But on the other hand, I didn't want her to destroy the bond she had with Levi. So I left things for a couple of days, took my cue from Rachel and whatever she wanted to do. She said she wanted to go to Cardiff, didn't you? You know, to spend more time with Jack, get to know him a bit.'

'Which we did,' says Rachel. 'And it was fine, it was good! It took a while, don't get me wrong. I mean, he was not a nice person when he knew my mum.'

David raises his eyebrows when Rachel says this and I wonder if there's a lot they're not telling me. She throws a glance his way. 'But it was years ago. People need the chance to change and I genuinely believe he has. He's okay, he tries his best now.'

'You say *now*,' I interrupt. 'Does that mean you're still in touch?'

'What?' Rachel looks confused, 'Oh, yes. Yes, we're still in regular contact. He visits once a year, we go down there a couple of times, but it's all very polite.'

'Yes, the relationship is sort of *tainted*,' explains David. 'Because in gaining Jack, she lost Levi.'

'And Levi was my real dad,' she whispers, and the tears begin afresh. 'And I never got to tell him that.'

David takes his wife's hand. 'It was so difficult for Rachel. Because of Levi going like he did. And never getting the chance to sort things out – none of it needed to have happened.'

He goes on to explain how they'd returned from Cardiff only to find that Levi was no longer there. He'd left a note in the house, telling them he'd gone away on his trip and that it would give them all some distance from what had happened.

'I was glad to begin with, if I'm honest. I didn't want to see him, wasn't ready to forgive. But time passed and I calmed down, started to see the situation more objectively. And I thought, okay, when Dad comes back we can talk. Resolve everything. But we never got the chance to do that. Because he never *did* come back,' Rachel adds sadly.

'We received a letter – the postmark was Glasgow – telling us that he was fine and safe and well, but that he just couldn't forgive himself for all that had happened,' says David, 'and that maybe it was best if we just forgot about him.'

Rachel gets angry. 'I mean, how ludicrous! How on earth did he expect us to do that? And how could I ever apologize to him? How could I ever get the chance to say sorry to him, to be his daughter again . . . he took that chance away from me, and now it's too late.'

It's all horribly sad. I can understand Rachel's frustration, but Levi, too – how terrible he must have felt to cut himself off from his only daughter and opt for such a lonely, isolated existence. All because he couldn't come to terms with what he'd done. The forgiveness was there. It just came too late. And maybe it wouldn't have done any good anyway. Because if Levi couldn't forgive himself, what use was Rachel's empathy?

I wish I'd known this man. I think I would have liked him. A lot. But what a terribly sad conclusion to their tale; what a sorry waste of life and love.

2018

65

Levi

It was a cash sale for a two-bedroom cottage on the Outer Hebridean island of Storrich. Levi had never heard of the place before. And he thought this was a good thing. To have no connection, no expectation, no acquaintances – a completely clean slate. He'd seen the advert online – a website selling simple homes in faraway places. The name of the cottage was Beannach Lodge: *after the nearby little lochan, Loch Beannach*. He bought it on spec – had no survey done – and paid up front. From what the estate agent told him, there would be little to do to the place, it having been well maintained by the previous owners, who'd rented it out as a holiday let. This was part of the appeal to Levi – the last thing he wanted was to have to get into conversations with carpenters and electricians. Though, considering the island was just under three hundred in population, maybe there weren't any there anyway.

He loved the fact that the nearest neighbours to Beannach Lodge were a good two miles away and that its 'centre' comprised a pub, a post office, a chandlery and a grocery shop. The less he had to be involved with anyone, the better. There was also a kirk, of course. Though he wouldn't be attending. He wanted nothing to do with God, either.

Because Levi wanted to hide.
Levi wanted to forget.
Levi wanted to be invisible.

It had been fortuitous that in anticipation of his previously planned road trip he'd spent months offloading and divesting himself of his possessions and handing over the house to Rachel. It meant he could literally leave behind the life he'd had. Leave behind the daughter who was no longer his. She'd been right – her words were still ringing in his head – *you've lost me now*. He'd never get rid of that pain, but at least if he never saw her again he could let her move on and stop the pain from getting worse.

On the day he left Inverness, he packed up his car with all the belongings he felt he couldn't live without, including the urn containing Diana's ashes, the photographs of the two of them on their wedding day, his bluestripe snapper fish painting and the box of mementoes he'd treasured over the years. He wrote a note to Rachel and David telling them he thought it best if he gave them some space in light of what had happened. He wept as he sealed the envelope, leaving it next to two sets of keys to the house. Shutting the door behind him, he didn't look back.

Next, he travelled to Glasgow, to the estate agent's office for an official handover of the keys and a signing of the paperwork. Whilst in the city he posted another letter to Rachel, knowing that the Glaswegian postmark would help disguise his ultimate whereabouts. In the letter he said he completely understood that she would want to build a relationship with Jack Blythe and that he didn't want to stand in her way. But even as he wrote the words he felt sick to his soul: as if he was giving away a part of himself that he could never reclaim.

When Levi disembarked the ferry at the little harbour in Storrich, the clank of the iron ramp as the car wheels ran over it seemed to signal his arrival like a welcoming gong. There were only three other cars and a post van in front of him. And in the harbour itself, a handful of fishing boats bobbed jauntily on the water. Not glamorous sailing boats, but working vessels that had seen better days. This place was certainly the opposite of a hubbub.

The estate agent had sent him a simple map. It would be difficult to get lost – there was just the one main road around the island and he knew he had to head west, then turn up a less-trodden single track. It took him twenty minutes without passing another vehicle to arrive at Beannach Lodge.

He climbed wearily out of the car, stood, and looked around him. The sun was still quite high in the sky and the light danced gently on the glossy seaweed cloaking the rocks just a stone's throw away. He turned around, taking in the full panoramic view. He couldn't see another house for miles.

What hit him the most was the tranquillity. Not the silence – it certainly wasn't silent: a gang of oystercatchers and curlews called loudly to one another overhead and the seals a little way up the shore joined in the coastal cacophony. It was just calm. Nourishing. He watched two herons in flight glide elegantly above the water and land on a far-off promontory. They spread their wings, drying their feathers in the hazy winter sun. The sight of them was unexpectedly comforting, along with the gentle lulling of the waves breaking politely on the shore. As if he was being reassured that he'd made the right decision in coming here. Closing his eyes, Levi took in some cool, refreshing breaths of Hebridean air and told himself it would all be all right.

As he made his way back towards his new home, he kept his eyes peeled for a 'perfect' pebble amongst the different shades of grey and pink and green beneath his feet. It was something he and Rachel had always done years ago on the many beaches they had tramped together. She would find one and hold it out to him. 'Look at this one, Daddy!' And he'd smile at her glee in finding it, never pointing out the tiny bump or the crack or the crevice. Or telling her that none of them could ever actually be perfect, because nothing in life ever was.

The cottage was open – the estate agent had told him of the zero crime rate on the island and how nobody locked their doors. He'd been expecting it to feel damp inside, but instead it was surprisingly welcoming – and clean. There were logs ready to be lit in the log burner and a list of instructions relating to the property. Levi stood in the doorway, looking out at the sea beyond.

If circumstances had been different, this could have been the start of a two-week family holiday in a beautiful part of the world. Instead, it was the start of a new life. At the age of sixty-seven. Or maybe this was just the return to who he used to be. Who he was before Diana. A solitary soul living a solitary life. Maybe this was what he was always destined to be.

He went back into the kitchen and sat, his head in his hands, finally absorbing the magnitude of what he'd done. The second time he'd run away. The first time he'd done it for the love of Diana; this time it was for the love of Rachel. It was right that he was here. But it was also desperately sad that his life had come to this. Taking in a deep breath, he wept for what he'd lost, and surrendered to the overwhelm of stark, searing grief.

2025

66

Linda

We leave the house both feeling drained. It wasn't really the conclusion I'd been hoping for. I gave Rachel the keepsakes box, but didn't want to wait around for her to look through it – that felt intrusive. And I explained to her about Levi's and Diana's ashes and that they were being safely stored at Murray's Undertakers in Boransay, for reclaiming when she felt ready. I omitted telling her about Lena Druinich and the mislaying of the urn – it didn't feel necessary. Plus, I would be so embarrassed in the retelling.

Neither I nor Brodie fancy a long car journey straight away. 'I think I need to blow the cobwebs away,' I say. Reliving Levi's story has had a profound effect. It's brought up all sorts of sorrow, and I don't like feeling like this. Brodie looks at his watch.

'We could have our lunch on the beach at Nairn? Only half an hour or so from here.'

'Don't you see enough of the sea in Storrich?' I joke.

'True. Tell you what, it's not that cold and the sun is shining, let's go for a walk along the Ness, have lunch, then maybe go see a film.'

'You're lovely, you are,' I say, and I take Brodie's hand and kiss him.

'I know,' and he smiles back at me.

'But you are a terrible driver,' I add.

'Am not.'
'So are.'

Dozens of joggers run past us as we sit on a slightly damp bench munching chicken sandwiches and left-over Christmas cake. We have a wonderful New Year's Day view of the city centre and the River Ness. This plethora of joggers I put down to people's New Year's resolutions and the obsession to get fit. All that 'new year, new you' mentality that the magazines, diet clubs and gyms capitalize upon so well. 'I wonder how long they'll keep it up,' I say through a mouthful of cake.

'I've never seen the appeal,' says Brodie, taking a swig of flask coffee.

'Me neither. All that jiggling.'

'Terrible for the knees.'

'Yep.'

We share a smile – the smile of the fitness-shy – and carry on people-watching, river-watching, contentedly scoffing away in both senses of the word.

'Do *you* have any resolutions for the year ahead?' I ask Brodie.

'Good God, no. Don't believe in them. All they do is set you up to feel a failure. If you're going to do something, then just do it. You don't need a date in the diary to be granted permission.'

'Very true!'

'How about you?'

'Well, I always make a vague promise to myself to lose weight. Every year I think, *this will be the year*. Never happens,' I laugh. 'I've tried more diets than I've had hot dinners, which is an ironic metaphor now I come to think of it.'

Brodie nods. 'I thought you weren't bothered about your weight.'

It's strange when he says this, I suppose because it's an out-and-out acknowledgement that he's noticed I'm fat. But there's also something reassuring about the lack of judgement in his observation. And I'm disarmed. And rather than doing my usual self-defensive comedy routine, I find myself being unexpectedly honest with him.

'Publicly, no, I'm not bothered. I'll wave the flag for us big girls till the cows come home and stand up to the fat-shamers like some sort of body-positive Boudicca. But inside? I can't bear it. I often feel really self-conscious and it's so uncomfortable at times. And then there's the theme-park fear.'

'The what?'

'Going on theme-park rides: the terrifying fear that I won't fit into the seat and they'll ask me to leave. Hasn't happened yet, but I'm always a couple of pounds away from public shame!' I laugh awkwardly.

He doesn't laugh back. Just takes my hand and gently says, 'I don't like thinking of you being fearful.' His compassion floors me and I cough too loudly, trying to clear my throat.

'I can't believe I'm telling you all this,' I mumble.

And I can't. Why am I making this humiliating confession to a man I'm attracted to and who I know is attracted to me? I want to keep it that way. Hardly sexy, going on about my lack of self-esteem. But his empathy and his tenderness are quite hypnotic, and everything comes tumbling out. We're both looking at the river, not facing each other. Maybe that makes it easier to confide.

'The number of people who've told me how *easy* it would be to lose weight. The number of times I've seen online adverts like, *Finally, the answer to your weight-loss quandary*. And all these thin people who think they know best, think they know how to solve it all. Eat more of this, eat less of that, move more, move less, eat this bar, drink this juice, medicate! Medi*tate*!!'

'Have you ever tried counselling?' he asks.

I'd been expecting him to laugh, and when he doesn't I'm a bit thrown by his seriousness, his refusal to collude with me in my self-deprecation.

'Oh yes, a few times. Including CBT and aversion therapy. That was fun – had to imagine a chocolate bar like a piece of carpet. Think about what makes me want to eat certain stuff . . . Thing is, I just find food . . . so . . .'

'Comforting,' he states.

'Yes.' And then I hesitate. 'Plus, it stops me from thinking. About things. Certain . . . things.'

He nods and pauses for a moment, as if digesting what I've said along with his picnic lunch. 'You don't have to tell me,' he says softly.

I stay silent. I feel like I'm venturing into very dangerous territory.

'But I know there's something. Saw it in you the first evening we met.'

And smack! I am suddenly hijacked by an overwhelming desire to cry. I try to speak, to explain. Nothing comes out.

He reaches over and squeezes my hand. 'It's okay,' he whispers. And we just sit there, as the determined joggers run by, some looking more depressed than others. I wait for this wave to pass. But it won't budge. I feel as if it will burst out of me, this behemoth pain that I've lived with all these years. I take deep breaths, willing it away.

'I never, *ever* talk about it! About . . . her,' I whisper, my voice strangled by emotion. And here I am, with a man I've known just a matter of weeks, on the verge of letting my heart crack open and spill the seething, broken mass of sorrow that lives within it. I splutter and I nearly choke. And the tears pour from my eyes, my chest aches and my nose runs. It's not a good look. But I do not speak. I do not tell him.

No.

'I can't,' I whisper. And he nods, then puts his arm around me, pulling me in to him and kissing the top of my head. 'I must look such a mess.'

He turns to me then, and takes my face in his hands. 'Yes, you do,' he says. 'But a bold, beautiful mess.'

He kisses me, oh, such a soft, gentle kiss, bursting with affection. And I'm torn between wishing I could be anywhere else except here right now and wanting to stay like this for good.

67

Linda

There are a thousand vivid images of her still living in my head. So many joyous, beauteous moments. Some have faded over the years but others are as clear as crystal water. One in particular, not long after her third birthday. It was one of those hazy May days and I'd picked her up from nursery and we'd had a picnic in the garden, just me and her; Doug was at work. And after our sandwiches and our orange squash, I suggested we make a daisy chain. She looked confused for a moment and then I realized why, as she held the little white-and-yellow flower between her thumb and forefinger. 'This not Daisy,' she said, with that quizzical little frown on her precious forehead.

'That's a Daisy Flower,' I explained. '*You* are a Daisy Angel.' And after that it became our special name for her. Daisy Angel.

And of course there are the baby memories that came before that: the first time she smiled, the first time she giggled, the thrill, in fact, of her making any sound whatsoever. Or when she rolled over, or when she found herself on all fours, or in the perfect yoga 'child pose', gearing up to start crawling, not quite knowing what she was doing or how this new form of travel was opening up to her, sticking out her left leg as she moved, delight on her face as she headed straight for her daddy.

The first time she said *I love you Mummy* I thought I would explode with bliss. The joy she brought. The pure, unadulterated, heart-bursting happiness every moment of her existence injected into our lives. For three precious years – three precious years, two months, one week and a day, to be precise.

All gone within the space of a few hours.

Vanished. Deleted. As if she'd never even been.

There have been fleeting moments since when I wonder if I imagined her.

It's not called cot death. They told me she was too old for it to be cot death. No, Daisy's was – in my view – clumsily acronymed to SUDC or Sudden Unexplained Death in Childhood. I remember thinking it a very inelegant term. Difficult to say, impossible even. I don't know why I focused so hard on something so irrelevant. What could be elegant about death? Why did I need a pronounceable term? How would that ease even a minuscule drop of the torture I was enduring?

In the aftermath, when they thought I could hear them (I couldn't), they tried telling me there could well have been a connection with the seizure she'd had some weeks earlier, but when I screamed at them, at Doug, at anyone who came near me, that it was my fault, they all said the same thing: *there was nothing you could have done*. I had tucked her up that night, read her her favourite story, and when she was just drifting off, her eyes half-closed, I'd kissed her goodnight and whispered, *I love you, Daisy Angel*. And that was that. She never woke up. She was no more.

And even five years later, when we were blessed with darling Struan and I thought the gaping hollow would finally be filled, I realized it never could be. It just became easier to hide, to cover up, to deny. And as long as no one mentions her or asks what she was like, I am fine. I am happy. I can carry on as if the worst thing that can happen to a parent never happened to me.

I have my little traditions – things I do to keep her memory alive. It's not that the memory of her will fade, but when I act out my rituals, it reinforces my connection with her, somehow. I visit the grave just once a year, on the anniversary of her death. Strange that we say the word 'birthdays' but not 'deathdays'. Struan comes with me, and Doug sometimes, though I think he has his own private little remembrances. I don't stay long, and I don't talk out loud and I don't take cuddly toys or other child-related emblems. Each to their own, of course, but I think I'd find it too tragic to go back a year later and see a weatherbeaten teddy bear left in solitude at Daisy's gravestone. I just pull up any weeds, tidy round the edges and lay a big bunch of giant daisies. And tell her how much I miss her.

The other thing I do, on her birthday, is go to a beach an hour's drive away, where I choose a nice pebble which I take home. I write her name on it and the year, and I add it to the rest of the pebbles, collected in a special basket. It's a way of marking the time that has passed since she went. To date I have thirty pebbles, soon to be thirty-one.

My darling Daisy Angel.

68

Linda

Zander and Struan have been gone two months already. Two months! How does it happen? How do the days just speed up like that as you get older? I mean, I'm under no illusion about stopping the hands of Time and I feel very grateful that I'm not someone desperate to halt the ageing process with Botox and fillers and implants and what have you – knock yourself out, if that's your thing. Me? I'm happy to sag in all the right places and keep smiling throughout, crow's feet, grey hair, the whole shebang. And one of the bonuses of being overweight is that fat flesh wrinkles less easily. No, it's just, I wish Time could go at least at half the speed it does.

To be fair to Struan, he's done a marvellous job of keeping in touch. Me, him and Zander Facetime at least twice a week and visit every fortnight. It's not the same, of course it's not, but I really do appreciate the effort he makes.

Last time they visited I tried to ascertain Struan's happiness level since the move. I can tell when he's just putting on a brave face and, at the risk of annoying him, I sat him down with a lemon drizzle and made him tell me how the land was lying. Because I'd noticed he'd stopped mentioning the possibility of a reunion between himself and Lauren.

'Has something happened?' I asked, and he sighed. So I knew my instincts were right.

'I don't know if you know this, but when me and Lauren first got together, she was sort of on the rebound. Her old boyfriend had dumped her after a really long relationship.'

'How long?'

'They'd been together since school.'

'Ah, I see. The old *first love* situation.'

'Yeah. Exactly. Anyway, she stayed friends with him – absolutely convinced me that that was all it was, even arranged nights out with him and his wife.'

'Oh my God, when I was babysitting? Who is this guy?'

'Kenny Robinson.'

I sank my teeth into a slice of the cake, as if by swallowing something sweet I could push down my anger at the deception of my son's wife with this man. 'I remember him!' I said. 'Shortish, with a beard, big Billy Connolly fan?'

'That's him.'

'Oh, love. So she had you being *all friends together* whilst behind your back . . .'

Struan shook his head. 'Actually, Mum, to be fair to Lauren—' *Oh, here we go,* I thought. *Jumping to her defence, as usual. Even now!* I looked at him in disbelief. 'At the start, that's what it was. We *were* all just friends. But it turns out Lauren has been, y'know . . . for the past eighteen months.'

I tried to process all this. Her behaviour, the way she'd made out that Struan was her soulmate – all that nonsense. And it was just an act. 'But I don't understand. Is *that* why you moved back to Bordgalsh?'

Struan sighed and put his head in his hands, rubbing his eyes. 'Sort of. She tried finishing it with Kenny.'

'God, do we have to call him "Kenny"? Any name with a "y" on the end always sounds so fluffy and cute. What's his full name, Kenneth?'

Struan smiled. 'It's Cenard, actually. Anyway, it didn't last, the break-up. And they admitted they can't live without each other. So . . .' His voice trailed off and I wanted to scoop him up like I did when he was little, take away the hurt.

'Why didn't you call me?'

'And what would you have done? Driven down and battered him?' It was a touché moment. At least it raised a little smile from him. 'We're divorced, after all. So technically she can do what she wants, can't she? See who she wants to see.'

The thing I couldn't bear was seeing him so embarrassed. Seeing how much of a failure he felt. 'You thought there was still a chance, didn't you?' I asked gently. 'For you and her, I mean.'

He nodded, unable to look at me, and I saw a big fat tear lollop on to his lap. My poor baby. I wrapped my arms around him and kissed his head.

'There'll be a time when you'll look back at this day and wonder why you were crying. Because there is someone there for you, my darling, lovely son. She's just biding her time before you meet her.'

I hope that's true. And if not, well, we all have to accept that not every story has a happy ending. I just pray little Zander doesn't bear the brunt of it all.

People go on about kids being resilient – I think that's non-sense. They're not resilient, just scared and unable to voice their worries. So all we can do is keep on reassuring the little man and playing happy families. I'm just glad my boy is still young enough to start again.

But as usual, I'm jumping ahead of myself and launching into a swirl of unhelpful *what-ifs*. Look at what's right in front of you, Linda Standish. And right now, in this moment, it's my retirement bash.

I'd thought it best to book it for the week before I actually leave, so that I can tidy my desk and physically leave the office in a low-key fashion. Somehow, getting all the bells and whistles out at the end of my last day in there freaks me out a bit and I worry that the come-down might be too big. I'm still looking forward to it, there's not a grain of dread or regret at my decision to retire. But I want to do it quietly on the day.

For now, though, the bells and whistles are abundant as I walk into the pizza restaurant to be greeted by twenty or so colleagues from the council as Katy Perry's 'Roar' blasts from the speakers. Fair play, Gillian has really gone to town. I do wonder if in another life she would like to have been singing and dancing on a West End stage. For someone so minimalist in her communications, so neat and curt and contained, there is something about Gillian that is so *out* there. Begging to perform and be applauded. In a good way. The private dining room is bedecked with 'good luck' balloons and flowers and a big banner that says *Thank you Linda!* Of course, I want to cry as soon as I walk in, but I manage to contain it and just laugh instead, hugging them all and receiving a huge bouquet of flowers.

The meal is great – I find myself not taking much advantage of the 'eat all you can' buffet because I am talking so much, there's barely room or time to stick any pizza in my gob. Once the ice-cream sundaes have been consumed, the lights are dimmed and the music starts up. And much to my absolute delight, Gillian comes into the room now changed into a leotard, fishnets and stilettoes, accompanied by four other colleagues – two female and two male. The guys aren't in leotards, which I have to say is a godsend – the fabric being so clingy and us not long having finished eating. They are all sporting feather boas and incredibly heavy make-up. Gillian appears to be in her element. They all start singing 'Big Spender', but they've changed the words to 'Dear Linda' instead. They *must* have been tempted to change it to 'Big Linda' but kindly chose not to go down that route, even though it would have been a funnier lyric. The ones they've written don't rhyme in the slightest and are completely out of rhythm, but it's the thought that counts:

> *The minute you walked in the office*
> *We could see you were a girl from Boransay*

> *A real Highlander*
> *Don't forget us*
> *In your paddleboard race*
> *We sure are gonna miss you, girl, around the place!*

It's absolutely awful, which makes it so, so special. Like nothing I have ever seen before in my life. Gillian really is one in a million and I wonder whether she's done this more for her own benefit than mine.

At the end of the song we all clap and the performers take three bows. Then Gillian calls everyone to attention by clinking her glass and launches into a speech thanking me for my work at Boransay Council over the last thirty-seven years. A showreel plays, depicting me in various fashions, various hairstyles and various body-shapes during the changing decades. And it's like it all goes into slo-mo. Thirty-seven years. Ye gods. Blink, and it's gone. I see one particular photo of me from the early nineties. I'm in a maternity frock and laughing, stood next to the Mayor of Boransay at some council event. I worked for a different department then and nobody in this room would have known me. Or that it heralded the happiest time of my life, followed three years later by my darkest time. I remember it. I remember being pregnant, for sure. And it wasn't Struan I was expecting then.

It was Daisy.

I've kept no photos at home of that particular time in my life. So seeing this one sneaking out to remind me is a real sucker-punch. My lovely colleagues weren't to know, of course. And I swallow hard and pray that the photos move on fast, pulling me out of the painful recollection. Sometimes the thought of Time standing still is unbearable. Thankfully, it's soon over and I applaud and laugh, a little too hard, but it's a self-defence mechanism. Nobody is any the wiser and I listen intently as various colleagues share memories of working with me. All the time I'm thinking of that photo and wishing I hadn't seen it.

I raise my glass of sparkling kombucha as the speeches draw to an end with a chorus of 'To Linda!' And cries of *Speech! Speech!* force me to jollify myself and gather my thoughts as I face all the anticipation of my beloved workmates.

'Well,' I say, when the cheers have died down. 'I'm still getting over the shock of those leotards. Who knew we had such talents in our midst?' Everyone cheers the performers again. 'You know, I've heard it frequently said that council workers are boring people. Well, this is just one of those myths. Because in all the thirty-seven years I've worked for Boransay Council, I've known nothing but joy working with a gorgeous, fascinating lot who care about the people they serve and the people they work alongside.' Aw heck, voice is cracking now – bloody emotions are a bugger when they hit you and you can't escape them.

'I mean, don't get me wrong, I will not miss the printer jamming or the wi-fi cutting out or expenses forms or the stationery cull. But I will miss the Monday-morning catch-ups, the silly jokes, the birthday cakes and of course not forgetting the times when we succeeded in making a difference to people's lives. It can be a sad arena we work in, but there are occasions, aren't there, when we bring about a reunion or a bit of joy, or fill in the gaps to make a person's life make sense.' I think about my final case. Of Levi Norman and his daughter Rachel, who *wasn't* his daughter, but *was*. There wasn't much of a happy ending there.

'Please all of you, do stay in touch. You may have trouble finding me, as I have plans for my retirement and none of them involve being predictable or sedentary. But once you track me down I'll be delighted to catch up. Here's to you all. Long may you thrive, long may you jive and long may you stay a-bloody-live!'

I raise my glass to the roomful of smiling faces and they all cheer. The booze has been flowing for some time now and people are starting to get a little leery. And I take this as my cue to leave. One thing I've learned as a lifelong sober person is that you do not need to say goodbye when you want to leave a party. Truth is, nobody notices you've gone, because they're all too many sheets to the wind. So I surreptitiously get my bag and my coat, and sneak off out into the February night air. It's been a fabulous farewell, and now it's time for bed.

EASTER 2025

69

Linda

My last day in the office was five days after my retirement bash and as planned, I left with as little fanfare as possible. I took my box of personal possessions, handed in my lanyard at reception, said goodbye to Mick on the main door and headed out of the building without so much as a backward glance. One positive that seems to have happened in the weeks since I finished work is that I've not had a single binge. No rhyme or reason as to why: I've not gone on some fitness drive, I still have my sweet treats – I just don't gorge on them. There's a family-sized Dairy Milk in the fridge that's been there a month and only had five squares broken off. I didn't even bother hiding it under the bed. Is it retirement that's having this effect on me? Who knows. I'm definitely a bit slimmer as a result – though I'm no stick insect. Just more of a curvaceous queen than a chunky unit.

I've been umming and ahhing about booking myself a holiday. Struan thought it would be a good idea. 'It'll soften the blow, Mum!' he said. 'Go and see Dad and Denise!' I laughed at that one. 'Or you could always go to Storrich – see Brodie?'

I stopped laughing then. It's a sore point.

Me and Brodie.

There were no bad words between us, we just stopped texting

and Facetiming. Actually, that's not strictly true. Brodie texted me. And called me. But I didn't reply. Fergus Murray, whose leg is now fighting fit I should add, has remained in regular contact with his Storrichian friend. And like my son, is always trying to persuade me to go see Mr McLeod. Is it pride on my part that stops me? Or something deeper? I suspect it's the latter. Because I really dare not go there. I do not want to be vulnerable. No, scrap that – I do not want to be hurt.

Because on that last day, that trip to Inverness, when I'd *nearly* opened up and started blubbing, something shifted in me and made me feel needy. And if there's one place I do *not* like to find myself, it's being needy.

'Brodie,' I'd sniffled, whilst reaching into my bag for a bit of tinted moisturizer to rescue my red cheeks.

'Yes,' he'd said, clearing away the remains of our picnic and screwing the lid back on the flask.

'I completely get that you have to, but I don't want you to go back. To Storrich, I mean.'

He didn't say anything at first, just carried on clearing away. It was hugely embarrassing when he didn't respond.

'Just saying, that's all,' I added.

And he eventually came back with a mumbled, 'I can't stay.'

'Yes, I know. I was just saying!' I snapped, totally wishing I'd kept my mouth shut, I felt so stupid and knew I sounded ridiculously defensive.

'Sorry,' he said, and he did actually look crestfallen.

I blustered then, desperately trying to change the subject, waffling on about popcorn and getting to the cinema and how I hadn't seen a film in ages. But the deed was done. I'd shown my true colours, worn my heart on my sleeve, and now I was squirming inside with humiliation and regret.

Thing is, the relationship is impossible. Brodie won't ever leave Storrich, and I won't ever leave Boransay. If I was going to move, I'd move nearer to Bordgalsh to be near my boys.

'It doesn't stop you visiting him!' Struan says, time and time again.

But it does. Because what the eye doesn't see the heart doesn't grieve over, and my heart has grieved enough in its long life. Also, I think I just misread the room. I'm not sure Brodie felt the same about me as I did about him, despite his trying to convince me otherwise. I'm a great believer in gut reactions. And when he didn't instantly take up my request to stay that day, I understood that there was an imbalance between us. Struan thinks I'm being childish, that I don't understand how men and women differ. But put harshly, Struan's hardly an expert when it comes to relationships. I do miss Brodie, though. I won't lie.

In order to get over my broken heart I tried a bit of internet dating, just to take my mind off things. 'Cos I thought, *Well, Brodie McLeod isn't the only Scot in the loch!* I've been on three dates now. All very nice chaps, but not for me. I think Ronnie was looking for a kindly soul to nurse him through his old age; Jim seemed beset with family problems, having been married three times and fathered or step-fathered a total of nine children, most of whom he had 'issues' with; and then there was Matthew, who was lovely. But if I'm honest, I'm not entirely sure he was straight. And much as I thought we'd get on very well, I really do need a bit of the old physical. I blame Brodie for that.

As promised to myself, I have been paddleboarding twice. The first time was a bit of a disaster and my pride took quite a bashing. But the instructor was very kind and patient and the second time I went, I found myself almost standing. Well, I say standing – that's how I looked in my mind's eye. It was more of a terrified crouch in reality.

Occasionally I get calls from the office asking for my help or advice on a particular case. Young Liam seems to be settling in to his promotion well, but there are some situations that only an old hand like me can resolve. This morning he called with a message for me from Rachel McKenna, which was a bit of a surprise as I thought all that had been sorted. 'She wants to talk to you,' Liam said, and gave me her number. I feel a little ambivalent about contacting Rachel again. I'm a big believer in keeping things moving, and despite most of my working life having revolved around digging up the past, in my personal life I'd like to move on. Still, it would be rude not to call.

70

Rachel

'Aw, look darling, see this?' Rachel holds up a gaudy medal on a red ribbon that she's found in the keepsake box and shows it to Ellis, her five-year-old son. 'Mummy won this in . . .' she looks at the date engraved on the front, 'Gosh, 1995! When she was twelve.' Ellis takes the medal from her and puts it on. Rachel takes a photo on her phone and WhatsApps it to David with a message. *Our son wearing my 100m medal from sports day in 95. So many lovely things in here.* She puts her phone down and takes out the blue velvet box that she instantly recognizes from her wedding day: her mother's pearls. Gently lifting them up, she runs her fingers along their tiny irregular shapes, blinking away the tears that threaten to fall. She worries that she might cry. A notification on her phone. The ticks go blue and David messages back: *Not making you sad sweetheart?* She replies *yes and no* and watches Ellis take out a postcard of the Eiffel Tower. Her flowery handwriting on the back makes her smile, remembering the type-set style g's and a's that she no longer does.

The guilt has eased a bit. With a lot of coaching from David and a few sessions with a bereavement counsellor, Rachel has finally begun to accept that her estrangement from Levi was not her fault: that ultimately, it was his decision to stay away. But occasionally it comes back to haunt her. That she should have made a different choice. 'That text I sent him. It was so cruel. He died thinking I hate him!'

David had smiled kindly when she'd said this. 'Darling, your father knew you. Knew your spirit, knew more than anyone – even me – who you really were and what a kind heart you have. At worst, he will have thought you were angry, yes, but never hateful.'

When the solicitor gave her the will and she found out about the cottage on Storrich, her first thought was to sell it. After all, it wasn't a place she knew or that she could associate with Levi, so surely it would be less painful to get rid of it? She also felt, somehow, that she didn't really deserve it: she had, after all, callously rejected this man who had only ever loved her. But as time passed and she could reflect on it all, Storrich began to feel more intriguing. And she began to wonder whether going there would bring her some peace.

*

'Who is that man and that lady?' Ellis asks as he stares at the wedding photo of Levi and Diana outside Inverness Town Hall.

'That's my mummy, and that's my . . .' she hesitates, unsure why, when for all those years Levi was indeed her daddy. 'He was your grampa.' Her voice cracks when she says it and she tries to hide behind an exaggerated smile. She worries for a moment that Ellis will ask about Jack and get confused. Jack was known to him as Bampa Jack – a name Ellis had created in his toddler days and which Rachel didn't want to take away. But her little boy has already found a new object to explore and lifts from the box a smooth, pebble-like piece of sea-glass, turquoise and opaque and shaped like a mini kiwi fruit. He holds it next to his eye, as if close up its mysteries will be revealed. 'What's this?'

'It's a very old piece of glass,' she says, holding it between her finger and thumb, momentarily transported back to the wildlife holidays she'd been taken on as a child, and the hours spent with Levi scouring shores for the ocean's treasure. 'The sea has made it smooth and round,' she says and holds it in her palm, her fingers wrapped around it, keeping it safe. It feels unexpectedly comforting, and for some reason she holds it to her lips and kisses it. Strange, she recognizes all the other items in the box, but not this one. Putting it in her pocket she tells Ellis, 'Your Grampa Levi probably found it on the beach by his cottage. He lived on an island and his house was right by the sea.'

Rachel watches as Ellis tries to process this new information before venturing to ask, 'Would you like to go there one day? To Grampa Levi's house?'

'Will he be there?' asks Ellis, and Rachel swallows hard.

'No, darling, not any more. But we can see where he used to live?'

'Okay.'

The phone rings and she welcomes the distraction.

'I got a message to call you,' says the bright and breezy voice on the other end. 'I would have rung sooner but I've been at the pool for another paddleboard lesson. I'm terrible at it. Keep falling off. Don't think I'll be going again but still, God loves a trier. I'll stick to ballroom, less demoralizing although the foxtrot is . . . Sorry, TMI, I'm waffling, it's because I'm nervous. Is everything all right?'

Rachel smiles. 'Hello, Linda, yes, all good. Thanks for calling back, it's just I never really thanked you properly for coming all this way back in January and explaining everything about Dad. I was in so much shock.'

'Of course you were,' says Linda. 'How do you feel now? Have you sorted Levi's estate? I hope the solicitors aren't dragging their feet, although probate can be a hugely long process, I'm afraid.'

'They've been great,' says Rachel. 'And I'm going to see the cottage in Storrich next week. Beannach Lodge. That's actually why I wanted to talk . . .'

71

Linda

The pub is busy with tourists and Brodie has his back to me, changing the optic on a whisky bottle as I creep up to the bar.

'Do you sell any non-alcoholic lager?'

The politeness lasts for a nanosecond, 'Aye, we've got—' and then he stops, realizes, and breaks into a big, beaming smile. God, he's gorgeous.

In another life he'd have leapt over the counter and swooped me into his arms *Officer and a Gentleman*-style, but come on, we're both in our fifties and martyrs to mild arthritis. Plus, although I've lost a few pounds since retiring – mainly due to the dancing – I'm still no Victoria Beckham. He comes around the side of the bar and stands looking at me.

'Well,' he says.

'Well, indeed.'

Because it's so busy, what with it being Easter, it's difficult to talk properly. 'D'you want a hand?' I ask as another group of walkers enters the Storrich Arms, and I don't wait for the answer. It's like I've never been away. In between pulling pints and mixing vodkas and Coke, we talk. I tell him about Rachel and how she decided to come to Storrich with her husband and little boy, to look at Beannach Lodge and the island that was her father's home for the past six years. 'She asked me to come too, I suppose for some sort of moral support.'

Brodie nods. 'Well, also you're an honorary Storrichian now, aren't you?'

'How d'you work that out?' I ask him.

'There are several criteria,' he says. 'Being born here, obviously, or at least living here since a bairn. Then like Levi Norman, if you move here and make it your home.'

'Right, but I'm neither of those.'

'No, but you fit into a third category,' he says, grinning. 'You've had sex with a local.'

'Damn – did Hamish Hamilton tell you about our sordid affair?'

'That he did,' laughs Brodie. And as he leans over to set a pint of Guinness pouring, he nuzzles into my ear and whispers, 'I miss you.'

An hour later things have quietened down, and the Australian barman has come back off his break to take over. 'Fancy a walk?' I say to Brodie. And we head off down the beach. Sitting on a flat rock looking out to sea he says, 'You didn't answer my calls. Or my texts.'

'No.'

'I took the hint. Eventually.'

'Yes.'

'But I've not given up.'

I feel quite a flutter when he says this. 'Why? I'm hardly a catch. A fifty-five-year-old grandmother who's three stone overweight.'

'Ach, stop fishing, Linda Standish. You know you're bloody gorgeous. And anyway, who d'you think *I* am?' he asks. 'Harry bloody Styles? I suffer from gout, my hair is thinning and I take Lisinopril every day for high blood pressure. I'm hardly a sex god on a plate!'

'I beg to differ,' I say. And there's a look between us that catches my breath.

We sit on the rocks in silence for a while, just looking out at the Irish Sea. I shut my eyes and enjoy the sun on my face and the warm breeze, salty-scented and rejuvenating. 'I need somewhere to sleep tonight,' I say. 'Fancy top and tailing in exchange for a shift behind the bar?'

'Sounds like a fair deal,' Brodie says. 'But it'll be top and topping, none of this top and tailing nonsense.' I smile and take his hand. Further down the beach we see three figures, barefoot, trousers rolled up and standing ankle-high in the water. It's Rachel and David and their little boy, Ellis. 'They have the ashes,' I say quietly, 'Diana and Levi.'

'Finally together.'

We watch them in silence, the distance between us sustaining a certain level of privacy for this very personal act, but offering Brodie and myself a small opportunity to honour the dead.

'Rest in peace,' he says, as we watch Rachel scatter the ashes, the sunlight glinting momentarily upon them as they arc high in the air, infusing them with something celestial and otherworldly.

'Yes,' I whisper, 'rest in peace.'

We watch as David comforts Rachel, and little Ellis holds his mother tight around her waist. Then they begin heading back towards the shore, towards us.

Rachel looks relieved, though her face is tear-stained and sad. 'Beannach Lodge is so beautiful,' she says. 'I felt some sort of connection with my dad as soon as I went inside.'

'Oh that's lovely, Rachel,' I say.

'I know it's a sore subject,' says David, with the caution that always accompanies the subject of holiday homes when talking to a local. 'But we reckon we'll be here a lot. And when we're not, we'll lend it out to friends.'

And before I know it, the words are out of my mouth. 'Well, I reckon my son Struan could be your first customer,' I say. 'He'd love to come here, with his own little boy.'

Brodie looks at me, puzzled.

'Sounds perfect,' says Rachel. 'We'll keep you posted.' And they head back up to the pub.

'Chicken pie on the menu tonight,' Brodie calls after them.

'And Minty's made a cranachan,' I add.

'Delicious!'

When they're out of earshot, Brodie turns to me. 'So you're planning your son's holidays for him now?'

'Kind of . . . I just think it's the perfect place for them to stay when they come to visit.'

Then I shut my eyes when I say the next bit, because it's a risk. I swallow hard. 'When they come to visit . . . *me*.' I slowly open one eye and peep at him to check his reaction. He's unreadable.

'So . . . what exactly are you saying, Linda Standish?'

'Okay, well . . . I haven't changed my mind about moving here.' Disappointment flashes across his face. 'But I thought there might be a nice sort of middle ground. Like, what if you and me go part-time? I come and stay here some weeks, help out in the pub, have lots of incredible sex in your bed . . .'

'With me or with Hamish?'

'Don't make me choose!' I laugh. 'Then you come and visit me some weeks. On the mainland. We don't need to go the whole hog, do we? We can just do a sort of semi-hog, can't we?'

'Yes,' he says. And pushes a strand of hair behind my ear. 'So what's changed your mind?'

'Oh, I dunno . . . Levi Norman, I think. He should have been braver in the end. Faced up to his mistakes and said, yes, I've messed up, Rachel, I should have told you from the start. And let her get cross, then let her forgive him and carry on. Rather than wasting all that time without her in his life. He never got to meet his little grandson.'

'Aye, that's a shame, I know. But him coming here wasn't a total waste of time. If he hadn't, then nor would you, and then you and me would never have . . .'

I can't resist him any longer and I shut him up with a juicy, windswept kiss that seals the deal before we make our way back to the Storrich Arms, ready for the evening ahead.

2018

EPILOGUE

Levi

He never forgot the date. November the third. The day he lost her. In previous years he'd taken a morning to be on his own with his memories, the happy ones, not the sad. He would travel to Nairn where they'd spent such joyful hours, and call in at the Caberfeidh pub, where he'd buy himself a large whisky, settle in a quiet corner and drink a toast. To his darling Diana and their short life together. He would close his eyes when he did it, conjuring up her image in his mind's eye, her features clear as day, her beauty still sparkling and vibrant.

As the date approached this year, he began to feel anxious. Should he just buy a bottle of malt and carry out his little ritual at home? Or should he brave the island's only pub? He decided on the latter, walking first along the beach where he gazed intently at the pebbles underfoot, searching for unusual driftwood or some ocean treasure thrown up by the receding tide. It caught his eye just as he was heading back: a beautiful piece of turquoise sea-glass, smooth and round, glistening in the November sun, a jewel amongst the duller pebbles. He picked it up and held it to the light before kissing it and putting it in his pocket. It made him smile: it reminded him of Rachel.

He entered the Storrich Arms tentatively, hoping he was too

early to encounter any locals. He was in luck. The place was deserted save for the landlord, who was restocking the bottle shelves. When he ordered his double malt, Levi took out some coins to pay. The piece of sea-glass fell out amongst the cash.

'We take sterling and euros,' the landlord said, laughing, 'but not pebbles.' Levi smiled back. 'You on holiday?'

'No. I'm over at Beannach Lodge,' Levi replied, desperately hoping he wouldn't have to make any more conversation than that.

'Ach, well if you need anything, give us a shout. We like to help each other out if we can.'

Levi nodded, gave a curt smile and took his whisky to a table in the corner. The landlord watched as the stranger lifted his glass in a toast, shut his eyes and whispered something he couldn't hear.

Acknowledgements

I have so loved the journey that *By Your Side* has taken me on. I feel I may at times have metamorphosed into Linda Standish and in my mind I believe Storrich actually exists, in a Brigadoon kind of a way . . . I hope you have enjoyed reading the book as much as I've enjoyed writing it.

I must thank my early readers: the wonderful author Hannah Beckerman, who gave me such invaluable advice and support from the start, as well as regular *Archers* therapy; my dear friend Nicola Merrigan, who let me sprawl out with my laptop in Casa Azul and offered such insightful suggestions; dear Emma Ralston – who, amongst other things, taught me about macaroni pies, Empire biscuits and fern cakes; and my precious little sister, Maria Cronjé, who amazes me constantly with what she does for other people – so for her to find time to read an early draft and give notes is beyond the call.

As ever, special thanks to my agent, Jonny Geller, for his support, friendship and just general brilliance. I am so lucky to know you, Jonny. And to the team at Curtis Brown: Sophie Storey, Ciara Finan, Natalie Beckett and Viola Hayden – super-efficient, patient and invaluable as ever.

A big thank-you to the lovely folk at Transworld: Sarah Adams, my superb editor who picked up the baton from the wonderful Frankie Gray and got me over the finishing line! Thank you, Sarah, what a journey! To dear Alison Barrow, who navigates the publicity of my books so brilliantly and is such a joy to spend time with. Here's to the tour – and thank you Bradley Rose, driver extraordinaire, for getting us there! Special thanks to Bill Scott-Kerr and Kim Young – I look forward to our future Transworld partnership. And thank you Larry Finlay for being at the start of this journey too. Huge thanks to my ever-patient copy editors Kate Samano and Helen Bleck; to Richard Ogle for creating such a striking jacket, to Sarah Ridley and Rosie Ainsworth for doing such an incredible job with marketing, and to Tom Chicken and the rest of the sales team. And, of course, thanks to the audio-book team, especially Tom McWhirter and producer Charlotte Davey, with a special thank you to Seumas MacFhionnlaigh for the Scottish Gaelic translation and pronunciation help.

Thanks to Jo James and all the team aboard the Cunard *Queen Mary 2* who took the Cheltenham Festival at Sea from Southampton to New York last November. What a blast that was. I learned so much from you all, and it was a joy to be in your company. I hope we get to do it again sometime. And I promise not to sing.

To booksellers around the country – thank you for stocking my books. I can't tell you what a thrill I get to see one of them on your shelves. Bookshops and libraries are such peaceful and nurturing places to visit. Long may they continue! Indeed, thank goodness for books and the enjoyment, enlightenment and company they bring to so many. Especially the mobile libraries in remote places – what an institution.

As always, thank you, dear family and lovely friends, for your constant support (through the highs and the lows). You know who you are! My immense gratitude to David for all that you have done for me, and for introducing me to the beauty of Sutherland all those years ago. And finally to the super special little ones – Frida, India, Nina-Hâf and Otis: thank you for bringing us all such joy and filling our hearts with love.

And finally, thank you to my readers. I am continually touched by your ongoing support. I absolutely love meeting you at events and festivals and I hope we get to say hello again soon.

Read on for bonus content from Ruth . . . and Linda!

Ten things that really annoy Linda Standish

1. People who use the word 'yourself' instead of 'you'. E.g. *I've got a selection of options to show yourself* or *I can talk through the most efficient tariff for yourself* or *What's the best contact number for yourself?* What does it achieve? Is it supposed to sound posh or something? It's almost as annoying as being called Madam. Just talk normal, for God's sake!

2. Misuse or lack of apostrophes. E.g. *it's* instead of *its* or *Jone's* instead of *Jones*: *Its a big problem for Mr Jone's who has examined the subject in all it's glory*. I know, I know, the Grammar Police are here. But it just sticks in my craw. (Whatever a craw is.)

3. People who video-call on buses or trains or, worse still, who watch TV on their phones or iPads without headphones. Do I want to watch what you're watching? NO. Do I want to be party to your conversation with your grandchild? NO!

4. The use of the expressions 'for my sins' and 'speak my truth'.

5. Snapchat.

6. Customers in restaurants who spend the majority of their meal taking either selfies or photos of their food or scrolling on their phones. Last week I witnessed a group of young women film themselves singing 'Happy Birthday' to their friend, who

then blew out the candle on her dessert. Which is fine. Except they then proceeded to repeat the process three times until they were happy with what they'd filmed! Talk about NOT living in the moment.

7. Midgies. I know being Scottish I should love all things Scottish, but when it comes to the evil little midge, I am livid. I mean, what is the point of him? He terrorizes us all with his minuscule bites that explode into red rashes overnight. Apparently BATS like eating them, but that's all they're good for. Bat food. Move on, midge. Nothing to see here.

8. Kale.

9. Never getting to speak to a human being when ringing up about a gas bill or a bank statement, and having to press about twelve different options only to be told *We are experiencing a high volume of calls right now but your call is important to us.* No. It isn't. And how comes you're ALWAYS experiencing a high volume of calls? Every time I ring. How comes it's not occasionally a mid-range volume of calls? In fact, why not just say *We're not actually experiencing that many calls, but we've got a few people off sick today so we're understaffed.*

10. Train managers' announcements. Look, I know you've got to inform people, but be honest, sometimes you do make unnecessarily long announcements *over and over again.* Is it because you enjoy using the microphone? Come on . . . admit it. Oh, and please don't get me started on *See it, say it, sorted.*

Ruth Jones MBE is well known for her television work, most notably BBC One's multi-award-winning *Gavin and Stacey*, co-written with James Corden, in which she played Nessa Jenkins. The 2019 and 2024 Christmas specials of this well-loved show garnered viewing figures of 18 million and 21 million respectively. Ruth also created and co-wrote several series of *Stella* for Sky TV, for which she was BAFTA nominated. Other TV work includes *Hattie*, *Nighty Night* and *Saxondale*. In 2024 Ruth played Mother Superior in *Sister Act The Musical* at London's Dominion Theatre. Her latest acting role is Elena Ravenscroft in Harlan Coben's *Run Away* for Netflix.

Ruth's novels have sold over a million copies. *Never Greener* was a *Sunday Times* bestseller for fifteen weeks, three weeks at number one, as well as WHSmith Fiction Book of the Year 2018, a nominated Debut of the Year at the British Book Awards, and a Zoe Ball Book Club pick. Her second novel, *Us Three*, and her third novel, *Love Untold*, were also instant *Sunday Times* bestsellers. *Love Untold* was a Waterstones Paperback of the Year, as well as a Richard & Judy Book Club pick.